6/17

SO-AQM-266

A CONTRARY WIND

A VARIATION ON MANSFIELD PARK

BY LONA MANNING

© 2017 Lona Manning

ISBN: 9781520374147

Independently published

Boyle County Public Library

"I shall think her a very obstinate, ungrateful, girl..... considering who and what she is."

Aunt Norris

"[I]f Mansfield Park had had the government of the winds just for a week or two, about the equinox, there would have been a difference. Not that we would have endangered his safety by any tremendous weather -- but only by a steady contrary wind...."

Henry Crawford

TABLE OF CONTENTS

"True courage is like a kite; a contrary wind raises it higher."

Jean Antoine Petit-Senn (1792–1870)

Synopsis of the first part
of *Mansfield Park*

A Contrary Wind *breaks off from Jane Austen's original text in Chapter Fifteen, at the point when the young people are casting the parts in the play* Lovers' Vows. *A very brief synopsis of* Mansfield Park *to that point is provided below for anyone who hasn't read this great novel.* A Contrary Wind can *be read without having read* Mansfield Park, *but I of course recommend that you read Austen's subtle and beautifully written novel. This variation references scenes and dialogue in the original novel, so knowledge of the original will enhance the enjoyment of this variation.*

Sir Thomas Bertram is a wealthy baronet with four handsome children, two girls and two boys. His estate, Mansfield Park, is in Northamptonshire, north of London. His wife was one of three sisters – she made a brilliant marriage when she snagged the baronet; her older sister, Mrs. Norris, married the neighbourhood clergyman. The third sister, Mrs. Price, married beneath her; she wed a lieutenant of marines and lives in squalor in Portsmouth with her husband, now disabled for active duty, and a large brood of children.

Mrs. Norris proposes to Sir Thomas that he take in one of the poor Price children to help that struggling family (this is so she may have the credit of being benevolent without any of the expense); he agrees, and awkward, timid little Fanny Price, aged ten, comes to live in the great mansion. She is overawed by everything and everyone, and only her cousin Edmund, the younger of the two Bertram boys, pays any attention to her or shows her kindness.

Lady Bertram is remarkable for her indolence and inactivity, so by default, the management of her household and the raising of her children has been taken up by Mrs. Norris, childless and widowed, who is a judgmental, self-important, miserly busybody. Fanny is particularly bullied by Aunt Norris. The novel shows us numerous scenes in which Fanny is established as the Cinderella of the household. Fanny is shy, humble and passive, but she is also very morally upright. Thanks to Edmund, she grows to love poetry and reading, and becomes an enthusiast for the sublimity of Nature. She grows up to be totally devoted to him and secretly in love with him. (This was at a time when first cousins could marry each other).

Sir Thomas must leave Mansfield Park to attend to his "plantations" in Antigua (that is, he is a slave-owner who owns sugar plantations, a very considerable source of wealth for England at this time) and he is away for almost two years. During his absence, his oldest daughter, Maria, becomes engaged to the wealthy but dim-witted Mr. Rushworth, who owns a large estate known as Sotherton. Then two new characters appear – pretty, witty and charming Mary Crawford, and her flirtatious brother Henry. They are the half-brother and half-sister of Mrs. Grant, wife to the local clergyman.

Mary Crawford first thinks that Tom Bertram, the older son and heir to the Bertram estate, might make a suitable husband but finds herself, unaccountably, falling for the quieter and more serious Edmund. When she learns that Edmund is going to become a clergyman, she tries to forget about him, as she, an heiress who is used to the glamor of London society, has no interest in being a clergyman's wife in some quiet country village. Meanwhile, Maria and Julia both fall under the spell of the captivating Henry Crawford. Fanny observes this dangerous situation, but worse, also has the heartache of watching Edmund fall in love with Mary.

A friend of Tom Bertram's, Mr. Yates, visits Mansfield Park. He has just come from another stately home where a scheme to put on a play was disrupted by the death of a relative of one of the amateur players. His enthusiasm for play-acting inspires Tom, his sisters, and the Crawfords, who decide they will entertain themselves by putting on a play.

This strikes Edmund and Fanny as disrespectful to Sir Thomas, especially considering that the play chosen, *Lovers' Vows* (a real play whose text is available on the internet) is about a woman who is seduced and has an illegitimate child, and it contains a rather saucy *soubrette*. Sir Thomas would not want his virginal daughters portraying women like this. (This was at a time when professional actresses were socially at the level of courtesans.)

The others disregard Edmund's warnings, and set about casting the parts of the play. The play has two storylines – one melodramatic and one comic. Both Maria and Julia want to play the dramatic part of Agatha, but there can only be one; Maria is chosen – she will play scenes with Henry Crawford (who is playing the part of her son, not her lover) and jealous Julia vows she will have nothing to do with the play. Mr. Yates will play the sadder but wiser Baron who regrets having seduced Agatha in his youth; plodding Mr. Rushworth is miscast as Count Cassel, an over-the-top Don Juan who boasts of his conquests;* Tom Bertram will play the Butler, a comic relief character who comments on the action of the play, in rhyming verse, and petite, sprightly Mary Crawford is well cast as the saucy Amelia in the comic storyline. Naturally she wants Edmund to play opposite her, but can she overcome his scruples?

As the variation begins, Fanny is being pressed to take one of the minor roles in the play. Leading up to this evening, Fanny has been tormented by watching Edmund fall in love with Mary Crawford, while Aunt Norris has been ordering her around and belittling her as usual.

* Contemporary readers of *Mansfield Park* would have been familiar with this play and would have appreciated the juxtaposition here – Mr. Rushworth is playing, incompetently, a sort of Henry Crawford character in the play, even as Crawford is busy seducing his fiancée Maria.

Author's Note: As the story begins, I have interposed some of Jane Austen's writing and she is occasionally quoted throughout the book. Her words appear in a different font.

Chapter One

Mansfield Park, October, 1808

"Fanny," cried Tom Bertram, from the other table, "we want your services."

Fanny was up in a moment, expecting some errand; for the habit of employing her in that way was not yet overcome, in spite of all that Edmund could do.

"Oh! we do not want to disturb you from your seat. We do not want your present services. We shall only want you in our play. You must be Cottager's wife."

"Me!" cried Fanny. "Indeed you must excuse me. I could not act anything if you were to give me the world. No, indeed, I cannot act."

"Indeed but you must," her cousin returned with a smile which signified to Fanny that he would not attend to her protests, "for we cannot excuse you. It need not frighten you: it is a nothing of a part, a mere nothing, not above half a dozen speeches altogether."

"It is not that I am afraid of learning by heart," said Fanny, shocked to find herself at that moment the only speaker in the room, and to feel that almost every eye was upon her; "but I really cannot act."

"Phoo! Phoo! Do not be so shamefaced. You'll do it very well. Every allowance will be made for you. We do not expect perfection. You must get a brown gown, and a white apron, and a mob cap, and we must make you a few wrinkles, and a little of the crowsfoot at the corner of your eyes, and you will be a very proper, little old woman."

"Oh Fanny, pray don't be so anxious about it," added Maria. "You needn't put yourself out to be *acting* – Mr. Crawford and I portray the leading characters, you need only support us."

"We will do everything in our power to render you as comfortable as possible," cried Henry Crawford, rising from his chair to make a half bow,

4

accompanied by his most engaging smile. "Should you feel yourself in doubt as to how this or that line may best be delivered, permit me to read your part aloud to you, by way of supplying you with a friendly hint. You need only mimic my expressions, my turns of countenance."

"And yours is a very trifling part," Mr. Rushworth put in. "Whilst I must come in three times, you know, and have two-and-forty speeches. That's something, is not it? But I do not much like the idea of being so fine. I shall hardly know myself in a blue dress and a pink satin cloak."

"And here, I suspect, is the *true* origin of Miss Price's reluctance – I fancy that she doesn't care to yield the honours of the pink satin to our Count Cassell, and grace the stage herself dressed in peasant rags and a mob cap," Mr. Yates interposed. "I can understand your feelings very well, Miss Price, and I will be your champion. I shan't let your cousin Tom paint crow's feet around those soft blue eyes. What say you to appearing as a little shepherdess or a milkmaid? You will look very fetching indeed, and what does it signify if Cottager's wife is young enough to be his granddaughter?"

"You must excuse me, indeed you must excuse me," cried Fanny, growing more and more red from excessive agitation, and looking distressfully at Edmund, who was kindly observing her; but unwilling to exasperate his brother by interference, gave her only an encouraging smile. Her entreaty had no effect on Tom.

"Here – here – Fanny," cried Tom Bertram, pushing an open manuscript across the table toward her. "You need only enter and say: *here's a piece of work indeed about nothing!*"

"What a piece of work *here* is about nothing!" exclaimed her Aunt Norris loudly. "I am quite ashamed of you, Fanny, to make such a difficulty of obliging your cousins in a trifle of this sort—so kind as they are to you! Take the part with a good grace, and let us hear no more of the matter, I entreat."

"Do not urge her, madam," said Edmund. "It is not fair to urge her in this manner. You see she does not like to act. Let her choose for herself."

"I am not going to urge her," replied Mrs. Norris sharply; "but I shall think her a very obstinate, ungrateful girl, if she does not do what her aunt and cousins wish her—very ungrateful, indeed, considering who and what she is."

Fanny turned crimson, then pale. Turning her back on the rest of the company, she bent her head over her needlework. The rest of the party were briefly silenced – Edmund was too angry to speak, Maria was chagrined that Henry Crawford was witness to this breach of decorum in their family circle and even Tom recognized that another word from him, either of comfort or censure, might destroy Fanny's composure completely.

Miss Crawford, looking for a moment with astonished eyes at Mrs. Norris, beside whom she was sitting, said, with some keenness, "I do not like my situation: this place is too hot for me," and moved away her chair to the opposite side of the table, close to Fanny, saying to her, in a kind, low whisper, as she placed herself, "Never mind, my dear Miss Price, this is a cross evening: everybody is cross and teasing, but do not let us mind them."

For the next quarter of an hour Fanny received Miss Crawford's warm praise of her needlework, and mechanically answered her enquiries and remarks, until rising feelings of humiliation threatened to overpower her altogether. To add to her distress, the knowledge that it was *Miss Crawford* who, of all the company, was the one endeavouring to soothe and revive her, was a mixed blessing, as it obliged her to think better of her neighbour than she wished to.

Fortunately, Miss Crawford's attention was called away by the other young people. Fanny was too discomposed to attend to the conversation but heard enough to understand that the subject was again *Lovers' Vows*, and which of them was to undertake which part, and she dreaded a renewal of those urgings and accusations which had destroyed her peace. She wanted to escape and go to her room, but she could not trust herself to make her excuses in a tolerably complacent fashion. As for leaving the room directly, her aunt's angry words – *considering who and what she is* – echoed in her ears again and again, humbling her too utterly to contemplate such a lack of ceremony.

Who was she, and what was she? A penniless relation, a dependent female, taken in as a child out of motives of charity. She had never resented her cousins for their superior beauty, dress, or accomplishments, and seldom did she bridle at the errands upon which she was forever being sent. But to be accused of ingratitude, obstinacy and willfulness – she who might as well not even have a will of her own, so seldom had she been given an opportunity to exercise it? At that moment, an unaccustomed sensation burned in her breast, rising until she felt it must choke her. It was anger; it was a burning resentment at being so misunderstood by those who should have known her best.

She had disapproved of the acting scheme, agreeing with Edmund that it was disrespectful for the younger Bertrams to engage in play-acting when their father was engaged on a perilous ocean voyage, when the most calamitous tidings could reach them at any hour until they were assured of his safe arrival on England's shore. As the youngest person in the household and a dependent relation, she would never presume so far as to lay down the correct course of conduct to her cousins Maria and Julia, who appeared blind to the indelicacy of representing on stage such women with whom their own father would have barred all association. She stood with Edmund in refusing to participate but had confided her feelings only to him. Unaware of her disapprobation and her forebodings of mischief, Tom laid her refusals to childish timidity, Mrs. Norris to a peevish disobliging nature. It was deference alone which prevented Fanny from raising those objections which could only be perceived as rebukes.

And yet, Fanny reflected, bending lower over her work, was it not true that she would still shrink from participating in the theatricals, even if were there no such objections to be met with as had occurred to her and Edmund? Did she not wish to avoid being contrasted on the same stage with the pretty, sprightly, Miss Crawford or her handsome cousin Maria? Was it not for this same reason that, when a child, she had refused, absolutely refused, to study piano and drawing – for fear of comparisons to her more accomplished cousins? Could her seeming modesty and reticence be, in reality, a species of pride?

Feelings of self-pity, mingling with feelings of self-loathing, struggled inside of her. She had only one wish: to escape from herself. She observed Miss Crawford returning to sit next to her, she saw Miss Crawford's lips move, something was "disagreeable" to her; Fanny nodded her head in seeming acquiescence, but she heard none of it. Although her disordered mind rendered all conversations into an unintelligible babble, she could yet observe – and she caught sight of Edmund's admiring gaze fixed upon Miss Crawford. Another glance, full of meaning, he swiftly bestowed on Fanny, one which said, "Miss Crawford, and she alone, was kind enough to soothe you, to comfort you, and I honour her for it."

Fanny had not thought it possible to feel more despondent than she had for the last half-hour, but now fresh well-springs of misery flowed forth. Edmund was giving every evidence of being a man in love. Her own humiliation at the hands of her aunt had brought it about – Mary Crawford's pointed attentions confirmed her in Edmund's mind as being without equal in compassion and goodness. It appeared then to Fanny that Edmund would inevitably take the fatal step that would bring him lasting unhappiness and disillusionment. Mary Crawford as a clergyman's wife in a small country village! The mind revolted! The kindest and the best of men so sadly deceived! And herself a helpless witness to it all.

With a trembling voice, Fanny finally excused herself for the night. The others hardly acknowledged her departure, which was at once all she desired and at the same time fresh proof of her insignificance to the household and her supposed nearest relations. Her resentment toward her Aunt Norris was now strangely benumbed, replaced by anger at herself, at who and what she was: a pathetic creature who could only go away and cry. She hurried up the stairs to the second floor to reach the back staircase and gain the privacy of her own modest room in the attic, where the sound of her sobs would not be heard over the bleak cold rain drumming against her narrow window.

***

The carriage was summoned to convey the Crawfords back to their sister's home. Edmund handed Miss Crawford in, and briefly made as though he might climb in beside her and accompany her to her own door, but her brother and a groomsman were sufficient escort and the lady herself was not welcoming. Edmund had angered Mary earlier that evening when, in a rather sententious tone, he pronounced that it was inappropriate for a clergyman (or soon-to-be clergyman in his case,) to portray one on the stage. But he was also turning down the opportunity to play the part of her lover. His indifference had wounded Mary's pride and she was very far from being ready to forgive him, barely acknowledging his cordial *adieux.*

"Well, sister," remarked her brother in a low voice, as the carriage pulled out of Edmund's hearing, "Perhaps we should make our excuses and go to Bath or London, rather than stay for this play-acting scheme. I think, for a party got up for pleasure, there were more long faces than happy ones at the Park tonight. Miss Julia spiteful, Bertram vexed with everyone, Edmund Bertram at his most insufferable, Miss Price near to fainting, and as for that aunt!"

"Maria plays the tragic part but *she* was looking particularly well pleased tonight, a matter I will leave for now to you and your conscience." Mary Crawford nodded meaningfully at her brother, who smiled, rather more gratified than abashed at the contemplation of the havoc he had wreaked in more than one female breast that evening.

"True – I *would* regret leaving off such a fair opportunity to play the tragic hero. To be authorized by the script to kiss Maria and press her to my bosom, in front of her future husband, is too irresistible!" Henry laughed.

"And as for Julia's pique, we also know where to lay the blame, do we not?"

"We do indeed – we lay the blame on female vanity and caprice– for despite my best efforts, Julia Bertram scorned to take any part but that of Agatha. In the face of such obduracy, reasoning is in vain and flattery useless. She must be first in consequence, and if she cannot, she chooses to be nothing at all."

"As for that last, are you speaking now of the play, or of your affections, Henry? At any rate, the foolish girl should have more pride and resolution. Heaven knows how *my* vanity has been mortified tonight, though I would confess it to no-one but you." Miss Crawford willed herself *not* to look out the window to see if Edmund was still standing in the sweep and watching the carriage as they drove away.

"When you gave Bertram your consent to apply to his friend Charles Maddox to take up the part of Anhalt, were you in earnest? Or do you object to playing love scenes with a gentleman with whom you are barely acquainted?"

"No, Charles Maddox is not objectionable – in himself. But I thought, I *had* thought, I had more power over –- " she stopped in vexation and let out a little laugh. "Perhaps I should enlist Mrs. Norris in my cause. She could scold Edmund Bertram into playing the part!"

"You remind me, I have hit upon an idea which will spare us any further scenes as we have witnessed tonight. Let us propose our own sister for the part of Cottager's wife."

"What a capital idea, Henry! She will be very pleased to be asked. And you know, Cottager's wife is a comic part, and although Miss Price has many fine qualities, I'm sure, I cannot discover that she has any wit about her."

"She is an earnest little soul, not a merry one," Henry agreed.

"Perhaps she has little enough to laugh about!"

"Yes, but we all must learn to laugh at ourselves and I fancy Miss Price cannot. Too delicate and scrupulous to walk on stage, in front of her friends!"

"But did you not perceive how she contrived to make herself the centre of attention tonight? I fancy she would have drawn less notice upon herself had she simply acquiesced! If she truly wanted to reject the role, she could have, with some justice, objected on the grounds that Cottager's Wife must half-carry your poor, expiring, wronged Agatha across the stage. Little Miss Price would be hard-pressed to do so," Mary laughed. "She might even have done herself an injury in attempting it. Maria Bertram will need the talents of a Mrs. Siddons to convince *me* that she is one meal away from death! There, you see, Henry, I can laugh at *others*, and in time, I promise you, I will resume laughing at myself. Only do not ask me to do so tonight. I am too chagrined."

***

The grandfather clock in the front hall struck eleven, then midnight, and Fanny still lay awake in her narrow bed, unable to console herself. As miserable as her present circumstances were, the future offered no hope of improvement.

At an age when most young ladies were beginning to seriously contemplate matrimony, she had already formed the resolution that she would never enter the state; it was impossible that she would ever meet another man who could be the equal of Edmund Bertram. She rejected with contempt the idea of marrying for money, and in her humility she could not conceive of receiving an offer from one who esteemed her well enough to overlook her lack of a dowry. Settling with her family in Portsmouth appeared to be as equally out of the question as finding a husband. Her parents had never, in the course of her nearly ten years' absence, expressed the wish that she return to them.

Fanny's visions of her own future had all centered on a plan concocted with her older brother William – namely, that they would one day live in a little cottage and she would keep house for him when he retired from the Navy. But what was she to do until then? Her cousins had paid little regard to her over the years, but how empty the great house would seem when Maria and Julia married and formed their own establishments. Tom was abroad more than at home and Edmund would remove to Thornton Lacey after his ordination. She would be left behind to grow old in the service of her aunts. A long twilight existence, fetching and carrying for Aunt Bertram and bearing Aunt Norris' slights and insults in silence, stretched ahead of her. She might have to endure ten, fifteen, twenty years of such a life before she could retire to a cottage with her brother.

And could she truly rely upon this solace, at long last? Although marriage formed no part of her brother's plans at twenty, could she expect him to regard the state with the same indifference at five or eight-and-twenty? What if William did marry, and his wife had no wish to be encumbered by a maiden sister? And whether in Mansfield, Portsmouth or her brother's cottage, was she not dependent upon the charity of others for every mouthful she ate and every thread upon her back? Were her comings and goings to be entirely at the command of others, her own preferences never consulted?

As Fanny tossed and turned for the hundredth time that long night, a new unbidden resolution suggested itself to her – *you are acquainted with one independent gentlewoman who earned her own bread.*

Your own governess, Miss Lee.

Why should you not do the same?

***

The following morning, Fanny escaped to the East Room after a half-eaten breakfast to ask herself how the thoughts she'd entertained the previous night appeared to her in the judicious light of morning.

The East Room had once been the school-room and had sat empty after the departure of their governess. It was now used solely by Fanny, the smallness of her own bedchamber making the use of the other so evidently reasonable, and Mrs. Norris, having stipulated for there never being a fire in it on Fanny's account, was tolerably resigned to her having the use of what nobody else wanted.

The aspect was so favourable that even without a fire it was habitable in many an early spring and late autumn morning to such a willing mind as Fanny's. The comfort of it in her hours of leisure was extreme. She could go there after anything unpleasant below, and find immediate consolation in some pursuit, or some train of thought at hand. Her plants, her books—of which she had been a collector from the first hour of her commanding a shilling—her writing-desk, and her works of charity and ingenuity, were all within her reach.

To this nest of comforts Fanny now walked down to try its influence on an agitated, doubting spirit. Could she, Fanny, take a position as governess? Of caring for children, she had had much experience. As the eldest daughter of a family of ten, she had been important as playfellow, instructress, and nurse until sent away to live with her uncle and aunt.

In the ordinary course of events, gentlewomen only became governesses out of necessity. It was the last resort of the genteel but poor.

11

It was a position entered upon with resignation at best, despair and resentment at worst, by widows and orphans, by persons whose expectations had been dashed and whose hopes had been overthrown – it was not to be wondered at that governesses and their faults were dwelt upon with much energy by ladies on their morning visits throughout the kingdom. While it was possible that some governesses become honoured and beloved members of the family, Fanny only knew that the profession never wore a happy face in any novel she had picked up.

Fanny paced unceasingly around the old work table, greatly agitated at her own audacity for even entertaining such ideas as now entered her head. She attempted to recollect, as best she might, any remarks dropped by Miss Lee concerning her opinions of the profession. But Miss Lee had been of a taciturn and formal disposition, a quality that recommended her to Sir Thomas, but was ill-suited for arousing lasting feelings of affection or confidence from her pupils.

Fanny had first met Miss Lee upon coming to Mansfield when she was but ten years old, and for many months was afraid of her, though anxious to win her approbation. The governess's biting remarks upon Fanny's backwardness, ignorance and awkward ways had often brought Fanny to tears. Almost a year passed before Miss Lee had realized that of her three pupils – Maria, Julia and Fanny – only Fanny loved learning for learning's sake; only her timidity before the others prevented her from showing that she had memorized every textbook laid before her, and thenceforward Miss Lee was more encouraging.

Maria and Julia were overjoyed to be released from the schoolroom upon turning seventeen, while Fanny, the youngest, continued for another year, sitting with Miss Lee for several hours every morning, studying French, geography and natural history, or walking the grounds of the park to collect botanical samples.

Although Miss Lee had less to do as a governess when she had only one pupil, she was required to devote her afternoons and many evenings to attending on Lady Bertram.

When Miss Lee was at last discharged from Mansfield Park, Fanny was old enough to supply her place as Lady Bertram's errand-runner and cribbage partner. Fanny wondered whether these tasks were rendered less irksome to Miss Lee by the knowledge that she was paid for performing them. Would living amongst strangers be preferable to living with her cousins, if she received a salary, however small, rather than paying for her bread and board with the coinage of duty, submission and gratitude?

12

A tap at the door roused her and her eyes brightened at the sight of Edmund. They had not spoken since Aunt Norris's cruel rebuke of the night before, and Fanny, her colour rising, anticipated the unlooked-for joy of a private conference with Edmund, in which he would declare his indignation at their aunt, and assure her of his esteem and regard. But no, it was the *play*, and worse, it was *Miss Crawford*, that occupied Edmund's thoughts and occasioned this rare, this precious conversation.

"This acting scheme gets worse and worse, you see. They have chosen almost as bad a play as they could, and now, to complete the business, are going to ask the help of a young man very slightly known to any of us. This is the end of all the privacy and propriety which was talked about at first. I know no harm of Charles Maddox; but the excessive intimacy which must spring from his being admitted among us in this manner is highly objectionable, the more than intimacy—the familiarity."

He came to the East room, he said, for her 'advice and opinion,' but a very few moments made it clear to Fanny that he had already made up his mind – he would yield – he would take the part of Anhalt himself rather than see a stranger admitted on such intimate terms. "Put yourself in Miss Crawford's place, Fanny. Consider what it would be to act Amelia with a stranger."

Fanny protested, "I am sorry for Miss Crawford, but I am more sorry to see you drawn in to do what you had resolved against, and what you are known to think will be disagreeable to my uncle. It will be such a triumph to the others!"

"They will not have much cause of triumph when they see how infamously I act," Edmund responded drily, adding that he hoped, by yielding in this fashion, to persuade the others to keep the theatricals private and not involve any others in the neighbourhood, either as performers or audience. "Will not this be worth gaining?"

"Yes, it will be a great point," Fanny said reluctantly. Then Edmund did, finally, refer to her humiliation of the previous night, but only as a further reason to yield to Miss Crawford and take the part of Anhalt, for: "She never appeared more amiable than in her behaviour to you last night. It gave her a very strong claim on my goodwill."

At this, Fanny could scarcely speak, and Edmund was only too willing to interpret her silence as consent.

He smiled, he spent a few moments looking over her little library with her, when he was clearly eager to be gone, to walk down to the Parsonage and convey his change of sentiments to Miss Crawford. Then he *was* gone, entirely insensible of the pain he had inflicted.

Had either circumstance – Aunt Norris' insult or this fresh proof of Edmund's infatuation – occurred separately, Fanny would surely have spent her morning weeping. But occurring within twelve hours of each other, the absolute misery of the whole was so stupefying that she could no longer weep and, resolving within herself that she would weep no more, Fanny jumped up from her seat and slipped downstairs to the breakfast room, unobserved by anyone.

Lady Bertram kept her recent correspondence in an elegant little desk there. All of Lady Bertram's acquaintance, including Miss Lee, had received a note from her Ladyship hinting at the engagement of her eldest daughter to the richest landowner in the county – and the former governess, Fanny knew, had recently replied, wishing her one-time pupil every happiness. The note was postmarked from Bristol, where Miss Lee's latest employers resided.

With a rapidly beating heart, Fanny retraced her steps to the East Room where she composed a letter to Miss Lee, imploring her to keep her secret for now, and asking her advice on whether she thought her last pupil at Mansfield Park might be suited to be a governess. No sooner had she sealed her letter than she was summoned to walk into town on an errand for her Aunt Norris, which happily afforded her the opportunity to visit the village post office without the letter passing through the hands of servants at the Park.

She passed by Dr. and Mrs. Grant's home on the way to the village, and she could hear the lovely rippling strains of harp music issuing from the sitting room. Miss Crawford was entertaining her cousin Edmund. With tear-filled eyes, Fanny hurried past the parsonage, followed by the faint sounds of Edmund laughing in response to something witty Mary Crawford had said.

Chapter Two

Julia, usually regarded as the more cheerful, lively and obliging of the two Bertram sisters, had lost her composure entirely when Henry Crawford intervened in the casting of the roles of the play; both sisters recognized his preference for Maria over herself in the part of Agatha as an unspoken avowal of particular regard for the eldest sister. Maria gloried in her triumph, and sought every opportunity to rehearse her Agatha with Henry Crawford's Frederick, whilst having as little as possible to do with her betrothed, Mr. Rushworth. Fortunately for Mr. Rushworth's peace of mind, *his* faculties were so heavily taxed by the demands of learning his two-and-forty speeches by heart, that he had little leisure to observe and less capacity to understand what his lady love was about.

Julia was in love with Henry Crawford and had believed he was falling in love with her. Why should she *not* believe it, when his eyes, his gestures, his whispers, had proclaimed his devotion? Now that the conviction of his preference for Maria had been forced on her, she submitted to it without any alarm for Maria's situation, or any endeavour at rational tranquility for herself. Henry Crawford himself had attempted to soothe her through flattery and re-doubled attentions – she scorned them, and him, and he soon gave up the effort.

Nor was Julia in any humour to accept the elaborate attentions and gallantries of her brother Tom's house guest, the foppish Mr. Yates, who, hailing her as "the divine Miss Julia," made a point of sitting by her at breakfast, fetching her morning dish of coffee, declaring his raptures over her dress and shoes and the arrangement of her hair, and soliciting her approval of his own choice of cravat and jacket. She knew not how, but she could not discern in his assiduous gallantries any true symptom of a lover. Her brother Tom acknowledged the unserious nature of Mr. Yates' attentions, although in terms she could not understand.

"Gentlemen must pay their due tribute to beauty, Julia, but I would be sorry to see you take Yates seriously. I was at Eton with him and……" he coughed. "Your estimable governess never taught you much classical literature, did she? Any Latin? Hadrian and Antinous? Zeus and Ganymede?"

Julia shook her head, bewildered.

"No matter. The point is, these pleasantries between ladies and gentlemen are all part of the game, don't you know, you mustn't believe Yates is falling in love with you."

"I pay no attention to Mr. Yates at all, Tom, except that he is your friend and our guest. Now go along and practise your rhyming Butler. Ask Baddeley to help you," Julia returned scornfully.

***

Fanny retrieved Miss Lee's reply a few days later, at the post office. Although Miss Lee was surprised to receive Fanny's enquiry, she was not discouraging. Miss Lee was a well-judging and discerning woman, and she recollected that Fanny loved the house, the gardens, the countryside, and everything animate and inanimate connected to Mansfield Park, with the possible exception of some of its inhabitants. She knew that Fanny had been only tolerated as a companion by her female cousins, and was intimidated to the greatest degree by the formal manner of her uncle Sir Thomas, who, although not absolutely cruel, and by no means as censorious as Aunt Norris, had nevertheless made her little pupil tremble in terror when he visited the school room to examine her in English and French.

Her upbringing at Mansfield Park had rendered Fanny too genteel for the rough-and-tumble life she had left behind in Portsmouth; but as a governess she would continue to live amongst the same set of people, and in the same style, to which she was accustomed.

Miss Lee refrained from counselling Fanny as to the wisdom or imprudence of her proposed course but did inform her that Mrs. Smallridge, a cousin by marriage of Miss Lee's own employers, was looking for a young lady of unexceptional character to undertake the charge of their daughter, who was not quite six years of age, and their son, who was old enough to start learning his letters and sums. Miss Lee offered to forward Fanny's application to Mrs. Smallridge, with her own testimony as to Fanny's good character.

To be the tutoress of very young children appeared to Fanny to be the most probable circumstance to suit her talents – which she rated as very low – as well as her inclinations. She composed a careful letter to Mrs. Smallridge, describing herself as a gentlewoman, the daughter of a lieutenant of Marines, but raised principally by an aunt, the widow of a country parson – this last a reference to Mrs. Norris, who, it could truthfully be said, had more to do with raising her than any other adult at Mansfield Park, for it was the admonitions and scowls of the aunt that had rendered a timid and awkward young woman from a shy and retiring little girl. Fanny felt it was best to sink Sir Thomas and his family into oblivion, as she reasoned that Mrs. Smallridge might wonder why the niece of a baronet sought employment as a governess. Fanny had never dissembled so much in her life before, but had observed from Maria and Julia the art of withholding information without actually stooping to deceit.

The letter composed, folded and sealed, it remained to post. Fanny's heart raced as she contemplated taking that step which would transform her secret musings into action. The bare fact of engaging in secret correspondence filled her with shame and guilt, for whenever Lady Bertram was kind to her, or when Edmund had time to talk with her, the thought of leaving Mansfield appeared to her like a species of treason. But, once admitted to her mind, the thought of departing recurred with increasing frequency and plausibility.

Although Fanny had disclaimed any talent for acting, her relations would surely have been astonished at the secret she kept to herself whilst preparation went forward for the production of *Lovers' Vows*. Fanny found, before many days were past, that it was not all uninterrupted enjoyment to the party themselves, and each having their own concern, were frequently blind to the concerns of others. Everybody began to have their vexation. Edmund had many. Entirely against his judgment, a scene-painter arrived from town, and was at work, much to the increase of the expenses, and, what was worse, of the éclat of their proceedings; and his brother Tom, instead of being really guided by him as to the privacy of the representation, was giving an invitation to every family who came in his way.

Fanny, being always a very courteous listener, and often the only listener at hand, came in for the complaints and the distresses of most of them. She knew that Mr. Yates was in general thought to rant dreadfully; that Mr. Yates was disappointed in Henry Crawford; that Tom Bertram spoke so quick he would be unintelligible; that Mrs. Grant spoiled everything by laughing; that Edmund was behindhand with his part, and that it was misery to have anything to do with Mr. Rushworth, who was wanting a prompter through every speech. She knew, also, that poor Mr. Rushworth could seldom get anybody to rehearse with him: his complaint came before her as well as the rest; and so decided to her eye was her cousin Maria's avoidance of him, and so needlessly often the rehearsal of the first scene between her and Mr. Crawford, that she had soon all the terror of other complaints from him. So far from being all satisfied and all enjoying, she found everybody requiring something they had not, and giving occasion of discontent to the others.

Mrs. Norris was, in her own way, as happy as she had ever been, for she was busy from morning 'til night, living entirely at Mansfield Park, directing the servants, ordering the dinners, and supervising the sewing of the costumes and curtains. She also felt it was necessary for her to stay at Lady Bertram's side in the event that doleful news arrived concerning Sir Thomas – perhaps he would perish at sea, or be stricken by the fevers and distempers which carried away so many of his countrymen in tropical climes – and in such case, she, Lady Bertram's elder sister, would naturally be the rod and staff of the stricken family. She was confiding some of her gloomier prognostications to Mrs. Grant, who was sitting with Lady Bertram and Mrs. Norris after the conclusion of a rehearsal of the first act of the play, while Fanny, quite forgotten, was stitching on Anhalt's costume by candlelight at her own little worktable. For a young girl, every trifling thing connected with one's beloved transmits pleasure, so the thought that she held in her hands a garment to be worn by Edmund gave her a sweet sensation, mixed with sorrow, that she would not have exchanged for the world. So abstracted was she in her thoughts, it was in fact a wonder that some portion of the conversation of the ladies attracted her notice.

"Dr. Grant tells me the price of sugar has now fallen so low, that it is now considerably below what would repay the grower for his cost to make the sugar and bring it to market. What a shame for Sir Thomas! He has laboured so hard, away from home, yet these events conspire against him, do they not?"

"Yes, indeed, Mrs. Grant," answered Mrs. Norris, learning forward and speaking in a loud whisper, with a nod of her head toward Lady Bertram, who lay, half asleep, on her settee, "I heard the same. There is a glut on the market – that is what they call it – too much sugar; and in addition, with the recent prohibition on importing new labourers from Africa, the future prosperity of the West Indies plantations is very much in doubt."

"Dear me! But I'm sure that Sir Thomas – "

"*If* he should return alive, he must come down with the marriage portion for Maria, of course, and fit up Edmund for his ordination – his new home at Thornton Lacey must be gotten into readiness – you will see now, my dear Mrs. Grant, why I am so particular about making what little economies we can at Mansfield and have done everything in my power to curb any waste or unnecessary expense."

"No doubt they are all very obliged to you, ma'am."

"I do not consider that, of course, for who else should I assist but my own sister and her family? I have told Lady Bertram that, as I have no children of my own, whatever I have been able to put away every year is for her dear children, but little did I imagine that the time might come when my paltry widow's mite would be so needful!"

"Matters are not so bad as all that, surely? The price of sugar may rise again? And the family is in general well provided for, I trust. There would be his income from the rents?"

"But, with his prolonged absence," countered Mrs. Norris, unable to give way to any ray of hope, "you may be sure his tenants are behindhand and dear Tom and Edmund are too good-natured – the returns will not be enough to meet the expenses of maintaining the estate."

"Pray, sister, do not distress yourself," said Lady Bertram drowsily, having half-awakened and hearing the word 'rent.' "Sir Thomas will never require you to pay any rent on the White house, not so long as you have need of it."

"No doubt, Lady Bertram, the family of Sir Thomas Bertram can rely on his generosity *and* his prudence – you are all in the best of hands," Mrs. Grant suggested, as Mrs. Norris was for a moment discomposed.

She rallied, however, and leaning forward again, said in a forceful, sibilant whisper, which carried to every corner of the room, "Of course, Sir Thomas is very capable, but what can even *he* do in the face of such calamities! Naturally Sir Thomas would not confide all the details of his financial burdens to me, and I am sure I am not one to pry, but there was the matter of poor Tom's youthful follies, which amounted to a not inconsiderable debt, so that Sir Thomas was unable to do everything for Edmund that he intended – ahem – " and here Mrs. Norris recollected that it was this very circumstance which led to the living at Mansfield Park being settled on Dr. Grant, instead of being held for Edmund, something Sir Thomas, out of delicacy, would not have wished her to allude to before Mrs. Grant.

Mrs. Grant betrayed no consciousness, however, and Mrs. Norris resumed her catalogue of the family's financial woes: "– and some years ago, he declared his intention to settle some funds on Fanny when *she* came of age, to enable her to live as a gentlewoman, so *that* promise must hang about his neck like a millstone, and, I have no doubt, contributes

19

greatly to his cares. Of course, if Fanny continued to live here, and endeavoured to make herself as useful as possible, I dare say he would think his generosity in bringing her up under his roof would be at least *partly* requited, and he would be spared the great expense of a separate maintenance for her."

Fanny gave no indication she could hear what had been said, but continued sewing placidly until summoned to the little theatre to act as prompter for a scene between the ranting Mr. Yates and the befuddled Mr. Rushworth. She was surprised to discover she was not crying – her eyes were perfectly dry, but she could feel a strange feeling in her stomach, as though a cold little stone had taken up residence there. Perhaps she should bless her Aunt Norris for helping her to reach a resolution, for although she suspected her aunt of exaggerating the financial peril in which the family stood, she would not stay to be resented for receiving monies from Sir Thomas that she had never asked for, nor expected.

The next morning, Fanny asked her Aunt Norris if she needed anything taken to her home in the village, or fetched from it. As it happened, the lady wanted her good pair of scissors, so Fanny was dispatched, with the warning, "but pray, don't make this your excuse, Fanny, to dawdle along the way – you are needed here to help finish these costumes, for I cannot do everything by myself. Don't suppose that by staying out of sight you can shirk your share of the work to be done."

Fanny called at the post office and sent her application to Mrs. Smallridge, care of Miss Lee, and then forgot Aunt Norris's scissors, so stupefied was she at the enormity of what she had done, and was halfway home when she remembered and had to hurry back for them. She endeavoured to be in good time to avoid her aunt's condemnation by running up the hill and arrived breathless, holding her side.

Edmund met her near the rose garden and gently remonstrated with her – "You have been running, Fanny, you are out of breath! Whatever are you about? You look knocked up."

"Oh, it doesn't signify," Fanny panted. "I have not been out on horseback as often as I should lately, we have been so busy with the theatricals."

"Bother the play," laughed Edmund. "I have a tonic for you, Fanny – can you guess what it is?"

Fanny brightened, and wondered if there had been a letter from her brother William.

"No, no, not that, but this did come with the post this morning – *The British Critic*," and Edmund happily flourished his and Fanny's favourite publication, a gazette that listed all the new publications, with reviews and extracts. "Shall we look it over and decide upon those books whose acquisition is essential to the preservation of our happiness?"

No invitation was necessary, and Fanny almost danced beside Edmund as they re-entered the house. With joy did she anticipate that much-loved activity – looking over descriptions of books along with Edmund, discussing them, and making a list of the most desired titles to be ordered, and *that* followed by the pleasure of receiving the books in the post, and reading and comparing views with her cousin! It was the most complete happiness she knew.

"Stay, Fanny," called Edmund as Fanny hurried ahead of him to the library, "we are in the breakfast room. I thought we should be more comfortable there."

We? Bewildered, Fanny spun about and followed Edmund into the breakfast room, where sat Mary Crawford, looking particularly lovely, preparing her ink and quill for the list of chosen titles. She looked up and smiled expectantly as Edmund entered.

"Yes, I invited Miss Crawford to join us," Edmund explained cheerfully as Fanny faltered at the doorway.

"Oh, come in Miss Price," cried Miss Crawford. "We had despaired of you before Mr. Bertram saw you dashing up the hill." Turning to Mr. Bertram, she added, "I hope we shall have some travel books! Wouldn't you love to visit Paris, Mr. Bertram? The Bonaparte has stolen the birthright of every patriotic Englishman and woman – the right to return from Paris to disparage the place of our birth and to compare our food, fashions and manners unfavorably with the French! It is monstrously unjust! This war seems never-ending!"

The sight of Miss Crawford preparing to perform the office *she* had always performed, hit Fanny like a blow.

"Why, Miss Price, are you well?" asked Miss Crawford, eyeing her with concern. "You look pale. It *is* true what your cousin says – any kind of exercise but horse-riding tires you too quickly – pray, sit down, sit down."

Fanny managed to stammer – "The scissors – Aunt Norris – I must give – " and, backing out of the room, she turned and fled up the back stairs to her own little bedroom, where she gave way to her anguish, muffling her sobs with her quilt.

Sometime later, with reddened eyes and pale cheeks, she found Aunt Norris in the drawing room and resumed her sewing work, reasoning that Edmund by now had assumed she had been kept behind by her aunt and so could not return to the breakfast room.

"At last! My scissors!" exclaimed her aunt. "Fanny, I have been looking for you these two hours! And after I particularly asked you to hurry! You are too provoking! You are worse than thoughtless, you must have kept away out of spite and willfulness! I have no patience with you!" And so on, until the two housemaids, bent over the green baize curtain being prepared for the theatre, furtively exchanged looks full of pity for the young lady between their furious stitches.

***

Fanny could not know how probable or improbable it might be that a young lady of only eighteen summers would be accepted as a governess, but two circumstances smiled upon her. One was that Mrs. Smallridge, being the daughter of a prosperous tradesman, who through marriage to Mr. Smallridge had been elevated into a much higher sphere, had the greatest admiration of excellent handwriting and propriety of composition, and Fanny's letter was very pleasing on that score. Secondly, Miss Lee was able to assure her that Fanny was a genteel young lady, but was not one to give herself airs, and after further enquiry was kind enough to particularize Miss Price's appearance: 'She could by no means be called a beauty, nor was she plain, but was not the sort of young lady whom gentlemen noticed or remarked upon, being retiring and modest to a degree.' Miss Lee's commendation soothed Mrs. Smallridge's apprehension about engaging a servant who might conceive herself to be superior in point of birth or breeding to the lady of the house, and a further, if unspoken, reservation which any woman no longer in the first bloom of youth must feel when introducing a young person into her family circle. Thus satisfied, she wrote out a note for Miss Lee to enclose in her own letter to Fanny:

Dear Fanny: (wrote Miss Lee), *I will honour your request for secrecy at this time because of my understanding of Lady Bertram's character. It is not to be doubted that should she learn you are* contemplating *accepting a post as a governess it would be a source of great uneasiness for her, and the kinder course is to inform her only if you have positively decided upon taking this position.*

My acquaintance with Mr. and Mrs. Smallridge is slight, but I have observed nothing which could suggest that living under their roof would be objectionable or ill-advised, and their children are still too young to have formed any habits that you yourself could not counteract …..

Should you decide to accept the post, you and I may meet in the course of the spring, but not before, as Mrs. Smallridge is expecting to be confined later this year and will not be travelling.

Yours, etc.

ps Mrs. Smallridge's letter does not name a salary. I suggest you condition for not less than 20 pounds per annum, with an allowance for clothing. Her relatives are drapers in Bristol, I believe, so the fabric for your wardrobe can be supplied to you at very little cost. It would therefore be advantageous for you to take some part of your salary in fabric in lieu of ready money. But your youth and inexperience does not justify requesting a greater sum than this.

Fanny was in her favourite retreat, the East Room, wondering whether she had gone mad or was she truly contemplating leaving Mansfield Park, when a gentle tap on the door revealed Mary Crawford seeking admittance.

"Am I right? Yes; this is the East Room. My dear Miss Price, I beg your pardon, but I have made my way to you on purpose to entreat your help."

Fanny, quite surprised, endeavoured to show herself mistress of the room by her civilities, and looked at the bright bars of her empty grate with concern.

"Thank you; I am quite warm, very warm. Allow me to stay here a little while, and do have the goodness to hear me my third act. I have brought my book, and if you would but rehearse it with me, I should be so obliged! I came here to-day intending to rehearse it with Edmund—by ourselves—against the evening, but he is not in the way; and if he were, I do not think I could go through it with him, till I have hardened myself a little; for really there is a speech or two. You will be so good, won't you?"

Fanny was most civil in her assurances, though she could not give them in a very steady voice.

"Have you ever happened to look at the part I mean?" continued Miss Crawford, opening her book. "Here it is. I did not think much of it at first—but, upon my word. There, look at that speech, and that, and that. How am I ever to look him in the face and say such things?"

Fanny thought privately that Mary Crawford had audacity enough to say and do anything, but lacking the courage to disagree or refuse the request, nodded in assent to both.

"You are to have the book, of course. Now for it. We must have two chairs at hand for you to bring forward to the front of the stage. There—very good school-room chairs, not made for a theatre, I dare say; much more fitted for little girls to sit and kick their feet against when they are learning a lesson. What would your governess and your uncle say to see them used for such a purpose? Could Sir Thomas look in upon us just now, he would bless himself, for we are rehearsing all over the house. Yates is storming away in the dining-room. I heard him as I came upstairs, and the theatre is engaged of course by those indefatigable rehearsers, Agatha and Frederick. If they are not perfect, I *shall* be surprised. By the bye, I looked in upon them ·five minutes ago, and it happened to be exactly at one of the times when they were trying not to embrace, and Mr. Rushworth was with me. I thought he began to look a little queer, so I turned it off as well as I could, by whispering to him, 'We shall have an excellent Agatha; there is something so *maternal* in her manner, so completely maternal in her voice and countenance.' Was not that well done of me? He brightened up directly. Now for my soliloquy."

She began, and they had got through half the scene, when a tap at the door brought a pause, and the entrance of Edmund, the next moment, suspended it all.

Surprise, consciousness, and pleasure appeared in each of the three on this unexpected meeting; and as Edmund was come on the very same business that had brought Miss Crawford, consciousness and pleasure were likely to be more than momentary in them. He too had his book, and was seeking Fanny, to ask her to rehearse with him, and help him to prepare for the evening, without knowing Miss Crawford to be in the house; and great was the joy and animation of being thus thrown together, of comparing schemes, and sympathising in praise of Fanny's kind offices.

She could not equal them in their warmth. Her spirits sank under the glow of theirs, and she knew she was on the point of enduring yet another unendurable circumstance; watching the bewitching Miss Crawford recite those lines which constituted very nearly a declaration of love, while Edmund played the part of a man who loved passionately but could not declare himself, owing to the disparity in rank between himself and his beloved Amelia. To add to her pain, if it were possible, Anhalt was Amelia's tutor in the play, the person who educated her and shaped her mind, and thereby won her respect and love – in just such a fashion had Fanny come to love her cousin.

When the stage lovers were done exclaiming over the similarity of impulse, the conformity of thought, and the delicacy of the motive, which had prompted both of them to seek Fanny's help, Edmund proposed that they rehearse together, and Fanny was wanted only to prompt and observe them. With exquisite self-consciousness then, on the part of all the parties, they rehearsed the dialogue:

Amelia. I will not marry.

Anhalt. You mean to say, you will not fall in love.

Amelia. Oh no! [ashamed] I am in love.

Anhalt. Are in love! [starting] And with the Count?

Amelia. I wish I was.

Anhalt. Why so?

Amelia. Because he would, perhaps, love me again.

Anhalt. [warmly]. Who is there that would not?

Amelia. Would you?

Anhalt. I—I—me—I—I am out of the question.

Amelia. No; you are the very person to whom I have put the question.

Anhalt. What do you mean?

Amelia. I am glad you don't understand me. I was afraid I had spoken too plain. [in confusion].

So sensitive were the two amateur players to each other, when embarking upon a dialogue of this nature, it was not to be wondered that they did not notice the occasional wavering in the voice of their prompter, who at one point lost the struggle to maintain her implacability of manner and had closed the page and turned away exactly when Edmund wanted help. It was imputed to very reasonable weariness, and she was thanked and pitied; but she deserved their pity more than she hoped they would ever surmise. She quite correctly imputed the warmth of Anhalt's responses to Amelia as more than play-acting, and while she could not answer for the sincerity of Miss Crawford's affections toward Edmund, she was in no doubt that Miss Crawford did not object to Edmund's being in love with her.

Left to herself again, Fanny retrieved the letter from Mrs. Smallridge and perused it once again with swimming eyes: *If Miss Price is able to Arrange her own conveyance to the Raleigh Inn, Oxford, on the 22nd inst., she will be Encountered by one Mrs. Butters, viz, Aunt to the Undersigned, who will conduct an Interview and, should Miss Price's answers and Appearance prove all that is Satisfactory, the said Aunt will Convey her from thence by private carriage thither to Keynsham Hill.*

25

Boyle County Public Library

Although the language of the letter hinted at an aspiration, on Mrs. Smallridge's part, to greater elegance of epistolary style than she might actually possess, this insight into her future employer's capabilities gave Fanny no alarm. The letter gave directions for writing to Mrs. Butters to confirm the arrangement, a *rendezvous* in Oxford now only two days hence. Fanny's despair made her reckless, and in the most daring act of her short life, she determined to be in Oxford at the appointed time.

She had received, over the years, gifts of pocket money from her aunt and uncle as they were in the habit of bestowing on all the young people for birthdays and holidays, but unlike Maria and Julia, who made a habit of exceeding their allowances, Fanny always saved more than she spent. Apart from small acts of charity and the purchase of some books, Fanny was building a nest egg against the day she and William could at last settle in their own cottage. She possessed sufficient funds to travel to Oxford by mail coach and a little further besides.

Even as she told herself that her proposed course was rash, dangerous, and worst of all to a temperament so sensitive as hers, ridiculous, she found herself already calculating in her mind what, if anything, amongst her few possessions she might be able to carry away from the household without detection. She would take several of her plainest gowns, and perhaps a second pair of shoes – but alas! – she would leave her beloved little library behind, as she had not the strength to carry all her books with her to the village. As she looked about the East Room at the pictures and gifts she had received over the years, she felt a fresh sensation of guilt and humility. The table between the windows was covered with work-boxes and netting-boxes, all gifts from her cousins at different times, principally by Tom. All must remain, and as she contemplated these kind remembrances from her family, her Aunt Norris's accusations of ingratitude struck her as forcibly as they had ever done.

Her alternative was to continue as a silent witness while Edmund courted Mary Crawford, and if, as Fanny devoutly hoped, Miss Crawford ultimately rejected him, it was after all only a matter of time before he fixed upon another woman as his wife. Fanny knew that the woman Edmund Bertram married could style herself, in all rationality, as the happiest and most fortunate of creatures. Fanny did not condition for happiness. At 18 years of age, she sought only peace of mind as the best that life could offer her. Despair had given her the courage to do what once had been truly unfathomable.

Her little stock of sealing wax was exhausted and Fanny descended to the main floor and slipped into her uncle's study to obtain some more for her letter of reply. She tiptoed through the billiard room, where the scene painter was putting the finishing touches on the painted stone walls of Frederick's prison cell, while a young housemaid watched in admiration as she pretended to be dusting the woodwork. The room smelt pleasantly of fresh-sawn lumber and wet paint. Fanny had just reached the door of the hallway when her Aunt Norris, looking into the theatre, called for her.

"Come, Fanny," she cried, "these are fine times for you, but you must not be always walking from one room to the other, and doing the lookings-on at your ease, in this way; I want you here. I have been slaving myself till I can hardly stand, to contrive Mr. Rushworth's cloak without sending for any more satin; and now I think you may give me your help in putting it together. There are but three seams; you may do them in a trice. It would be lucky for me if I had nothing but the executive part to do. You are best off, I can tell you: but if nobody did more than you, we should not get on very fast."

Fanny took the work very quietly, without attempting any defence.

Presently, her aunt Norris exclaimed "Bother! I came away this morning without the green thread for the curtains. Fanny, go to my house and ask Betty for the green thread — stay, come back, take this bit of pink satin with you, I can use this little leftover piece to repair a cushion on my sofa."

Thus Fanny was able to run upstairs, and seal her reply to Mrs. Jos. Butters, care of the Raleigh Inn, which assured that lady of her attendance in two days' time. Fanny hurried to the village, the letter was posted and the green thread retrieved. She debated whether she should reserve her seat on the mail coach, but to do so she would need to give her name, which might cost her the absolute secrecy she required. It would never have occurred to Fanny Price, as she then was, to give a false one.

Chapter Three

A dress rehearsal of the three first acts of Lovers' Vows was to take place in the following evening: The players were all assembled in the billiard room and were waiting only the arrival of Mrs. Grant and the Crawfords to begin. With great bustle and satisfaction Mrs. Norris entered, followed, as a sovereign by her attendants, or a peacock by his tail, by two housemaids carrying the green baize curtains over which she had bestowed so much care.

"All the rings are sewn on, and we may hang the curtains now. Now you shall have a proper theatre!" She glanced up at the ceiling and her look of triumph disappeared, to be replaced with a mortified expression.

"Tom! Tom! To what were we supposed to attach the curtains?"

"The ceiling, Aunt? I – I don't know, the thought had never occurred to me. Send for Christopher Jackson, what has he been about? I told him I required a theatre."

As everyone waited, some exclaiming about the absolute necessity of having curtains, while two of the party privately sighed over the needless additional expense, the housemaids began to sink under their burden and Mrs. Norris, growing increasingly vexed, ordered them to fold the curtains in a neat pile on a corner of the stage.

Jackson swiftly arrived from the servants' hall. "Your pardon, Mr. Bertram sir, but you told me you wished me to build a stage, but constructed so as not to mar the paneling or the floors. No-one as told me you wished to hang curtains."

"Of course we did, you tiresome fellow," interposed Mrs. Norris. "Every stage has one of those – one of those...." she gestured overhead.

"A proscenium arch, ma'am?" asked Jackson.

"Whatever you may call it! A means to hang the curtains!"

"I'm very sorry ma'am, sir, for this blunder, but I did build as I was asked to build and no-one –"

"Never mind that now," interposed Tom Bertram. "Tomorrow morning, at first light, I want you to fetch more lumber and build a proscenium arch."

"Very well, sir. It shouldn't take more than a day or two, sir. And a fair quantity of lumber, sir."

"See to it."

Mrs. Norris was extremely put out that the rehearsal would take place on a bare stage with no curtains, and many a reflection on Christopher Jackson and his sly, lazy, cunning ways was needed to dispel the worst of her vexation. She was still expostulating when Henry and Mary Crawford arrived, but without their sister Mrs. Grant, who could not come. Dr. Grant, professing an indisposition, for which he had little credit with his fair sister-in-law, could not spare his wife.

"Dr. Grant is ill," said she, with mock solemnity. "He has been ill ever since he did not eat any of the pheasant today. He fancied it tough, sent away his plate, and has been suffering ever since".

Here was disappointment! What was to be done? After a pause of perplexity, some eyes began to be turned towards Fanny, and a voice or two to say, "If Miss Price would be so good as to read the part." She was immediately surrounded by supplications; everybody asked it; even Edmund said, "Do, Fanny, if it is not very disagreeable to you."

"And I do believe she can say every word of it," added Maria, "for she could put Mrs. Grant right the other day in twenty places. Fanny, I am sure you know the part."

Fanny could not say she did not; and as they all persevered, as Edmund repeated his wish, and with a look of even fond dependence on her good-nature, she must yield. She would do her best.

Their audience was composed of Lady Bertram and Mrs. Norris. Julia stayed pointedly away. Mr. Rushworth, resplendent in his pink satin cape, watched glumly through the first act as his affianced Maria explained to her son, as portrayed by Henry Crawford, how she had come to be seduced by the Baron Wildenhaim; Frederick knelt before the anguished Agatha, took her hand, and pressed it against his heart as she declaimed:

Oh! oh! my son! I was intoxicated by the fervent caresses of a young, inexperienced, capricious man, and did not recover from the delirium till it was too late.

Fanny, watching from the wings, thought Rushworth would exclaim aloud, but his scowl merely darkened.

The second and third acts brought Fanny's time of suffering, as she watched Miss Crawford – in her guise as the impudent, bewitching Amelia – make love to the noble-minded Anhalt. The words of love spoken to each other, while powerfully painful for Fanny to hear, were yet not so tormenting in the billiard room, as they had been in the quiet and intimacy of the East Room, not with the distraction of the feathers on Lady Bertram's headdress bobbing about as she dozed and awakened, and Mrs. Norris's constant fidgeting – but they were tormenting enough.

For her own stage debut she could barely speak above a whisper, but she cared not. This was to be her last night amongst them, the last night she would stand close enough to Edmund to brush against his sleeve, to hear his voice, to see his dark hair as it curled gently just over his collar, to see him bestow a sympathetic smile on her as she spoke her lines.

What with the fits and starts, and the patient coaxing of Mr. Rushworth through his two-and-forty speeches, and the impassioned bellowing by the Baron, the final curtain, had there been one, would not have been rung down until after nine o'clock. Lady Bertram had been gently snoring since the beginning of Act II, but Mrs. Norris was all enthusiasm and full of the warmest praise for the players. Mr. Yates declared himself tolerably satisfied (in truth, he was being polite, for the efforts of the others were far from the mark of excellence he himself had set). Tom proposed a bowl of punch and supper in the dining room, and Mary and Henry Crawford were earnestly desired to stay the night. The servants, some of whom had been listening to the play by lingering in the hallway without, scattered like a flock of pigeons to bring victuals, candles, and hot punch, and to prepare enough beds for all the guests.

The young people, still with the exception of Julia, retreated to the dining room to drink, eat and be merry, and Lady Bertram and Mrs. Norris retired for the evening, soon followed by Fanny, under plea of a slight headache.

Fanny encountered Julia on the staircase. "I see that you have given in at last, Fanny," her cousin said scornfully.

"It was only for a rehearsal, Julia. I don't wish to act, as you know."

"Ah, even when you do wrong by your own admission, you do no wrong. Have you never succumbed and done what you knew to be wrong? No? I will tell you why. It is not because you are more virtuous than the rest of us – though I know you think you are. It is because nothing tempts you. You are too frightened of everything to attempt anything. Whatever is not tame and insipid is disgusting to you. Wherefore then, can you hold yourself out as better than the rest of us?"

"Julia, I never – "

But Julia brushed past her carelessly and went up to her own room.

And so, farewell, cousin! Fanny saluted her silently, and retired to her bedroom, but not to sleep. She sat instead, at the rickety little table that could barely support her washbasin, to compose a final letter to Edmund. But how much of her true feelings could she, ought she, reveal to him?

It was her intention, as she felt it to be her duty, to try to overcome all that was excessive, all that bordered on selfishness, in her affection for Edmund. To call or to fancy it a loss, a disappointment, would be a presumption for which she had not words strong enough to satisfy her own humility. To think of him as Miss Crawford might be justified in thinking, would in her be insanity. To her he could be nothing under any circumstances; nothing dearer than a friend. Why did such an idea occur to her even enough to be reprobated and forbidden? It ought not to have touched on the confines of her imagination. She would endeavour to be rational, and to deserve the right of judging of Miss Crawford's character, and the privilege of true solicitude for him by a sound intellect and an honest heart.

Only when her final letters were composed and sealed did she blow out her candle, climb into bed and attempt in vain to fall asleep.

***

Downstairs in the dining room, Mary Crawford laughingly congratulated her brother on his artistry. "Undoubtedly, Henry, you are the best actor among us. Your Frederick was truly affecting! However, I maintain that comedy is more difficult to portray than tragedy. Did *I* acquit myself creditably?"

"Yes, you were of course excellent – and I won't bother to deny that I was too, but, Mary…" her brother looked around before continuing in a lower voice. "I think this will be my final performance. It is time to put some distance between myself and the fair Maria. Our little game has become too serious. I fear I may have become somewhat entangled, and should she lose her head and renounce Rushworth, I shall be at some difficulty to extricate myself."

"Would marriage to Maria Bertram be so terrible? You know our sister wants us to marry into this family. Think of the general joy it would bring – I, myself would be very happy to see you settled. She is a handsome girl – why do you resist?"

"As though you need to ask, Mary. Matrimony forms no part of my plans at present."

"Yes, but Henry, you speak as though you wish never to return," and Mary glanced across the room at Edmund Bertram

"Alas, Mary, if I don't get away, I fear the consequences."

"Yet you were as ardent as ever, if not more so, with Miss Bertram tonight! Could you not simply be more discreet? Or turn your attentions back to her younger sister?"

Henry shook his head. "Tonight must bring a close, I fear. I predict that tomorrow our uncle will have suffered a gouty spell and will have written, requesting my attendance on him. At any rate, Lord Delingpole has invited me to join his hunting party."

"You cannot mean to leave me here with only my sister and Dr. Grant to talk to!"

"Come with me, then! Lady Delingpole will welcome your company."

"Only for the pleasure of abusing Lord Delingpole to me. I think not, Henry. Not now."

Miss Crawford soon excused herself to retire for the night, which seemed to signal a general break-up of the party; Maria Bertram made her *adieux*, Mr. Rushworth yawned and took his leave, and Henry Crawford slipped away quietly. Only Tom Bertram and Mr. Yates remained behind.

Mary Crawford paused at the second floor landing and stood at the tall windows overlooking the path which led down the hill past her temporary home at the Parsonage. For the past four months, the young Bertrams, her brother, and she had come together almost every day— walking, talking, riding, dining, reading, singing, laughing and flirting. But, should her brother make good on his promise and leave them on the morrow, she feared the immediate effects of such a change. She saw herself isolated at the Parsonage. The sisters, while professedly her friends, had not truly formed an intimate tie with *her*, clearly preferring her brother's company to her own. She, in turn, while not disliking the Bertram sisters, was, it must be confessed, only interested in being on an intimate footing with them as it brought her into contact with their brother Edmund. Henry's removal would make this fact, disguised by the frequent comings and goings of both households, all too evident.

After some moments of calm deliberation, Miss Crawford quietly glided along the passageway to Julia's bedroom, and found Julia awake, still dressed, also searching for solace by gazing out the window.

"How now, Julia!" she cried. "Shall I call your maid, or can I assist you? I promise you, the world will wear a better aspect tomorrow morning, after a good night's sleep."

"A good night's sleep!" Julia exclaimed scornfully. "They say that a troublesome conscience keeps one awake, but in my experience the opposite is true. *I* have not wronged anyone, *I* have not deceived anyone, and I cannot close my eyes. But *she* sleeps soundly at night, after making a fool of her future husband before his very face!"

"As for *sleeping soundly*," Mary said with meaning, "Just now, I went to your sister's bedroom to wish her goodnight, and there was no answer. The door was slightly ajar, so I peeped inside – her lady's maid was sitting there asleep by the fire, but of Maria, there was no sign."

"Where is she then? With the others?"

"No, she was not in the dining room when I left. And," – with an earnest look, "And – neither was my brother...."

Further hints were not necessary. Julia took a candlestick from her dressing table, slipped out of the room in her stockinged feet and glided down the stairs.

The servants had banked all the fires and retired for the night, save for a solitary yawning footman who stood at attention in the pantry, ready to serve Mr. Bertram and his last remaining guest. The clocks were striking eleven and Tom Bertram and Mr. Yates were still holding high revel in the dining room, having opened their fourth bottle of wine.

Yates was half sitting, half lying at his ease across several dining room chairs, entertaining himself by flicking playing cards at, but seldom into, the upturned hat of his Baron costume.

"This is what happens when I go out shooting, drat the luck," Yates took another long sip of wine. "My aim is atrocious. Not like Charles Anderson. D'you remember when Anderson shot the cork off a bottle of champagne at twenty paces in the old Duke's gallery? Shame about the bust of Diana, of course."

"Nonsense, Yates. That statue wasn't an antique, but once Anderson took her nose off she looked like she'd been dug up out of Pompeii. Did the Duke a favor."

"Gave it that very.... veritable.... verisimilitude..... *in vino veritas*," Yates was cheerfully assenting, when a strange commotion arose. A woman's voice, raised in anger, another's in alarm, followed by a man's voice – "hold your tongues, both of you! You'll bring the entire household down upon us!"

"I'll NOT hold my tongue, you – you – blackguard! You cur!" It was Julia, and the argument seemed to be proceeding from the theatre room.

"They're not still rehearsin', are they?' Mr. Yates queried, the wine cup half raised to his lips. His host exclaimed something in an undertone, and bidding his guest stay where he was, Tom ran to the billiard room in the opposite wing of the house.

There, in the dim light of a solitary candle, a desperate situation met his eyes – Maria *en dishabile*, her limbs exposed, reclining on the pile of green baize curtains, Henry Crawford in the act of pulling up his breeches, his shirt tail untucked, hopping across the stage toward Julia who, like an avenging virago, stood poised, one hand holding her candle aloft, with the other hand pointing toward her guilty sister. Tom Bertram, hearing more footsteps in the corridor, closed the door firmly behind him.

"Is everything all right, sir?" He heard the sleepy voice of Baddeley, the butler, through the door.

"We won't require you any further tonight, Baddeley," said Tom. "T'was only a – "

"Only a play?" suggested Julia scornfully. "Only playacting? Tis too true, isn't it, Mr. Crawford? Tell her that you were only playing a part. Did you vow undying love? Did you tell her you would perish unless she gave herself to you? Let us have a repeat performance!"

"Good night, sir," came from the other side of the door. Baddeley retreated.

Henry Crawford's eyes met those of the brother of the girl he had seduced. "Bertram, my friend, what can I say? You're a man of the world, aren't you?"

The effects of two bottles of wine evaporated and Bertram felt himself to be fully sober. "Crawford, you and I shall speak in my father's study. Julia, you shall assist your sister and escort her upstairs as swiftly and quietly as you can."

"No! That I shall not! I shall never speak to her again so long as I live!"

"Come with us then, let me get you some brandy to calm your nerves. Maria, you have nerve enough for anything, I apprehend. Get yourself to your room and for heaven's sake, let no-one see you."

Julia took a deep breath and was on the point of screaming her defiance when her brother seized her by the shoulders and shook her roughly.

"Have a care, Julia. If you bring ruin and disgrace upon your sister, you will ruin yourself as well."

"*I* bring ruin. *I?*" Julia hissed, shooting a look of pure venom at Mr. Crawford. "Serpent! Cad!"

34

"Will everyone please leave me?" Maria asked, in a tone, Tom thought, more imperious than ashamed. Julia set down her candle and allowed Tom Bertram to pull her across the stage and through the door into his father's adjoining study, where Henry Crawford followed. The only light was from the faint crescent moon and the three could only see each other in silhouette, Julia's heaving breast giving testimony to the fierce passions that contended within.

"Well then, Bertram," offered Crawford coolly. "I am at your disposal." Julia gasped and moved to place herself in front of him, but he pushed her aside.

"If you are hinting at a duel, Crawford, don't be ridiculous. I find, when it comes to the point, that I've no wish to risk my life for my sister's honor – not when *she* has chosen to fling it away. But you will oblige me by telling me, how do you propose to dispose of yourself, Crawford?"

The door from the billiard room opened and Maria, hastily dressed, with her hair tumbling down her back, flew into the room and flung her arms around her lover.

"I see," said Mr. Bertram. "Very well. Julia, I promised you some brandy. Crawford, you will oblige me by staying out of my sight until I ask for you. I am not inclined to discuss this matter further tonight and I want in particular to consult my brother."

"I surmise that your brother will not be as…. philosophical about this turn of events as you are, Bertram."

"Don't be a fool, Crawford. All Edmund – or anyone save ourselves – need know is that Julia and I have seen, shall we say, undoubted proofs of affection, between yourself and Maria. And tomorrow morning, Maria, Mr. Rushworth will be informed that your understanding with him is at an end – unless *you* can bring yourself to look him in the face."

"I can look him in the face if I am assured it will be the last time I must ever do so," was the rejoinder, and Crawford felt Maria's arms tighten around him further.

Julia's outrage had subsided to wracking sobs which she muffled with her handkerchief; her carriage now spoke more of defeat than of anger as she allowed her brother to lead her away. The guilty lovers parted in the hallway, but not without a fond caress and a whispered "My Henry! My own!"

Mr. Yates remained, forgotten, in the dining room, addressing another bottle of wine. After waiting some three quarters of an hour for his host to return, he finally took a bottle with him to bed.

Fanny, lying in her garret bedroom, awoke briefly. She thought she had heard a quarrel but perhaps it had only been part of a dream. She had been dreaming of Henry Crawford, seeing him in prison, as his character Frederick was in Act Four of the play. Maria, as Agatha, pleaded for his release, but it was to her own father, Sir Thomas, that she pleaded in Fanny's dream, not to the Baron in the person of Mr. Yates. Fanny hovered on the edge of sleep, listening to the household clocks strike midnight, then one, then two, waiting for the hour of four o'clock, when she would arise.

Chapter Four

It would be hours yet before anyone by the name of Bertram, or any of the guests sheltered under their roof, required hot water, or hot chocolate, or curling tongs, or breakfast, or a morning paper, yet the corridors and offices of Mansfield Park were by no means deserted, even before the first hints of dawn. Fires were laid, chairs dusted and all was set in order for when the household should come to life. Unnoticed among the underservants, who scurried to and fro on their duties, there passed a slight figure, muffled up in a dark green travelling cloak, wearing a close bonnet and carrying a small portmanteau. No one challenged Fanny as she left the house through the tackle room and detoured around the stables, where she was unlikely to be noticed from the house. It was an unseasonably cold morning, and Fanny's breath mingled with a morning fog which enveloped the park and gave a ghostly aspect to the bare trees. Frost lay thick on the ground, and the shallow puddles in the rutted lanes were covered with a thin dirty film of ice.

Had she been able, Fanny would have paused to turn around and take a last look at the beloved house, and she longed to go into the stables and take affectionate leave of Edmund's gentle little mare, the one he had bought specially for her use, but fear of detection prevented her from doing so.

Fanny was passing carefully behind the outbuildings, when Christopher Jackson, driving a cart pulled by a reluctant old pony, overtook her.

"Why – Miss Price? What are you about at this hour, Miss? Are you going to the Parsonage or to town? You had best climb up here with me, don't be walking through the dews and the damp like that."

Fanny had no choice but to comply and climb up beside the tradesman.

"What brings you abroad so early Miss Price?" Jackson persisted. "Is anything amiss? Are you a-going to the White house? Is your aunt unwell?"

"My aunt Norris is in good health, I believe." Fanny countered. "Mr. Jackson, please do not trouble yourself on my account. Please let me down at the crossroad before we reach my aunt's house."

"Of course, Miss Price, but I can just as easily take you to her door. It'd be no hardship." Jackson looked again at his passenger and observed with alarm that she was wearing, in addition to her travelling cloak and bonnet, two dresses, one on top of the other, and any quantity of petticoats.

"Why Miss Price, for all the world, you look as though you was planning to..."

Fanny could say nothing but looked straight ahead, her face framed by her bonnet, so that Jackson could not see her countenance.

Jackson whistled thoughtfully and the pair proceeded in silence for some minutes. Finally, he spoke to her in an undertone:

"Miss Price, we folk who serve your family may be silent but we're not blind. We know what a life you lead. That lady, who out of respect to *you*, I will not name – and Jackson spoke with angry emphasis – "insulted my son, my own little boy, as much as calling him a thief – just because he was bringing a piece of lumber to me, at my bidding, at the same time that the upper servants were sitting down for their dinner. He had no more idea of what time it was than any boy of his age, but she must scold him in front of everyone, call him a sneak and a sly fellow trying to cadge a meal and tell him to run home again! A lady who has eaten how many fine dinners at your uncle's table? A lady who, let me tell you, never leaves her sister's house for her own with empty hands! Who walks through the kitchens as she goes, supposedly to bring instructions from my Lady Bertram, but really to help herself to anything she pleases out of the pantry and larders, so Cook tells me! To accuse me and mine of taking advantage of your uncle's generosity!" Jackson recollected himself and urged his pony on a little faster. "It may seem a small thing, to be spoken to in such a manner, but one small thing builds on another, I know all too well, and – and I reckon you do, as well. And I'll say this – though I'd say it to no-one but you – if you are going away in secret, then it's nobody's business, as I reckon, but your own."

Fanny could only nod her head in acknowledgement and thanks. She half felt that she was dreaming. They passed by the Parsonage, and her luck held; the windows were still dark; Mrs. Grant and her servants were not yet astir. They passed by the hedges, trees, fences, and scattered dwellings she had passed hundreds of times before, usually on some errand for her Aunt Norris in the biting winds of autumn or the glaring heat of summer. She had seen the trees clothed in the tender green shoots of spring while she tottered on her pattens through the mud, seen the fences lined with hollyhock in the height of summer, seen the winds of autumn toss the dry leaves before her down the road, and reveled in the beauty of new-fallen snow on the meadow, but never had she beheld these familiar scenes in the earliest light of dawn, through the tendrils of an October fog. She had the sensation that everything and everyone she knew was dissolving into a mist, leaving only her, Christopher Jackson, and the sound of the pony's hoofs on the half-frozen road. The enormity of what she was doing, actually doing, made her feel oddly detached from her own body. It was as though she could see herself in the wagon but yet it was not herself, it was some other person.

"Mr. Jackson, you will not speak to anyone about this?" she finally ventured.

"Well, I've been thinking on this, Miss Price, as we were getting along, and I believe I have hit on it. I would never tell your uncle, Sir Thomas, a falsehood, were he here, nor out of respect to him, any member of his household. If someone was to tell him that you was seen in my cart this morning, I would never deny it. But all I *know* is, I offered you a ride to your Aunt Norris's door, and you rode with me so far as the crossroad and you bade me not to go out of my way, but to let you down. And so I will and that's all I need say about the matter. So God bless you and keep you safe, Miss Price."

Fanny thanked him fervently and they maintained a companionable silence for the rest of the journey. Fanny had lain awake half the night, wondering if she had the strength to carry her portmanteau to the village, not daring to arrange for a ride or to borrow Edmund's pony, which she knew not how to saddle – oh, was there no end to her ignorance and helplessness! But the ride with Christopher Jackson had saved her a quarter of an hour and she walked as swiftly as she could through the quiet streets to the coach house well in time for the early morning mail coach to Oxford. Her luck held there, as she was able to obtain the last empty inside seat. Her name was entered in the station master's book, who evinced no surprise that a genteel young lady was travelling alone, without a companion or servant, and if he knew of her connexion to the great house on the hill behind the village, he betrayed no sign of it, or indeed any interest whatsoever beyond collecting her fare.

***

Tom Bertram could not long endure being the only soul, apart from Julia, who knew what evil the day must bring. He woke his brother Edmund before six o'clock and gave him enough information to comprehend that

Maria and Henry Crawford had secretly formed an understanding while Maria was still pledged to Mr. Rushworth.

"What would I give not to have to perform this interview with Rushworth, Edmund. I would almost condition for my father to be here, rather than have this fall to my portion!" Tom exclaimed.

"But our father is expected every day, and I grieve to think of how imperfectly we have discharged the trust he placed in us, to superintend his daughters – "

"Stop! Stop, don't preach to me now, for pity's sake, Edmund!" cried Thomas. "We have enough to do. We must break the news to our mother, we must manage Julia somehow. Can *she* reconcile herself a marriage between Maria and Mr. Crawford? What think you?"

"Perhaps, if given enough time. I can hardly take it in myself and I never fancied myself in love with Crawford, as I fear Julia has. But as awkward as this situation is, matters may yet tend for the best. You know what misgivings I was harboring about Maria's union with Rushworth. Crawford is inferior to Rushworth in point of fortune, but his superior in understanding, education, address, wit – "

"Surpassing Rushworth in wit would be about as challenging as surpassing our dear mother in enterprise."

"Yes, yes, and perhaps this augurs well for Maria's happiness, once the scandal attached to the sudden dissolution of her engagement to Rushworth passes over. However, can an understanding formed under such circumstances be expected to prosper? Whatever intimations Crawford has given to Maria of his attachment to her – "

(*May you never know about the intimations Crawford gave to our Maria, old boy*, Tom thought to himself.)

"– he knew she was promised to Rushworth. What's more, considering matters in this new light, I think Crawford's manner was a little too warm with *Julia*. I was disposed to like Crawford, but, taken all in all, I doubt that Maria will find lasting happiness with him. How can she rely upon his constancy, faithfulness, honour? I will always regret how this came about, as should they. Even though – " Edmund could not but consider the effect upon her who was always foremost in his thoughts – "even though I have reasons of my own for desiring closer ties to this family. But happily for us, Tom, we may defer any decision regarding a union with Crawford until our father's return, which will accord with *our* inclinations and *his* principles. He asked that Maria not marry until he returned, and this condition should abide even if the bridegroom changes."

Tom suddenly had a happy inspiration. "You are to become a clergyman soon, Edmund. Bearing sad tidings will be no small part of your future duties. Who better than you to separate Maria from Rushworth?"

Fortunately for Tom Bertram, nothing so reconciled his brother to the performance of an unpleasant task than the hint that it was a moral duty. Edmund charitably disregarded the motive that prompted it, and saw matters as Tom could have wished – if he shrank from addressing the follies and sorrows of others, he was perhaps unsuited for ordination. With a heavy sigh, Edmund arose and dressed and sought out Mr. Rushworth for the first of many unpleasant interviews that must be held before the morning was over. He had never before had such cause to be thankful that his mother was not in the habit of early rising, and that Mrs. Norris preferred to take a dish of hot chocolate in her room before joining the family at breakfast.

He cared not a jot for the loss of the connection to Mr. Rushworth's grand estates and fortune, and he hoped, rather than believed, Maria would feel more regret for the pain she would be causing Mr. Rushworth, than the loss of Sotherton and all the consequence and distinction attached to it. But above all Edmund wondered, how would *Mary* – for so he thought of her – bear this news? Would she be chagrined, as he was, that their near relations had engaged in secret intrigues – Maria, breaking her pledge to another, and Henry, requiting the hospitality of the Bertrams in such a fashion? Or would Mary welcome the joining of the two families as a precursor to another, more intimate tie?

Edmund found Maria's fiancé – or so poor Mr. Rushworth still fancied himself – pacing up and down in the little theatre, attempting to memorize one of his two-and-forty speeches, beating time with one hand as he furled and unfurled his copy of the script.

.....:*In a gay, lively, flimsy*.....hang it all! *In a gay, lively, inconsiderate, flimsy....... gay, lively, inconsiderate, flimsy, frivolous coxcomb...... such as...... such myself, it is... excusable.* No, *it is* in*excusable: In a gay, lively, inconsiderate, flimsy, frivolous coxcomb such as myself, it is inexcusable. For me to keep my word to a woman, would be deceit: 'tis not expected of me. It is in my character to break oaths in love.*

A quiet shuffling, an *ahem*! brought Mr. Rushworth to order. He brightened at the sight of Edmund. "Is everyone awake? Is breakfast ready?"

Although Edmund had never congratulated himself on the prospect of having Mr. Rushworth as a brother-in-law, it was with genuine shame that he explained the connexion between the families was not to be, – if Mr. Rushworth wished to hear confirmation from Maria's own lips he should have it, but circumstances had arisen which compelled the Bertram brothers, acting *in loco parentis,* to state that they could not, in honour, countenance the proposed union. Maria had transferred her affections to another – Mr. Rushworth could not be in doubt as to whom Edmund referred – Mr. Rushworth was held in too high esteem by them all, not excluding, of course, Maria, for any of them to be a party to the marriage going forward under the present circumstances. Edmund observed Mr. Rushworth's countenance change slowly from perplexity, to surprise, to indignation, before Edmund's concluding 'greatest esteem and very great regret.'

Rushworth cleared his throat, and asked for his carriage. "I think I shall go away. I believe I shall, Mr. Bertram. I believe I shall go home to Sotherton."

"Without," he added, after some additional thought, "Without seeing Miss Bertram. Or having breakfast."

Edmund stayed with the disappointed lover until his manservant was summoned, his valises were swiftly packed and his carriage was brought round, and Mr. Rushworth left Mansfield Park, never to return. Although Maria's rejected suitor does not appear in this story again, the reader may kindly wish to know that by the time he reached the outskirts of Mansfield village, he was as angry as he had ever been in his life; by the time he crested Sandcroft Hill, he was wanting his breakfast very much indeed, and by the time he reached the long avenues leading to Sotherton, he was reflecting that, all things considered, he was tolerably relieved that he would not marry Miss Bertram, as for many months past she had been cold and careless in her manner, rejecting even the touch of his hand, and causing him to doubt whether she was of a truly amiable disposition.

***

The sound of hammer and saw drew Tom Bertram from his unhappy meditations over his morning coffee, and hastening to the billiard room, he found Christopher Jackson hard at work, as directed, building the proscenium arch. Jackson was abruptly dismissed, with orders to return later that day and "take the whole d—ned thing apart – take it away and burn it." The scene-painter was dismissed, having spoilt only the floor of one room, ruined all the coachman's sponges, and made five of the under-servants idle and dissatisfied.

Tom then retreated to his father's study, where, with his head in his hands, he recollected his brother's objections to the amateur theatricals, which he, in pursuit of his own amusement, had ignored, while knowing that Edmund's representation of his father's disapproval was correct, and further, acknowledging to himself that the *denouement* of the scheme was worse than Edmund's grimmest predictions.

Maria appeared before him, pale but determined. "Have you spoken to Henry this morning, Tom?"

"No, I have not spoken with our amiable guest and if I were to do so, it would be to inform him that Edmund and I have agreed to defer the question of your marriage to our father, upon his return. You shall not have long to wait, although *waiting* for matrimony is clearly a trial for you."

Maria's features contorted in ugly passion. "How dare you, brother, stand in judgment over me. How *dare* you! You, who have had had the freedom to ride and roam all over the United Kingdom, you who have been away to school, to Oxford, to Bath, to London, to every fashionable resort and race track, you who have poured out our father's money, on gaming, and drink and – and – other forms of pleasure, which are too foul to be named – whilst I – " Maria's tears were flowing freely now, "Whilst I have stayed here at home, doing my needlework, playing the pianoforte, unable to go anywhere, or meet anyone. You *dare* preach to me? You cannot know what it is to be buried alive, to awake every day to the same companions, the same routine, the same evenings, and the day after that, and the day after that. I dared to follow my heart for just one day – just one night – and I am threatened with ruin, and disgrace and exposure for all my days. Where is the justice in that?"

"Maria, it is not *I* who condemns you, it is the World, it is Society, it is the established modes of our religion – "

"It is one rule for men, and another for women! I defy you all! Tell me that *you*, Tom, have never, ever – "

"The world *is* unjust, Maria," her brother acknowledged. "But recognize who your friends are. To publish the news of an understanding with Crawford, immediately after dissolving your agreement with Rushworth, would only expose you to malicious speculation."

Maria startled, her lips quivered as though to say something more, but she quit the room.

A little while later, another conference was in progress in the breakfast room, which the Crawfords had to themselves, the appetites of all the younger Bertrams being so disordered as to make it impossible to contemplate pork chops, eggs, or kippers with equanimity.

"Am I to congratulate you now, brother?" Mary enquired. "Is this the end of your flirtations and intrigues? Mr. Rushworth has been seen off, I understand."

"Mary, you are being very charitable to refrain from saying 'I told you so.' Had I listened to your warnings, I would have given up the game with Maria Bertram and left this place weeks ago. Now I'm in a fairly delicate position. However, I take pleasure in informing you that I've obtained a stay of execution – we await the return of Sir Thomas. Perhaps he will conclude I am not good enough for his daughter."

"Maria means to have you, so in the eyes of the world, you are in honour bound. Ah, what a picture the wedding will be! Maria blushing in bridal lace, eyes downcast, I as one of her attendants, and Julia as the other – oh! my poor Julia! What did Benedict say of Beatrice? *She speaks poniards, and every word stabs!* Beware you turn your back on her, Henry, especially if she is holding a sharp instrument! So what do you propose to do while waiting for Sir Thomas's verdict?"

Henry yawned and stretched. "Life here is too hectic for me. I yearn for the tranquility of a fox hunt. And you? Can I convey you anywhere?"

"You mean to avoid the Bertram sisters for now?"

"Shall Maria Bertram, so lately, so publicly engaged to Rushworth, become the acknowledged bride of Crawford? Tongues would wag, insinuations would be made. I could not stand idly by and allow the honor of the fair Maria to be besmirched. T'were better if there were some time and distance between us."

"She will be anxious until your return."

"Ah well, as the Butler says in our play:
Then you, who now lead single lives,
From this sad tale beware;
And do not act as you were wives,
Before you really are."

"But Henry, if you refuse to marry Maria, then.... then consider how it places *me*. You know that I have grown more than commonly fond of Edmund Bertram."

"I had no idea you entertained any serious notions, Mary. He is a good enough sort of fellow, but will you throw yourself away on a second son?

44

He is to be ordained this winter, is he not? Do you yearn to become a clergyman's wife in a little country village? Without even a Mansfield Park nearby to provide society and amusement? You know yourself better than that."

"He is not yet ordained."

"Oh, well then. You will stay with the Grants and exercise your charms over Mr. Edmund Bertram. He, by the by, knows nothing of the... epilogue to the play that Maria and I performed last night. Out of charity to *you*, I will never breathe a word about it to *him*, and I'm sure my lovely Maria will likewise remain discreet. Julia may need some wise counsel from you."

"Yes, I can point out the two paths she may choose – she could expose you and share in Maria's disgrace, as no respectable man would marry into the family, or she can pipe a tear at your wedding, accompany you and Maria on your bridal journey and enjoy the season in London, under the chaperonage of Mrs. Henry Crawford."

"If you were a man, you could have a brilliant career at the Old Bailey, dear sister. Now, whilst you are arranging your future with Mr. Earnest – pardon me, Mr. Edmund – I shan't do anything to bring the wrath of Sir Thomas down on my head. Let me know when Sir Thomas returns. Send me a line when he desires a conference with me. From Bath, Norfolk, London, York, wherever I may be, I will return from any place in England, at an hour's notice. I won't publicly deny that there is an understanding between Maria and myself, but I will try to dance just out of her reach – for a time. "

"When will you make your *adieux*?"

"This morning."

And so it was that both of Maria Bertram's suitors were gone from Mansfield Park before Lady Bertram and Mrs. Norris appeared in the breakfast room. It fell to Edmund's lot to apprise the ladies of the rupture between Maria and Mr. Rushworth; Lady Bertram was perplexed and very near to agitation, her older sister was stupefied to learn that the match was dissolved, on which she had concentrated all her guile and energies, and which in her own imagination would serve either as a welcome-home offering to Sir Thomas on his safe return, or the family's consolation should he perish on the homeward journey. Because his mother and aunt could not understand why so eligible a match had been broken off, Edmund was compelled to unfold the further news about Maria and Crawford.

So astounding was this revelation, that the further disclosure that Tom had rung down the last curtain on his amateur theatre, before the said curtain had even been hung, was received with submission, even by Mrs. Norris. The curtain in question, over which she had presided with such talent and such success, went off with her to her cottage, where she happened to be particularly in want of green baize.

The last member of the theatrical company to appear in the breakfast room, enquiring dolefully for coffee and ham, was Mr. Yates. Of all of the members of the late theatrical troupe, surely he was the most to be pitied. His ambitions once again to be annihilated on the eve of his public triumph as an actor. It was with more obduracy than politeness that he proposed to summon two or more of his particular friends to Mansfield to take over the roles abandoned by Mr. Rushworth and Mr. Crawford. Even Tom grew weary of his friend's tenacity and was truthfully not sorry to hear Yates speak of shortening his visit amongst them to merely another fortnight or two.

The inhabitants of Mansfield Park, each with their own wishes, regrets, and cares, were not assembled together until dinner was laid upon the table. The silence that enveloped the gathering was complete. Maria was wrapped in her own reflections of her parting from her beloved, who had insisted, as he embraced and kissed her, that it was almost fatal to him to leave her, but it was necessary to protect her honour.

Julia was not speaking to most of the members of her family, and her looks proclaimed she would entertain no sallies from Mr. Yates. Mary Crawford contented herself with sending speaking glances to Edmund, wishing to ascertain within herself that his undoubted anger toward her brother did not extend to her. Lady Bertram was anxious and confused, and Tom Bertram was struggling with remorse, a feeling he hoped to overthrow tolerably soon as it was a d–-ned uncomfortable state. It was only when the first course was being served that Edmund, looking around, enquired:

"But where is Fanny?"

Chapter Five

Fanny was at that time, miles away on the Oxford Road, sharing a seat with a friendly but generously proportioned lady from St. Albans. The curtains were partly drawn against the morning chill, but what little she saw of the landscape was not worth craning her neck for – it was October, clouds stretched from horizon to horizon, and a persistent light rain fell all around. She had made this same trip almost ten years ago, as a timid child, and had travelled under the protection of the coachman until delivered up, at Northampton, to her Aunt Norris, a first meeting she still vividly remembered. *Let me never frighten the children in my care as my Aunt Norris frightened me! May I always be patient, and be not quick to find fault! And concerning Aunt Norris, may I learn to forgive and, so far as I can, forget!* Fanny prayed to herself.

At times waves of doubt and remorse washed over her, and she trembled guiltily at the thought that any of those she left behind might be angry with her for leaving Mansfield Park with so little ceremony.

No-one of Fanny's tender disposition could abscond from home with the intention of hiding herself forever from her relatives. She calculated, however, that those at the Park would assume she was headed to Portsmouth and, once it was discovered she was not with her mother and father, she would have arrived at Somersetshire. If she successfully entered the Smallridge establishment as a governess, she would send word to her family, and trusted that no-one could, or would, oppose her. She had never been legally adopted by Sir Thomas, so he had not the authority of a parent over her, and her own father, she felt tolerably certain, would not be so angered by her removal from one place to another, as to demand that she return to a home which by all accounts had no room for her. She had never received a single line directly from her father in ten years, and had only received an unsatisfactory and infrequent correspondence from her mother, whose letters always spoke of haste, and duties which called her 'to conclude her message,' more than of affection or longing.

The one family member on whom she could rely to return her affection equally was her brother William, currently at sea on *HMS Antwerp* and not expected back in port for another month or more. His approbation, indeed, meant a great deal to her and she trusted that her modest earnings toward their future home together, accumulated patiently over the years, at twenty pounds or more per annum, would contribute materially to his future comfort.

Fanny attempted to stop worrying about what she left behind her, by contemplating what lay ahead of her. She revolved in her mind a passage from Miss Lee's last letter: *The governess is neither a member of the family, nor is at the level of the other servants, although a well-judging, competent housekeeper is no mean companion. A governess exists between upstairs and down, and therefore might hear or receive the confidential remarks of both servant and master. The most essential qualification for being a governess, in my estimation, is an ability to endure a solitude of mind, whilst being occupied from morning 'til night. Do you understand me? I think, Fanny, that you can.*

She calculated to herself as every mile or half-hour passed, – by now, they will have missed me, by now they will have looked through the house in search of me, by now they will have found my letters…. will they be angry? Will they be worried on my behalf? Will *he* be worried?

***

Neither Maria nor Julia were in spirits to wonder at anything that did not concern their own fates, and not even the unexplained absence of their cousin could rouse them from their seats, but Mary Crawford instantly volunteered to help find Miss Price. She first went, naturally enough, to the East Room, where she fully expected to find Fanny sitting morosely by the fire. But the grate was cold – in fact was completely bare, as though no fire had been lit during the whole course of the autumn – and there was no Fanny. Mary descried a letter lying on the school table. She snatched it up and saw in Fanny's neat, elegant hand, the inscription: "To Cousin Edmund."

Mary was instantly convinced that Fanny had left Mansfield Park. The letter would provide some explanation, but what if – what if that explanation involved her brother Henry and his unguarded behavior toward Fanny's cousins? Fanny had often sat in the theatre and acted as prompter for many of the rehearsals between Maria and her brother. What if the silent watchful Miss Price, had, like Julia, been a witness to the indiscretions of her brother and Maria. Mary herself had left her uncle's home in London in disgust last spring because he had chosen to live openly with his mistress. Would not Fanny Price, who appeared to be the picture of female rectitude, flee from Mansfield Park rather than live with a cousin whose passions were stronger than her virtue? What if the letter contained a condemnation of her brother Henry's behavior with Maria? Fanny's testimony could only further damage the successful conclusion that Mary Crawford now sought to bring about.

These speculations took less time than it has taken to relate them – the seal was broken – the letter opened – another, smaller, note addressed to "Sir Thomas Bertram" fell out, which Mary set aside, giving her full attention to the letter addressed to her *"dear cousin Edmund,"*

You, cousin, who have always been my chief friend, advisor and protector, will defend me again I know, if any defense for my conduct can be made. I have tried to do what I thought was right, and if my judgement has erred, you will still understand my motives and my sentiments. If anyone can understand why I have left Mansfield Park, it must be you, dear Edmund. Upon your candour I must rely.

The time has come for me to recognize "who and what I am." I am not a Miss Bertram, and I vow before Heaven I have never had any expectation of assistance from your uncle beyond all that he has generously provided to me, ever since I was sent to live among you.

I always have been – and should I remain at Mansfield Park, always will be – accused of ingratitude! Can it really be so! My faults are many – faults of weakness, timidity and foolishness, but Edmund, I am not sensible of ever feeling less than the purest gratitude to your family for sheltering and educating me. Gratitude I do feel and will always feel, but I must confide this to you, that I can no longer endure being accused of not feeling, or showing, sufficient gratitude. I would rather put an end to this burden, this debt that is impossible to satisfy, than to continue as I am.

"Ingratitude indeed," murmured Mary. "Baited and scolded for years by that interfering aunt – only someone as meek as a Fanny Price could have borne it! And yet, even *she* has not borne it, she has broken her tether and run away! How extraordinary!"

Yet how much more shall I be accused of ingratitude now that I leave you all without making my farewells in person! But I am a coward, as you know, and could not endure a conscious parting. Please give your dear mother my apologies and my heartiest wishes for her continued health and happiness. Beg her pardon on my behalf, if you can! I enclose a note to your father, but again, I implore you to speak on my behalf, as I am unsuited to speak for myself. I am greatly grieved if I have caused any offense.

Satisfied that Fanny's letter contained no damaging intelligence concerning her brother and Maria, Mary hastily began to fold up the letter, even as she perused the final postscript.

Farewell, my dear cousin. The memory of your kindness, your guidance and instruction, will be all I need to sustain me in the future. We may not meet again for many years, so may I say in parting, as your happiness is more dear to me than my own, I implore you, do not bestow your affections on anyone who is not worthy of you! Please remember those misgivings of which I have hinted. I cannot say more. God bless you.

Mary froze in surprise. There could be no doubt that Fanny was referring to herself, Mary Crawford, as being unworthy of Edmund Bertram. A wave of vexation overtook her and a hot flush stained her cheek. Who was Fanny Price to presume to call her 'unworthy'? The poor relation, the daughter of nobody, whom she, Mary, had graciously flattered and befriended. What was that kind and elegant compliment she had recently bestowed – oh yes, 'She fancied Miss Price had been more apt to deserve praise than to hear it.' She thought Miss Price had been happy, even honoured, at the notice Mary had condescended to take of her. And instead, behind those modestly lowered eyes, that mild countenance, Miss Price was finding fault with her and confiding her thoughts to Edmund? Here was a most unexpected enemy!

If Mary Crawford was not worthy to marry Edmund Bertram, then who, pray, *was* worthy? A new suspicion darted into her mind just as familiar footsteps in the hallway announced that Edmund had followed her to the East Room. There was no time to re-seal the letters. With a rapidity of thought and gesture perhaps only possible for a Mary Crawford, she tucked the letter to Edmund in the folds of her shawl and regained her composure just as he crossed the threshold.

"There, Mr. Bertram, there. On the table."

"What! – a letter from Fanny to my father? Does this mean that Fanny has left Mansfield Park? And without protection?"

"The letter will confirm the fact, I fear. But perhaps she has gone no further than the village, or your aunt's house."

A swift exchange of knowing glances proclaimed without words how unlikely it was that Fanny would have taken refuge *there*.

"Then I will lay you any odds she has returned to her family in – where? Some seaside city, as I recollect."

"Portsmouth."

"Oh yes, Portsmouth. I would have looked into her bedroom," continued Mary, "to see if she has packed her clothes, but knew not which is her chamber."

"Yes…. yes. How quick-thinking you are, Miss Crawford! I admire your composure and presence of mind more than I can express. This is what a true Englishwoman should be! Julia is in weeping again, I fear. Would you be so kind – could I ask you – could you speak to her, endeavor to calm her, while I search Fanny's room?" And without waiting for a reply, he snatched up the letter intended for his father and ran out. She heard him running upstairs to the servants' quarters.

So, Fanny was placed in the attic with the servants, Mary remarked to herself as she hastened to the main staircase, tucking the letter to Edmund in her bosom. *As she was evidently so little regarded by the family she will be soon forgotten, I fancy.*

An errant thought froze her in mid-step. Fanny had said "I enclose a note to your father," in her letter to Edmund. What if Fanny alluded to her letter to Edmund, in the note to Sir Thomas? But, the message to the uncle was but a single piece of lady's writing paper, much shorter than the letter to Edmund. Fanny had been brief – she could not have aired any doubts or accusations.

At any rate, it was now impossible, without exposing herself to embarrassment and recriminations, for Mary to return the letter to Edmund without acknowledging that she had opened it. Even if she re-sealed the letter, she could not replace the note to Sir Thomas within it.

But what if? – what if Fanny had more guile than Mary had ever given her credit for? Was she running away only to be pursued? Was Fanny foolishly hoping for a reunion with Edmund, and a tender *eclaircissement*? Viewed through the lens of jealousy and resentment, Mary now considered her interception of Fanny's letter as fully justified, even providential.

It had been the work of an instant, of impulse, but Mary had prevented Edmund from receiving what she now regarded as a declaration of love from Fanny, and she resolved that he should never know of Fanny's true feelings for him.

***

As every mile and every quarter hour placed more distance between herself and Mansfield Park, Fanny was able to drift into a light sleep, her small neat head sometimes resting against the plump shoulder of the genial Mrs. Renfro. She dreamt of her brother William, of playing and running with him along the ramparts overlooking the sea in the days when she lived with her family in Portsmouth. William's smiling face was before her, her older brother, whom she had seen once only in the intervening ten years since leaving Portsmouth. She had written to William faithfully in all the years of their separation, and he to her. In his letters, he was interested in all the comforts and all the little hardships of her home at Mansfield; ready to think of every member of that home as she directed, or differing only by a less scrupulous opinion, and more noisy abuse of their aunt Norris, and with whom all the evil and good of their earliest years could be gone over again, and every former united pain and pleasure retraced with the fondest recollection.

In her dream, freed from the stifling air and restricting walls of their small home, invigorated by the ocean breezes and the cries of the seagulls overhead, the children larked about freely. William challenged Fanny to a race to the Union Jack, and he kindly curbed his own speed so that his little sister could reach the flagpole just before he. Breathless and laughing, she looked behind her and saw her younger brothers John and Richard, having thrown off their mother's hands, running to catch up. Little Richard stumbled and fell to the paving stones, but William ran swiftly to him and scooped him up with a laugh and a smile, and Richard, who had opened his mouth and drawn a deep breath in preparation for sobbing, forgot his sorrows and joined William and Fanny in the general laughter.

She awoke with a start, and fearfully wondered whether her family would be called to account for her abrupt departure from Mansfield Park. Over the years, Sir Thomas had done what he could for his wife's sister's plentiful family: he assisted Mrs. Price liberally in the education and disposal of her sons as they became old enough for a determinate pursuit. John was now in London and Richard was serving on an Indiaman. Would Sir Thomas put a veto on any future benevolence to Sam, Tom and Charles, the brothers still at home, to punish them for the actions of the sister? *No, no, that could not be*, she thought. *I think too well of my uncle to believe he would show resentment towards innocent persons.*

52

Recalling William's cheerful, blunt, confident manner, so different from her own, Fanny felt solace. She believed that, no matter what she did, and no matter what the consequences, William would be kind to her, support her and encourage her.

Fanny smiled to herself and drifted back to sleep, moving ever farther away from her past and toward an unknown future. Until she had a new home, she could not send William a direction to write to.

***

To make some small amends for all that Edmund had endured, and would yet endure, in arranging matters between Maria, Julia and the Crawfords, Tom Bertram, accompanied by Mr. Yates, had volunteered to ride to the village and confirm that Fanny had indeed travelled on the mail coach, as they surmised. When they returned, with the certain intelligence that she had boarded the morning coach to Oxford, they found a reduced party gathered in the sitting room. Maria and Julia had gone up to their bedchambers after tea. Edmund and Miss Crawford were talking intently by the fireplace, and his mother was lying on the settee, obviously in a fretful mood, stroking her pug dog for comfort, while his aunt Norris plied her needle with energy.

"*Why* has she gone away?" exclaimed Lady Bertram, still struggling with her puzzlement. "When I retired to my bedchamber last night, Maria was engaged to Mr. Rushworth and Fanny had promised to tack up my new dress pattern. I wake up to learn Maria is engaged to Mr. Crawford and Fanny has left us. How I wish your father were here!" Mrs. Norris, who had returned to the Park to support her sister in this time of crisis, had not yet reconciled herself to Maria's throwing Rushworth over, although, as Maria was her decided favourite, it would take but the operation of time for her to discover that Crawford was to be preferred and that she had both foreseen and approved the match. Her censures, therefore, were directed to Fanny. "Why indeed, Lady Bertram? She was met with nothing but kindness here."

"We opened Fanny's letter to father," replied Tom, "as he authorized Edmund and I to do with all his correspondence in his absence. Here is the letter, aunt," he added, offering it to Mrs. Norris with a significant look. "Perhaps *you* would like to read it to my mother."

Mrs. Norris took the letter reluctantly and read the following:

To Sir Thomas Bertram,

Honored uncle, dear sir,

This letter will surprise you and, I greatly fear, injure me in your esteem. Allow me to thank you for making Mansfield Park my home for these ten years. I am now 18 years of age and, as I am not entitled by birth or fortune to live as a Bertram, nor ever presumed to be other than who and what I am, I have resolved to return to my own sphere. I will ever remain,

Your grateful niece,

Fanny Price

PS – please give my respectful regards to my Aunt Bertram.

A thoughtful silence passed, punctuated only by the crackling of the fire in the grate. Tom waited for either of the ladies to recognize in Fanny's letter an allusion to the unkind words spoken by Aunt Norris. Then –

"But why has she gone away? Why?" from his mother, and "Humph. No mention of me, I see, although I superintended her upbringing as much as anyone. Ungrateful girl!" from his aunt.

Feeling that any remonstrance would be both futile and disrespectful, and feeling as well that his own callous treatment of his young cousin could ill bear scrutiny, Tom retrieved the letter and made no remark upon it, referring only to what he had discovered in his trip to the village.

"There can be no doubt then," Tom concluded, "She bought a ticket to Newbury and by the time we discovered she was missing, she had already been on the road for eight hours."

"And from Newbury it is only another day's journey to Portsmouth," Edmund explained for Miss Crawford's benefit.

"No prospect of overtaking her, then. Mother, could you please send a note to your sister Price, asking her to inform us of Fanny's safe arrival?"

"I daresay *she* wrote to her family in advance to advise them of her coming," Mrs. Norris ventured, who appeared to be chiefly annoyed that she had not been consulted on the scheme, or asked to organize the trip herself, for she could not be supposed to object to Fanny's departure from the household. "Such secrecy and double dealings, I never expected to see! Baddeley," she enquired of the butler, who had entered to remove the tea things, "did Miss Price give you any letters to post in the last fortnight?"

Baddeley paused, "I believe, ma'am, she sent a letter to her brother, the midshipman. Aboard the *Antwerp*, ma'am."

"She writes him every month, I think," said Edmund. "but she has no other correspondents that I know of, outside of her family."

"If you would be so kind as to give me the direction to her parent's home in Portsmouth, Mr. Bertram," Mary interposed. "Would it be officious of me to write to her directly – as a friend?"

"You are too good," Tom answered, "but I expect Maria or Julia to....."

"Oh, but they have cares of their own, and – and, am I not soon to become your sister, that is – once Maria and Henry are united?"

Tom said nothing, but Edmund's countenance, as he thanked Mary for her kindness, was all she could desire, and she accepted his offer to accompany her back home to the Parsonage, where, despite the chill of the evening, they chose to walk, so that they might have a longer *tête-à-tête*.

"You do not appear to be angry with me, Mr. Bertram."

"Angry? No. Did you suspect me of being so?"

"Thank you. I wanted to assure myself. I know that my brother has behaved selfishly, imprudently. I cannot expect you to countenance his behavior, whatever the outcome. And I feared... I feared...."

For answer, Edmund drew her arm within his.

"While my brother certainly behaved rashly, in the end it will all be for the best. As for poor Mr. Rushworth, he is better off as he is. You were kind enough to undeceive him, but the truth would at last have dawned upon him sooner or later."

"While I cannot defend either of our relatives, I think the first error was on my sister's side. When Maria discovered her feelings for Rushworth were not what they ought to be, she should have ended the engagement."

"You have heard of the expression, 'a bird in the hand,' Mr. Bertram? Many women would not relinquish the first plump little bird until she was assured of the second."

"Night is falling and I cannot clearly see your face, Miss Crawford. I don't know if you are jesting or are in earnest. If you sincerely believe this, then your opinion of womankind is a degraded one."

"You are too severe upon our sex, Mr. Bertram. Kindly recollect, if you please, that we women generally are not as bold as Amelia to her Anhalt; custom deprives us of the freedom to make declarations of love. The alliance with Mr. Rushworth was not a thing to be thrown away lightly unless she was certain she had secured my brother's affection."

"By 'alliance' you are referring, I suppose, to his property and his fortune?"

"Any sober-minded woman would weigh a proposal from such a man very carefully before refusing. You shake your head. But we have debated this point before, have we not? Please," she leaned lightly on his arm, "let us not quarrel about the prudence of marrying well. We have had enough discord for one day! I flatter myself I was of *some* use today in soothing both your sisters. To succeed with them, only to quarrel with you, makes me doubt my abilities as a conciliator. But pray believe me when I say that I respect your opinions. You cause me to think and reflect, as perhaps no other person has.... you have a solidity, a constancy, so different from the sort of man one meets in London."

"If I could lay myself out for a compliment as artfully as some ladies do, I would prefer to hear some encomiums on my wit."

Mary laughed, and Edmund had never heard a sound half so enchanting. "Your wit, Mr. Bertram, could be used to start a fire, so dry as it is."

And Edmund was almost ready to forget that not half a minute ago he had been distressed to hear Mary speak of her brother's imprudence, merely imprudence, and not his honour. He thought to himself that he would have to relate some part of the conversation to Fanny, as was his habit – then startled slightly when he remembered that Fanny was gone.

"Yes, what is it, Mr. Bertram?"

"I own myself surprised that Fanny would go away without confiding in me...."

"Yes! It shows such a want of consideration and respect for you, as must astonish anyone who knows of your kindness to her. So patient with her timidity! So indulgent of her dependence on you! Can you speculate on her reasons for leaving so abruptly?"

"I think I can. She has been living amongst us since she was a child, and yet has not always felt herself to be *one* of us, and you were recently a witness to an instance of why this is so. I think it has, at times, been difficult to bear – even more difficult than I supposed."

"She may have resented being left at home to protect your good mother from *ennui* while your sisters were attending balls and dinner parties?"

"I do not mean to imply that she felt resentment. You have seen how truly modest and retiring she is. I recollect when you said that Fanny seemed almost as fearful of notice and praise as other women were of neglect. Your powers of observation are remarkably acute."

Mary was pleased that her companion had stored a casual remark she had dropped in his memory, and even more pleased that he did not list jealousy of herself as the reason for Miss Price's departure. He seemed to be entirely unaware of his cousin's regard for him. She shivered delicately, as though she required protection from the cold night air, and hung upon his arm even more closely. "You know her best, of course, Mr. Bertram. I think her a dear, queer, little thing, in some respects like a child of eight, in others like an old woman of eighty, but very unlike the young ladies of eighteen that one ordinarily encounters! Recall her raptures at the trees of Sotherton, her quaint way of talking: 'to look upon verdure, is the most perfect refreshment'!" She began to laugh, then checked herself.

"While I can say nothing in defense of her *mode* of leaving your household, it may be for the best – yes decidedly it is for the best – for her to spend some time among her own people, of her own class, wouldn't you agree? As direct as your dear aunt can be, she spoke the truth – Miss Price is not one of you, not by birth, or fortune, and while the education and manners she has acquired under your roof may help her attain a station in life above her expectations, it would be cruel to allow her to think that she could win the affection of any gentleman of consequence."

"Are you speaking of matrimony? Fanny married? In my imagination I always pictured her residing here with my family. But now that you broach the topic, I must say that the man who sees Fanny's worth, and takes her for his wife, will have chosen wisely."

Miss Crawford stumbled a little here, and Mr. Bertram placed his arm around her waist, briefly, while she steadied herself. She looked up at him, slowly, and his breath caught in his throat.

"Do not imagine such a thing – yet, Mr. Bertram. She is still very young, and younger still in knowledge of the world. I wish her a safe and speedy journey to Portsmouth! But I cannot judge her too harshly for leaving you as she has done, as selfish and thoughtless as it was. Her yearning to see her own family is very natural. Having lost my own parents at an early age, I can imagine no greater felicity than being with those I love, knowing that I belong to them and they belong to me!" This last was uttered in such low, thrilling tones that Edmund might have spoken there and then, had he not recalled that the great dispute between them – his determination to become a clergyman – had not been resolved.

***

Fanny had paid for a fare to Newbury, in an attempt to convince any pursuers that she was proceeding on to Portsmouth. It was late afternoon when the coach reached Oxford, and Fanny alighted, her limbs stiff and her spirit subdued. She bid a quiet farewell to Mrs. Renfro and, carrying her portmanteau through the cobbled streets, walked for about half an hour to find the Raleigh Inn where she sought the landlord to enquire after Mrs. Butters. Oh yes, he knew the lady, and she travelled through twice a year at least, but she was not there, and yes, this was the only Raleigh Inn by that name in Oxford and if the young lady had no more foolish questions he would go about his business.

Fanny was at a loss, and she felt the familiar tears stinging in her eyes. Sighing, and resolving to compose herself, she found a quiet corner in the inn's dining room, and pulled out her letter from Mrs. Smallridge to confirm the name, date, time, and place, everything she had read above fifty times before. Putting up the letter, Fanny reasoned that Mrs. Butters might have been delayed in her journey from London, and that she, or some communication, might appear on the morrow.

Fanny forced herself to consider the possibility, however, that she had fled her home to meet with a woman who might never appear. What ought she to do? She attempted to steady her fluttering heart with deep breaths, retreating deep into the hood of her travelling cloak to avoid meeting anyone's gaze. To return to Mansfield would be ignominious. To find other employment in a strange city where she could not give a good accounting of herself, appeared utterly daunting.

She finally concluded that, supposing she never heard another syllable from Mrs. Butters, she would continue on to Portsmouth and visit her family. Perhaps they would have some use for her, or help her to some employment. However, she resolved, at the very least, to spend the following day in Oxford, and walk about the ancient city as a tourist in the place where her beloved cousin had attended college. Having made her resolution, she composed herself enough to walk outside again, past the high courtyard walls of the Inn, to watch the setting sun, as it finally emerged through the rain clouds at the end of the day and lit up the spires of the chapels and colleges, until an enveloping dusk fell over all.

She didn't know the price of a private room for the night; she was too timid to enquire, too modest to share a bedroom with strangers and afraid of being laughed at. But by observing the other guests, she learned how to place her request for some ale and pigeon pie, which in turn bought her the right to remain where she was. She spent her first night in the great world, nodding and stirring and nodding again in her chair, her portmanteau clutched in her lap, enveloped in her travelling cloak, and occasionally weeping silent tears.

It was not to be wondered that her thoughts were all for Edmund during that long night. She had never felt so utterly alone, and it was all her own doing.

***

Warming himself by the fire after his walk across the Park, Edmund wondered at the coincidence of Fanny leaving the household on the same night that the others had been preoccupied with Maria's affairs. Had she known of the intrigue between Henry Crawford and her cousin? Hadn't she, in fact, once hinted about it to him, and hadn't he dismissed the possibility? What else had his quiet, watchful cousin observed that he had not?

And again, why no note, no final word to him, whom she had always acknowledged as her best friend, her supporter and protector? Had he given offense somehow? Was she vexed with him? He had seen Fanny in tears on more occasions than he could count, he had seen her frightened, or worried, or nervous, or uncertain – had he ever seen her in a temper? Her letter to her uncle – while its language was calm, while there was neither accusation nor complaint, its brevity alone was a reproach to Sir Thomas and all the family, and its firmness of tone was so unlike Fanny that, if he did not recognize her handwriting as well as his own, he would have denied it could have come from her hand. Did he know his young cousin as well as he thought he did?

Ah well, he reflected. Another few days would bring a reply from Portsmouth. And so a long, miserable, uncertain day drew to its close.

Chapter Six

Leaving word at the inn for Mrs. Butters, and leaving her portmanteau in the care of the landlord's wife, who, busy and harassed though she was, was not unkind, Fanny left the Inn, intending to walk all the morning. The light rains of yesterday had given way to fresh sunshine and the city beckoned. As she made her way along High Street to Magdalen College, she began to discover the curious elation that comes on the traveler who has left behind anyone who knows ought of them. She had never walked along such a busy street; she had never looked through shop windows like a little vagabond child while eating warm gingerbread purchased from a street vendor. She had never had such freedom of choice in her life before, and perhaps the ability to make choices would lead in time to a more discerning, more confident Fanny Price. She prayed it would be so.

Fanny was a little light-headed, not merely from lack of sleep or proper food, but from the intoxication of actually seeing the spires of Oxford and all the well-known buildings of which she had heard so much from her cousins. She thought with reverent wonder of the antiquity of the great colleges, the brilliant scholars who had studied there – who had, perhaps, walked where she was herself walking, until the many sensations flooding her breast threatened to overpower her.

She was craning her neck to look upward at the handsome tower of the Church of St Mary the Virgin when to her mortification, she collided with a well-dressed gentleman who, after the initial surprise, seemed not at all discomposed by the accident. He silenced Fanny's profuse apologies with an eloquence and an assurance of address that Fanny had never before encountered – he was delighted to meet someone as enchanted by the beauties of Oxford as he. He had spent the happiest years of his life studying here. But surely the young lady was being neglected by some errant brother who was coming to meet her?

"No, indeed sir, that is…. my cousin is, that is to say, my cousin *was*…." Fanny could barely stammer a reply.

Without knowing what happened, she found the stranger's arm supporting her own, and herself being guided away from the main thoroughfare. "William Elliot, madam. At your service. And I have the honor of addressing....?"

An inner voice whispered to Fanny: *Governesses do not walk arm-in-arm in the street with strange men.* She pulled her arm away as though she had been scalded. Mr. Elliot raised an eyebrow and smiled; a most engaging smile. "Forgive me for my presumption. Your scruples do you great credit, but please be assured that I offer myself as your guide *and* protector." Once again her arm was pinioned against his side. "Did you know that you are standing only a few steps away from where the great martyrs of our faith were burnt at the stake? *We shall this day light such a candle, by God's grace, in England, as I trust shall never be put out.* Pray, allow me to show you the way."

His eye was so mild, his tone so reasonable and his manner so agreeable that Fanny briefly wavered, but again her inner voice counselled her: *If you do not have the self-assurance to tell this man to desist, then you must get back on the coach and return to your refuge in the East Room. You have not the courage, nor the presence of mind, to be a governess.*

"Sir! Thank you, but I must decline your offer. We are not acquainted and – and I have pressing business."

"Only a little further this way, and then you can decide if you wish to appoint me as your guide or no."

"If, sir, you *are* a gentleman, you will release my arm immediately."

Fanny had never addressed anyone in such a fashion in her life, and she prayed that Mr. Elliot could not feel how violently she trembled as she spoke. The stranger stroked her arm, feeling the slenderness of it, insolently running his fingers down her forearm, to firmly hold her delicate wrist. Fanny grew truly alarmed; he felt her pulse fluttering under his grasp, and suddenly he released her.

"Did you think yourself in danger? Do not flatter yourself, solemn little lady. I find on closer examination you are a little minnow that I would just as soon release back into the pond. Perhaps in a year or two you'll be worth what a man must lay out in bait, hook and tackle."

Fanny ran away, with the faint laughter of William Elliot chasing after her.

***

Mrs. Butters and her maid, coachman, and groomsmen, having been delayed in their journey from London by an accident to one of her carriage-wheels, arrived at Oxford at about dinner-time. She was between fifty and sixty, in possession of a good fortune from her late husband, active and energetic, inclining to stoutness, decided in her opinions and confident in sharing them. During her married life she had lived in Bristol but, to be closer to a married son, now dwelt in Stoke Newington on the outskirts of London. As her niece, Mrs. Smallridge, was expecting her confinement at Christmastime, the kindly widow had agreed to pass the holidays in the retirement of the countryside, where her anticipated reunion with many acquaintances from her earlier life in Bristol was some compensation for leaving the metropolis.

The landlord of the inn saw to her every comfort and soon she was installed in a private dining room overlooking the thoroughfare, whereupon she lost no time in ordering an early dinner. As he was retiring, the landlord spied Fanny, very tired, thirsty and extremely footsore but completely gratified by her morning's sojourn in Oxford, walking slowly up the street.

"There's the young lady as was enquiring after you, Madam."

Mrs. Butters had been in receipt of Fanny's letter upon arriving at the inn and as she desired to interview the prospective governess immediately but did not want to wait for her dinner, Mrs. Butters spoke for more food to be sent up and bade the landlord bring Miss Price to her.

Now came for Fanny the moment when she hoped to impersonate a self-possessed, capable young woman, and not the frightened, tired child whom she really was. The landlord chivvied her impatiently upstairs, she was not to keep Mrs. Butters waiting - a quick trip to the privy was the only preparation he would countenance - and Fanny, who had had perhaps five hours' sleep in the previous eight-and-forty, unable to wash, brush, or arrange her dress, was ushered in to meet the aunt of Mrs. Smallridge. Her exhaustion contributed to the feeling of unreality, of moving through a dream, which had pursued her since leaving Mansfield Park.

A subdued "how do ye do?" was followed by an uncomfortable silence as Mrs. Butters took her survey of the demure applicant. "You look as though you could do with a hearty meal, Miss Price. Pray have a seat. Do not thank me, I intend to eat too much dinner and then I intend to fall asleep until tea time, so this is the only convenient time for our interview."

Prompted by Mrs. Butters, Fanny answered her queries, interspersed with mouthfuls of roast beef, turnip, and onions, and found herself growing more comfortable than she could have imagined. Mrs. Butters' manner was abrupt, but not unkind, and when she learned that Fanny was the daughter of a lieutenant of marines, her face brightened. "Is he indeed? In Portsmouth, you say. My late husband was a shipbuilder in Bristol, so we are both from sea-faring families. Where is the gravy boat? Dear me, that's the only boat I have anything to do with nowadays. That was a jest, child. That's better."

Mr. Smallridge, Fanny learned, was seldom to be found at home. He was of an old and eminent family, had no profession, and had obtained his estate and his independence through his judicious marriage. Mrs. Smallridge desired her children to acquire sufficient education to enable them to mingle in society but, cautioned Mrs. Butters, "We want no prodigies, no bluestockings or eccentrics fiddling about with home laboratories and dephlogisticated air or nonsense of that sort. What is your philosophy of education, Miss Price?"

"I... that is.... "

"Have you read *Emile*'s Rousseau? Or was it Rousseau's *Emile*?"

"Yes ma'am, I have."

"In the original French?"

"Yes ma'am."

"Well, I haven't and I dare say I never shall. My lady's maid tells me the book has to do with education."

"Yes ma'am, as I recollect, Rousseau believes that if the child is led with love and kindness, he will develop according to the dictates of nature, and a love for learning will unfold within him."

"And what do you think?"

"I have observed that learning one's letters is a drudgery, and if not compelled to do it, most children would not be put to the trouble of learning to read, but of course reading is the means whereby we may acquire all the published knowledge of the world. Rousseau's thoughts are impractical, I conclude. And I was told that his own children were not schooled in the fashion he advocates, so his advice should be regarded, I think, with some misgivings, as he never endorsed them by actual application."

"I was informed that this Rousseau believes it is better to praise a child into acquiring knowledge, rather than beating it into him."

"Oh, as a general principle, ma'am, I must agree." Fanny thought of the unsmiling and meticulous Miss Lee presiding over the school room at Mansfield Park. "However, ma'am, a governess should lead by example in being strictly self-disciplined herself, the better to enforce the same expectation in her pupils."

"Very well. Now let us turn to your accomplishments. Do you play the piano?"

"No, ma'am."

"Do you play *any* instrument?"

"No, ma'am."

"Can you draw?"

"No, ma'am."

"Paint in watercolours?" Fanny's heart sank at being thus exposed.

"No, ma'am."

"Mrs. Smallridge asked me to enquire. But I don't believe in the efficacy of these so-called accomplishments as some do. Where there is real aptitude and inclination, of course, masters can be engaged. But in my opinion the nation has its full complement of accomplishment – " she paused to see if Miss Price would smile at her wordplay, but she did not – "mediocre painters and sketchers, that is. And how many excruciating recitals in various drawing rooms have I suffered through! Have you been to London?

"No, ma'am. If you please, ma'am, I can instruct Mrs. Smallridge's daughter in her needlework – I can make lace, netting, fringe, filigree, do carpet work, and embroidery and cross-stitch of all sorts."

Fanny had had the forethought to bring with her a cunningly made little housewife, covered with ornate embroidery, as an example of her skills with the needle, which she presented to the widow. "And I am adept at plain sewing also, Ma'am. If you would care to examine the hem of my handkerchief, you will see the evenness of my stitches."

"Now *here* is a useful talent." Apparently satisfied with both her dinner and Fanny's answers, Mrs. Butters slowly rose from the table, followed with rather more alacrity by Fanny.

"Your youth is against you, or rather, your youthful appearance. Do not think I resent your youth! If you were attired in grey bombazine perhaps you would look more the part. But we are not expecting to engage an Oxford don for children barely out of leading strings. The boy, of course, will go away to school when he reaches the proper age. Caroline will be your charge alone. English, history, geography, natural history, some arithmetic, penmanship, dancing, needlework, and, when she is a little older, French. If you feel you can undertake this much then perhaps we will take you on trial. You may share a room tonight with my lady's maid."

Fanny was so astounded that she forgot – in fact it was a matter of days before she recollected – she hadn't asked about the wages the Smallridges would pay.

***

After her brother's hasty departure from Northamptonshire, Mary Crawford was anxious to see the Bertrams but she judged it best, given her brother's indiscretion and the folly of Miss Price, to remain quietly at the Parsonage for a few days, and make no calls unless invited to return. Without Edmund's grey mare at her disposal to ride, she was confined to taking many a turn in the garden beside the house, an exertion that suited the revolutions of her mind. She felt tolerably certain that her brother would acknowledge his duty to marry Maria Crawford in due course, but would Edmund undergo ordination before the tie between the two families became permanent? He had announced his intention to take the step with a friend of his, around Christmas-time, which was just over six weeks away. The thought filled her with something approaching disdain but she could not contrive an alternative, however many times she paced around the shrubbery. She and Edmund had canvassed this point before – he was too old for the Navy, expressed distaste for the law and soldiery, there was no interest to get him a seat in Parliament, but he must have *some* profession as a second son, as an unjust Providence had ordained that his brother Tom, and not he, was the heir to Mansfield!

When she thought of Miss Price, Miss Crawford's uncertainty gave way to resentment and jealousy. She had never heard Miss Price venture an opinion on anything much beyond the weather or the beauties of the shrubbery. To find herself held up by this mere nobody from Portsmouth as actually *unworthy* of Edmund Bertram – when in fact, any candid observer would have said the opposite – that a second son with no independent fortune was presumptuous to aspire to the hand of an heiress and acknowledged beauty such as she – this was not to be borne. Some remonstrance was called for. Miss Price should be warned, should be reproved, should be corrected, for her own benefit.

Mary recollected how Fanny tended to agree with anything Edmund said, how her light blue eyes followed him around the room. The two of them were undoubtedly very close. The more Mary thought of it, the more resentful she grew of all the past confidences that Edmund had no doubt shared with his cousin Fanny. How often had they talked of *her*?

She was called out of her thoughts by a visit from Maria Bertram, who sought her out that morning as the only person who could discuss the anxious topic of Henry Crawford with anything resembling sympathy or approbation.

As soon as she had reached the age of reason, Maria had taught herself never to wish or expect anything of consolation or advice from her own mother, because Lady Bertram could barely be made to attend to anyone for more than a few moments before her attention wandered, and at best would murmur absent-mindedly, "is it really?," or "poor dear," before her thoughts would completely revert to her own cares and idle occupations, an habit which, while not designedly unkind, had the effect of further depressing the spirits of her children who went to her hoping for someone to take a warm interest in their distress.

Aunt Norris had always praised and flattered her, and for that reason, Maria was as indifferent to her praise as she was to her censure – and for now, Aunt Norris was still angry at her for throwing Rushworth off. Her sister Julia's vexation with her had subsided into sullen grief; Julia spent her waking hours at the pianoforte, playing "Dido's Lament" over and over again. They were not even speaking to one another.

With no one at home then, to calm her spirits, Maria went to Henry's sister at the parsonage.

"Miss Bertram? Or, may I at last call you Maria? How good it is to see you! You are wondering, perhaps, if I have had a letter from my brother. Do not punish this messenger who has no message to deliver!"

"I recollect that you have said that your brother is no correspondent, Miss Crawford."

"I undertake to write him this very day for you, and to insist upon an early reply – should my letter find him, for he may be at Hill Street with my uncle, or gone fox hunting with Lord Delingpole, or heaven knows where. But wherever he is, I am certain he is thinking of you. And do not forget, you are not the only sufferer in Henry's absence. My poor brother-in-law has had no excuse to order extra dishes for dinner or drink claret for a week. Spare a thought for Dr. Grant's trials, in the midst of *your* distress! Pray, is there any news of Sir Thomas – or of Miss Price?"

"No, we have heard nothing from either, but we do not expect to have word from father until he is on our doorstep. Once he has reached an English port, he will travel to us more rapidly than the mail coach, I am certain."

"And no word from your cousin in Portsmouth? No assurance of her safe arrival?"

"I think not. It is most unaccountable, is it not? I never would have thought that my cousin Fanny had more daring than either Julia or I. We would never have gone abroad without a chaperone, in such a fashion."

"Ah, but surely there is no comparing the Misses Bertram with Miss Price, so far as the expectations of the world are taken into account? *She* may come or go, and is not noticed by anyone out of the little family circle, whereas, if the two first young ladies of the county were to decamp, we cannot doubt that Dame Rumour and her attendants Envy and Malice would follow in their wake, human nature being what it is. Everyone looks up to the Miss Bertrams for showing the world what female conduct should be, while Miss Price sets the pattern for nobody."

"Even so, I had not thought my cousin capable of it."

"Perhaps your Aunt Norris is correct that Miss Price is a sly, subtle creature. I always thought she was as she appeared to be – quiet, retiring, even timid, but evidently she harboured secrets. Did she ever confide anything to *you* of her innermost wishes?"

Maria looked startled by the question. "Fanny? Confide in me? No, I think not."

Miss Crawford flattered and pressed, and suggested that Miss Bertram, with her superior intelligence and penetration, must be in the secret of Fanny Price's true character and her unspoken longings. But she finally had to conclude, from Maria's answering entirely by rote – *speaking* of anxiety for Fanny while *showing* none, that she was almost entirely indifferent about her cousin, and was not in the least curious about what had driven Fanny to leave Mansfield Park! Fanny's heart, Fanny's woes, were but of little interest, at least in comparison with Maria's own concerns, which she soon took up again.

"Mr. Yates has left us, Mary, did you know? So we are all alone. You cannot conceive how lonely and solitary we are, after all the bustle of the play-acting! There are to be no more dinner parties or card parties either, as Edmund and Tom are being so hateful. They say the entire neighbourhood is speculating about me so I should not go abroad, either." She sighed. "They, of course, may go wherever they please, whenever they please."

"And when Mr. Edmund Bertram goes to Peterborough to be ordained, as it *apparently* pleases him to do so, our little circle will be even smaller!

Will you wait until your brother is in orders, so that he can perform the wedding ceremony for you and Henry?"

"Edmund? No, that would seem odd to me, somehow. Dr. Grant will suffice. Only....."

"What is the matter, Maria?"

"As I now recollect, your brother has not asked me to marry him. He said we would be reunited soon, and all sorts of wonderful things, but he did not, in point of fact, ask for my hand."

"Oh, pray do not worry. Perhaps he is waiting until he can speak with your father. Henry is quite old-fashioned in some ways, you know."

"In no way that I have observed!"

To turn Maria's thoughts to a happier train, Miss Crawford began to speak of Everingham, her brother's estate in Norfolk, and how handsome Henry had made the park and shrubberies all around it, and how it lacked only a mistress to make it all that was elegant and comfortable. Maria took her leave, feeling tolerably reassured, and with a promise to Miss Crawford that she would petition her brother Edmund to allow the use of the little grey mare to ride out if the weather continued fine.

Miss Crawford then went upstairs and composed a reproachful letter to her brother: *Oh Henry, when will you be serious at last?* She then, impulsively, pulled out another sheet of letter paper and composed a longer letter to "Dear Miss Price," directed to the Price home in Portsmouth.

Chapter Seven

The journey to Somersetshire was accomplished in a little over three days (Mrs. Butters preferring to spend no more than six hours every day on the road), and late in the afternoon, five days after Fanny had left her home, the carriage turned into the drive of Keynsham Hill, the estate of Mr. and Mrs. Smallridge, near Bristol. Three days' companionship in a closed carriage and at wayside inns had raised Fanny yet higher in the older lady's esteem. Miss Price was an attentive and courteous listener, faultlessly polite in her ways, tidy and regular in her habits, unobtrusive when Mrs. Butters was dozing in her seat, and conversable when her hostess was inclined to speak. Fanny could well tolerate long periods of silence on the journey, as she had so much to reflect upon, and was passing through country she had never seen, and although nothing could be viewed to its best advantage in the damps of late October, she was sometimes carried out of herself by the contemplation of a fine prospect or a cheerful town, as to make her forget she was now among people who called her "Miss Price" but never "Fanny," and that every mile drew her further away from all that was familiar and beloved.

However, when the carriage pulled up in front of the neat and modern home, fronted with fine white columns and large windows, Fanny was nearly overcome with trepidation and remorse. She was as frightened as she had been throughout her journey, not excluding the commencement of it, and heartily desired herself back at Mansfield Park, and was even, silently formulating her protestations and apologies for having falsely imposed herself upon others as qualified in any respect to be a governess! Her inner struggle to maintain her composure must have shown on her face, or betrayed itself by a trembling hand and a faltering step, as the lady's maid gave her an encouraging wink and a smile, and the groomsman fetched her portmanteau and gave her a little bow. Upon finding she had not the fortitude to speak out to end the masquerade, – indeed, she was at that moment too overcome to speak at all – she uttered a silent prayer, and followed the broad back of Mrs. Butters through the front door, where smartly dressed footmen in blue and gold livery stood at attention and so on to the sitting room where the mistress of the house awaited their arrival.

Keynsham Hill was smaller than Mansfield Park, but it was modern-built and all new-furnished and landscaped in the Capability Brown style. Mrs. Smallridge, to whom Fanny was presented, gave the impression of being landscaped in the old style, being so festooned and ornamented and emblazoned with ribbons and bows and silk flowers that she resembled an Elizabethan knot garden more than an Englishwoman of nine or eight-and-twenty. This was perhaps owing to modesty, Fanny surmised, as she was in an interesting condition and the stiff embroidery and embellishments to every part of her dress helped to conceal, or at least distract. She was a handsome woman, if no longer young, with dark eyebrows and eyelashes and the direct gaze of her aunt.

She welcomed Fanny not unkindly, expressed some dismay at her youthful appearance, and waved her away to be escorted to the nursery to meet her new charges. Fanny escaped, grateful to have avoided an interview, for it seemed Mrs. Butters, having made the choice of Fanny, would do the talking on this occasion. Mrs. Butters had overruled her niece, who desired a governess who could paint, draw, play and sing, but had armed herself with the argument that firstly, the children were too young to study these pursuits seriously, secondly, the lack of these accomplishments meant that Miss Price could not expect to command the salary that their cousins the Bragges were paying to Miss Lee, and thirdly, should little Caroline show promise as an artist or musician, Miss Price could be discharged and a new governess hired. "And, Honoria," Mrs. Butters pointed out, "These so-called accomplishments are on display only for a season or two and are abandoned by most ladies upon marriage. When did *you* last sit down to your pianoforte? And can we demonstrate that a gentleman chooses a wife because she can cover a screen or play a cross-hand piece? So much effort and expense for so little proven return. A knowledge of cookery and all the branches of housekeeping will better enable your daughter to become mistress of her own house one day. Of course she will never perform these offices herself, but she will know how they are to be done, and that's what signifies."

"I understand you, ma'am, and am vastly obliged to you for fetching Miss Price to us – but isn't she rather too young for the responsibility of looking after my children?"

"In many ways, she has an old head on those young shoulders. She can talk better *extempore* than I can write, and she is almost amusing when she starts prosing on in her quaint fashion! And, you know, she will do very well when you invite the vicar or any other superfluous gentlemen for dinner. She is very genteel, without appearing above herself." Privately, she added to herself, "But she's as unworldly as a day-old chick, for all that."

In the nursery, the ceremony of meeting the two children who were to be her charges was less of a trial on Fanny's nerves. Caroline was six years old, and Edward had just entered his fourth year. There had been another little boy, who, to the grief of his parents, had not survived his second summer, while the cradle in the corner of the nursery testified to the expectation of another little Smallridge.

Caroline at first showed herself indifferent to the new governess, being absorbed in play with her dolls, and only looked up briefly to regard Miss Price without expression or reply to her greeting, before returning her attention to Polly and Molly. Edward ran and hid behind the nursery-maid's skirts and refused, despite Anna's coaxing, to come out and say 'how do you do.' Fanny was a little disappointed that she was not loved at first sight, but knew enough about children and their ways to let them become accustomed to her presence.

Madame Orly, Mrs. Butter's lady's maid, kindly gave Fanny a tour of the principal rooms of Keynsham Hill. Her new home was built on a low prominence that had received an elevation, in name if not in fact, to a hill. There were several adjoining sitting rooms and a large dining room, all done in shades of rose and blue with gilded mirrors. In lieu of ancestral portraits, Daphne and Echo, Venus and Mars, Paris and Helen, clad in the flimsiest of draperies, chased each other across wooded groves. There was a small study, and a billiards room, and an imposing formal entrance hall and staircase that led to an open hallway above. This, with the offices at the rear of the house, comprised the ground floor. Fanny was struck by the fact that there was no library, nor any substantial bookcases in the study. The idea that some families did not consider books to be as essential a furnishing in the home as chairs or knives had never occurred to her. In every home she had entered – the Parsonage, even the White house, and of course in Mansfield Park, books were to be found on every side table and mantelpiece. Her uncle maintained a substantial library. At Keynsham Hill Fanny noted only a family bible, a *Pilgrim's Progress*, and a half-decayed bound volume of *The Spectator*. The absence of books, to Fanny's eye, made the house feel half-empty and cold, as though the occupants were merely temporary dwellers. She enquired, and learned that Mr. Smallridge took *Baily's Magazine of Sports* and the local newspapers, Mrs.

Smallridge studied the fashion plates, but neither were in the habit of reading for pleasure or improvement. This information had the effect of rendering her employers less intimidating in the young governess's mind, for her respect and admiration were all for the well-informed and the educated, such as her uncle and her cousin Edmund.

Fanny's new domain on the second floor comprised the schoolroom, the nursery and her own little bed-sitting room, adjoining them both. This room, with its little fireplace and a window overlooking the park, was in fact superior to her bedroom in Mansfield Park. She had a narrow bed, a rug, a wardrobe, two chairs and a little table that also served as her writing desk.

Fanny had tormented herself with many fears upon entering into the Smallridge's employ, not the least of which was her trepidation concerning the children — would they obey her, and would she win their affection and her employers' approbation? She had, as is so often the case in human affairs, and most particularly in the case of inexperienced, timid 18 year-old females, worried to no purpose. Fanny first recommended herself to the children by offering to tell them a bed-time story that evening. Recalling the little tales she used to tell her younger sisters in the cramped bedroom they all shared in Portsmouth, Fanny spun a tale of a little fairy family that lived at the bottom of their garden, who used foxglove flowers for cups and toadstools for tables, and so entranced were the children that they extracted a promise from Fanny to go and search for the fairies when the warm weather came.

In those early days, Mrs. Butters often breakfasted with Fanny and the children, explaining that Mrs. Smallridge was feeling particularly indisposed and tired, and while the old widow could be blunt to the point of incivility in her remarks — she did not scruple to teaze Fanny for her formality of speech — her reproofs did not sting like the condemnations of her Aunt Norris. Perhaps this was because Fanny knew herself to be sincerely liked by Mrs. Butters and the older lady was in a fair way to becoming a most important guide and friend. Mrs. Butters had favourable reports to give to her niece concerning the new governess, who appeared to be naturally adept at commanding the obedience of her charges without resorting to scolding or punishment, could make their lessons tolerably interesting to them and best of all, awaken in them enough affection for her so that they desired to please her.

Fanny was in the schoolroom with her young charges when an unfamiliar tread in the hallway announced the arrival of the master of

Keynsham Hill. Caroline's pencil and Edward's alphabet cards were abandoned – they swiftly ran to meet him at the door, and Edward was scooped up with one strong hand while Caroline's curls were affectionately caressed by the other.

Mr. Smallridge was well above the middle-height, with a large forehead, small penetrating eyes set rather close together, an aquiline nose, and thin lips. His dark, hard, satirical gaze made Fanny wish to look down at the floor, the table, the fireplace tools, anywhere rather than look her new employer in the face. Fanny felt herself to be an imposter, rather than a real governess, and she feared that here was the person who could instantly discern her inexperience, her ignorance, her lack of accomplishments – and proclaim her unfit for her post.

Fortunately for Fanny, Mr. Smallridge, while genuinely fond of his children, never spent any time in the nursery or the school room, and having just returned home after several weeks' recreation that had left him more in need of rest than when he left, had little to say to the new governess except that 'he supposed she had settled in comfortably,' and that 'she was not to allow this one' – and he tossed Edward up on his shoulder, to the child's screams of delight – 'to give her any trouble.'

Fanny nodded and curtsied, and was just trying to formulate an intelligent reply when Mr. Smallridge deposited Edward back on his chair, and unwrapped Caroline's little arms from around his leg, adding, "Capital – capital. Well, then. Good day," and left as abruptly as he had come.

Lest the reader's imagination give rise to a supposition in which this first meeting was the precursor to other, longer, more interesting interviews, in which two lonely souls discovered an irrepressible and mutual sympathy, allow me to state that not then, nor subsequently, did Fanny ever injure the peace of the household or betray her own principles by fancying herself in love with the master of the house. This happy escape was by conviction as well as by inclination, and despite the traditions prevailing for young governesses so situated. Mr. Smallridge, while a gentleman in appearance as well as air, had nothing to say to Fanny, in the ensuing weeks, that softened her first impression of him, and she could barely be said to have made an impression on him at all.

Fanny was accustomed to the solitude of her own thoughts, so a day spent with no other companions but the children and the nursemaids, and an evening passed alone, did not distress her. She dined with the family twice, when Mrs. Smallridge was entertaining company and was in need of another lady to even out her table, but since her employers and their guests spoke only of trivial matters and local gossip, there was little that could interest or engage her, and naturally she never volunteered any information or opinions beyond the most commonplace. She was grateful for the self-absorption of the others in that no-one ever felt themselves under any compunction, out of ordinary politeness, to see that she was included in the conversation, or to seek for topics of general interest. She was therefore spared the necessity of ever answering questions about herself, her background, or her family in front of them all, questions which would have forced her to evade the details of her life as a baronet's niece, and perhaps drawn the keen eye of Mrs. Butters upon her, for she felt that she would have dissembled but poorly.

Fanny had fully intended to write to Mansfield Park and explain herself within a week of arriving at Keynsham Hill, to reassure the family of her safety, but she intended to withhold the knowledge of her whereabouts. She wanted to post the letter from Bristol, without giving particulars of her new address, or having her correspondence pass through the hands of the Smallridge's servants. Her letters to Mansfield and Portsmouth were prepared and sealed – they consisted mostly of apologies and a reiteration of her determination to live independently – but she omitted the details of her situation, stating only that she had taken the post of governess. She thought it best to let some months elapse before revealing her location, in the hope that Sir Thomas and her parents would be reconciled to her choice in time. She was surprised by her own fortitude in foregoing any possibility of hearing a word from Edmund. She yearned for news of him, to know whether he had taken his orders as a clergyman, and if so had he given up Mary Crawford, or she him, or was he still torn between his affection for her and his stated purpose?

Almost a fortnight passed, and Fanny was growing anxious for the opportunity to relieve any anxiety her families in Portsmouth and Northamptonshire might be feeling on her account (and in her humility she imagined that that they could not, after all, be extremely distressed), when Mrs. Butters announced she was travelling into Bristol on the morrow, and that she would take Fanny along, the better to select some fabric and trim for a dress suitable for a governess. Fanny happily retired that evening in anticipation of new sights in a city she had never seen, but awoke to the news that Mrs. Smallridge had been brought to bed some weeks earlier . than expected. The midwife was summoned, urgent messages were sent to Mr. Smallridge, who was visiting friends in Bath, and Mrs. Butters of course would not stir from her niece's side.

All day the household moved about in hushed suspense. Madame Orly was all agitation and tears, and as the hours went by, Fanny found herself growing truly concerned for her mistress, and many a silent prayer on her behalf was made as she looked down at the little heads of Caroline and Edward while they played, insensible of the hazards their mother was facing. Finally, in the late afternoon, as the pale setting sun was tangled in the branches of the bare hazelnut trees, came tidings of twin daughters, small but healthy, and Mrs. Smallridge was as well as could be expected.

***

The expected letter from Fanny, or from her mother, to announce her safe arrival in Portsmouth had not arrived. Lady Bertram and Edmund had each written to Mrs. Price, and Mary Crawford had also written, as promised, but their enquiries were met with silence. Every day Lady Bertram enquired of Baddeley, "Any word from Portsmouth, Baddeley? Has my sister Price written to me?" and every day the butler answered, regretfully, in the negative.

After dinner, almost a fortnight after Fanny's departure, Edmund was about to propose that he ride to Portsmouth to assure the family of Fanny's safe arrival, when Julia burst into the drawing room and exclaimed, "Our father is come! He is in the hall at this moment."

The arrival of the master of the house was met with expressions of joy and satisfaction on all sides. For Maria, indeed, it meant that the arbiter of her future happiness had arrived. Tom and Edmund were truly pleased to see the man to whom they could resign the mantle of *paterfamilias*, yet were uneasy at the prospect of having to impart uncomfortable tidings to him.

Sir Thomas greeted every family member with smiles and embraces, overcoming his habitual reserved manner to a degree that surprised his household. He was older, his face thinner and somewhat drawn, he was browned from the tropical heat, and he had lost some flesh, but he declared himself, and appeared to be, well. His joy in seeing his family was indeed heartfelt, and he rejoiced to have survived his lengthy sojourn in the West Indies, whose climate had proved so fatal to so many of his countrymen – and, more than that, to have left behind scenes which had affected his peace of mind to no small degree.

He had inherited the sugar plantations in Antigua from his father, and had visited them once before, as a young man, and for many years they had enriched the family, enabling them to live with comfort and consequence and to build their spacious and airy home at Mansfield Park. But his prolonged sojourn on the island, during which time he had managed the plantation himself, had left him without the power of denying what it meant to rely on the labour of slaves. For it was one thing to contemplate these circumstances from half a world away, to regard them as regretful necessities, and another to see, before his eyes, the high cost in human lives, and the use of fear, threat and punishment to keep the slaves at their miserable toil. Not only were the slaves themselves made brutal and coarse through their treatment, but their English overseers were also degraded thereby.

Sir Thomas had privately resolved to find a buyer for his plantation, which would, he acknowledge, not ameliorate the evil, and could, in all likelihood, increase the suffering of his slaves, for while *his* plantations were acknowledged to be free of some of the worst excesses, he could not speak for the good conduct of any new owners. He believed that sugar plantations and the evils they engendered would exist so long as Englishmen wanted sugar; but he desired to wash his hands of the business. However, the recent precipitous fall of the price of sugar, and the banning of the slave trade, had rendered his holdings less valuable than heretofore, and he would not realize one-half of what he might have done a few years ago. But these reflections he kept to himself during his homecoming; he might later speak with Tom and Edmund about them, but for now his looks, his smiles and his thoughts were all for his family.

Sir Thomas took his place by Lady Bertram, and looked with heartfelt satisfaction at his wife, sons and daughters all collected together exactly as he could have wished. But, he added, after a pause, looking around him, "where is Fanny? Why do not I see my little niece?"—

"Indeed, sir," exclaimed Tom. "She will be very sorry to have missed this happy reunion. She desired to see her family and so she is gone to Portsmouth." The reply satisfied Sir Thomas and his sons forestalled any others by asking him for particulars of his voyage, with Sir Thomas ready to give every information, and answer every question of his two sons almost before it was put. He had an opportunity of making his passage thither in a private vessel, instead of waiting for the packet but his return to Liverpool had been delayed about two weeks by a contrary wind across the North Atlantic, and all the little particulars of his proceedings and events, his arrivals and departures, were most promptly delivered.

At length there was a pause. His immediate communications were exhausted, and it seemed enough to be looking joyfully around him, now at one, now at another of the beloved circle; but the pause was not long: in the elation of her spirits Lady Bertram became talkative, and what were the sensations of her children upon hearing her say, "Sir Thomas, Maria's intended husband is not at Mansfield at present, but Maria assures me he will come back and wait upon you promptly, now you are returned."

"My dear, in my satisfaction at being home again, I could desire no addition to our family circle, with but one exception – the welcoming of a new son-in-law, an exception I may, I think, countenance without reservation. I look forward to making Mr. Rushworth's acquaintance at the first convenient opportunity, and in no short time thereafter, I trust we may be able to determine the date for that happy occasion which, if our best poets and authors are any guide, will be not less welcome for having been delayed by my extended absence."

An awkward pause followed Sir Thomas' speech, as conscious looks were exchanged among some of his children. Maria hoped, perhaps unreasonably, for one of her brothers to make the necessary communication, and when Tom remained mute she turned to Edmund with an imploring glance. She dared not, of course, meet Julia's eye, but Julia had regained sufficient mastery over herself since the hour she had discovered her sister in the arms of the man she loved, or once loved, that only the twisting of her handkerchief in her hands betrayed the inner agitation of her spirit.

"Sir, Maria *did* have an understanding with Mr. Rushworth," Edmund finally ventured, "but upon discovering that she had been mistaken in her regard for him, she judged it best to end the engagement."

Sir Thomas' brow contracted, and looking from face to face in the little family circle, he fancied he beheld an unease, a holding back. "Your mother spoke, just now, of a husband-to-be. My dear," he said, turning to his wife, "you cannot be in error on a point as material as this. There is something in this which my comprehension does not reach."

"I am now engaged to Henry Crawford, father," Maria finally ventured. "He is the brother of Mrs. Grant, wife of Dr. Grant."

The parental brow contracted further, and awful was the suspense of his daughter. "Maria, the choice of the gentleman on whom you choose to bestow your hand is, as it ought to be, a matter of no small significance to me and to everyone associated with you. You will understand that I have many enquiries to make as to how it came to be that you severed a connection so eligible, so suitable, so promising in every respect. Further, I doubt not that this dissolution has been canvassed in every household from here to Sotherton, attaching a degree of notoriety to your name – to our name, which is highly regrettable. And, without paying me the compliment of consultation, you have promised yourself to a man of inferior birth and consequence. But in deference to the delicacy of your situation, we will continue this interview after tea, in my study."

He turned then, to questions about the Park, and the village and the tenants, which his sons were able to answer to his satisfaction and to give him, at least for that hour, the sensation that nothing else had gone seriously amiss in his absence. Poor Sir Thomas! How brief was this interval of peace to be!

Mrs. Norris was the first visitor to the house to congratulate Sir Thomas on his safe return, having hurried up from the White house when news of his arrival by post chaise had spread through the village. She was vexed that she had not been in the entry hall to greet him first, where her imagination had always placed her. Mrs. Norris felt herself defrauded of an office on which she had always depended, whether his arrival or his death were to be the thing unfolded. She endeavoured to compensate, however, for being robbed of that which was her due, by now trying to be in a bustle without having anything to bustle about, and labouring to be important where nothing was wanted but tranquility and silence. Would Sir Thomas have consented to eat, she might have gone to the housekeeper with troublesome directions, and insulted the footmen with injunctions of despatch; but Sir Thomas resolutely declined all dinner: he would take nothing, nothing till tea came—he would rather wait for tea. Still Mrs. Norris was at intervals urging something different; and in the most interesting moment of his detailed recitation of his passage to England, when the alarm of a French privateer was at the height, she burst through his narrative with the proposal of soup. "Sure, my dear Sir Thomas, a basin of soup would be a much better thing for you than tea. Do have a basin of soup."

Sir Thomas could not be provoked. "Still the same anxiety for everybody's comfort, my dear Mrs. Norris," was his answer. "But indeed I would rather have nothing but tea."

"Well, then, Lady Bertram, suppose you speak for tea directly; suppose you hurry Baddeley a little; he seems behindhand to-night." Baddeley appeared almost instantly, but instead of bearing a tea board, he brought a letter, addressed to Edmund Bertram, to whom he delivered it, with the apologetic remark: "Pardon me, sir, but I judged it best, to interrupt you now with this letter, rather than reserve it with the other letters of business." Edmund saw the direction and excusing himself, opened the letter, expecting to read a note from his aunt Price with another letter from Fanny enclosed within. Instead he held a single sheet of paper, with what appeared to be a smear of butter and jam on one corner and a small sketch of a cat, drawn by a childish hand, on another. He read:

Dear Mr. Bertram:

My Apologies for not replying sooner to yours of the past week, but since your Letters informed me that Fanny was coming to stay with us, I have been Waiting for her these four days. And I have been too occupied with the cares of my Household to have the Leisure to enquire why my daughter did not Write to me herself, while you have Written repeatedly, for I expected that Fanny would Explain all when she finally did Arrive.

But I have got yet another Letter from you, telling me positively that Fanny is with me in Portsmouth, and several Letters from Mansfield addressed to Fanny besides, and rather than continuing to Pay for all of these Letters, I send you this note to Inform you that Fanny is not here, at least not at as I Write this.

I don't know what to make of this Affair. I was going to enquire of Fanny if you had cast her off, and I feared that she has Disobliged you in some particular, but I cannot satisfy my curiosity for she is not here. However, Sir, if you and my sister Bertram both believe Fanny to be here, then she most assuredly is not there at Mansfield Park. And if she is not with you, nor with us, then where is she? Please Advise,

Your much-obliged aunt,

Frances Price

pps – I instructed our Servant to bear this letter to the Post Office three days ago, and Discovered it this Morning in the entry hall. My daughter Susan is taking it to the Post directly. We still have no Word of Fanny, and yet another Letter from Mr. Edmund Bertram!

A brief cry escaped Edmund's lips – his countenance told of utter calamity – there could be no withholding this shocking intelligence. His father held out his hand, Edmund surrendered the note, which Sir Thomas read silently, once, twice and three times.

"What is it, sir?" "What's the matter, Sir Thomas?" came the anxious enquiries. Finally, Sir Thomas looked up, and his response was all the more startling because of the uncustomary brevity with which it was delivered.

"Fanny has gone missing."

Chapter Eight

All of the interest of the Smallridge household now centred on the new little visitors. The twins had been consigned to a wet-nurse and were kept in their own separate nursery. Mr. Smallridge, it was said, was extremely pleased to have fathered twins, for all that they were both girls, and he made an handsome present to his wife of a pearl necklace and earrings upon his return from Bath.

Although Caroline and Edward were vaguely aware that their parents did not bestow as much attention on them as heretofore, before the advent of their younger sisters, their growing affection and confidence in their governess helped remedy the loss. For Caroline, Miss Price was a friendly confederate who could sew the prettiest dresses for her dolls with the tiniest of doll-sized stitches, and she had Edward's respect because she could name all the sails on a man of war.

Fanny was tolerably cheerful and busy every day and it was only when dusk settled over Keynsham Hill that she found herself fighting a tendency to lowness, to having to suppress a sigh, and preventing herself from idling away an half-an-hour gazing out the window as the shades of night closed around the house. Had she been at home, the family would be gathering in the parlour, with Fanny making and serving the tea, while Edmund read aloud to them. In her imagination it was always just their little family circle, with no unwelcome visitors from the Parsonage!

Fanny might have passed all the gloomy afternoons of November in solitude in her little room, her mind miles away with thoughts of Northamptonshire, except for the fact that Mrs. Butter's lady's maid, Madame Orly, had more leisure to bestow upon Fanny. Her mistress was more than usually indifferent to perfecting her *toilette*, and was making and receiving no calls but to her niece's bedside. The lady's maid was at leisure to bring her sewing basket and sit together with Fanny as they stitched caps and baby linen for the new daughters of the household.

Madame Orly was a petite and voluble woman admitting to the age of five-and-thirty, whose cheerful demeanour, despite the hardships and reverses she had suffered as an émigré after the overthrow of the monarchy, served for Fanny, who was naturally of a melancholic

81

temperament, as an object lesson in how to be happy. Even if half of what Madame Orly had told her was true – the riots in the streets, the cruelty of the Jacobins, the loss of her family, property, fiancé, and very nearly her own life – she had suffered enough for five lifetimes, and yet she appeared to enjoy serving her English mistress, and find an inexhaustible fund of interest and amusement in the doings of all the households in the neighbourhood and indeed, wherever her sparkling dark eyes glanced. Fanny had never met anyone from France and benefitted from practicing the language she had studied under Miss Lee. Madame Orly complimented her effusively on her accent and declared her to be *comme une vrai Parisienne*.

Although she had much to occupy her hands and head, Fanny naturally had some time to reflect upon those persons so dear to her heart. She was in daily hopes of a letter from her brother William. Soon after her arrival in Keynsham Hill, Fanny had penned a long letter to her brother, beseeching him to understand and support her, and expressing the hope that they could see each other someday.

As for that *other* most precious to her, and the well-being of all under the roof of Mansfield Park, she yearned for news, but had deliberately placed herself out of the power of receiving any.

***

Sir Thomas' return was of course known to their neighbours at the Parsonage – everyone had remarked on the hired chaise as it passed by – and Mary Crawford, strolling out for a short walk after tea, saw almost every window in the great house lit up, confirming that its master was safely returned. Mrs. Grant was prompt in dispatching a polite congratulatory note to Lady Bertram, and Mary did not spend the following morning looking out of upstairs windows in vain – she was rewarded by the sight of Edmund Bertram strolling down soon after breakfast to deliver his mother's reply. But scarcely had Mary and Mrs. Grant begun to congratulate him on the safe return of Sir Thomas, when his newest intelligence that his cousin had disappeared stopped them in the full flow of their civilities.

Edmund perceived how Miss Crawford's countenance gave every testimony of her alarm and distress. It was no slight consolation to him that the young woman whose principles and character he had sometimes doubted was so taken up with the fact that Fanny was not in Portsmouth.

She looked, she spoke, in such a way as to recommend herself irresistibly to his anxious heart. He stayed with them above half an hour until finally, recollecting his true errand, asked if Mr. Crawford would soon be returning to Mansfield? Mary undertook to write to her brother that very morning, and modestly declined to return with him to the house, 'as she supposed Sir Thomas would want to be only with his family at such a time,' giving such further proofs of her sweet nature as materially lessened Edmund's cares, and he returned to the great house in a much better frame of mind than when he left.

"What can this mean, Mrs. Grant?" cried Mary when their visitor left. "It is impossible to suppose that Fanny Price, of all people, has eloped. She had no admirers that I know of."

"I don't know what to make of it, Mary," came the reply. "Did she not positively write that she was going to Portsmouth? Oh, I dread to think – but no, we must not look for the worst, but hope for the best."

"We all believed she went to Portsmouth," answered Mary thoughtfully. "And so I wrote to her there. Oh, do you suppose that her family there – no one there would open a letter addressed to Miss Price, would they? They would return the letter to me, would they not?"

"Upon my word, I don't know," her sister remarked. "But depend upon it, Sir Thomas and his sons will do everything in their power to recover her. Let us not speak of this outside of our own little circle – it may be that the family does not wish the world to know of Miss Price's disappearance."

Mrs. Grant was correct – Sir Thomas had judged it best not to advertise the fact of his niece's absence amongst his friends, or to place a notice in any newspaper. The consequences of giving such notoriety to a lady were undeniable and evident; the consequences of refraining from publishing the news, less certain, and only the event would prove whether he had been correct in maintaining an embargo on the subject outside the family circle.

Mary Crawford did apprise Henry Crawford of this astonishing turn of events when summoning him back from their uncle's home in London – no one could expect such a degree of female taciturnity as to keep the interesting subject from her brother – and when he arrived at the Grants' doorstep, two days later, he appeared to be more animated and interested in the mystery surrounding Miss Price, than in his own future with Miss Bertram.

"Mary, what's the news? What has been done to recover Miss Price?"

"Edmund Bertram enquired at the post office, and he learned that she did receive and send some letters before she left, but the stupid old postmaster does not recall the directions. He also interviewed the driver of the mail coach. *He* is certain she left the coach in Oxford, not Newbury. Tom and Edmund Bertram are in Oxford now, I believe, making enquiries."

"Have they stopped at all the coach houses along the route?"

"They intended to do so, and I am sure they have. They promised to write twice daily at least."

"A missing young lady! Has she been abducted? Does she have a lover? Has she been deceiving the family or has she fallen and knocked her head and forgotten her very name?"

"The family assumed she had gone to Portsmouth but, upon re-reading the letters – the letter, that is, that she left behind – she does not say so in so many words. She spoke only of 'returning to her own sphere.' So, for my part, I think she has deliberately misled everyone – her secrecy about her correspondents would suggest so – although I would be the first to agree with you that it strains all credulity to think that Fanny Price had the guile to impose on everyone in this manner."

"Ha! This is a mystery peculiarly suited to my energies and talents."

"Have a care, sir," Dr. Grant cried. "You look positively cheerful. This is the gravest matter. Consider, Miss Price has been gone, no one knows where, for a fortnight! I hope you will compose yourself into a different frame of mind should you discuss this awful circumstance with any of the Bertrams."

"But of course, my dear sir," returned Henry. "In fact, you will acquit me of any charge of levity once you understand that I intend to offer my services in finding the young lady. There is not a moment to lose. My own happiness must wait until Miss Price is recovered. My fair bride would not countenance the thought of a wedding ceremony, I know, if the whereabouts of her cousin, the playfellow of her childhood days, the young lady who is almost a sister to her, remains unknown. So, I will pay my respects at the Park, enjoy a brief reunion with my Maria, then prepare for another journey, perhaps an extended one, until I can return Miss Price safely to her family."

"Are we going to start the search at Portsmouth? Will we visit her family there?" Mary asked.

"If the one thing we know for a certainty is that she is *not* in Portsmouth, I don't see the necessity of going there. Perhaps we should –

but Mary, what are you saying? Are you determined to accompany me? With the greatest pleasure, I am sure, but why?"

"Ought not you to reconsider, Miss Crawford?" Dr. Grant cautioned. "'Tis almost mid-November – should you be travelling to who-knows-where at this time of year, my dear? Enduring bad roads, uncomfortable lodging and infamous dinners at roadside inns?"

"I thank you for your kind solicitude, Dr. Grant," responded Mary, "but knowing of Miss Price's reserved and formal nature, I do not believe that, once located, she could be prevailed upon to travel with Henry unaccompanied."

"By heaven, that's so," Henry agreed. "Pack your trunk, Mary. We shall commence tomorrow at first light. First to Oxford to overtake the Bertrams, then we will act upon any intelligence they may have gathered. We will search the length and breadth of England if we must!"

"But first," Mary replied, "you, Henry, shall meet *the* Sir Thomas himself. How I wish I could be present to watch as you exercise all your abilities on him! But *my* introduction to him shall await another day. My vanity requires no less – I will not have him divide his attentions between wayward nieces and the latest claimant for his daughter's hand – and me. Go, go and make them all love you."

* * *

Sir Thomas judged that, from a pecuniary and worldly view, Maria's union with Mr. Crawford was inferior in every respect to the now ruptured engagement with Mr. Rushworth; and having heard nothing but the highest praise of Mr. Rushworth in letters from home when he was in Antigua, he was perplexed that this paragon among men had failed to retain his daughter's affections, until Edmund had privately given him a better understanding of Rushworth's deficiencies in sense and education. But the substitution of Crawford for Rushworth did not placate him; he suspected that the young man lived beyond his means, and lived purely for pleasure. An old friend who lived in the City, upon being applied to by Sir Thomas on the very day of his return, sent no good report of his reputation, describing him as an idler and a man who raised the hope and expectation of marriage in many young ladies, conquering one heart after another for his own amusement, and hinted that Miss Bertram was not to depend upon being married to Henry Crawford unless they were actually at the altar, with the church doors locked securely behind them!

Sir Thomas greeted Henry Crawford, therefore, with even more than his usual dignity and formality, as his daughter Maria could not fail to perceive. However, when once seated at dinner, Sir Thomas could not but allow that Henry Crawford's powers of address were superior to what is generally met with, not excepting his own two sons, for Crawford had more ease of manner than Edmund and more sense and information than Tom.

When Mr. Crawford petitioned to be permitted to go and search for Miss Price on the family's behalf, in a manner so determined, with a countenance so truly manly and resolute, expressing himself so warmly and yet so properly, speaking of his ties of affection to the Bertrams, the need for discretion and dispatch, etc., Sir Thomas wondered if his old friend from the City had confused *this* Henry Crawford with some other gentleman!

Indeed, Crawford little suspected with what misgivings Sir Thomas first greeted him, or he would have congratulated himself still more on his ability to captivate. He hoped that any marriage to Maria would remain a distant event, but to know himself to be the centre of attention, to watch as the father's *hauteur* slowly dissolved, and to see the mother wipe away a tear as he spoke of the lost niece, so young, so innocent; to observe the glow of Maria's countenance, to feel her little stockinged foot beneath the tablecloth, rubbing against his leg, and best of all, to know that Julia, though feigning indifference, was as taut as a bowstring, and attending to his every word and gesture, was for Henry Crawford one of the chiefest pleasures that life has to offer.

As the meal concluded, Sir Thomas, with a significant look at their visitor, announced that he was going to retire to his study to prepare a letter to his sons, to advise them that Henry Crawford would join the search for Fanny.

Henry instantly understood this as an invitation to follow his host and make his formal declaration for Maria's hand, but he pretended that he did *not* understand, and instead asked if Miss Bertram might be so kind as to write a little note to Miss Price, to assure her that she should not hesitate, on any point of modesty or decorum, to return to Mansfield Park in the company of Mr. Crawford.

"Come with me into the breakfast-room," Maria murmured to him, "we shall find everything there, and be sure of having the room to ourselves."

And indeed they did.

Not twenty minutes later, Mr. Crawford was at the front door, and with a respectful bow and hearty handshake for Sir Thomas he was gone, while the eldest daughter of the house, evidently much discomposed by the necessity of parting with her beloved, retired swiftly to her bedchamber.

Later that evening, Sir Thomas' complaisance was a little clouded by the realization that Mr. Crawford had left the house without asking for a confidential interview with him. Yet, regarding himself to be a good judge of men, he was not displeased with his prospective new son-in-law, and the satisfied countenance of Maria as she re-joined the family circle that evening confirmed his favorable views.

***

A fortnight after Mrs. Smallridge's *accouchement*, the trip to Bristol was revived, to Fanny's great relief. She and Mrs. Butters were to go on the morrow and spend the better part of the day there.

The carriage departed Keynsham Hill for Bristol directly after breakfast, with Fanny, Mrs. Butters and Madame Orly – for the widow was also indulging her lady's maid with a change of scene – seated comfortably inside with blankets and mufflers. It was a mild day, and Fanny dared to lower the window a little to admire the passing view. The groves of newly-planted trees surrounding the estate, while yet to reach maturity, were picturesquely arranged over the park, and every turn in the lane brought a new view to admire, either screening or revealing the house behind them and the countryside before.

"The evergreen! How beautiful, how welcome, how wonderful the evergreen!" exclaimed Fanny. "When one thinks of it, how astonishing a variety of nature! In some countries we know the tree that sheds its leaf is the variety, but that does not make it less amazing that the same soil and the same sun should nurture plants differing in the first rule and law of their existence. You will think me rhapsodising; but when one is out of doors, one cannot fix one's eyes on the commonest natural production without finding food for a rambling fancy."

"Good gracious!" cried Mrs. Butters, turning her head to look at Fanny in amused disbelief. "Pray do not speak in such an affected manner, Miss Price. You are sometimes quite an odd creature, I vow. But there, there," she added, reaching over and patting the little governess's hand affectionately. "I perceive that you are one of those who have not conversed with a wide variety of persons, but have acquired your knowledge of the world from books. Life in Bristol will cure you of talking

87

like a poet in a garret. But then again, speaking of poets in garrets..." she added, then seemed to drift away in thought.

Fanny, though a great deal abashed, resolved to take Mrs. Butters' advice as kindly meant and to curb her rhapsodic tendencies where Nature was concerned, at least in certain company. With Edmund, (and here a sigh was stifled) she could always speak as she felt, save on one important point.

Soon the streets of Bristol were gained, and Fanny forgot herself in comparing this seaport city with the Portsmouth of her childhood, the sailors striding along in their wide-legged attire, the plentiful sight and smell of fish, oysters and whelks, and the red-faced, loud-voiced women who bargained over them. The widow's first stop was at the draper's shop owned by Mrs. Smallridge's own family, and Fanny had all the pleasure of admiring bolt after bolt of fabric, and enjoying Madame Orly's transports over lace and ribbon and *le dernier chose*. Mrs. Butters selected some sober grey for a dress for Fanny and, at Madame Orly's urging, a periwinkle blue muslin as well. Fanny asked for some fabric scraps to make doll's clothes for Caroline. Well pleased with their purchases, the ladies stopped at a tea house, and at last Fanny a post office across the street and excused herself to mail her letters.

Fanny returned from her errand as Mrs. Butters was commencing her second cup of tea. Fanny knew that Mrs. Butters took no sugar in her tea, but, with her mind full of those she had left behind at Mansfield Park, she absent-mindedly offered her the sugar tongs. Mrs. Butters declined, adding, "if you knew, Fanny, where sugar comes from, you would not want it any more."

"You mean the West Indies, I suppose?" asked Fanny.

"I should perhaps say, how that sugar came to be."

"You are referring to the slave trade, I fear."

"I would take no pleasure in enlightening you, no pleasure at all, believe me, as young and innocent as you are." Here Mrs. Butters sighed and looked out the window toward the masts of the ships in the harbor, just visible in the distance, as though recollecting long-ago days.

And Fanny thought it best to turn the subject to the weather.

The carriage returned as the ladies were finishing their tea, and they resumed their seats within. Fanny, looking eagerly at everything around her, timidly expressed a hope that they might see something more of the dockyards and the sea while in Bristol; Mrs. Butters didn't reply but instead directed the coachman to stop at St. Thomas Lane in front of an old, low ceilinged, gabled building that appeared to be a tavern.

"I will stop here a little while, you may accompany me or wait in the carriage, as you please," she said. Fanny, surprised, elected to follow her benefactress, while Madame Orly declared her intention to rest in the carriage. Mrs. Butters boldly entered, and, looking around the large, empty room, maneuvered through a tangle of tables and chairs to a heavy table, piled high with broadsheets and books, where several earnest men and a woman were deep in conversation.

"The point is, that we should not be drawn into defending a proposition we have never made – no one ever claimed that the Negroes are a species of angel. They have faults and human failings like the rest of us," exclaimed an older gentleman, quaintly garbed all in black, vigorously tapping the table for emphasis as he spoke, and leaning forward so that his glasses were in danger of slipping from his nose.

"But, the moods and caprices of this woman are being used, and not ineffectually, to discredit her testimony about the cruelties of the plantation system," replied the gentlewoman he was addressing, a respectable-looking, dignified older lady whose simplicity of attire did not diminish her air of quiet authority. "I do not deny that if *I* had suffered one hundredth of what she has suffered, and continues to suffer – repeated floggings, half-starved, forced to toil from before sunrise to after sundown, her health broken, separated from her family – I too would be of an uneven temperament. By what right the public expects a former slave to be cheerful, humble, and perpetually grateful, I know not. But Mary will not conform to this expected pattern, and it damages our cause."

"If she could be provided with regular employment that did not overtax her strength, I feel certain – " a tall, slender young man was beginning to suggest, when his gaze fell on Mrs. Butters and Fanny. His face lit up in a most engaging fashion. "My dear Mrs. Butters! How good to see you at last! We wish you joy, by the by – what happy news! Twins!"

"Thank you, Mr. Gibson. We had our alarms, of course, but the little ones are thriving, and Mrs. Smallridge is doing as well as can be expected. She is following my advice and refraining from all bathing for the winter. My dear Miss More, allow me to present Miss Price, recently engaged as governess at my niece's home. Miss Price, these are my friends Mr. Thompson and Mr. Gibson."

After Fanny quietly greeted her new acquaintance, she looked down bashfully, as was her habit, and became transfixed by the engravings on one of the broadsheets, which showed an African, bound hand and foot to a large carriage wheel, over whom stood a man with a whip. The youngest man, following her gaze, explained in an undertone, "This is one of the methods of punishment in the West Indies for slaves, Miss Price. Our Society is endeavouring to educate the British public about the cruelties of slavery."

"Ah, you are Abolitionists, Mr. Gibson. I have read a little about your movement."

"Mrs. Butters is one of our chief patronesses, were you aware?" Drawing her a little aside from the others, who continued their conversation, he added in a low tone, "Her late husband built the ships, the very ships, which were used to transport these unfortunate souls from Africa to the Indies. But she, bless her, has renounced her past and put no small part of her husband's fortune in the service of ending this abominable trade."

Fanny looked concerned, and doubtful. Her respect and awe for her uncle, Sir Thomas, prevented her from even thinking critically of him – whatever he deemed to be correct and just, must be so; yet, the bald fact of humans in bondage, taken by force from their own country to toil in another, could hardly be considered by her with anything approaching equanimity. "I understand that the trade in slaves itself has been, or is to be, abolished. But how shall industries established on this system be reformed, Mr. Gibson? Shall the owners be compensated, if they are compelled to release those persons that they have paid sums to transport thither? Shall workers be found to replace the slaves? I do not ask this in defense of the sugar plantations, but merely ask for information."

"Permit me to give you some of our literature, Miss Price. But," he added doubtfully, eyeing the slight figure before him, "it is of a truly distressing nature, and as such, perhaps not advisable for persons of delicate constitution."

"I shall take care that the children do not see it. But I have long wished to learn more about this question on my own account." She looked up again, and beheld a young man, with a most arresting countenance; a long, slender, handsome face, framed by dark curls around his high, broad forehead. His smile was gentle and peculiarly pleasing, but it was the vitality and intelligence of his expressive deep blue eyes, which twinkled behind small round glasses, which held her attention. "At any rate, I shall be pleased to have something new to read, because Bunyan and Addison have been my only diversions for a fortnight or more."

90

Mr. Gibson laughed, "Indeed, you deserve to have some sweetmeats in this diet of wholesome gruel! Have you read *Marmion*? Yes? Let's see..... There is a bookseller's in the next street. Mrs. Butters, may I escort Miss Price to the bookseller's?"

Mrs. Butters broke off from her animated conversation with the others and consented, so long as Fanny was ready in time to return home before dinner, and her new companion bowed, and offered his arm to the little governess. Fanny observed that his cuffs were frayed and his jacket was old and worn, though clean and well mended. He started eagerly for the street, without pausing to put on a greatcoat – Fanny thought it quite likely that he did not own such an article – then he realized he had to check his gait, as Fanny came barely up to his shoulder and could not keep pace with him without a struggle. They were soon talking volubly of books, favourite authors, favourite works, histories, novels and poems, and Fanny delighted in meeting someone whose love of reading equaled hers and whose knowledge of literature far surpassed her own. They had just reached the door of the booksellers, when Mr. Gibson gave her to understand that he himself was a writer, one of the editors of the Abolitionist's *Gazette*, and also had seen several of his poems published in the *Gentlemen's Magazine*. Fanny had never conversed with an actual published author before, and her look of unfeigned awe caused Mr. Gibson to feel that today was a propitious day indeed.

The sight and even the smell of a roomful of books was welcome, more than welcome, to Fanny, and her attention was diverted between her interesting new friend and the offerings for sale, both new and second-hand.

"I believe you said Cowper was your favourite poet, Miss Price. Here is an amusing satire on Woodsworth – *The Simpliciad*. I think you would enjoy it. Ah, here is something new in the Gothic line!" And, holding up a volume, he pronounced in exaggerated horror, "*The Ruins of Rigonda: or, the Homicidal Father.*"

Fanny smiled and shook her head. "These novels are too expensive for the passing entertainment they provide, I fear. A governess cannot afford them."

"Never fear. I shall write a three volume novel featuring a ruined castle and an evil prior and publish under it a woman's name and make prodigious sums of money. And you shall receive a presentation copy, of course."

"As you like, sir," laughed Fanny, "but I should prefer to read some of your own productions."

Instead of a three-volume novel, Fanny selected a well-worn book entitled *Stories for the Young*, as a welcome addition in the nursery. Mr. Gibson deftly plucked the book from her hand and examined it. Fanny found herself admiring his long fingers as they turned the pages, which were slender but gave the impression of much strength and dexterity. "Well, here is a happy coincidence, Miss Price," he smiled. "The gentlewoman who was conversing with us as you entered the tavern is – the authoress of this book! Are you acquainted with the works of Hannah More?"

Fanny was speechless. That she should have stood in the same room with not one, but two, writers, and one of them a lady, was a circumstance so wonderful that she could scarcely comprehend it. She recollected herself only when she observed Mr. Gibson attempting to purchase her selection for her, but he yielded to her gentle remonstrance and permitted her to lay out her own monies, as she thought only proper, but her gratitude at his kindness, artlessly but fervently expressed, caused him to laugh at her, and Fanny blushed and laughed in return, until their friendly confederacy was brought to a close by the sound of Mrs. Butter's approaching carriage. Fanny was compelled to bid a hasty farewell to Mr. Gibson and climb in beside a slumbering Madame Orly, feeling that her trip to Bristol had been memorable indeed!

Chapter Nine

The sight of Mary Crawford standing by the large and welcoming fireplace in the dining room of the Royal George Inn, after a fruitless day of visiting various hostelries around Oxford, was a blissful tonic to Edmund's spirit and caused him to acknowledge that despite his current distress, she was never far from his thoughts – her eyes, her smile, her countenance, frequently appeared before him, and her materialization in the flesh seemed almost to be in response to his unspoken wishes.

Edmund thought Tom seemed rather more eager than otherwise to let the Crawfords continue the search for Fanny unaided, so that he could return to his usual habits and haunts. Edmund warmly offered to accompany the Crawfords anywhere in their pursuit of Miss Price. But although Miss Crawford's lovely dark eyes eloquently told him how welcome his company would be, her brother argued that by taking separate routes, they might cover more ground. "You say you have learned the name of the lady – a Mrs. Renfro – who was in the coach with your cousin, and that she is a native of St. Albans. Should not one party pursue her, to enquire if Miss Price confided in her, while another traces your cousin's supposed path to Portsmouth?"

"By Jove, that's sensible, " offered Tom. "The Crawfords and I can go to St Albans – you know my particular friend, Hedgerow, lives just outside the city - Edmund, you have heard me speak of Hedgerow -and you can go to Portsmouth and placate our Aunt Price. We've never met her, Crawford. Do you suppose she is as much of a Tartar as Aunt Norris?"

Upon this, Miss Crawford protested that she and her brother should accompany Mr. Edmund Bertram to Portsmouth. But, objected Tom Bertram, it had already been established that Fanny was *not* in Portsmouth, and he had no doubt that the Crawfords, with their skills of address, would obtain a more sympathetic audience with Mrs. Renfro. Edmund could not gainsay the observation, and moreover it was *his* duty to pay his respects to his aunt, who, he had no doubt, was beside herself with anxiety over the fate of her daughter. Mary felt some resentment that Edmund could not contrive an irresistible reason why she and her brother should not go to with him to Portsmouth, but as she could not put forward one herself, she gave up disputing the point.

It so happened that Mr. Crawford was always in the habit of using the Raleigh Inn when in Oxford, and when the Crawfords retired there for the night, he happened to enquire of the landlord if any errant young women had come through recently. He received a description of a timid, tired, shrinking young lady as left no doubt that the innkeeper had indeed seen Miss Price. When eagerly questioned as to her whereabouts, the innkeeper added that 'she was in no danger,' and when further pressed, allowed that she had left Oxford in the company of a wealthy widow of great respectability, but more the host declined to say, fearing reprisals either from Mrs. Butters herself, for having given her name to a stranger, or from the family of the wayward Fanny Price, for having aided a runaway girl.

"It appears that our little missing bird is safe enough, Mary," ventured her brother after they had found a quiet corner in the dining room. "However, I see no reason to alter our plans for the morrow – let us proceed to St. Albans with Mr. Bertram. Haven't you always wanted to see the Abbey there? I understand it has the longest nave of any church in England."

"Really Henry, you are incorrigible! Do you really intend to keep what we have just learned from the Bertrams? You will seize upon any stratagem to delay coming to the point with Maria Bertram. Very well, I shall not betray *you*, if you will assist *me*. I wish to retrieve a letter."

"Where is this letter?"

"In Portsmouth."

"Could you have chosen a more salubrious place to misplace a letter? Ah, very well. After St. Albans, we will visit Portsmouth. And afterwards, London. A man may lose himself in London."

"You will return me to Mansfield, if you please."

"Where you will convey my regret to the Bertrams – say that I had no time to wait upon them, because the most urgent business called me to my own estates in Everingham."

"The better to place everything in readiness for your wedding, I trust?"

"Do not importune me, dear sister!" Crawford laughed. "

The Crawfords, brother and sister, took their leave of Oxford the morning after they had entered it, with plans to meet with Tom Bertram in St. Albans. Mr. Crawford was in the habit of sitting beside the coachman and either directing his driving or taking the reins himself, as he enjoyed nothing more than driving four-in-hand, but a cold pelting rain rendered the box seat less hospitable, and so he sat with his sister, who seemed ill-disposed for conversation. Mary's agitation and impatience increased as the morning drew on, until her brother finally exclaimed, "When you will tell me *why* we need to retrieve a letter in Portsmouth, Mary? I think I deserve to know."

Mary succumbed to the relief of confiding one part of the secret which had been weighing on her conscience. "I wrote to Miss Price, when we all supposed her to be in Portsmouth, and in that letter I said some things which were not.... *entirely* true and which, upon reflection, it was unwise of me to commit to paper. You know my impulsive nature, Henry. I was carried away by my feelings and, in my defense, I believed I was acting for the best. Miss Price had formed a foolish infatuation for someone very far above her station in life, and to extinguish any hopes she had in that quarter would truly be the office of a friend. Further, I was let into the secret of some of her sentiments towards *me*, and my temper got the better of me, as it sometimes does. I intended the letter as a much-needed corrective. Had she received it, I am sure she would not have mentioned it to anyone, knowing her timid nature. But, as she was *not* in Portsmouth, the letter never came to her hand, and heaven knows what has become of it. I should be placed in a very awkward situation indeed, were that letter to come to light now...."

"So you will not name the gentleman upon whom Miss Price had fixed her affections?" he asked, after some moments of silence between them.

"What woman of feeling and delicacy would betray the confidence of a friend in such a fashion?"

At first, Henry naturally supposed that *he* was the person with whom Miss Price was in love, and he silently reviewed what he had said to her, and she to him, in the brief course of their acquaintance at Mansfield and discovered that, apart from the most commonplace remarks, they were entire strangers! She had never, to his recollection, sought his company, never smiled at him, or made a point of catching his eye, and while he may have missed *some* symptoms of love, as occupied as he had been with the Miss Bertrams, he was in general so alert to these overtures that Miss Price must be a most extraordinary young lady indeed if she could cherish tender feelings toward him while appearing so utterly indifferent – nay more than indifferent, as he could almost declare that she had avoided his company.

More moments of silence. Since the matter did not concern himself, he would not ordinarily have cared about the identity of the man the silly girl had fallen in love with, but the carriage ride was long and too slow for his liking, he was bored, and he loved a mystery. So far as he knew, the list of gentlemen of Miss Price's acquaintance was not a long one, as she almost never stirred from home. Rushworth? She had spent a great deal of time with him, helping that dull-witted fellow learn his two-and-forty speeches for the play. That fop Yates? Could a plain brown wren fall in love with a gaudy bird of paradise? Surely even the sheltered little Miss Price could understand that Mr. Yates was immune to female charms?

Henry eyed his sister narrowly. "You have been particularly distracted ever since Mr. *Edmund* Bertram decided to visit Portsmouth while we went to St. Albans."

Mary looked out of the window and shook her head in vexation. "We may already be too late."

Henry placed a consoling hand on hers and out of consideration for her mood, said nothing more.

Two more days saw the conclusion of their errand in St. Albans. The widow Renfro, while affable and open-hearted, and recalling Miss Price perfectly, could not recall anything the young lady might have said concerning her journey or its purpose. The Crawfords then resumed their travels and reached the environs of Portsmouth just before tea-time on the day after parting from Tom Bertram. After consulting several passers-by, something Mr. Crawford was loath to do, but upon which his sister insisted, – "or else we will roam about this dreadful town 'til nightfall, Henry!" – the correct street and house were located. The narrow, dark lane, with its antiquated over-hanging buildings, smelt of the sea, and fish, and tar and rotting cabbage. Mary dismounted from the carriage and frowned in dismay, feeling ill.

"Henry, this horrid place *cannot* be where the Prices live, for heaven's sake, do not leave – " the door was opened by a young girl, who confirmed that Lieutenant Price and his family dwelt within. Mr. Crawford ordered his driver to continue and promised to return for her in a quarter of an hour, and Mary Crawford, pulling her cloak tightly about her, was ushered into a small, cramped abode where she was greeted by the younger sister of Lady Bertram, whose path in life had differed so profoundly from the mistress of Mansfield Park, that in comparing the tired features and contracted brow of Mrs. Price with the placid expression of Sir Thomas' wife, Mary felt here was a triumphant vindication of her maxim that it was a duty to look out for oneself and marry well.

Mrs. Price gave her a civil welcome when she introduced herself as a friend of the Bertrams, and urged Susan, for such was the name of the girl, a younger sister of Fanny, to quickly move the mending and the cat so Miss Crawford could have a place to sit, and halloo'd to the kitchen for someone to bring tea. In answer to Miss Crawford's enquiry, Mrs. Price confirmed that, unfortunately, Fanny had sent them no further word. Her sister Bertram had written her several times concerning the efforts made to recover her, and Mr. Edmund Bertram had left them only yesterday, so the Prices had already heard the Crawfords spoken of most highly – how Mr. Crawford was sparing no efforts on their behalf, and how Miss Crawford had left the comforts of her own home to assist him.

"We were not quite certain why it was that Fanny told no-one where she was going. Pray, Miss Crawford, did they part on bad terms? If Fanny has behaved poorly, I hope that Sir Thomas will still be inclined to assist my youngest boys, as he has been so obliging with William, John, Richard and Sam! It was owing to his influence that John works as a clerk in London, you know, and Richard is with the East India Company, thanks to Sir Thomas."

"I could not tell you why your daughter left Mansfield as she did, Mrs. Price, but from all I understand of Sir Thomas, I think you have nothing to fear from that quarter." Miss Crawford then civilly wished good fortune to all of Mrs. Price's children, and received in reply an enumeration of all six sons, their ages, states of health, habits and pursuits, as could tire the patience of the most doating relative and was stupefying to one who was, in fact, entirely indifferent to the entire Price tribe. The youngest girl, Betsey, then made her appearance and stood and stared fixedly at Mary, without intermission, despite Susan's efforts to draw her away.

"Pray, Mrs. Price," Miss Crawford asked, as Mrs. Price finally reached the end of her recitation with the doings of young Charles, "as we will doubtless locate your eldest daughter without any further loss of time, may we convey her letters to her? Did Mr. Bertram collect her letters while he was here? I know he and Lady Bertram sent letters to your home for Fanny, and as it happens, I myself – "

"Oh yes," answered her hostess, half-listening as she pushed the workbasket across the floor with one foot so that it covered the worst worn spot on the carpet, "we did receive some letters for Fanny, but Mr. Bertram did not enquire for them and I never thought of it. Let me see...." she pulled at the top drawer of a battered sideboard, which refused to open. A firmer tug and the drawer yielded, nearly spilling all of its contents on the floor. Mrs. Price pawed and rummaged, pulling out bits of ribbon, parts of a broken mantelpiece clock, and stubs of candles, more than once exclaiming to herself, 'THERE it is!;' but Miss Crawford came to realize it was not Fanny's correspondence she was referring to but some other long-lost object. After a few moments, Mrs. Price abandoned the effort and apologized but, she was sure, she had placed the letters there in the drawer. The careless servant might have started a fire with them, or Betsey may have taken them to draw upon, or they might turn up again at some point, and if they did, she would be certain to keep them for poor Fanny. She then excused herself to discover what was delaying Rebekah in bringing their tea and Susan followed her to the kitchen, from whence a loud and somewhat rancorous conversation could be heard.

Mary was left alone with little Betsey who continued to regard her with fascination. Mary smiled prettily and whispered to her, "Now be a good girl. Here is a shilling for you if you can give me any letters that came for your sister Fanny." Betsey understood her only imperfectly, and eagerly ran in and out of the parlour, bringing Miss Crawford every piece of paper in the household, including letters from their midshipman son, a laundry list, and the demands of the greengrocer that his account be paid, but despite Miss Crawford's fervent hopes, no letter from herself to Miss Fanny Price was ever produced by the willing child.

After an interval of some minutes, Mrs. Price returned from the kitchen, followed by a trollopy-looking servant with a tea tray, just as Mary heard her brother's carriage pulling up without. With polite reluctance, Miss Crawford made her farewells, barely stifling a shudder.

She was just stepping into the carriage, and consoling herself that in such a household, the letter would in all probability never find its way to anyone, when Rebekah came running out, begging her pardon, but here was a letter for Miss Price that the mistress had just found on the mantelpiece.

Miss Crawford took the letter, and recognized Edmund's strong, elegant hand. "No other letters, then?" she enquired, endeavouring to appear disinterested, but there was no one to hear or reply, for the servant had gone in, slamming the door behind her.

In the privacy of her hotel bedchamber, Mary read over the following, composed shortly after Fanny's disappearance.

My very dear Fanny,

You cannot conceive of the anxiety your departure has caused me and all the family. Had you told me that you wished to visit your family in Portsmouth, I would have conveyed you there myself. Your leaving in this manner, and your letter to my father, can only suggest that you were very unhappy living amongst us. Had I known of your sorrows, I would have done everything in my power to assist you. Can you doubt it? Do you not know of my regard for you? I have told you that you are one of the two dearest creatures I love upon this earth, and Fanny, I must own myself hurt and surprised that you did not confide in me on this occasion.

Please write to me, if only a line, to assure me of your well-being. But Fanny, please, in remembrance of the many happy hours we have spent together, open your heart to me. If you have been offended by something or someone, please explain the cause and I will work to remove it. If you bear some secret sorrow, please share it with,

Your affectionate cousin,

Edmund Bertram

Then Mary held the letter over a candle and watched it burn to ashes, not without some regret, because it contained an avowal of Edmund's love for her.

Having intercepted first her letter to him, and his to her, and knowing that a meeting between the two cousins would bring her actions immediately to light, Mary was haunted by the necessity, the absolute necessity, of marrying Edmund Bertram before Fanny returned to their midst. Although she felt assured of his regard for her, she could not deceive herself about his reaction to any hint of *escobarderie* on her part. He would not be complacent about being thus practised upon – he would condemn her actions and she might well lose him forever. All because she had not the time to enclose Fanny's letter to her uncle within the letter to Edmund, and re-seal the whole, and place it back on the school room table, before Edmund entered the room! And now it was far too late for excuses and apologies. A half-minute would have made all the difference, and she would not be forced upon the path she now trod!

Mary resolved to return to the Parsonage, from there to finally make the acquaintance of the redoubtable Sir Thomas and try her charms upon the man whose word and will had such sway with all of his children. If she had the love of both the father and the son, perhaps a way forward to marriage could be contrived.

***

The regularity of her new life, her assured place in the household, as well as Mrs. Butters' occasional encouraging remarks, all did much to help

Fanny overcome the timidity and shyness which had always afflicted her. Her employer, Mrs. Smallridge, though tending to be aloof, or so Fanny thought, was not unkind to her, and in fact, Fanny was as free from slights, snubs, neglect and insults, as she had ever been in her short life.

With the Smallridges, Fanny was not expected to fetch or to carry, or to drop one task, such as untangling needlework, to take up another at the whims of her aunts. She had the dignity of a title, and in fact was in a position of authority, in charge of the welfare and education of children. When she looked at her reflection in the little mirror in her bedroom every morning, as she smoothed her hair and prepared for a new day, she thought she saw a new composure and assurance dawning there.

Fanny had also worried that her strength would not be equal to her responsibilities, but her health appeared to be unimpaired. At Mansfield Park, she had taken regular exercise on horseback and it was believed that nothing was so efficacious for her. But for the time being, her exercise consisted of chasing after little Edward. Being placed in charge of her own small sphere, though only fifteen paces from door to door, animated Fanny to a degree which surprised her.

After the birth of her twin daughters, Mrs. Smallridge had briefly, very briefly, basked in the sunshine of her husband's praise and affection, but that was now forgotten and he had resumed his usual habits – careless and indifferent when at home, and more frequently absent than not. Further, she had been slow to regain her health since the birth of her infant daughters – there was thankfully no specific malady, but her spirits were low, and although Mrs. Butters made light of it, saying that many new mothers experienced the same, the kindly widow determined to extend her visit for at least another month. Through the banter of the nursemaids and upper housemaids, Fanny knew that the mistress of Keynsham Hill was more than usually captious and fretful and even spent one morning in angry tears upon being informed that her husband had invited his cousins, the Bragges, for dinner.

Fanny was invited to the table with the Bragges, and was secretly amused to note how perfectly their names accorded with their natures, for the Bragges were inclined to speak only of their own affairs. Whatever new topic was introduced, it was sure to be quickly turned back into an anecdote concerning themselves, with both husband and wife vying to be the foremost speaker, and sometimes both speaking together, he to his end of the table and she to hers. Having only to listen and observe, Fanny also came to see that Mrs. Smallridge was almost silent in their company, and not merely because the only way to join a conversation with the Bragges was to interrupt them emphatically, but because Mrs. Smallridge's sullen countenance proclaimed that she interpreted the praise the Bragges bestowed on themselves as condescension towards their hostess.

Fanny was astonished when she finally comprehended that her mistress was herself anxious and self-conscious when in company. That anyone but herself, let alone a handsome, well-married woman of eight-and-twenty, could feel unease amongst others, was a revelation. With the self-centredness of youth, Fanny had thought only she felt awkward when called upon to converse with people of fashion. Unlike Fanny, however, whose timidity took the form of self-abasement, Mrs. Smallridge assumed a false air of *hauteur* when in company, which had at first deceived her governess into thinking her chilly and proud.

Upon further reflection, Fanny concluded that the source of Mrs. Smallridge's unease arose from the fact that she was the daughter of a tradesman, and in marrying Mr. Smallridge she felt herself to be at a disadvantage in education, manners and address. Her own relatives, the drapers, were not welcome at Keynsham Hill when any of Mr. Smallridge's friends or relations were in residence, with the exception of Mrs. Butters.

This better understanding inclined Fanny's heart sympathetically toward her mistress, and while she took no liberties, she was better able to bear with and understand Mrs. Smallridge's habitual reserve.

One evening, only a few days after their trip to Bristol, Mrs. Butters entered the nursery where Fanny was sitting and stitching on her new grey dress. "Here is a little something for you, Miss Price, from my friend Mr. Gibson. He has collected some of his poetry and his writings on the slave trade and asked me to submit them to you for your comment." Fanny, blushing, began to anxiously disclaim all abilities as a critic, at the same time reaching eagerly for the proffered parcel.

"Of course you are no critic, Miss Price, and I am tolerably certain that Mr. William Gibson, a man who has been to Cambridge and who can speak Latin and Greek, does not wait anxiously upon the judgements of an eighteen-year-old girl. When a man asks you to comment on his writing, you can be pretty sure he means, that your *admiration* would not come amiss. He doesn't want you to write up a review for the *London Gazette*."

Fanny began to apologize for being so apologetic, then checked herself as Mrs. Butters laughed and left the room. She felt chastened indeed but perceived that Mrs. Butters' intentions were kindly meant, as always. Fanny meditated on whether she tended to be excessive in her self-abasement, and whether her frequent disclaimers and professions of humility were always necessary. She had enough self-knowledge to understand she had acquired the habit because of the disapproving scrutiny of her Aunt Norris, who so frequently accused her of trying to put herself forward, who reminded her that "wherever she was, she must be the lowest and the last." From the time of her arrival at Mansfield Park at the age of ten, she had imbibed the notion that she was only residing there on sufferance, and if she displeased anyone, she would be sent packing back to Portsmouth in disgrace. Given her sensitive nature, it was not to be wondered at that she had lived in perpetual fear of causing offence. But amongst new acquaintance, perhaps she appeared as someone who exaggerated her own humility, and therefore was set down as one who, far from being truly humble, was actually full of self-consequence! Being amongst a new set of people enabled her to perceive herself through different eyes.

She thought again – how was it that she thought? – of Mr. Gibson's twinkling dark blue eyes, alight with intelligence and humour, and wondered if she would meet him again soon. Propriety forbid their establishing a direct correspondence with one another. He could only address her through Mrs. Butters, and she could only respond in kind. But she felt, very sensibly, all the compliment of his sending her a package of his writings, and his promptness in so doing told her that she had remained in his thoughts after their brief meeting. When she read his poems and articles carefully, she imagined hearing them read aloud to her, and she could with pleasure recollect the sound of his voice.

Her budding friendship with Mr. Gibson could only be named as friendship, as her heart was, and would always be, entirely Edmund's. Nevertheless, it was pleasant to form such a friendship and very gratifying indeed that he thought well enough of her, to desire her acquaintance!

***

The family at Mansfield Park at last received Fanny's letter from Bristol. All of the apologies and protestations contained therein, however, did her no service in the eyes of Mrs. Norris, who condemned her for ingratitude and want of respect in terms so severe that even Lady Bertram was moved to remonstrate with her sister – as Fanny was always so very biddable and even-tempered, Lady Bertram could not recognize her in the monster delineated by Mrs. Norris and added, "I am sure we would never have kept her all these years, sister, if she was as wicked as you *now* say you *always knew her to be*, but, you know, it was you who suggested that we take one of our sister Price's children – I must own the thought would never have entered my head, but for you."

Sir Thomas had last seen Fanny as an unformed, exceedingly timid girl of sixteen, and so could not reconcile his image of her as she was two years ago with the portrait of a young woman so independent of spirit as to leave home without the sanction and protection of her guardian. He was very much affronted, but as Fanny had left him with no means of replying, he could only look his displeasure, and said little. She was well, and in a genteel profession, and off his hands, and if he regretted the entire experiment of taking her under his roof, he confided to no one.

The receipt of Fanny's letter did away with all the suspense and nearly all the interest that Maria and Julia felt in the matter, and from that time they only mentioned Fanny to complain between themselves that, in her absence, it fell to their lot to wait upon their mother – to untangle her fringe, prepare her tea and play cribbage with her in the evening.

However, Henry Crawford was unwilling to abandon the search, declaring that he would look from John O'Groats to Lands' End before he gave up the hunt for Miss Price. He had stopped in Mansfield only long enough to return his sister to the Parsonage and he was gone again, no-one knew where.

Edmund, upon returning from his penitential visit to the Price household to apologize for mislaying their daughter, recollected that his mother had mentioned that Miss Lee, their former governess, was in service near Bristol. But when applied to, his mother could not locate the few letters she had received from Miss Lee, and could not recall the name of her new employers or their direction. "How strange! For Fanny always put my letters away in my little desk here."

Edmund looked in at the East Room, to search amongst the belongings Fanny had left behind, and was saddened to see that Fanny's geraniums on the windowsill were all brown and withered, as no-one had thought to water them.

Chapter Ten

As November turned to December, Fanny could reflect with satisfaction on the progress and industry of her pupils, and even congratulate herself on her management of them. Fanny noted that Caroline could not keep away from the pianoforte when allowed into the parlour. Fanny had lately regretted that she could not play an instrument, and reasoned that she was not too old to learn, so with the consent of Mrs. Smallridge, the governess and the little girl sat side-by-side every day, practicing scales, after her mistress had gone upstairs to dress for dinner.

Fanny's brother William had become a frequent topic of conversation between Fanny and little Edward, who was entranced by everything to do with the Navy, so Fanny soon learned to reward his diligence at his lessons with tales of 'William the gallant midshipman.'

Shortly before the holidays, she had the joy of a reply from her brother William in Gibraltar, giving his warm-hearted approbation for her decision to become a governess:

You were afraid, I think, he wrote, *that I would scold you for leaving the Bertrams – but I know my sister well enough to know that she would not have taken such a step without good cause! And I know whose ill-treatment has occasioned it. However, I am sorry that Sir Thomas has been away from home for so long; I think that, had he been there, matters might have been different. From your letters, I received the impression that he is the only one who can keep Aunt Norris in order.*

But never mind it, my Fanny. One day we shall have our own little cottage by the sea and we can bid defiance to all overbearing aunts and cold-hearted cousins.

One night when Fanny was invited to dine with the Smallridges and their guests, as happened not infrequently, and there happening to be an excellent wine served with dinner, Fanny observed with trepidation as Mr. Smallridge, partaking freely, grew ever more satirical in his remarks, while his glittering eyes followed every speaker around the table, until finally, interrupting his wife, he gestured at Fanny and said, "have you noticed, Honoria, how seldom Miss Price speaks, but, when she does speak, what good sense she utters? Is not her voice soft and pleasing? Have you observed, supposing you capable of noticing these nice points, that her grammar is unfailingly correct, her words well chosen, her discourse elegant and modest? *That* is the mark of a true gentlewoman, 'pon my word.

"Miss Price," he said, addressing her directly, "you will please to see to it – I charge you straitly – that Caroline will learn how to speak and to comport herself as a gentlewoman, as you do. My wife, for all of her advantages, was not bred up to it." Fanny looked down at her plate and flushed crimson, out of embarrassment for herself and mortification for her mistress. But her host had turned his attention back to his wife.

"My advantages?" his lady returned sharply. "I can only suppose you mean – "

"Your beauty, of course, my dear, and your complaisant air, Honoria. Ah, Honoria!" and Fanny perceived he was not addressing his wife but meditating aloud on her name, something he perhaps had done many times before, judging by the way Mrs. Smallridge quietly sighed and laid down her fork. "What an appellation! It is only the lower orders which give their daughters these presumptuous Christian names, coupled with family names such as – such as – pray dear, what was your name before you took mine? I do not recollect."

"When you was courting me, you could bring yourself to say my name without a sneer, I *do* recollect."

"Oh, yes – who would not take pleasure in coupling the super-fine, elegant name of Honoria with, with – Blodgett! Honoria Blodgett! Honoria Blodgett! There is a music in the sound! Well, my dear, now that *we* are coupled together for all eternity, I trust you are not unhappy to exchange your initials for mine? I think you were delighted to seal your end of the bargain and sign "Blodgett" for the last time on our wedding articles.

"As *you* were delighted to receive my father's settlement on me!"

"Alas, my charming simpleton, you can leave the name behind, but you can never leave your origins behind. You betray yourself with every movement, every word, in every choice that your taste, if it can be so called, dictates in the way of dress, hair and ornament. How *do* you contrive to spend so much money to so little good effect?"

Wounded silence was his wife's only rejoinder and to Fanny's infinite relief, Mrs. Butters interposed, "pray, Mr. Smallridge, when do you think the new stables will be ready?" To Fanny's astonishment, her host took up the new theme as though his insults to his wife were not still hanging heavy in the air in front of them all, and horses and stables, paddocks and breeding formed the balance of the conversation until the ladies withdrew.

Fanny soon excused herself to take a solitary cup of tea in the schoolroom, leaving Mrs. Smallridge to recover her dignity in the company of her aunt and the other female guests. While Mrs. Smallridge gave no indication that she resented Fanny for being singled out for praise, Fanny reasoned that her company could not be wanted.

Sheltered as she had been, Fanny could not even conceive of a married couple who saved their bitterest upbraidings for just such times as there were witnesses to hear them. Fanny was accustomed to the measured, steady tones of her uncle regulating the discourse at every family dinner. She had never seen him affected by strong drink. Her cousin Tom only grew more jovial after his customary half bottle, while Edmund was nearly indifferent to ardent spirits and never overindulged. She had vague memories of her own father, and his horrid breath after he returned from drinking punch with his old sailing comrades, but in her childish recollections his voice, though invariably loud and alarming to one of her tender sensibilities, was not raised in anger, and while he had often *spoken* his irritation at one or another of his children, and predicted their sorrowful but deserved ends, his tone had never betrayed true vexation or malice.

Mr. Smallridge's cruelty, his suddenly unleashed vituperation, was something new, something she had heard of but never witnessed – the abrupt change of temperament, the sudden gathering of the storm clouds, unpredictable and unwanted, which can sometimes be averted but more frequently must be endured. She was to be the unwilling witness to a number of family quarrels in the ensuing weeks, or to hear raised voices echoing in the hallways, which gave rise to the conviction on Fanny's part that no woman would knowingly marry a man of such temperament, and that no material comforts, or elevation in the world, could compensate for the uncertain footing the wife of such a man must endure, not knowing from one night to another if she was to be praised and caressed, or insulted and belittled, and studying in vain for the secret which would enable her to obtain the former and prevent the latter. Such a woman must harden herself to ignore his insults as proceeding from nothing more than the overthrow of his reason by liquor, and, if she was at last successful in becoming indifferent to her husband's censure, would inevitably become disgusted with his praise. Once a wife lost respect for her husband, or a husband for his wife, no true sympathy or confidence could exist between them, to say nothing of more tender feelings. The sight of such domestic unhappiness, so readily avoidable by common sense, decorum and good

106

principles, even where true affection did not exist or had subsided, gave Fanny much material for meditation.

Fanny's reflections enabled her to regard Mrs. Smallridge with even more sympathy than heretofore. Fanny now understood her bitter remarks, her suspicious air, her discontent when Mr. Smallridge was away from home and her cold demeanour when he returned.

She would not have wanted to trade places with her mistress, no, and if a sympathetic genie suddenly appeared and offered to whisk away the school room, the tedious sameness of the long mornings bent over multiplication tables and map puzzles, the long evenings without intelligent companionship and only the prattle of the nursery maid for company, in exchange being thus harnessed, she believed she would decline and send him back to his lamp.

The faults of her host only served to summon to her mind more frequently the perfections of Edmund, and it was with more poignancy, more tender gratitude, that she contemplated every moment she had spent in his company. His even temper, his rational and well-judging mind, his candour, his quiet wit, his gentleman-like courtesy, coupled with his unaffected delight in all that elevated the mind, such as music, poetry and nature – all taken together, was to Fanny a portrait of masculine perfection. When her mind wandered, as it frequently did, to scenes of the past, she could sometimes fancy him suddenly appearing before her, entering the schoolroom, or, when she walked on the terrace with Caroline and Edward, she imagined his form, far in the distance yet instantly recognizable to her, astride a horse, drawing ever nearer, until at last he was close enough to bend down to greet her. Their eyes would meet and his expression would tell her that he understood all, forgave all, and he would ask her, nay beg her – – but here she would shake her head and return all her attention to the children.

***

Observing the settled melancholy which hung over Maria and Julia, which no holiday excursions in the neighbourhood could alloy, Sir Thomas, after much deliberation, resolved upon a change of scene and formulated a proposal such as could not fail to delight both his daughters. Although he had seen no profits from Antigua in recent years, and the future appeared even more uncertain, owing to the prohibition of the importation of new slaves, he resolved on the expense of taking a house in London after Christmas, so his daughters could enjoy the Season in that great metropolis. He could not but acknowledge that, had his wife's spirits, health and inclination been other than they were, the family would no doubt have lived half the year in London for these many years, particularly after Maria's coming out. Remaining in the country had deprived his daughters of meeting many eligible young men, and he desired to see Julia well settled, especially after the scandalous failure of Maria's engagement to Mr. Rushworth.

The problem arose: who was to chaperone his daughters when they attended the various soirées and balls that the Season offered? As Sir Thomas pondered the question, it appeared inevitable that his sister-in-law, Mrs. Norris, and not his own wife, would be the one to sit with the other dowagers and mothers until the small hours of the morning, watching the couples dance and flirt, as Lady Bertram's disinclination for exertion exceeded her interest in her children's doings. Thus Sir Thomas resigned himself to Mrs. Norris quitting the White house, where she nominally lived, for indeed she spent more than half of her days and nights at Mansfield Park, to serve as the female head of the proposed London establishment.

Sir Thomas also asked Edmund to postpone his ordination to escort his sisters about London. The delay would be inconsequential, and in fact should a brief residence in London serve to confirm Edmund's preference for the country, it would strengthen his ties to Thornton Lacey and his intended profession. Sir Thomas made no secret that he reposed greater confidence in Edmund's judgement and propriety of conduct than in his elder brother's, and reasoned that the welfare of his daughters was better placed in Edmund's hands.

Sir Thomas consulted his old friend in the City for his recommendation for an address just fashionable enough to support the dignity of a baronet's family but as moderate as to expense as possible; an elegant but compact residence on Wimpole Street was decided upon, the news imparted to his family at Christmas dinner as a sort of Christmas present, and Sir Thomas had all the satisfaction of seeing his daughters restored to more than their usual vivacity, and Mrs. Norris's pleasure in the prospect was very little less than her nieces. Lady Bertram, once she comprehended the scheme, and understood that it was to remove every creature from Mansfield Park but herself and her husband, was inclined to pity herself very much, and sighed anew for the missing Fanny who, had she been there, would certainly *not* have been one of the party going to London. But on the whole, Sir Thomas believed he had chosen wisely and the benefits were in evidence weeks before their departure, for the joyful news helped to heal the breach between the two Misses Bertram. Their former habitual good understanding was almost completely restored as they exulted over every detail of the proposed stay, where they would go, what they would wear, and who they would meet. They pictured themselves at Almack's and Vauxhall Gardens, and wherever they went, being acknowledged as among the foremost beauties of the Season, with clouds of admirers trailing in their wake, and for Maria, there was that added anticipation of appearing, at long last, as the acknowledged future wife of Henry Crawford!

The sisters were swift in communicating their happy prospects to their neighbour, Mary Crawford, who discovered that she, too, had intended to return to London for a time, as her good friend Mrs. Fraser had invited her for many weeks and could no longer be put off. She exulted in the thought that Edmund's ordination was to be postponed for months, as it afforded her more time to persuade him to choose another course in life.

Dr. and Mrs. Grant and their sister were invited to a farewell dinner, and Sir Thomas discovered it to be an occasion for regret that he had not made his neighbour Miss Crawford's acquaintance heretofore. She was seated at his right, and at first he thought she talked a little too much and a little too fast for his liking, but he could not help but observe that as they spoke together, she grew ever more fascinated with his remarks, and thereafter said little, except to invite him to expound some more on whatever topic he chose to introduce, and her modest, respectful demeanour, so becoming to a young woman, recommended her to him even more than her undoubted elegance and beauty.

Edmund, who was seated at the other end of the table, had to content himself with admiring Miss Crawford's profile as she turned and looked up at his father, and the admiration and respect on her countenance; the obvious mutual sympathy and friendship that so quickly developed between his father and the woman he loved was more than sufficient consolation. He could picture her seated beside his father, at all the special family dinners to come, as dear to him as any of his daughters. He saw the introduction of a grandson and a granddaughter to gladden his father's heart, and the vision of the years of felicity that beckoned from the future, filled Edmund with a longing such as he had never known.

Mary herself finished the dinner tolerably satisfied with her performance. She had made the error, when first sitting down, of chattering gaily, as she was wont to do when entertaining Dr. Grant, but quickly adopted herself to Sir Thomas' more measured tones, and soon discovered that she need do little but listen and nod and encourage the quaint old gentleman, and she flattered herself that she had won yet another conquest by the time the final course was laid.

Sir Thomas escorted her to his carriage at the end of the evening, and expressed the wish that his children might have the pleasure of meeting her in London during the season.

"What, Sir Thomas, will we never see *you*?" enquired his fair guest, hanging on his arm with every appearance of regret.

"Perhaps, and only briefly, Miss Crawford, from time to time, as either my daughters' calendar requires or my own business interests may direct. But I trust that my son, Edmund Bertram, will prove to be a not unacceptable substitute in London when my duties keep me here at Mansfield, and I have no doubt Mrs. Norris looks forward to welcoming you at Wimpole Street, when you can be spared from your many social engagements elsewhere." Sir Thomas parted from the young lady in a very benign mood. While disdaining even as a littleness the being quick-sighted on such points, he could not avoid perceiving that his son Edmund was earnestly attracted to the heiress, and so Sir Thomas was well-pleased at the prospect of the young people meeting frequently in London, a circumstance that would, he trust, compensate his son for the sacrifice in postponing taking up his career.

Mary had a further, final, smile and nod for Edmund, and so the two families parted, with the conviction on Edmund's part that their future meetings in London must conclude matters between himself and Miss Crawford, one way or another. He would, he must, ask her to be his wife, and now he had only to ask himself, how far could he bend, how much could he give way, for her to say "yes"? He *would* be ordained, Thornton Lacey *would* be his home, but – was it, after all, essential that they reside there *every* month of the year if he engaged a competent curate to assist him in his duties? Could a compromise be reached between himself and the lady? If she should prefer to reside in London, relying upon her own income, for some part of the year – could *his* pride endure such an arrangement? He could not find an answer but he hoped, he almost believed, she was as desirous of finding a solution to their dilemma as himself.

***

Shortly after the New Year, Mrs. Norris, with angry triumph, baited Sir Thomas in his study one morning, carrying the urgent news that one of the upper-housemaids was with child, and had named her partner in shame –

the scene painter from London! Mrs. Norris waited expectantly for Sir Thomas' thanks and his assurance that the young person would be turned from the house before nightfall, but to her dismay he replied, "Scene-painter? I do not know of a scene-painter from London. Are there to be some theatrical exhibitions in the vicinity? How did a scene-painter gain entrance to my home to make his insinuations amongst my servants?"

For in her zeal to denounce the servant, Mrs. Norris had forgotten that the entire episode of the Mansfield theatricals had been successfully kept from Sir Thomas' notice, save an absent-minded remark or two from Lady Bertram, which Sir Thomas had interpreted to mean that the young people had entertained their mother with dramatic readings in the evening. Now, in consequence of the acuity and persistence of Sir Thomas in asking questions and drawing inferences, Mrs. Norris had to reveal the truth, so within a quarter of an hour he was pretty much apprised of the entire episode from start to finish – the selection of a play whose central theme was the seduction of innocent maidens, the building of the stage, the monies laid out on the scene-painter, etc., and he also came to the realization that, had Tom never proposed this means of diversion, his daughter Maria might be the respectably married Mrs. Rushworth today.

Mrs. Norris was a little confounded and as nearly being silenced as ever she had been in her life; for she was ashamed to confess having never seen any of the impropriety which was so glaring to Sir Thomas.

Her only resource was to get out of the subject as fast as possible, and turn the current of Sir Thomas's ideas into a happier channel. She had a great deal to insinuate in her own praise as to general attention to the interest and comfort of his family, much exertion and many sacrifices to glance at in the form of hurried walks and sudden removals from her own fireside, and many excellent hints of distrust and economy to Lady Bertram and Edmund to detail.

After this unsatisfactory interview, Sir Thomas also understood why he had been quietly revising his estimation of Mrs. Norris, to her disadvantage, since his return from Antigua. She had always insinuated herself into the affairs of his household, owing chiefly to the complacency of his wife (he would not name it as indolence, not even to himself), and he had professed himself grateful for her solicitude for his family and his concerns. But during his extended absence, his sister-in-law had come to regard herself as the chief superintendent of Mansfield Park, a role which she would not or could not easily relinquish. And not only had she made herself irksome to his servants, her overbearing and censorious manner to

Fanny, he speculated, may well have caused his sensitive niece no small amount of discomfiture. Mrs. Norris' removal to London would at least take her from under his roof at Mansfield Park for a time, but as she would be standing *in loco parentis* for his daughters, he knew that her conception of herself as the guiding force of the family would be strengthened, rather than diminished. It was to be regretted, but he could see no alternative.

***

Mrs. Smallridge was churched in the New Year; the infant daughters were christened Amelia Mary and Sophia Anne, and Mrs. Butters announced her intention, now that matters were in so smooth a train, to return to her own establishment in London. Fanny was very sorrowful upon hearing the news, as she privately considered the older lady to be her best friend and guide in her new life.

However, an unexpected pleasure awaited her, for the Smallridges declared their intention of visiting with their friends the Sucklings for a few days, leaving Mrs. Butters in command of the household, and authorizing her to invite and entertain any of her Bristol friends as she pleased, not excepting her abolitionist set. Mrs. Butters invited Fanny to make a fourth at the table with Mr. Thompson and Mr. Gibson – Miss More having returned to her own quiet country village – and the young governess was in a happy flutter all week, anticipating the dinner party and the evening to follow. She wore her new periwinkle blue muslin, which made her light blue eyes appear rather darker. Madame Orly offered to dress her hair, and allowed that it was a pleasure to wind the ribbons and arrange the braids just so, for the dear old Madame always wore her widow's cap and *entre nous*, a wig under that, and what could be done with that, *hélas*?

Fanny looked at herself in the mirror and saw a stranger.At first she worried that her hairstyle was too *outré*, but after examining herself in the glass for a longer period, decided that the elaborate topknot Madame Orly had bestowed on her gave her some added height, and some judicious pinching of the cheeks and lips completed her toilette. Mr. Gibson, of course, was the sort of man who was oblivious to fashion, and she had never set herself up as a beauty and much preferred, in fact, the compliment of being thought a worthwhile companion, than a creature to be admired. But – but, she was glad to know that she was in good looks that evening. Feeling very happy but conscious, she joined Mrs. Butters in the drawing room to welcome their guests.

112

Mr. Gibson handed her in to dinner, resplendent in a red velvet jacket, such as was worn by a previous generation of English gentlemen, much faded and worn, but the fact that he was not wearing his customary patched dull brown jacket was clearly intended as a compliment to his hostess and to the evening. Mrs. Butters had ordered enough dishes for twice as many as sat down at table, because she knew Mr. Gibson – poor man! – lived on bread and stale cheese, and could acquit himself very well at such a banquet as the Smallridge's cook was proud to provide.

Fanny perceived that Mr. Thompson, a lawyer of about five-and-fifty, was one of those philanthropists who love mankind in general, but are not overly fond of its individual specimens, being easily irritated by the faults of others. His Quaker garb and his white whiskers, together with his zealous expression, put Fanny in mind of an energetic Scots terrier. Mr. Gibson, with his mild yet witty manners and friendly countenance, formed an agreeable contrast to his sterner companion. However, the erudition of both of the gentlemen, and the respect and affection with which they treated their hostess, made the dinner that followed more than answer Fanny's longing for stimulating discourse. The talk between the three friends providing a striking contrast to the usual insipidities at her employer's dinner table, or worse, the studied coldness of the wife and the cutting sallies of the husband. Fanny ventured few remarks herself, but listened eagerly. She had expected the slave trade to comprise the whole of the conversation from the first course to the fruit and cheese, but in fact Mrs. Butters and her guests touched on many topics – the health of the King, the incompetence of Parliament, the state of the roads, the doings of their mutual friends, the latest publications, the education of the poor, and the army's reverses in Spain, and whether the new commander, Wellesley, could turn the tide against the Corsican. Here Fanny was able to speak of the activities of the Navy, adding information supplied to her by her brother, and his cheerful prognostications of complete victory in the New Year.

The talk reminded Fanny of the act of skipping stones over a broad lake, as the speakers moved swiftly from one topic or allusion to another, but leaving the listener in no doubt of the depth of the knowledge supporting the discourse, or, as she fancied, the depths of the water beneath the sparkling surface. And as plentiful as were the courses laid before them, the richness of the talk amazed Fanny even more – she felt herself to be at a banquet where she could sample only the smallest portion of the learning on offer. And through it all, the delicious, the novel, consciousness that Mr.

Gibson was at no small pains to please and entertain her, that he was as aware of her presence at the table as she was of his.

The last dish being tasted, the ladies then withdrew but were swiftly rejoined by the gentlemen who, being neither smokers nor heavy imbibers, had no other business at hand but to continue to pay their respects to their hostess and patroness of their cause.

"And now, my dear lady," Mr. Thompson bowed to Mrs. Butters, "allow me to present to thee the first volume of the newly-published history by Mr. Clarkson." Fanny caught the reverent tone with which Mr. Thompson pronounced the name of Clarkson, and Mr. Gibson explained, "This is a history of the successful abolition of the slave trade, written by a chief instigator of our movement."

"Do not say successful, Mr. Gibson," cried Mr. Thompson, "for thee knows that the trade continues, with the Portuguese, the Spanish, the French, aye, and with the English as well — for laws alone will not make men obey, without power to enforce the law."

Mrs. Butters exclaimed with pleasure and asked Mr. Gibson to please read aloud to them all. He took the volume in his hands, and he proved to be an excellent reader. His affecting descriptions of the Africans torn from their homes, of families separated, of slaughter and raiding parties, brought tears to Fanny's eyes and she could not help wondering again, if it were possible that all of this could be known to her uncle? She heartily wished that Edmund was there, to help her in her perplexity.

After Mr. Gibson had read for three quarters of an hour, and then begged a brief respite, Mrs. Butters challenged everyone in the party to recite from memory a favourite speech from Shakespeare. She began, laughing, with Emilia from *Othello*:

> But I do think it is their husbands' faults
> If wives do fall: say that they slack their duties,
> And pour our treasures into foreign laps,
> Or else break out in peevish jealousies,
> Throwing restraint upon us; or say they strike us,
> Or scant our former having in despite;
> Why, we have galls, and though we have some grace,
> Yet have we some revenge....

Mr. Thompson assumed the role of Richard the Third before Fanny's eyes and gave out with *Now is the winter of our discontent made glorious summer by this sun of York…* Fanny was quite transfixed and when he exclaimed *'dive thoughts, down to my soul…. here Clarence comes!'* she looked anxiously toward the door, expecting Clarence, and everyone laughed at her but so merrily and fondly that though she blushed, she also laughed, at herself.

Mr. Gibson then stood, and with twinkling eyes and a confiding smile, declaimed:

I know a bank where the wild thyme blows,
Where oxlips and the nodding violet grows,
Quite over-canopied with luscious woodbine,
With sweet musk-roses and with eglantine:
There sleeps Titania sometime of the night….

And when her own turn came, she could not meet the eyes of her auditors, but looking into the flames on the hearth, softly recited the only Shakespeare speech she had read often enough to know by heart:

Then, I confess,
Here on my knee, before high heaven and you
That before you, and next unto high heaven,
I love your son.
My friends were poor, but honest; so's my love:
Be not offended, for it hurts not him
That he is lov'd of me: I follow him not
By any token of presumptuous suit;
Nor would I have him till I do deserve him;
Yet never know how that desert should be.
I know I love in vain, strive against hope;
Yet, in this captious and intenible sieve
I still pour in the waters of my love….

and so on through the rest, until she fell silent.

There was a moment's silence…. then – "Oh well done, Miss Price!" exclaimed Mr. Thompson. "We shall have a poetry-reciting contest between thee and Mr. Gibson one day, to learn who has the most prodigious memory!" Fanny was starting to exclaim, "Oh no, you must excuse me, I cannot – " when she caught Mrs. Butters looking at her significantly, a look that clearly said, 'don't apologize for yourself, Miss Fanny Price.' Instead, Fanny coughed, and blushed, and nodded, and said "thank you, sir," and coughed again, and Mrs. Butters smiled and Mr. Gibson rose and fetched her a glass of wine with water.

Finally, Mrs. Butters and Mr. Thompson fell into an involved conversation about the regulation of a colony for freed slaves, how it would be financed, how governed, how defended, whereupon it appeared that Mr. Thompson was so intense on every detail, from the crops that should be grown, the clothing and tools that should be issued, the modes of religious instruction provided, the recreations that would be permitted or forbidden, that to Fanny he appeared to be building his own perfect kingdom in which the inhabitants, while nominally free, would be so surrounded by well-meaning strictures that they could decide nothing for themselves. From this discussion the two young people in silent accord withdrew, and found themselves drifting away from the circle of light by the fireside and moving toward the tall windows which overlooked the broad lawn.

"The night is too cold to take a turn upon the terrace, Miss Price," Mr. Gibson offered. "But I think we can watch the moon rise if we stand by the window. You will not be too cold? Allow me to place your shawl for you." Thus half shielded by the drawing room curtains, the young people alternately admired the gathering night and each other. Mr. Gibson talked of himself, as a young man with a pair of sympathetic eyes fixed upon him is wont to do.

"I was intended for the law, Miss Price, and I do not deny that had I persevered in that profession, it might have been of some service to our cause, but, for better or worse, I found that I could not endure it. If you know what it is to be impelled by an irresistible force, then you will know that I cannot do other than what I am doing – although I know perfectly well it means" – and here was a significant glance at his fair companion – "I cannot afford to settle or marry, not with the life I now lead. I am indifferent as to worldly ambition, in the sense of becoming a foremost parliamentarian or leader of society; money I value only as it may assist our cause – but," he laughed, "I will confess that fame has its appeal."

"But I think sir, you are not eager to win the approbation of others, if to do so you were compelled to conform to society against your conscience?"

"How well you know me – or rather, how well you have discerned my particular form of vanity! I do not know how to temper my convictions to suit society, nor how to view with complaisance what ought to be condemned with horror and detestation by every man who calls himself a civilized gentleman. There must be many, I know, who follow the path of

116

duty and in so doing, must turn away from following their heart's desire, but I am a selfish fellow – I cannot do other than what I feel I *must* do, and cannot be silent when I must speak, cost what it may."

"To dedicate your life in such a manner can only bring you the respect and admiration of those who deserve the name of friend," Fanny declared loyally. "It is only to be regretted that there are not more persons like yourself and Mr. Thompson, those who give their lives to an important cause, rather than living merely for pleasure, or merely for themselves. Those who are aware of a higher calling, who put their hand to the plow and do not look back, have surely been called by Providence to do some great thing!"

Mr. Gibson looked at her and smiled his gentle smile which made her feel, delightfully, that he must enjoy conversing with her, even if they differed on some points. "Providence, you call it? Do you believe 'there's a divinity that shapes our ends'? That somewhere there sits an eternal auditor who watches over all, and graciously stoops to alter this man's path or change that woman's destiny in response to their humble petitions?"

"Of course – can anyone doubt it?"

"I can think of many millions who could doubt it, starting with the men and women kidnapped from their homes, shackled and beaten, who beg aloud for the intercession of a – but I shock you, I perceive. My dear Miss Price, I would never wish to give you pain. If *you* were to promise to remember me in your prayers, I would deem it an honour. 'Nymph, in thy orisons, be all my sins remembered.'" He gazed at her earnestly, and could see, even in the dim light, that a deep blush suffused her cheeks, nor could she speak; to spare her embarrassment, he turned away to the window again.

"And as we observe the beauties of the universe on a night like this, my heart cannot deny a yearning for the consolations of faith, even as my head cannot admit the inconsistencies, the illogic, even the barbarity of our scriptures. Have you read, actually read, the entirety of the Old Testament, Miss Price? Have you ever read Thomas Paine on the subject? No? – well, never mind, I think Paine would be too abrasive for one who has never encountered such writings before."

"If I understand you correctly, Mr. Gibson, you are in doubt as to the first Author of our morality, yet you are such a very moral man yourself. In the portion of Mr. Clarkson's book that you gave to us, we heard a beautiful exposition of the moral laws of charity, which explains why the loudest opposition to slavery is to be found among Christians. If there is no

117

divine law, why are *you* so perturbed by cruelty? From whence arises the strength of your convictions?"

"I do not attempt to deny, or even discount as inconsequential, the fact that most of the leaders of this movement are people of strong religious conviction. Between you and me and the moon, it is sometimes wearisome to hear the confident pronouncements of Wilberforce and his Clapham Saints on exactly what God does or does not approve of. I can only say that it appears self-evident to *me* that injustice on this earth can be clearly seen and felt, and, being seen, must be opposed, without reference to any supernatural being who *cannot* be clearly seen or felt, at least not by me. But again, do not let me distress you. If it is any consolation, our mutual friend Miss More has been trying to help me see the error of my ways for some time, and – who knows – she may succeed. By the bye, how did you like her book?"

"Oh! Very well, I suppose, but it is mostly allegorical, just like *Pilgrim's Progress*, so it is not the diversion I was hoping for."

"Then I will not be able to resist the temptation to send some Thomas Paine to you."

"You will give me Paine after all?"

Gibson laughed aloud, and Fanny realized she had made a pun, and laughed along with him, even though she was a little disappointed and confused to learn that he was not an adherent of that faith she had known and imbibed from childhood. And yet, his eyes were so gentle and merry, and his smile so warm, and his intentions so undoubtedly good, that she would not turn away from his friendship on that account.

Not long after this pleasant evening, Mrs. Butters returned to her home in Stoke Newington, north of London, and she took an affectionate farewell of her niece's family and left more than a kind word and a thought for the governess, for she invited Fanny to correspond with her. Fanny would gladly have done so for the pleasure of communicating with the blunt old widow for her own sake, but knew, also, that every letter from Mrs. Butters might also bring her news of Mr. Gibson's doings, and that he in turn would receive news of Miss Price, and she could almost suspect that this was Mrs. Butters' intention.

Chapter Eleven

Miss Crawford heard nothing from her brother Henry all through December and the New Year, apart from a brief note at Christmas. He was supposed to be scouring the countryside, looking for Fanny Price. Her correspondents, and she had many, told her that Henry was here, there and everywhere during the holidays. Had she been able to send a letter to him, she would have told him that his design to weaken Maria Bertram's affection for him by staying away was in vain; Maria regarded herself as a woman engaged, and looked forward to their reunion in London. Mary continued to feed her hopes, reasoning, as always, that close ties between the Crawfords and the Bertrams augured well for her own eventual marriage to Edmund, and she heedlessly flattered Maria with pictures of her coming triumph in the great metropolis, and the jealousy it would engender among the fashionable ladies of London.

"My dear Maria, you cannot have an idea of the sensation that you will be occasioning, of the curiosity there will be to see you, of the endless questions I shall have to answer! Poor Margaret Fraser – the stepdaughter of my good friend – will be at me forever about your eyes and your teeth, and how you do your hair, and who makes your shoes. Ah! poor girl, she never had a chance of succeeding with him."

"I am not surprised that many young ladies should have esteemed Mr. Crawford, but what of *his* affections?" Miss Bertram could not forebear from asking. "Did he ever show any particular regard for anyone?"

"Henry is generally agreeable, as you well know, but I can honestly state that he cared for no one more than he cares for you," Mary answered stoutly and truthfully. "He was never tempted into contemplating matrimony, I do assure you. I have three very particular friends who have been all dying for him in their turn; and the pains which they, their mothers (very clever women), have taken to reason, coax, or trick him into marrying, is inconceivable!"

The effect of these conversations was not entirely as Mary intended; instead of gratifying Maria's vanity, the thought of Henry's many admirers awoke alarming sensations within her breast, and she resolved to watch her beloved carefully when they were together in London for any symptom of particular regard for any young lady who had made his acquaintance before he came to Northamptonshire.

The New Year came, and the long-awaited day arrived, and the Bertram sisters, with their aunt and brother, took possession of their home for the next six months, a compact but elegant residence on Wimpole Street.

Mrs. Norris' triumph in being the acknowledged chatelaine of a townhome in a fashionable part of London could be readily imagined by anyone acquainted with the lady, and she was no less eager than her young charges in commencing her residence there, in getting her cards printed and even laying out some of her own money in ordering new dresses and bonnets. The dining room in Wimpole Street was smaller, indeed, than the corresponding room in her old home, the Parsonage, but she nevertheless saw herself as she would be in a few weeks' time – a sought-after hostess, presiding over a table as elegant, and bountifully laid, as Sir Thomas' money and her own ingenuity could supply.

Sir Thomas, owing to his years in parliament, had a goodly acquaintance in the City. He made his round of visits, left his cards, and established invitations for his family wherever he could. He did not need frequent reminders from his daughters to obtain tickets to Almack's Assembly Rooms. And with rather more difficulty, because the time was so short, he got his daughters on the list for presentation at St. James Court. It was only fitting that the daughters of a baronet make their curtsey to Queen Charlotte.

Maria cherished the idea that the day of her presentation at Court would be the ideal day to publicly announce her understanding with Henry Crawford. It would be coming only twelve weeks after she had dissolved her engagement with Mr. Rushworth. She made it clear to Mary Crawford that she expected Henry to attend at St. James on the important day.

But there were many other diversions around London to enchant the Bertram sisters – shopping along the Strand, viewing the Panoramas, walking in Hyde Park, riding on Rotten Row, attending the theatre and the concerts, and drawing the attention of new admirers, so Maria was by no means always pining for Henry. The business of shopping and dressing, of going out visiting and receiving at home, occupied her most agreeably.

**

Fanny regarded the New Year as an occasion for self-improvement, and had determined within herself to profitably use any spare time that fell to her, so in addition to practicing her scales on the pianoforte alongside little Caroline, she studied dressmaking, a pursuit that finally gave her a topic of common interest with Mrs. Smallridge, who, as a draper's daughter, was very knowledgeable about fabrics. Before she left Keynsham Hill, Mrs. Butters had highly praised the two new dresses Fanny had made for herself but had been exasperated when Fanny blushed and demurred, saying to her, "You must be prepared to accept the truth, Miss Price, and that is, you have a talent, my word, indeed you do!" and then fell to seriously commending her skill as a seamstress – how well her new garments fit and moved and the simplicity and elegance of her design. Out of habit, Fanny's heart fluttered, she grew nervous, and she almost looked over her shoulder to see if Aunt Norris was standing there.

Fanny reasoned that she had acquired the habit of panicking when she was singled out for praise because she would invariably receive a corrective, administered by Aunt Norris, that depressed her spirits further than the compliment had ever elevated it. To draw notice at Mansfield Park was to expose herself to her Aunt Norris' resentment and scorn. But here at Keynsham Hill, where, if she had few friends, she had at least no enemies, she need not be so afraid of attracting notice or receiving compliments and praise. This realization materially lessened her fears, and she schooled herself to receive compliments quietly and calmly, without flurries of panic and denial.

Mrs. Butters had been a valuable teacher indeed! And with her departure, Fanny keenly felt the absence of a sympathetic person with whom she could converse unreservedly on larger topics, as the Smallridges never thought or spoke of anything but their own doings and those of their neighbours.

She secretly amused herself by encouraging the habit of daily reading for them both. She had first stimulated Mrs. Smallridge's interest in novels by reading aloud to her in the evening, from *The Ruins of Rigonda*, which Mrs. Butters had given to her for Christmas. She set the volume down and was gratified to see Mrs. Smallridge pick it up and finish reading the story herself. She followed that experiment with reading aloud from books describing travels to Scotland and Europe, and she also had the happy thought of sometimes asking Mr. Smallridge for his opinion of current events, so that he was compelled, out of vanity at being thus applied to for his wisdom, to pick up the newspaper to inform himself of the matter in question.

One evening, when she was not in the parlour and Mr. Smallridge actually happened to be reading the newspaper, he saw a small item among the Notices.

"Honoria! Where is Miss Price from? What country?"

"She is from Portsmouth, my dear. She has one or two brothers at sea, I think. Why do you enquire?"

"There is a notice here in the paper for a 'Miss F.P.' It reads, "The friends of Miss F.P., formerly of Northamptonshire, would be greatly obliged if she would contact them by post, signed 'E.B.'"

"Ah. That could not refer to our Miss Price, then."

***

Henry Crawford finally returned to London, after repeated urgings from his sister, and from that time forward the Bertram sisters sought separate amusements. It was Maria's first object to go where Henry went, as it was Julia's desire to avoid him whenever possible. It fell out somehow, without any conscious discussion, that Mrs. Norris was Maria's chaperone, and Edmund was Julia's. Maria was the acknowledged favourite of her aunt and further, when Mrs. Norris felt herself to be too occupied with looking after the house or visiting some of her own acquaintance, Maria could safely be entrusted to Mrs. Fraser, the friend and protectress of Mary Crawford. Maria had only to mention that Mrs. Fraser had invited her to do such-and-such, and her aunt would happily give her consent – the grandeur of the Frasers, their wealth and consequence, and the connection with the Crawfords, were the only recommendation Mrs. Norris required to suppose that Mrs. Fraser was an appropriate chaperone for a young lady.

Although Henry Crawford was not eager to marry Maria Bertram, he was exceedingly eager to find some means of being alone with her again, a fact which surprised him, because in his experience the pleasure to be derived from arranging a secret assignation with a young lady from a good family did not repay the time and trouble it took to bring about. One had to first overcome their reluctance, of course, and that was pleasurable in itself, but then one had to get the girl away from duennas, mothers, jealous sisters, and trickiest of all, prying servants. And in the end, married ladies, such as Mary's friend Lady Stornaway, were to be preferred, being both more experienced and discreet.

That Henry Crawford worked diligently to obtain his pleasures, none could deny. He had first come to Mansfield last July and had stayed on with his sister Mrs. Grant and her husband in the Parsonage far into late October, save for a fortnight at his estate during the hunting season, during which time his chief occupation was to assiduously court and charm both of the Bertram girls; by turns flattering one and rousing the jealousy of the other, then turning to placate the jealous one; so that by September he had both of them in love with him. To seduce *both* at the same time would have been an unparalleled triumph, but his hand had been forced during the casting of the play *Lovers' Vows,* when both sisters expected to be chosen for the part of Agatha, and he had favoured Maria. Blessed by nature with a cheerful and optimistic temperament, he did not entirely despair of serving Julia in her turn, for so long as she showed resentment she was not indifferent to him. But he had always preferred Maria, and the delicious amusement of making love to her in front of the stupid fellow she was engaged to marry happily occupied the month of October.

But for all of his efforts, and the long weeks invested at Mansfield Park, and the slow patient progress from gallantry, to insinuation, to long, intense looks full of meaning (and he believed that no man was his equal in this art), to stolen kisses, to quick grapples in the shrubbery or behind the draperies, he had had only three opportunities to be alone with Maria Bertram. At Sotherton, the estate of the unlucky Mr. Rushworth, he and Maria had slipped away into the park, and matters were in a fair train until they had spotted Julia in hot pursuit of them; after the rehearsal of *Lovers' Vows*, he had given in to temptation, only to be interrupted once again by Julia, who almost brought disaster on them all, and finally on the day he met Sir Thomas, his daring was rewarded with a brief and delicious encounter in the breakfast room. Maria was ripe and willing, he was hungry for more, and it was deuced difficult to stay away from her, even though he was threatened with matrimony.

Being Henry, he hit upon a solution, and with the cheerful connivance of his sister, put his scheme into action. He took a room at one of London's most elegant hostelries. Mary, in Mrs. Fraser's name, sent Miss Bertram an invitation for a weekend visit. Mrs. Norris escorted her to Mrs. Fraser's door, then bid her a complacent farewell. Then Mary summoned a sedan chair to carry Maria to her rendezvous with Henry.

They embraced, he removed her cloak and heavy veil, she started to speak, and he silenced her with a kiss.

"No, no. Don't speak my love, my angel," he whispered fiercely, pushing down her sleeves to bare her lovely shoulders. "I am dying for you. I must possess you, now. Don't deny me."

And this is where he finally reaped the reward of his patient effort – the conquest of Maria Bertram was not simply the work of the present hour, or a day, or a week. Maria had been thoroughly seduced, and his to command, for weeks before.

Later, when Henry was drowsily calculating how much time would elapse before he would be able to start the dance again — very little time indeed, in fact — his partner raised herself up on one elbow and, brushing her hair back from her face, whispered softly,

"Henry, Henry, when shall we be married?"

"Married, madam?" Henry answered without opening his eyes. "What, are you proposing marriage to me? Can you so forget the modesty of your sex?"

"Don't tease me, my love — we have been engaged these three months."

"I never read anything about it in the papers. Are you sure?"

"But Henry, you cannot mean, we are *not* engaged? Did you not vow that you loved me?"

"'Lovers' vows'? Where have I heard that before? I may have said something of that kind, but my dear," Henry yawned and stretched, "in my defense, how could any man keep his head when in your company?"

He opened one eye and watched, amused, as the colour drained from her face and she scrambled out of bed, wrapping the bedsheet around her.

"Henry! I gave myself to you. You must make me your wife. What is to become of me?"

"My dear, if you had not spent your life mewed up in your father's house, then you would know the words of that French fellow are true — 'hypocrisy is the homage that vice pays to virtue.' Did you honestly believe that healthy young people in the prime of life, in the pride of their beauty, wait until marriage to sample the delights that you and I have known?" Henry was on his feet now too, and deftly sliding his shirt over his head.

Many gentlewomen would have fainted at this point, but Maria Bertram had more spirit, which he rather admired. He had to grab her wrists to keep her from clawing at his face and her strength surprised him.

"My g-d, Henry! By heaven, how could you do this to me! As g-d is my witness, I would never have lain with you if you — if you —"

"Well, not to quibble over a trifling point, my love, but I never offered you marriage. As for the rest, d'you not expect me to take what *you* so freely offered to *me*?"

Another attempt to scratch his eyes out and Henry changed his tactics slightly. He was feeling generous. He had enjoyed her thoroughly, wished to enjoy her some more, and perhaps, possibly, she *would* be the woman he would marry, and he supposed that he would marry, one day. He knew of no one he would prefer to marry, that he could recall.

124

"My dear Maria, calm yourself. I did not say that I would *not* marry you, only that I had *not yet* proposed to you — but how can a man go down on his knees when he is in danger of being blinded or scarred for life?"

That was better. He might regret his impulsive actions on some future day, but for now he reveled in his power over her — the proud, the elegant Maria Bertram, naked and weeping before him, begging him for a word of comfort…. he embraced her and gently led her back to bed to pass a delightful afternoon.

***

Edmund's hopes of feeling secure enough in Mary Crawford's affection to ask for her hand had received a material setback since they had both taken up residence in London. He had first made her acquaintance in the country, with few other admirers to contend with, but now she was returned to her native element, like a gaudy tropical bird returned to the wild jungle, surrounded by swarms of loud and assertive young men and women, all rapidly firing their merciless wit upon any of their acquaintance as chanced to be absent. His quiet, droll asides, that used to amuse her so greatly when they walked or rode horses together, went unheard in the crowded drawing rooms of London.

He was more admired by the other young ladies at these gatherings than he was perhaps aware of, for though he did not put himself forward, his height, air, and handsome countenance drew many eyes, and had he been an heir, and not merely a second son, he would have won yet more attention. But *his* eyes were all and only for Mary.

For her part, Mary was woman enough to want to show Edmund how admired she was, but not so much of a coquette as to wish to dishearten him entirely. She wanted him to be as seduced by her world, as he had been seduced by her, so that she might lure him away from his resolution of becoming a clergyman. But nothing availed to alter his determination on that head.

Mary asked Henry to invite Edmund to dine with their uncle, the Admiral, in the hopes of strengthening the ties between the two families, and speeding the day when Mary Crawford became Mary Bertram and Maria Bertram became Maria Crawford.

Mary and Henry, orphans from an early age, had been raised by this uncle and his late wife. The aunt had been almost a second mother to Mary, and her unhappiness in married life with the Admiral had rendered Mary more cynical than most young women concerning matrimony, declaring it to be 'of all transactions, the one in which people expect most from others, and are least honest themselves.'

Mary had left the Admiral's roof and gone to live with her half-sister, Mrs. Grant, when, after the death of his wife, the Admiral began living openly with his mistress. However, her brother Henry continued on very good terms with his uncle, who in turn loved him better than anyone.

On the appointed day, therefore, Edmund Bertram was presented at Hill Street by a jovial Henry Crawford. It was to be a bachelor's dinner – the admiral's mistress did not descend from her private apartments to be introduced and Edmund of course did not enquire.

Admiral Crawford was a shrewd, bluff man of five-and fifty with a booming voice and a choleric colour that suggested a fierce temperament. He provided, as Henry had promised, an excellent dinner with very good wine, but the coarse expressions of the host caused no little discomfort for the honoured guest.

The Admiral was also in perpetual peril of losing his false teeth, especially when expressing himself with vigor. The Admiral cursed them volubly, complaining they were very ill-fitting, although the teeth themselves were those of healthy young men from the battlefields of Europe. His misfortunes in no way diminished his devotion to his dinner, and as a dining companion, Edmund reflected, he must have disgusted his elegant niece.

Henry Crawford was obviously amused and entertained by his uncle, and the affection between the two was evident. "This rascal nephew of mine has two dangerous hobbies – women and horses. Dangerous and expensive, aye. Did you know he has taken up coach driving – here is a gentleman, born and bred, who, for his own amusement, dresses up as a common coachman and flies about the countryside on top of his barouche, four horses in hand. We Crawfords are never happier than when risking our necks! "

"Nonsense, uncle, I can always control my team. Reins in one hand, whip in the other."

"Are we speaking of the ladies or the horses, now boy?" the Admiral laughed and poured Edmund some more wine. "And the flattery he pours into their ears! Nonsense, I say. A needless waste of breath. Speaking now of the ladies, that is. Once a woman sees what we Crawfords have stored in our breeches, no further *badinage* is necessary. The virgins are near to fainting and the married ladies' eyes light up, don't they, boy? The lad is a true Crawford in that regard." Edmund could hardly gainsay the remark, as the Admiral then casually stood up, unbuttoned himself and, turning to a nearby cupboard, opened a door and pissed in a chamber pot, affording Edmund a view of the organ in question. "The peacekeeper, I used to call it, when your old aunt was alive. At sea they used to call me 'Long Nine Crawford.' If you know what that refers to, Bertram. No short barreled carronade for the late Mrs. Crawford. Well, here's to her memory." And the glasses were topped up again.

"They say old Boney can't come up to the mark with the ladies – his cock, they say, is the size of my little finger. Poor Madame Josephine, hey? But they say she finds consolation elsewhere."

Remembering the occasional indelicate remarks that his beloved Mary had made in the past, including a vulgar pun about *rear* and *vice* Admirals, Edmund could now only wonder that her manners were so very excellent as they were, after having spent much of her girlhood with such a guardian, and he recollected as well an occasion when both he and Fanny thought Mary had spoken disrespectfully of her uncle – he wished he could tell Fanny that he now acquitted Mary entirely – Mary was in fact a marvel of self-restraint so far as speaking the truth about her uncle was concerned.

"But hey, I recollect," cried the Admiral, breaking in on his guest's reverie, "Bertram, you are to turn clergyman. Will you not reconsider? Can't you turn your hand to some honest work – become a highwayman, for example, or a grave robber?"

Edmund smiled weakly but said nothing and Henry Crawford thanked his lucky stars that at least his friend had the good sense not to start prosing away about the virtues of the clerical life, as he had heard him do with poor Mary.

"You mustn't take offence, Bertram, at anything I say," the Admiral laughed and refilled his glass. "We sailors are not diplomats. Still, a damned dull life you'll lead, by g-d. I hope you sowed your wild oats while at Oxford – had a little friend there, or knew a friendly widow?"

Edmund startled, because, in fact, he *had* had an intimate acquaintance while at college, the respectable young widow of a tradesman with whom he had privately succumbed, for the better part of two years, to the agreeable pastimes that ardent young men will resort to when the opportunity arises. And while he was rather more philosophical than remorseful about his past, he was not accustomed to canvassing the subject openly.

"Sir," he turned the subject neatly, while raising his glass, "whatever I may accomplish on this earth, I own without reservation that it will in no way compare with the perils you have endured, in your service to our country."

This was more than pleasing to the Admiral, who then regaled his guest with tales of past engagements with the g-d-damned French, and he pressed the salt cellar and all the cutlery into service to re-enact some of his victories, so that Edmund's knife tacked nimbly past the soup ladle and fired a broadside at Henry's fork – and when at last the gentlemen retired to the parlor for a snifter of brandy, he regaled the young men with tales of prizes won, hurricanes encountered and mutinies suppressed, until sleep claimed him in the middle of recalling the first time he'd rounded the Horn.

***

The presentation dresses for Maria and Julia, with their hoop skirts and heavy trains, their white silk and extensive silver embroidery, stood poised on wire frames in the middle of their shared bedchamber. Because the hoops commenced just under the bosom (for the fashion of the day was for raised waists), the dresses looked like nothing so much as large dinner bells. The dresses had cost Sir Thomas a great deal of money, and were to be worn only once – at the presentation on the coming Monday. The hairdresser was engaged to call on them very early that morning; they would then be corseted and sewn into the dresses, their hair would be arranged with large, dazzling feathers crowning all, and they would be armed with enormous feather fans and high-heeled shoes. Once garbed, they would be transported to St. James Palace, where they would stand and wait for hours until summoned for their few minutes before Her Majesty. No wonder the daughters of England's finest families did not eat or drink anything on the day of their presentations, for to relieve themselves they must resort to a little coach pot held under their skirts, and no wonder so many fainted before the end of the day!

Maria and Julia were now too anxious to be happy, and too happy to sleep. On Saturday night, they both attended a ball at Mrs. Stanhope's, and it was hours after midnight when they returned, yawning and footsore, to the bedchamber they shared, but they lay talking together of the ordeal of the coming Monday – the announcement of their names by the Chamberlain, the advance and the deep curtsey, the brief conversation with the Queen, the final curtsey, and, most difficult of all, the retreat, backing away while facing Her Majesty, the train gathered up and draped over one arm.

Finally, Julia exclaimed, "Oh, Maria! We *must* go to sleep – look, it is already dawn!"

Maria looked, perplexed. "But Julia, our windows do not face the east but the south." Curious, she got out of bed and stuck her head out of the window. "I believe there is a fire in the distance." Soon both girls, all pretence at elegance forgotten, and with their hair in curling rags with shawls around their shoulders, were leaning as far out of the window as they could without falling into the street. The distant sound of pealing bells reached them, soon followed by the appearance of a wheeled cart, filled with long handled axes and grappling hooks, pushed by a group of panting young men, toward the distant blaze. A servant hallo'd down to them, to ask whither were they going and came the answer –

"St. James – St. James Palace is on fire!!"

The early morning brought confirmation of the dismal fact. Large crowds milled around the edges of the Park to view the sight – half the Palace lay in smouldering ashes, and no-one could deceive themselves that there would be any receptions hosted there this season.

Upon hearing the news that morning, Mary Crawford quizzed her brother on his whereabouts the night before – whether he had been in the vicinity of St. James Court with a torch, and to what lengths was he prepared to go, indeed, to avoid a public announcement of the understanding between himself and Maria Bertram? Mr. Crawford joined in the joke, but explained that he was, as always, the child of good fortune, and counted on that luck to continue to preserve him from wearing the matrimonial yoke.

The overthrow of all their hopes of meeting royalty, of distinction, of being the object of all eyes at the reception, was a bitter blow indeed for Maria and Julia, and no less so for the father who had laid down money, in the form of convivial dinners and gifts of sherry, to bring it about, and moreover, had had his pockets emptied by the most exquisite dressmakers London had to offer. Sir Thomas hoped he could persuade his daughters that with some alterations, the presentation gowns could be wedding gowns one day.

Chapter Twelve

Mrs. Butters was loyal to the fashions of her youth, feeling that the high-waisted gowns then in vogue looked ridiculous and immodest on a woman of her proportions. At her age, the necessity of wearing her corset and stiff bodice, and sitting at the sidelines of a ballroom until well after midnight, listening to tedious talk and watching foolish young people behaving foolishly, had lost no small amount of its charm. But the good-natured widow had agreed to escort the daughters of an old friend who was indisposed, and thus she found herself at Lord and Lady Delingpole's ball, with her fellow chaperones, watching over the new crop of Society beauties and the men who pursued them.

"There – that is Miss Crawford, is it not?" She asked her companion, Mrs. Grenville. "I haven't seen her for this age. How lovely she looks. Her partner is very handsome. Do you know him?"

"I believe he is the son of Sir Thomas Bertram, the baronet – you may recollect – he used to be the member for _____ borough. What a fine-looking couple they make! One of his sisters is here as well, the tall girl with the golden hair, in the next set of couples."

"Hmmm, very striking. Is this her first Season?"

"Yes, and she has an older sister also making her debut. They both will have ten thousand pounds."

"And young Mr. Bertram? What are his prospects?"

"He is not the heir. I am not certain."

"Miss Crawford appears to like him nonetheless, I perceive."

"Wasn't there something – something about Miss Crawford last season? I cannot recollect...."

"I think, my dear Mrs. Grenville, you are referring to rumours concerning Miss Crawford and the Earl of Elsham. I am told that Lady Elsham once met her at a reception and gave her the cut direct."

"Of course, I give no credence whatsoever to rumours."

"No, they only serve to entertain us until we can go home and be comfortable again. Blast these stays!"

"Oh, my dear Mrs. Butters, only look. There is the Earl himself."

Edmund Bertram and Miss Crawford were in the thick of a crowded throng, attempting to dance – though sometimes buffeted by persons moving through the ball room to gain the card tables or tea tables on the other side – when a tall, distinguished man of aristocratic mien, whose hair was shot through with grey but whose trim figure spoke of health, discipline and vitality, accosted her thusly:

"My dear Miss Crawford! At last! I feared we would not see you this season. You appeared to have buried yourself in the country, most utterly."

Mary startled, and paused in the dance. "My Lord, what an honour and a pleasure to see you again," Quickly recovering, she made a graceful curtsey. "Lord Elsham, may I present Mr. Bertram, the son of —"

"Your servant, sir." Elsham bowed, but if ever expression said, "I am no servant of yours, sir," his did.

"And yours, sir." Edmund managed with more grace.

Then Lord Elsham, without another word, took Mary's gloved arm and walked away with her, leaving Edmund alone among the dancers.

"My Lord," Mary remonstrated, "we will be remarked upon."

"I am always being remarked upon." he replied. 'I am the Earl of Elsham, after all. And you, Miss Crawford — you would be quite put out, I think, if you were not remarked upon at such a gathering as this. Now, when may I see you, Miss Crawford? When may we resume our delightful acquaintance? My wife is out of town, visiting her sister. She will be away these three weeks."

"I am greatly obliged to your lordship, but, my circumstances are such that, I can no longer — we must leave the past in the past."

"The past? I was not aware that we had parted. My dear, can you not continue to be my very good companion when you are in London? I do miss you extremely."

"As I will miss you, my Lord, but, I do beseech you, allow me to go my own way now, and let us part as friends, and perhaps — perhaps one day, we may meet again."

"I have many friends," Lord Elsham responded testily, "and don't require any more. If you are going to keep company with that Mr. — Mr. Beechnut over there, I suppose I must wish you well, but I see no occasion for you to withdraw from me in this fashion. Can you not find time for someone who admires you as I do? One who, if I may flatter myself, did so much to introduce you into the highest rungs of Society, to say nothing of the private lessons I gave you, which you gave every evidence of enjoying?"

Miss Crawford's face still wore a smile, as she looked about the room, as though she and the Earl were discussing the weather. She tried to find Edmund in the crowd.

"I hope we may part as good friends, my Lord," she repeated. "You have been very generous to me, I own. But you know as well as I, that reputation is a bubble and I must guard mine very carefully at this time." She stressed 'at this time,' in the hopes of placating him – she knew not if she would ever allow the Earl such liberties as he had taken in the past, but she did not wish to antagonize so powerful a man.

"With the greatest regret, then, my dear Miss Crawford," the Earl kissed her hand affectionately, and kept his hand possessively around her slender waist until Mary was able to locate her partner again. Edmund Bertram had to be satisfied with her explanation that the Earl was a particular friend of her uncle, and had known her since she was a child, etc., and Edmund tried to persuade himself that the look he had seen the Earl give Miss Crawford was an avuncular one. *Nay, it is but an Uncle*, he told himself.

***

"I declare, can it be? Yes, it is! 'Tis the divine Miss Julia!" Mr. Yates exclaimed cheerfully as he claimed a place next to her at the supper table. Her dancing partner looked up from his dish of white soup in irritation that someone was flirting with his partner, saw that it was Yates, and returned his attention to his meal.

"Mr. Yates, how good to see another friendly face amidst this sea of strangers," Julia returned his salute.

"And how fortunate are *we* that you have come to London to enchant us all with your beauty," Yates enthused. "A blooming country rose fresh from Northamptonshire. I have told my friends Sneyd and Anderson about you, do y'know. They declare that there never was a female possessed of a good sense of humour, who could tolerably understand their wit, and I told them, 'no, no, no, you have not met the divine Miss Julia, she is a girl who loves to laugh.'"

"I think all young ladies claim to prefer a gentleman with a ready wit," Julia offered, "but wit can be so dangerous, Mr. Yates. It aims its barbs in all directions."

"Fear not, Miss Julia, I will be your shield and protector for so long as you are in London. Stay by my side."

"So long as you don't shield Miss Bertram from Cupid's darts, Yates," put in her partner. "You and your particular friends must not engross her."

The two men fell to joking about arrows and quivers and targets and butts and soon Julia, while affecting to laugh, found she didn't understand them at all.

While Julia Bertram collected admirers, her sister was at pains to keep only Henry Crawford by her side, wherever they appeared together.

It was not at all unusual for Henry Crawford, when attending a reception or a ball, to be surrounded by two or more jealous females who aimed venomous looks at one another, and in the ordinary course of events he not only accepted such attentions as his due, he took amusement in the havoc he created in the breasts of the young ladies in his circle. He watched as sisters turned into enemies, best friends turned into implacable rivals, and it had only served as food for his vanity.

But Maria Bertram, with her superior, though as yet, unpublished, claims to his affections, was of a different order. When in public with him, she would not suffer him to address or even smile at any other lady under the age of five-and thirty, she fixed a glare that Medusa might have envied on any young woman who approached him, and as for dancing with anyone but herself and his own sister, he had first to seek her permission, confirm that the young lady was the daughter of an old family friend, and, as anyone could see, so far inferior to Maria in point of beauty that it was almost a punishment to stand up with her, etc., and during the said dance, his fair Maria would not take her eyes from him, nor, he sometimes thought, even breathe, until he had returned the young lady to her seat.

At times he rebelled, and made a point of giving flattering attentions to the most beautiful, most sought after women in the room – such transgressions were met by Maria with first, a whispered promise to end their clandestine meetings, and secondly, a whispered promise to attend the next clandestine meeting and smother him with a pillow when he slept and thirdly, she would fall to berating and insulting the unfortunate object of his gallantry in a fashion that drew the attention and derision of the lookers-on. In short, Maria was passionately jealous; she could not help or control herself, and the prospect of a lifetime under such scrutiny was unthinkable to a man of Henry Crawford's independence of spirit. By g-d, was she out to geld him? To make him into a tame lap dog? It was not to be endured.

But even as he internally resolved that he could not make Maria Bertram his wife, owing to her shrewish temper, she remained the most desirable, willing and passionate lover he could ever recall. And no sooner had he pleasured himself with her to the point of exhaustion and packed her back to her family or to Mrs. Fraser's, than he began to hunger for her anew and start to contrive the next *rendezvous*. It was dangerous, it was foolhardy, but what man could have done otherwise, given the inducement?

***

And so the month of February passed away, in novelty and pleasure, with some pangs of pain for those who, like Julia, were stubbornly forgetting forlorn hopes, and those, like her brother Edmund, who could neither advance nor retreat from their goal.

So far as he could allow himself to judge, Mary Crawford preferred him to any of her other suitors, and spent more time in earnest conversation with him, than in light bantering with the others.

One afternoon in mid-February they met, as they often did, in an overheated and overcrowded reception room. Mary was in attendance with Mrs. Fraser and her set of friends, a coterie whom Edmund had learned to distrust, suspecting them of being careless as to reputation and worse, contemptuous of morality, and he longed to see Mary brought out from their influence. He suspected that some of her cynical views were just those as she heard expressed amongst her friends, and it was they who were poisoning her mind against the idea of marrying a clergyman.

On this occasion, the afternoon began promisingly enough. Upon spotting him, Miss Crawford went to his side, would not be parted from him, took his arm and strolled about the room with him, and gave him her sauciest smiles. However, he had information for her that he feared would end those attentions for a time, if not forever.

"Mr. Bertram, there is to be a harp recital next week at the Argyll Rooms. While you have politely endured my playing for many an hour, wouldn't you care to listen to a true proficient? I am going with your sister – won't you come with us?"

"Alas, Miss Crawford, as much as I would enjoy accompanying you, I have determined on completing my ordination as a clergyman. My father will be here in London on business, and we thought it an opportune time –

"Oh!" She pulled apart from him. "So soon? You will leave us next week?" Miss Crawford looked shocked. "I thought you had determined to stay here with your sisters until July?"

"My father will not object to my leaving for a week while he is here."

"That is not what I meant, and you know it, Mr. Bertram. I meant, are you going to take this step? Have you no second thoughts? You know that *some* of your friends would be very sorry to see you settle for the life of a country clergyman."

"I trust that those of my friends who know me will understand that even if I could afford to choose a different career, or no career at all, I do not desire any other, and that I would rather, at the end of my days, look back upon a life of some utility to my fellow creatures."

"Come, Mr. Bertram – you cannot mean it. Are you truly going to do this? Will you condemn yourself to this dreary exile? Will you become a country parson, marrying and burying for a few shillings apiece, handing out the school prizes, taking your afternoon nap after your Sunday mutton? A man of your parts, your excellent understanding, your wit – will you throw yourself away in this fashion?" Mary's voice quivered with derision, but her eyes filled with tears as she spoke.

Edmund looked grave. "I see that it is useless to attempt to persuade you, Miss Crawford. I recall suggesting to you that you have been accustomed to speak lightly of the cloth, as you have heard others speak, but I *had* hoped that upon further examination and reflection, you would come to acknowledge that, for all their faults, the clergy play an essential role in a civilized nation. And I have explained that of all the professions open to me, the Church has long been my choice – by conviction – and not, as you seem to insinuate, out of any desire for a soft and idle life. Furthermore, obscurity holds no terrors for me, at least, not so long as I could believe myself esteemed by those I love."

She could only toss her head in vexation, more angry than wise. "It is a profession for those who cannot succeed in any other."

"Believe me," he went on, taking her hand. "Believe me, you have left me in no doubt as to your opinion of men of the cloth. If you cannot bring yourself to respect the *majority* of my fellows, I deeply regret that you cannot make an exception for *one* clergyman. With all my heart, I wish you could acknowledge me to be sincere in my commitment to this life – and I can only add that my sorrow over this essential difference between us, is just as sincere, and will be just as everlasting."

"Oh! Mr. Bertram!"

"I think you know my sentiments, Miss Crawford, though I have not had the courage to voice them. But it is better, perhaps, for us to remove all doubt, all suspense, and in my case, all hope, than to continue as we are?" he raised her hand to his lips and kissed it solemnly, while looking directly at her – his gaze, beseeching, threatened to overpower her, but she could not yield.

"My dear Miss Crawford," he added, still holding her hand, "pray, allow me to escort you to your friends." He led her to Mrs. Fraser's table, and there left her. She could not, would not, say 'farewell' to him.

Edmund could contain himself no longer, and swiftly left Lord Delingpole's residence without bidding farewell to his host. He walked for several hours through the streets, attempting to regain his composure. He found himself wishing he could talk to Fanny, and realized that he *was* speaking to her in his mind as though she were there, and in his imagination, he heard Fanny agreeing with him, and sympathizing. He stopped in the middle of the pavement, startled with a sudden thought – did he miss Fanny so much because of genuine regard for his cousin, or, because Fanny could always be relied upon to agree with him completely, on every point? Was *that* the reason he missed talking with her? Was he so spoiled and indulged, from having Fanny as the perfect confidante, always ready to listen, never inclined to disagree, that he could brook no opposition from any other woman? Did Fanny, in her innocence, feed his vanity to such an extent?

It was a troubling thought, and the conviction rushed suddenly upon him that he *had* been too inclined to take his cousin's approbation for granted. But, perhaps it did not necessarily follow that his vanity alone prevented him from reaching an accord with the woman he loved. The essential point of difference between Mary and himself was no minor matter, not a disagreement over whether Italian or German opera was to be preferred, or even the pleasures of country over city life, but, the utility and even sanctity of the clergyman's role. She wished him to abandon his planned career; she had made it, though unspoken, a condition of winning her hand; he knew it as well as she.

Therefore, his dream of marrying the only woman he had ever loved, was over.

Chapter Thirteen

Fanny delighted in all the first signs of spring, even when she was not among the beloved and fondly remembered gardens and groves of Mansfield Park. When she took the children outdoors for a walk to search for snowdrops, or to cut some switches of forsythia to bring indoors, she was sharing what she had used to do when a young girl, when Edmund was home from school for the Easter holidays. These moments, therefore, were suffused with precious memories and the tenderest feelings. Sometimes Fanny's eyes were swimming when Caroline brought her a little crocus or an early primrose and she explained that many people were affected this way by the flowers of spring, but they loved them nevertheless.

On a warm day in early March, when the promise of spring and freshness and sunshine was a tonic for the spirit and heart, the children were to have a day's holiday because Mr. Smallridge had decided to take them to St. Nicholas' Market in Bristol, for a special treat. Mrs. Smallridge was expecting a visit from Mrs. Bragge, and as their two governesses were acquainted, Mrs. Bragge kindly brought Miss Lee with her.

Being reunited with Miss Lee after an interval of three years brought many agreeable sensations to Fanny – her old governess was the first person she had seen who knew of Mansfield Park, its occupants, its ways, since she left it more than four months ago, and furthermore she was indebted to Miss Lee for finding her current situation. She found herself able to converse with her old governess with a freedom and ease which she had not expected. Now that they were no longer tutoress and pupil, Miss Lee – in the past so reserved, so formal – was decidedly more open, commiserating with Fanny over the loneliness and tedium of their shared occupation, and not averse to sharing something of her own history. This last was a revelation to Fanny who, if she had ever thought on the matter before, tended to imagine Miss Lee as springing forth fully formed, like Athena from the brow of Zeus. As a child, she had not even asked herself how old Miss Lee was, or whether she had birthdays, or brothers and sisters, but now perceived her to be a woman of between forty and fifty. Now, gathering assurance from Miss Lee's encouraging friendliness, she dared to enquire, 'how did she come to be a governess'?

"I grew up in Hertfordshire, the only surviving child of a poor clergyman," Miss Lee related. "There was a young gentleman with whom our family was acquainted, unlike any other I have met before or since. He was not a man easy to come to know or to understand, but of all the gentlemen of my acquaintance, he was the one I could most wish to have married. He was not handsome, but he was well-educated, with a most singular wit. If you will read *Tristram Shandy* (a book I could not have recommended to you when you were still in the schoolroom), you might receive some idea of his whimsical nature. In this, indeed, he was very different from myself, but I am one of those who believe that sympathetic natures, not identical ones, are best paired in marriage. We often spoke, when we met, of poetry and literature and I flattered myself that he desired a companion for life who could engage him on these points.

"But, in our little circle there was another young lady more practiced in the arts of flirtation than I. She was very pretty and lively, and younger than I (I was in fact several years' the gentleman's senior) but, without malice may I say I thought her too ill-informed to be the wife of such a man. The disparity between them was too great for understanding on her side, or respect and confidence on his. However, he made his choice of her, for better or for worse, and so my hopes were ruined. I understand that they have five daughters now and, my village correspondents tell me, have nothing put aside to settle on them. Perhaps there will be five more governesses in time! I cannot help but feel that had *I* been his wife, I would have managed his affairs more carefully. But (resuming her usual brisk tone) that was many years ago."

"Please tell me what pleasures have most consoled you, Miss Lee?" Fanny asked with interest, for she had never suspected that Miss Lee, like herself, was divided from the man that she loved.

"Oh…… playing the piano, reading, and walking out on a lovely morning such as this. I have maintained a large correspondence with my girlhood friends."

"May I hope that you took some pleasure in enlightening young minds?" Fanny asked with a little smile.

"Oh, perhaps, when I had a student who was truly interested in learning," Miss Lee nodded at Fanny significantly. "But I would caution you, especially as your pupils are at such an endearing age, not to become over-fond of them. You must always part with them in the end, and although you live together on terms of the greatest familiarity, you are not a member of the family; yours is a mercantile relationship. You must not lose sight of that essential point. Furthermore, overpartiality is an enemy to good discipline."

Fanny said nothing to this, as she could not find it within herself to agree entirely. She asked, instead, "Miss Lee, I trust you were you happy at Mansfield Park?"

"I was not *un*happy, and Mansfield Park is a beautiful home. Could anyone, knowing of the misery and poverty we see all around us, pity someone who lives in such a place as Mansfield Park? When thousands are fainting for bread shall I ask for pity, while I was dining on roast beef and fish?" And here Fanny looked down, and blushed. Seeing this, Miss Lee added, "Nor was *I* ill-treated by anyone there. But I shall not speak familiarly of your relations before you."

"And may I ask, when did you enter into the occupation of governess?"

"Not long after my hopes were disappointed. My father died, I was left with almost no income. My destiny, my fate, was clear and I resolved to face it. That was some five-and-twenty years ago, and I have served in three households, which is tolerably few, but – you cannot have failed to observe I wear a false fringe on the front of my cap. Under it, my hair is all grey. Once my duties end here, no doubt I will be cast once again on my own resources."

"Now for you, Fanny. You do know that Lady Bertram still corresponds with me, occasionally. She seldom mentions you, to own the truth, though it is not to be wondered at that she would have more to say about her own sons and daughters. But if I were to write to *her*, and ask for particulars about you, what would she say?"

Fanny blushed and hung her head. "I have told them that I am a governess but have not given them any particulars. I did not wish them to have the power, or should I say the means, to compel me to return. Although this decision has, I own, caused me great pain and remorse, I feel it has been for the best. But the inevitable consequence is, that I have no idea what Sir Thomas and – and all the family think and feel about my quitting them so suddenly. Sometimes I feel that they must be worried about me; at others, I fear they must have forgotten me already. So, in truth, I do not know what Lady Bertram would say to you."

"Before you ask me, I will assure you – I will not betray your confidence. Not because I think it advisable or courteous for you to deceive your own family in this fashion, but because I respect and honour that desire for independence and self-sufficiency which you have demonstrated."

Her interview with Miss Lee was instructive to Fanny. Despite Miss Lee's formality of manner, she recognized that her old governess wished her well, and she was sensible as never before that even the most resolutely composed persons of our acquaintance, while presenting a placid face to world, may, unbeknownst to us, have secret trials, regrets and sorrows. She thought of her uncle Sir Thomas, likewise so formal and reserved in his manner, and felt that she had little understood him or done him justice.

Mr. Smallridge was so late in coming home with the children from the Market that Mrs. Smallridge met the carriage in front of the house and, to Fanny's discomfiture, scolded him immoderately in front of the servants. The two sleepy children were bundled from the carriage and prepared for bed, half-asleep, while telling their governess, between yawns, of Punch and Judy and jugglers and gypsies and a wheel of cheese as large as a carriage wheel and other wondrous sights.

Fanny bade the nursery maid let the children sleep as late as they wished the next morning.

***

Miss Crawford was, to all the world, as gay and light-hearted, as lovely and delightful, as she had ever been. She adorned the best drawing-rooms of London, her hand was sought for as a dance partner, she received, as always, the gallantries brought by her admirers with wit and charm, her conversation sparkled at the card table. But twenty-four hours had not passed since Edmund had bid her farewell before she began to blame herself for having thrown away the one man she could love, out of stubbornness and pride. Underneath her sparkling façade of merriment, she was anxious and unhappy.

Ever since the death of her father, coming at an early age, followed soon thereafter by the loss of her mother, Mary had longed for the feeling of security she had once known as a child, before her removal to the unhappy house of her uncle, the Admiral. Mary could scarcely remember her father, but reverenced her few memories of his kindness, his calm temperament, and how his presence had made her feel that no evil in the world could touch her. Her growing affection for Edmund Bertram had rekindled those long-lost feelings – here was a man who would protect her, esteem her, a man of substance, intelligence and character. His announcement that he was to take orders had taken her by surprise, and she had not been able to check her temper. She wished she had not spoken so warmly in their last conversation. She was afraid she had used some strong, some contemptuous expressions in speaking of the clergy, and that should not have been. It was ill-bred; it was wrong. She wished such words unsaid with all her heart.

But she was not helpless, she could act, and she could make amends.

She was fortunate in having a means of coming at Edmund, through his sisters. She did not leave off her regular morning visits at Wimpole Street just because Edmund, the real object of her solicitude, was gone from London; she appeared to be as sincere a friend and well-wisher of the two Bertram girls as she had ever been. Miss Crawford could speak of Henry, and the Misses Bertram could speak of Edmund, and even this was some comfort. But, she discovered, upon guileless enquiry, they did not write to Edmund, nor he to them, in the ordinary course of events. There was no way to send him a hint through his sisters to let him know that she was a penitent.

She consoled herself by doubling her flirtatious attentions to Sir Thomas, who was staying with the household particularly while Edmund was away. She feared that the son had shared his disappointment with the father, and had told him of their quarrel; but so far as she could judge, Sir Thomas greeted her with the same old-fashioned courtesy, and escorted her into the parlour and to her carriage as she came and went, as he had ever done. He was in fact more animated in her presence than with his own daughters, whom he habitually addressed in the most formal terms, while they, with their lowered voices and downcast eyes, were quite different creatures when he was in the parlour than when he was not! No doubt, Mary reflected, his formal manner toward his own children inhibited them from taking him into their confidence, Edmund not excepted.

Mary was also more than typically gracious and attentive to Mrs. Norris, and had the happy thought of asking that worthy lady about *her* methods of managing the Parsonage in the bygone days when she was its mistress, asking for her advice as to management of servants, poultry, pantry, and etc., and this line of questioning, while it brought forth some uncomplimentary reflections on Miss Crawford's sister, Mrs. Grant, which Mary affected not to understand or hear, was well calculated to win Mrs. Norris' very good opinion of her. She hoped that some portion of their conversation would be repeated to Edmund, when he returned, for he would instantly understand its purport.

Every passing day strengthened her conviction that life was somehow dull and meaningless without Edmund Bertram. She missed the sound of his voice, she missed his hand holding hers in the ballroom, she longed for him to look at her in the way that he had used to do, before her sharp tongue had driven him away. All other young men of her acquaintance were fops or fools, drunkards or gamesters, danglers or liars; she was intelligent enough to recognize the solid worth, the manly virtues and the sensible principles of an Edmund Bertram, and she longed to secure them to her side for the rest of her life, even if it meant doing something she would have thought impossible only a few weeks ago – she would become the wife of a clergyman.

She still did not despair of making something of Edmund Bertram – perhaps he would become another Blair or Fordyce for eloquence and fame – or perhaps she could hire a scribbler to write something to be published under his name – it hardly mattered, so long as the Rev. Mr. and Mrs. Edmund Bertram were not condemned to wear out their lives in obscurity in the country. She told herself that with her determination and ingenuity, she could shape him into the man he deserved to be.

***

Two days after his visit to the St. Nicholas' Market, young Edward complained of a sore throat, and soon grew feverish. By nightfall, Caroline was in the same condition. Anna, the nursery maid, and Fanny sat up with them, watching in the greatest dismay as a tiny red rash appeared all over their bodies. Before daybreak Mrs. Smallridge and her two infant daughters were packed off to stay with their neighbours, the Sucklings.

The apothecary came, examined their rashes and looked at their tongues, and declared it to be scarlatina and not smallpox, which brought some slight consolation to the family, yet how many little ones had been carried away by scarlatina? Mr. Forrest, the noted physician, was called to bleed the children, which he did most thoroughly, until their little eyes rolled back in their heads. Then he ordered all their hair to be cut off, and Anna and Fanny wept. Day and night, they sat beside the children, sponging their heads with cool water, fanning them, talking and singing to them softly. They could sometimes hear Mr. Smallridge pacing up and down in the hallway outside the nursery, and sometimes sense his presence in the doorway but Fanny, at any rate, could not take her eyes away from the two little forms in their beds.

The physician returned and bled them some more – Fanny doubted the efficacy of this treatment, but could not oppose herself against his authority – and little Edward grew fretful, at which the women rejoiced, for it was a sign that the spark of life was in him, while Caroline lay still, her eyelids twitching, with only her slow breathing giving proof that she was still alive, while a fire raged in her little body.

Fanny lingered in silent prayer over Caroline, begging that the family be spared a tragedy that seemed inevitable, that would likely end with husband and wife permanently estranged; she, hating him for exposing their children to the crowded throngs at the Market, and he, seeking what consolation he could in ardent spirits, which, as Fanny had already observed, transformed him from an English gentleman into a snarling tyrant.

Nor was Edward considered out of danger as yet, for his throat was seriously inflamed and very painful, and Fanny and Anna suffered to watch him suffer, and defied the physician in his absence, because he had forbidden that the children be given chips of ice to suck on, nor even much water to drink!

And, as thoughts of self will intrude even at such times as these, Fanny meditated on the reverses and sorrows of her own life, and berated herself for ever thinking that she had endured anything that deserved the name of hardship, as compared to the anguish of a mother who had already lost one child, and was not permitted to attend the deathbed of another for fear of contagion, and who, because of the pride and the ill-will that had built up between them, could not even seek consolation in her husband's arms. Fanny thought of her own mother, who was considered lucky to have brought ten children into the world, and had lost *only* one of them, and she wondered how often her family thought of poor Mary, whose time had been so brief on this earth. Or, even considering Caroline herself, who lay between life and death, at only six years of age – would those six years be all that she ever knew before death closed her eyes? How did suffering the pinpricks of an Aunt Norris compare to having to quit this earth after only six years? Fanny made a solemn pledge to her Creator to combat her besetting sin – which she now identified as, if not self-love, then excessive solicitude for herself – if only, if only, little Caroline would keep breathing! If she could only give a small answering squeeze of her tiny hand!

In the middle of the night, Fanny became aware that Mr. Smallridge had entered and was kneeling at the foot of Caroline's bed. She could smell the brandy on his breath. He wept and watched helplessly, and asked if there was any hope, and Fanny promised to send for him if there was any change, for better or worse. After about an hour, he went away, still weeping. Fanny kept applying cool cloths and fanning the little girl, and speaking words of encouragement and exhortation to Caroline in low tones, and the minutes crept slowly by, with hours to go before the dawn.

Maria privately applied to her father for his blessing on her marriage with Henry Crawford, but Sir Thomas would not relent. He had determined that July, four months away, would be the earliest month on which he would pronounce on the matter; the end of July being when the lease of their London town home expired and the London Bertrams would rejoin the Mansfield Park Bertrams once again. With so many doubts raised against Henry Crawford's *constancy* in love, a three months' courtship was hardly sufficient to put that constancy to the proof, especially considering Crawford had absented himself for most of that time. And in that further interval, Sir Thomas sincerely wished to find reasons to like his proposed new son-in-law better than he did, and to feel secure in entrusting his daughter's happiness to him. He could no longer deceive himself – he saw that Henry Crawford was indifferent in his attentions to his daughter, he was lured away from her side by numerous other pleasures, and while he was an engaging and intelligent young man, he was not a serious one. He therefore hoped that Maria herself would tire of her suitor's neglect and put an end to the match and for that reason did not make a point of insisting that Crawford apply formally for her hand, as he ought to have done last autumn.

Sir Thomas had another reason for delaying the match – the returns from his Antigua plantations continued at a loss; the lack of labour, owing to the restrictions on the slave trade, began to be felt (for the unhealthy climate, and the rigorous toil, took more lives than were ever born on those islands) and he determined that he would sell part or all of his interests, if a ready buyer could be found. It would be from the proceeds of this sale that he could come down with the funds for Maria's dowry, which he would rather do than diminish the funds held in investments for that purpose.

With such a holding back on the part of the father, Henry Crawford resumed thinking of his wedding to Maria as a very distant thing, which might, after all, come apart in the end. His affection for his sister Mary, and her continued interest in Mr. Edmund Bertram, guaranteed his continuing good behavior toward the Bertrams in public, and he could not find sufficient reasons to put off his irregular secret meetings with Maria Bertram – such as solicitude for her honour, or respect for himself – so long as he could derive some fresh pleasure from them.

It was on a gloomy Tuesday afternoon in March, with a thick rain making all indoor occupations both desirable and pleasant, and Maria was supposed to be visiting with Lady Stornoway in Richmond but was instead lying abed with Henry Crawford, her unbound and tangled hair giving witness against her, and Henry was feeling particularly affectionate and careless about parrying her hints for an elopement.

"My dear Maria," he laughed, "I know you better than you know yourself. A trip to Gretna Green may satisfy your romantic notions for a time, but soon, you would sorely regret that you were not married in St. George's, Hanover Square, as you should be – nay, you have a duty to be married in London. Why were you born so beautiful, why were you born a baronet's daughter, if not to serve as an example to the world? Why be married at all if you do not arouse the proper degree of envy in others? Why be married if you can have no bridesmaids? There will be my sister, and Julia, and any other of your friends, perhaps even that little cousin of yours, if she can be found."

"Yes, I'm sure I'd like to see Fanny at my wedding," Maria responded absently, "and I know that Edmund truly misses her." She surmised also that if Henry Crawford located Fanny, her father might be better reconciled to their union, while Henry was not averse to anything that would give him an excuse for putting off naming the own wedding date. Although he thought to himself, *I hope Edmund does not wish little Miss Price to be a bridesmaid at his wedding. She would undoubtedly weep through the entire ceremony, and Mary would not care for that.* As Maria could hardly refuse his assistance in finding her cousin, lest she appear indifferent to Fanny, she agreed that he could make some further enquiries.

"Very well. Let us review the letter your cousin sent to your family from Bristol – I believe it was about a month after she left you – the one in which she was most grievously, sincerely, pray-excuse-me sorry. Your lady mother supplied me with a copy of it – it is here in my travelling trunk." He leapt agilely from the four-poster, and Maria admired the symmetry of his compact figure as he bent over his luggage, throwing his linen around the room as he searched for the letter. "Ha, here it is."

Resuming his place beside Maria, he read the letter over again attentively, murmuring.... *"so sorry...... regret...... apologies......* – a-ha!" He looked up, triumphant. "Here is a detail, a morsel buried in the mountain of remorse, the needle in the haystack, the diamond in the coal mine. Your cousin wrote, *"an important event occurring in the family who are now my employers, made it impossible for me to send this letter to you in as timely a fashion as I fully intended."* Mmmm-hmm. She did not wish to give her letter to one of her fellow servants to post – yes? Just as, prior to her departure from Mansfield Park, she visited the post office not far from your gentle Aunt Norris's abode in the village, not once, we have learned, but several times, to prevent the faithful Baddeley or one of the footmen from observing that she was receiving correspondence from a new and unfamiliar quarter. She is saying here she was prevented by the important event, from reaching a post office."

"Well, obviously," Maria retorted impatiently, slowly stroking his chest.

"My dear, the 'important event' is the key here. What are the important events in life? Marriage – " he leaned over and kissed her nose – "birth – death. The three occasions, we are told, when a lady's name may with propriety appear in the newspaper."

He sat bolt upright. "In the newspaper!"

She looked at him, wonderingly.

He flung the letter to the floor. "You have no idea how fortunate you are, Maria. Very few gentlemen can exhaust all their resources and yet recover to meet the demands made on their talents as rapidly as I."

"You will renew the hunt for my cousin?"

"I was not referring to that, but yes, I shall."

While Henry Crawford was, in truth, perfectly indifferent as to the question of whether Fanny Price would return to her family, he was still intrigued by her disappearance, in that he flattered himself if anyone could locate her, it was he. The information he gleaned from the landlord of the Raleigh Inn, that Miss Price had left Oxford with a wealthy widow, had fallen into his lap too easily, and in fact he had not pursued the clew, but now that he had bethought himself of another avenue of investigation, he was eager to try it.

Henry Crawford knew of a coffee house in Cowper's Court that catered to seafaring merchants and captains. Shortly after his interlude with Maria, he visited the Jerusalem, whose subscription room carried all the newspapers from the port cities – Bristol, Portsmouth, and Liverpool. He was able to order a bowl of thick, bitter coffee which he left untouched, take possession of a quiet corner, and thumb through the November and December editions of the Bristol *Journal* and the *Gazette*, armed with a pencil and a scrap of paper, perusing the notices which disclosed the names of various Bristol families whose titles or estates confirmed that they were wealthy enough to employ the services of a private governess. Miss So-and So was married, Mr. Thus-and-So died, much lamented, and ah, here – '*At Keynsham Hill on the 10th* inst*., the lady of Horace Smallridge, Esq., safely delivered of twin daughters.*' The Smallridges joined a select list of genteel families around Bristol for whom last November had been notable.

Chapter Fourteen

All of fashionable London was supposed to be gathered at the fortnightly receptions in the palatial London mansion of Mrs. Stanhope, so Edmund had searched, from one end of her drawing rooms to the other, but he had not seen the light and graceful form, nor heard the enchanting laugh, of Mary Crawford. He had hoped he would, that very afternoon, be reconciled with her, would see in her eyes and in her face and in her voice, a supplication and a relenting as would answer his fondest hopes, but she was nowhere to be found.

He was disappointed, but he was not entirely downcast because against all probability, hope had been reborn in his heart.

He was now a clergyman; the Bishop had blessed him and pronounced him fit to perform the offices of the church. He could marry, bury, and christen, and could preach the gospel every Sunday morning – according to an elegantly scribed parchment he'd received. But he had undergone the ceremony with his spirits in such perturbation, as humbled and confused him, and rendered him, as he then felt, unfit to think of himself as a leader of the faithful, or even as a dispenser of common wisdom. How could he preach to his new flock that "virtue was its own reward"? His reward for being a dutiful son was to perform more duties. His reward for taking the cloth was to lose the one woman he could rationally and passionately love. He acknowledged to himself that, however much he had intended to forget Mary Crawford, she would not be forgotten, and for some time, the pain must be severe.

He felt as a man at the dock, sentenced to spend at least three purgatorial months in London, escorting his sisters, acting on behalf of his father, before he could gain his release and bury himself in the countryside. He anticipated that he would see Miss Crawford repeatedly, would see her in company, laughing and surrounded by her admirers, belonging to them, and to everything that was glittering and bright and unlike himself. This was to be endured, and more besides. He did not seek to lessen his pain by reflecting uncharitably on the prize he had lost – on the contrary, in his recollection her faults had dwindled to nothing, and while he was naturally of a calm and sanguine temperament, it was at times a desperate calmness, as he contemplated the aridity of his future.

Then he learned that while he was away, Mary had spent many mornings in the parlour at Wimpole Street, she had spoken of him often, and with warmth and affection. His aunt related how assiduously, how respectfully, Mary Crawford had waited upon her, how intelligently the young woman had plied her with questions about the proper manner of running a Parsonage – lessons indeed, which she could never have learned from her own spendthrift sister, whose expenditures on wages for her cook, on meat and butter and brandy and claret and asparagus and artichokes, must severely drain Dr. Grant's purse. He nodded his acquiescence at all that was said upon the subject of the Grants, while his heart fluttered with joy. The intelligence received from his aunt provided assurance, almost as reliably as though he had heard confirmation from Mary's own lips, that, by some miracle, she had consented to become a clergyman's wife.

On his side the inclination was stronger, on hers less equivocal. His objections, the scruples of his integrity, were all done away, nobody could tell how; and the doubts and hesitations of her ambition were equally got over—and equally without apparent reason. She had made her preference known as clearly as a well-judging and intelligent young lady could, and he was wild to speak to her again. She was not to be found today, but found she would be, and soon, and he would not hesitate to put the question to her, once and for all.

"Pardon me, sir, but aren't you Mr. Edmund Bertram?" said a voice at approximately his elbow. He broke from his reverie, looked around and then down, and saw a young lady who appeared to be no more than one or two-and-twenty addressing him. She was well below the middle height, inclining to plumpness, with dark heavy brows which rested incongruously on her round, rosy face. She alternated between looking up at him imploringly – and how she had to crane her neck back to do it – and furtive glimpses around the room.

"Edmund Bertram, at your service, ma'am. Whom have I the honour of addressing?"

"I am Margaret Fraser. I believe you are acquainted with my step-mother. She is the intimate friend of Miss Crawford. May I speak to you for a moment, sir, in confidence?"

Edmund instantly extended an arm and escorted Miss Fraser through the French doors to a small interior courtyard where she sought out a stone bench supported by little carved cupids and screened by tall palms.

"Miss Fraser, shall I presume that what you have to say to me, concerns Miss Crawford? Because, if so, please understand that I wish to hear no communication which would betray a confidence."

Miss Fraser rolled her eyes, impatiently. "I think you *do* wish to know what I know, although I have hesitated to tell you. My step-mother will be so very angry with me, should she hear of this! It concerns your sister, Miss Maria Bertram."

With a wrench, Edmund pulled his thoughts away from Mary and recollected that Mrs. Fraser had indeed extended many invitations to both of his sisters, but principally to Maria. "Yes, I understand from my aunt, that my sister has been much in your mother's company this spring. Are you acquainted with my sister?"

"Of course. You have supposed her to be a guest in our house very frequently, have you not?"

"Not less often than once a fortnight, I should say."

Miss Fraser looked down at her feet as though she were earnestly studying her little kid slippers.

"Oh yes, she *arrives* at our house, but more often than not, she does not *rest* there."

"My aunt, Mrs. Norris, is always informed if your step-mother escorts my sister and Miss Crawford to a concert or some other outing. I believe what you are telling me is not unexpected, Miss Fraser."

His companion shook her head. "No, no, you misunderstand me. Your sister – when she *says* she is visiting my step-mother – she leaves – she goes – she goes to see – " a deep breath and then – "M-Mr. H-Henry Crawford."

Edmund flushed and the hairs on the back of his neck stood up, but he forced himself to respond calmly, almost indifferently. "Miss Fraser, are you speaking from your own knowledge? Are you quite certain of where she goes?"

"Oh yes, for she speaks of it openly. And when she comes back to our house," – Miss Fraser's chin began to tremble, and she struggled in vain to keep her voice even – "she speaks of 'Henry this' and 'Henry that' and how they are to b-be married."

"You say this has occurred more than once."

Miss Fraser nodded solemnly, still looking down at her shoes. "And last week, when your sister was invited to accompany my step-mother to Richmond, in reality, she went to Twickenham, where Mr. Crawford's uncle has a small cottage." This last declaration evidently awakened such painful thoughts, or such bitter memories, that Miss Fraser fell silent, struggling to hold back her tears.

A short thoughtful pause ensued and Edmund reached into his pocket for a handkerchief, which he pressed into the young woman's hand. She dabbed at her eyes, obviously agitated, perhaps with more to reveal, but she remained silent.

"My sister went to visit your step-mother only yesterday, I believe." Edmund ventured. "I think my aunt spoke of escorting her there."

"Yes, and my step-mother isn't even at *home.* She is still in Richmond. She will be away for a fortnight." Having made the communication, the young lady appeared relieved, and began to speak more rapidly. "I wanted to tell you this before, but I had no opportunity – I am always with either my step-mother, or with Miss Crawford, but today I came away with my aunt."

"I am obliged to you, Miss Fraser, and if our conversation has caused you any pain, or will expose you to any difficulties at home, I am most sincerely sorry. But please be assured of my gratitude. If I may presume to offer reassurance on the *propriety* of confiding this information, you have done as you thought was right, and your judgment did not err."

She nodded, still doubtful.

"May I ask, if your step-mother was not at home to receive my sister during this last visit, who *was* there? Yourself?"

"Yes, I saw her.... and Miss Crawford was there, of course," the girl answered simply, with a helpless shrug of her shoulders.

A dozen anxious questions came to Edmund, but he saw that Miss Fraser was trembling with suppressed feelings, he guessed, of anger, and relief, and worry, and he did not wish to expose her before such a multitude as were collected at Mrs. Stanhope's mansion. "Let us take a turn around this courtyard, Miss Fraser, and then rejoin the others. I trust you are not too cold without your wrap."

"You won't tell anyone I told you, will you!" The tear-filled eyes flashed their alarm.

Edmund reassured her and walked with her while she dabbed at her eyes and then blew her nose. *It is not an easy thing,* he thought, *to be in love with someone when there is no hope of a return. But whether or not Margaret Fraser has acted out of motives of revenge, I am afraid that I believe her.*

***

Fanny had lost count of the days and nights, but it was later reckoned as the sixth day, when Caroline's fever at last subsided, and she began to cry to be loosed from her restraints – for, the children had been wrapped firmly in torn bedsheets so that they might not scratch themselves, and Anna said that her old Scottish granny had always used an oatmeal poultice for soothing the skin, and the satisfaction of being able to do something for the children which brought them present relief, and the joy of seeing them return slowly to their rational selves, called forth more prayers of thanks from their grateful governess.

The children were sleeping a sweet peaceful slumber, and the crisis was passed, when Fanny allowed herself to leave their bedsides and go for a walk outside, singing silent hosannas as she breathed the fresh air of the park. The green lawn, bathed in the slanting rays of the late afternoon sun, had never looked lovelier. It was good to be alive, it was wonderful that Caroline would live to see more sunrises and sunsets, and perhaps grow up and fall in love and marry...

Fanny thought, unaccountably, of placid Lady Bertram, who seemed untouched by any knowledge of true calamity or sorrow. Life, love, marriage, childbirth, childhood, all had their risks. Had Lady Bertram been afraid when brought to her childbed four times? She was blessed with four handsome adult children – had she ever knelt in anguish over a sickbed? There was hardly a family in England that didn't know the misery of losing a child, or a mother dying in childbed, or children left orphaned, like her friend Mr. Gibson, who had been brought up by a puritanical uncle, Mrs. Butters told her. And yet, for all its risks and sorrows, life was a miracle, it was glorious just to be alive at that moment, to smell the grass beneath her feet and hear the raucous cry of the peacocks in the garden.

At moments like this, when she was carried away by the sublimity of nature, she thought of Edmund. He was with her every time she arose to a particularly beautiful sunrise, she could hear his voice when she re-read a poem he had taught her, she could see his smile when she recalled a private joke they had shared, every time she hummed a piece of music they had both admired, she felt every tender sensation of her love for him. Now, she thought, she must find a way to distill the pleasure from these memories, and try to leave the pain behind. From the time she left Mansfield, she had nurtured her thoughts of Edmund, as though any diminution of her sorrow concerning him must be a type of disloyalty, but here she was, walking through the shrubbery, alone with her thoughts, consciously happy, consciously at peace, and Edmund was still lost to her forever. If she could survive her broken heart, perhaps some future happiness awaited her.

**

Henry Crawford was feeling sorry for himself. Why were the pleasures of the flesh so all-consuming and yet so fleeting? Why did he have to expend so much of his time to obtain them, through weeks and even months of patient gallantry, and, having finally achieved his desire, did boredom and disillusionment replace ardour and passion so swiftly? His once-enchanting Maria now seemed to him to be a common trull, no better than one of the blowzy little actresses he picked up at the theatres, and with the devil of a temper.

He had done his best to keep his distance from the silly girl, his supposed betrothed, at no small inconvenience and exertion neither – he denied himself the pleasures of several receptions and gatherings, upon receiving the intelligence that she would also be there, and on several occasions he watched for her and Mrs. Norris to set out on their morning visits, before dashing to their front door and leaving his card with the butler. He contrived to always be where she was not, and to not be where she was, but had still succumbed to his weakness when it came to entertaining her privately in his hotel room.

She had insisted on coming to see him today – only a few days having passed since their last *rencountre* – because with her brother Edmund's return to the city, another pair of eyes would be watching her comings and goings. She found Henry distracted and distant, to which she responded with pride and resentment, and the worst of their tempers were soon on display to each other.

"I must leave London for a time, my Maria. When I return, we can talk some more."

Henry pushed her back into the bed, pinned down her shoulders and began nibbling on her neck, working down to those delicious breasts. He was tired of Maria, but he would miss those breasts.

"Henry, how long will you be away? Let us set a date for our wedding *before* you go – ow! Not so roughly!"

Henry released one fat pink nipple and replied, "Set a date? We are a long way from being able to set a date, don't you think?"

"What do you mean?"

L-rd, the woman was aggravating! Deciding to eschew further preliminaries, Henry pushed her legs apart with his knee and entered her without ceremony.

"Well, firstly – there is the question of your -- wedding settlement – from your good father. --- Rumour has it --- about town, I am – sorry to say – that Sir Thomas is – somewhat embarrassed at – the present and – may find it difficult to – come down with – all of your – dowry.

"Secondly, and – by no means of lesser import – is that Sir Thomas does – not smile upon me – and I scorn to – join in an alliance – with a household that – does not welcome me – with the due consideration – that any self-respecting – gentleman would expect.

"So -- on both – these points – the remedies -- are – in your – hands – rather – than – mine – and – I – shall – not – trouble – myself – any –further – to – give – my -- good – name – to – a – little -- slut – who – has – ahhhhhhhh! Sorry, m'dear."

Maria sat up and pushed him away, her eyes blazing.

"You dare call me a slut!" She slapped him hard, across the face.

His eyes narrowed, he rubbed his cheek. "You shall regret that, Miss Bertram." He paused, sorely tempted to teach her a lesson right there and then. But, as he reminded himself, *la vengeance est un plat qui se mange froid.*

***

"Good day. Is Miss *Bertram* within?"

Mary heard Edmund's voice in the hallway, talking to the butler, and she dropped her newspaper and jumped from her seat.

He had come to Mrs. Fraser's looking for his sister – nothing could be more natural, except of course, she wasn't there – the butler opened the door and presented "Mr. Bertram." Mary gave him her most dazzling smile and rose to meet him.

"Mr. Bertram. What a pleasant, pleasant surprise. Welcome back to London."

"Miss Crawford." He took her hand and held it for a moment. She looked up at him – she loved to look up at him – his person, his height, his air, were all excellent, and she felt a tingle which had nothing to do with the alarm which was making her heart beat faster. *How to explain Maria's absence?*

"Well, Miss Crawford, and how did you and Mrs. Fraser enjoy the concert last week?" he smiled.

"Oh, very well, I suppose. The crowd was insupportable, but we secured tolerably good seats."

The friendly light died from his eyes.

"Miss Crawford, I must explain the reason for my lack of ceremony. My aunt tells me that Maria has been a frequent guest here at Mrs. Fraser's, and that upon Maria's return to our London home, she describes the suppers she has eaten here, the games of cards she has played, the parks and the concerts she has visited and so forth, with Mrs. Fraser and you and her other guests. But.... " he released her hand and walked over to gaze out the window, though he saw nothing of what passed outside. "Miss Crawford, I have heard from a source I do not doubt that Mrs. Fraser has been away from London these past two weeks. I shall be perfectly candid with you – can you, without giving me the pain of enumerating them, understand the doubts, the fears, and the suspicions which now prey upon my mind?"

"Oh, surely, Mr. Bertram, there must be an explanation."

"Do you mean, an innocent explanation? Please give me one, I beseech you. I know that Maria has been telling us falsehoods. Who else is a part of her confederacy? That Mrs. Fraser is such a one, I have little doubt. But it wrings my heart to have to ask myself – Mary – "

She gasped, for it was the first time he had called her by her Christian name.

"Mary, tell me truthfully, have *you* lied to me?" Words failed him, and he looked at her in anguish.

Mary hesitated. Should she show resentment at the question, or should she appear wounded? She decided on a show of anger at first. It was a point of pride with her that she did not resort to tears as often as did most other women, and she felt it to be good policy also, as to cry too frequently inevitably led to disgust and weariness, at least so far as she had observed with her friends and their lovers and husbands.

"Mr. Bertram – you are insinuating something so improper – so indecorous – that I can hardly comprehend – words cannot express...." Mary clasped her hands together and walked about the room, feeling his eyes follow her. "I say again, there must be some explanation. Pray, let us wait for an explanation from Maria before making vile accusations. I had not thought you capable of it."

"Miss Crawford," he said gently. "Did you, or did you not, go to a concert last Tuesday afternoon with my sister and Mrs. Fraser? Was *she* not to have been your chaperone?"

"I? I – who can recall?" She laughed lightly. "When I am not in your company, I hardly care where I am or who I am with."

"I *believed* you did," he continued, in the same gentle but remorseless tone, "because, as you may recall, you told me of the concert before I went away, and that you and Maria were to attend."

"Ah yes! Yes, I do recall now," Miss Crawford's reply was rapid. "*Now* I understand you. Due to the crush of people, we were compelled to sit apart, I a few rows ahead of Maria, so I could not observe her. I looked for her during the interval, but did not find her. We were reunited *after* the concert."

"But did you not also say that Mrs. Fraser attended with you?"

"I don't recall." *Was it time to weep yet?* Maria asked herself. *No, wait a moment.*

"Not recall? I asked you if Mrs. Fraser enjoyed the concert not two minutes ago."

Mary was silenced for a moment, trying to remember exactly what she had said. She thought she had only said 'we', and had not mentioned Mrs. Fraser by name in her reply, but was she certain? Not waiting for her reply, Edmund pressed his point:

"Mary, are you in league with your brother to arrange secret assignations with my sister? Have you conspired to help your brother seduce her? Can your morals possibly be so corrupted?" Edmund looked at her as though he might well cry himself.

Now was the time! Tears welled up in her dark eyes, one perfect tear slowly traced down one cheek. To her relief, she saw Edmund visibly waver.

"That you could even begin to suspect me – that you could give voice to such foul insinuations – oh, Edmund, my heart is broken."

But what to say next?

"Yes" – *the chin wobbled, the voice wavered* – "I love my brother immoderately, and I know that he is impetuous. His love for your sister is past all bounds. But *he* has not asked me – it was Maria – Maria who asked me to say that I was at a concert. Out of friendship and love for her, I did not question where she went! Must we assume the worst? Perhaps they enjoyed being together, simply talking together, without the constant chaperonage of Mrs. Norris – pardon me, but to be alone with the one you love, is delightful above all things, to confide in him who holds your heart –
"

He looked at her, aghast. "Now I know that you can look me in the face, Miss Crawford, and tell me falsehoods. It is impossible for me to unlearn this knowledge." He looked as though he wanted to say more, a great deal more, but he turned, and slowly made his way to the door.

Both resentment and tears had failed her. *I will stake my last like a woman of spirit*, she thought. *No cold prudence for me. I am not born to sit still and do nothing. If I lose the game, it shall not be from not striving for it.*

"Edmund," she pleaded, running after him and placing her hand confidingly in his. "Edmund, I *must* tell you something, I must breach the bounds of decorum and speak to you from my heart. If you asked me – if *you* had asked me to meet you in secret, I would deceive Mrs. Fraser, my friends, my brother, anyone, to be with you. I could not resist you. There. I have told you the truth. I love you. I love you. Will you judge me, and Maria, so very harshly, or will you understand that we are young and in love and we cannot help ourselves? Are you so cold?"

She stood on her tiptoes, placing her hands on his chest, imploring. He closed his eyes in pain, and gently but firmly grabbed both of her upper arms, and she feared he was going to set her aside and walk out the door. She brushed her lips against his cheek, trailing to his ear. "And they *are* engaged to be married, Edmund – oh, Edmund, 'tis better to marry than to burn,'" she murmured in his ear. She wrapped her arms around his neck and pulled him closer – she felt his entire body stiffen for an instant, then – thank heavens! – he yielded. His eyes were full of pain as he stroked her face with one finger, traced the swell of her lower lip, his arm was like an iron bar around her waist, her eyes implored him, his lips descended on hers, her breath caught in her throat, and she gave herself up to his kiss. After a delicious moment, he broke away.

"Mary!" He cried hoarsely, grasping her face between his hands, raining kisses on her hair, her eyelids, her forehead, her cheek, her lips. "I *am* burning. I love you so, I love you utterly, I will love you until my last breath. But – "

"If you love me, you must forgive me, Edmund! Forgive me!" He tasted the salt tears on her soft lips. She was nearly fainting in his arms. "Edmund, I would do anything for you. I am like Amelia, and you are my Anhalt. You make me want to be a better person, I *need* you to help me. I love you, my love for you has made me reckless, shameless. Please, Edmund, please help me."

He embraced her tightly but briefly, then cupped her face again in both of his hands, tipping her lovely face upwards so that her eyes met his. The pent-up feelings poured out of him, the things he had longed to say spilled out, "Mary, if you love me, you must understand I cannot abandon my profession, or transform myself into what you desire. If you want London, fashion, wealth – I cannot give you that life. Please, Mary, please say you will be content with such a life as I can offer you? I swear to you that I will not claim one shilling of your fortune – it will be yours to spend on what you wish, to go where you wish, to do as you wish – my love, my Mary, so long as you come home to me. More I cannot offer you. Please, Mary – no, no, don't speak, not yet, let me kiss you again, my love! I cannot give you up! I will not!"

Now the sparkling tears in her eyes were in earnest.

Chapter Fifteen

A few days after their fevers had broken, the Smallridge children were permitted to sit up in bed and have their warm milk and bread, and Fanny was quickly stitching up more night caps for Caroline to cover her little bare head, when she became aware of feeling oppressively hot. She had been more than a week with only scattered sleep, had only paused to wash her face and drink a cup of tea before returning to the children's bedside, and so it was no surprise that the rocking chair she sat in seemed to be rocking of its own accord and the nursery started to spin. She tried to stand up but a swirling darkness overtook her, and her next distinct sensation was of waking in her own narrow bed, with the housekeeper peering down at her anxiously, and asking the physician, "Will she live, Mr. Forrest?"

Over her feeble moans of protest, Mr. Forrest exposed her arm and stuck her with his lancet, to release a dark stream of blood into a basin. "We will do everything for her that we can, Mrs. Campbell. My course of treatment has cured the children completely, as you can see, so we can hope for no less with Miss Price. I did not prescribe emetics for the children, on account of their youth, but Miss Price ought to be purged twice a day. I will return tomorrow to bleed her some more and in the meantime, keep her away from drafts —on no account open the window."

The next few days were a nightmare. Foul tasting medicine was forced down her already sore and inflamed throat, despite her tears and protests, which caused her to vomit again and again, when she had nothing to bring up. She had never experienced such dread as she felt whenever a wave of dry heaving wracked her exhausted frame, subsided, and then started again. She was kept in sweltering heat and tightly wrapped from neck to foot, and the doctor drained several basins of blood from her. He had no difficulty locating the blue veins on those thin arms! The nursery maids began to mutter about keeping Mr. Forrest locked out of the room, but Fanny could not hear them; she was in a delirium, sometimes calling for Mrs. Butters, sometimes for 'cousin.' Her hair was cut very short, but not shaved, and she lost a good deal of what little flesh she had, so that the nursemaids could count the ribs on her narrow chest when they changed her wrappings. Sleep brought her no peace, for she dreamt of Aunt Norris, who told her she must sew enough green baize curtains to wrap around Mansfield Park, and have it done by nightfall, or she would be a most ungrateful girl. Fanny's wasted frame shook with rage – she screamed back at her aunt, screaming out years of deeply buried anger and resentment, but no sound came out of her mouth. Aunt Norris just continued sitting and sewing, ignoring her.

Fanny came to herself long enough to hear someone say, "Does she have any family? Shall she be buried here, then?" and the thought occurred to her it didn't really matter where she was buried, so long as she caused as little trouble as possible.

***

Edmund alternated between being in a happy daze, as regards his own engagement to a woman of uncertain candour, and dire disapproval for his sister Maria's proven deceit. He forbad Maria to leave the house without Mrs. Norris or himself – she was never to cross the threshold of Mrs. Fraser's door, and she could only see Mr. Crawford if he came to visit them, in the parlour, with a chaperone. Maria chafed and raged, but had to submit. She mostly kept to her room, and saw as few morning visitors as possible. With every passing day, she grew more fretful.

To her increasing distress, Mr. Crawford didn't come to visit. A week went by, and there was no word from him. Tom Bertram, who had come up to London before heading to Suffolk for the Newmarket races, was not very sanguine as to Maria's chances of leading him to the altar.

"This is like last winter, Edmund. He was, as we supposed, riding all over England, looking for Fanny, so no-one could write to him, or bring him to the point. Now he has left his hotel, with no forwarding address. Unless his sister knows his direction."

"It's not fair to Mary to expect her to hold his chain, as though he were a tame bear," Edmund snapped, uncharacteristically ill-tempered.

"I beg your pardon."

"No, I beg yours, Tom, I'm sorry. Mary says she has no idea where he is, but that it is not unusual for him to fly about, particularly in the spring – rather like yourself."

"But *I* am not an engaged man – and I'm looking for proof that Crawford considers himself to be one."

"I wager he'll appear on our doorstep once my father has deposited Maria's marriage settlement in the bank for him," said Edmund bitterly. "Ten thousand pounds is a fair inducement."

"Well….. about that…."

"What, the rumours are true?"

"I don't know about any rumours, Edmund, but our father has been arranging the sale of a controlling interest in the Antigua properties to some new partners, to have the ready cash for both of our sisters and... for other projects that are coming along, rather than draw down the principal on the invested funds."

Julia, who had been practicing a new piece on the piano as her brothers spoke, looked up, startled.

"What? Is father in difficulty for money? How can this be? Why did he permit us to spend so much on our presentation dresses – and – rent this house, and rent a pianoforte for me, and let us buy so many new dresses, if he had not enough money?"

"Please don't worry yourself, Julia," Tom assured her. "Father told me that when he sells a majority share of the plantation, he will have enough ready funds for dowries for both you and Maria. Mother's jointure will remain untouched, the harvest at home should be plentiful this year, and our affairs are going well at Mansfield."

"But, surely," Edmund persisted, as Julia, satisfied, went back to her music, "with matters as they are now in Antigua, he will not realize a good price? The passage of the anti-slave trading bill has caused great uncertainty, has it not? I have heard that many smaller plantations have sold out to larger landowners."

"He has told me he wants to wash his hands of the entire business, but it's d-mned difficult to sell at a good price at this time, so yes, he has taken an offer from a company of investors," Tom affirmed, "he will be a minority partner – no need for him to return to Antigua, we trust – his partners will invest in other prospects, which should yield better returns in the future. Cotton in the Georgia colony looks more promising, for example. There's rice in the Carolinas, and I have my eye on horses in Virginia."

"Do you really? Tell me about it."

Edmund poured some wine and served his brother. The plantations in Antigua, like the lies that Mary had told him, were something he preferred not to think about, and he would be happy if they were sold out of the family, even if they fetched a disappointing price.

Fanny felt someone sponging cool water on her face, and murmured, "Thank you, thank you, thank you," until someone said, "ssshhhh." She sank back into a deep sleep and dreamt she was at Sotherton, the estate of Maria's former fiance, standing in the the little chapel with her cousins and the Crawfords. She heard the soft, insinuating voice of Mr. Crawford saying to Maria, '*I do not like to see Miss Bertram so near the altar.*' She saw again the face of the elegant Mary Crawford looking truly aghast when she first understood that Edmund was to be a clergyman. She walked with Edmund and Miss Crawford in the woods at Sotherton. Then they tied her down, laughing, to a bench, and they ran away. She frowned, trying to remember the actual day. She remembered when Edmund and Mary left her behind on the bench, but had she in fact been tied down? If not, why hadn't she gotten up? Why had she sat there, a helpless spectator, as everyone else came and went? Then along came the surgeon to force more of his emetic down her throat, and the torture began again.

Later, she dreamt again, and found herself back on the ramparts in Portsmouth with her brother William. It was a sunny day, the kind of day when you almost had to squint to watch the white foam on the waves billowing beyond the harbor. He told her that if she ran and jumped, she could fly over the walls, over the water, over the sails of the ships. She tried. She ran and jumped, and for a time she floated upward, and looked down over the Portsmouth harbor, and the bobbing ships, and the twinkling waves in the Spithead, and then felt herself sinking through the air, and gently falling, and the cold sea came rushing up to meet her, but she wasn't frightened, and she gently plunged into the water and began to sink, down, down through the murky currents, feeling relaxed and weightless. She watched herself sinking, arms and legs spread out, and saw that she had a little smile on her face and her eyes were closed, and her brown hair bobbed about her like seaweed, and she felt free and contented, and nothing mattered anymore.

***

Mary Crawford seldom read the shipping news, but one morning not long after her engagement to Edmund, she happened to be sipping her hot chocolate and saw a notice saying that *HMS Antwerp*, after many adventures, hazards and prizes won, had triumphantly returned to Portsmouth, to the accolades of the townsfolk. "Henry, is not the *Antwerp* the ship on which Miss Price's brother was serving?"

Henry Crawford, a guest who was welcome at Mrs. Fraser's at any hour, looked up from his sausage and eggs. "Yes, I believe so."

She handed the paper to him. "I believe that Midshipman Price is now returned to England. Undoubtedly the Bertrams will see this information as well."

"And the significance of that is......?"

"William, you may recall, was the only topic that Miss Price would prattle on about back at Mansfield Park. Her older brother, the dashing midshipman. And – I recollect this point in particular, for that humourless girl never could understand when I was speaking in jest – although he was her brother, he would write long letters to his sister – unlike you."

"Ah, yes, I recollect now! The faithful correspondent! He may know precisely where Miss Price is to be found."

"Exactly. And I should far rather *you* were the one to locate Miss Price, before anyone else."

"Of course. I've no objection to playing the hero. But would not he refuse to reveal her true whereabouts to us?"

Mary Crawford shrugged her lovely shoulders. "I can try, if you will take me to see him."

Henry laughed. "To Portsmouth again, then – and the elegant home of Mr. and Mrs. Price, no doubt, where a certain letter is still mislaid somewhere."

"You will not be sorry to leave London?" she teased.

Henry laughed. "As a matter of fact, you are asking a great deal of me. Tom Bertram may be helping his father, and Edmund Bertram may be – " he coughed discreetly " – keeping his sisters away from unscrupulous cads here in town, but I have weightier matters on my mind. I have been nominated for membership in Mr. Buxton's society of gentlemen coachmen, the Four in Hand Club. I am waiting to learn if that exclusive body will enroll me amongst its members. As for you – will it not destroy you to be torn apart from your beloved Edmund?"

Mary rolled her eyes coquettishly. "I had better avoid temptation until my wedding night."

"Good. At least one of you should behave like a timid virgin."

She wanted to fling the tea pot at him. "Never say anything like that again, Henry. Why must you be so unguarded!"

***

On the fifth day of Fanny's illness, Mr. Forrest was called away to a serious carriage accident and it was the misfortunes of others which perhaps saved Fanny's life. Spared of his ministrations for a few days, allowed to simply rest, without purging or bleeding, able to drink cool boiled water and to kick off her heavy blankets, Fanny came to herself.

"What day is it, Martha?" She whispered to the housemaid who came to change her wrappings.

"Why, it's Sunday, Miss. Can't you hear them church bells?"

163

"I mean, what is the date?"

"Oh, I don't rightly know. It's the fourth Sunday of Lent. Easter has come so late this year! There, the rash is all gone and the crusts are falling off. I think we can have these wrappings off you now, if you promise not to scratch yourself!"

Fanny tried to calculate.... when did she last write to her brother William? She wrote to him faithfully every month, but her time for writing had coincided with the children's falling ill. She hoped he was not worried about her. She was still far too weak to hold a pen.

The next day, the children were allowed to visit Miss Price for a few moments, and Fanny rejoiced in seeing them looking so well. She had recovered enough of her own strength to refuse to be bled any more – indeed, she turned Mr. Forrest away with a firmness and calmness which would have surprised anyone who knew the shrinking Miss Price of Mansfield Park. Mrs. Smallridge herself, once assured that Miss Price was no longer a source of contagion, visited her and tearfully thanked her for helping to preserve her two children. All of her former reserve and *hauteur* was gone as she pressed Fanny's hand gratefully.

"I was in such agonies, Miss Price, and when they told me that you never left my children's bedside, I dared to hope, and I cannot thank you enough. My husband and I are so extremely grateful..." and truly she did repeat herself in a similar vein, and truly could not thank Fanny Price enough, and Fanny for once in her life was able to accept the compliments and thanks – if only because she was too tired to summon the energy to refuse them. Mrs. Smallridge's remarks about her "dear husband" also gave Fanny hope that the misery of the past month had knit the couple more closely together, rather than the opposite, and so it proved to be, at least for a time.

Fanny was cared for with tender solicitude by the housekeeper and the nursery maids, and was promised she should have her own chaise, made of basket-work, to rest in the garden when the days were warm enough, and she was plied with beef tea and calves'-foot jelly and even oranges, fetched by Mr. Smallridge from Bristol. A friendly letter of enquiry came from Mrs. Butters, although she was still too weak to respond, followed by another note, slipped into her hand by a giggling housemaid, and Fanny opened it and saw for the first time the loose scrawl of William Gibson, writing to her directly –

Miss Price:

164

I have learned from Mrs. Butters that you have been very ill and that for a time your life was despaired of. Mrs. Butters was very concerned about you. Naturally she has heard some details from the Smallridges, but – between you and me and Mrs. Butters – they are not the most eloquent, or should I say, coherent, of correspondents. We did learn that even in delirium, you frequently apologized to everyone for having fallen ill, and Mrs. Butters says, that much she can well believe. But you don't mind a little badinage *from that kind lady, I trust.*

I accordingly volunteered to call upon you and to write up your own account of your recovery. May I visit you tomorrow afternoon and bring you some reading material (no Paine, I promise!) to entertain you while you recover your strength?

Your servant,

Wm. Gibson

She paused, affectionately, over his sprawling signature, tracing it with her finger. Then she thought about letting him see her, as she then appeared. Alas for female vanity! She pulled the little mirror from the drawer in her bedside table, and looked at her butchered hair, the dark shadows under her eyes, the hollow cheeks, the pale, chapped lips, and the dozens of small scabs on her face, neck and limbs.

Mr. Gibson would have to wait.

***

Mary Crawford made a show of unhappiness when her brother climbed into the box seat and took the reins from the coachman for the first stage of their journey to Portsmouth, but in truth she did not object to having the barouche to herself because she wanted time to think.

First, she was better reconciled to her exile to Thornton Lacey after her marriage because of what Henry had told her of the parsonage there: "I never saw a house of the kind which had in itself so much the air of a gentleman's residence, so much the look of a something above a mere parsonage-house. With some simple improvements, you may give it a higher character. You may raise it into a place. The residence of a family of education, taste, modern manners, good connexions. All this may be stamped on it; and that house receive such an air as to make its owner be set down as the great landholder of the parish by every creature travelling the road."

Her brother had sketched for her some ideas for alterations to the house and changes to the surrounding plantations, to which she had happily assented before consulting her husband-to-be.

Then, her parting from Edmund had been so tender, so delicious. There was something glorious in feeling her power over such a strong, upright man, to feel the way he struggled to control himself when she slipped into his arms and turned up her face for a farewell kiss. Their wedding day – and night – was less than a month distant.

The one aspect of their farewell which displeased her not a little was the fact that his thoughts seemed to dwell upon his cousin Fanny too much for her liking. She carried with her a little parcel from Edmund for Fanny – and Edmund's parting words had been to remind her to tell his cousin, could she be found, of his love for her and how he missed her.

But both she and Henry were in snares of their own making – Fanny had been Henry's excuse for delaying any talk of a wedding with Maria, and he had promised to find her. And unless Mary could keep Fanny and Edmund apart until after she married him, the fact that she intercepted her farewell letter to him would come to light. She intended to call on Mrs. Price while in Portsmouth again, and enquire if any letters had been found, but surely to do so would raise even Mrs. Price's curiosity – why was it so important to retrieve letters when the writer and the recipient would soon be reunited in any event?

Perhaps she would be unable to persuade William to reveal where his sister was to be found. However, she doubted that he would disoblige his own parents, and surely they would demand to know, and faced with betraying a sister's confidence or obeying his parents, what would any young man do?

"I wonder if young Mr. Price resembles his sister?" She called out to Henry.

Henry turned and smiled over his shoulder. "I have yet to meet a modest, retiring sailor, I believe."

Mary laughed. "Imagine, if his temperament *were* the same as his sister's, and his captain were to ask him to climb the rigging – *I'm so sorry, you must excuse me, indeed I can't!*" They laughed together.

Well pleased with herself and the world, Mary wondered if the time had come to set matters aright between Edmund and his cousin Fanny. Could she bring herself to confess that curiosity led her to open the note from Fanny, that only the lack of time *then* and jealousy of Fanny *subsequently*, had prevented her from doing what she now regretted? What man,

Edmund being no exception, would fail to be flattered by knowing that his lover was jealous of everyone who held a place in his affections? Would it not be better to confess all now, and enter upon marriage with a clear conscience, than to take her vows with this secret – this secret which must, after all, come to light – weighing upon her? She pictured what she would say to Edmund, how she would explain herself – this would definitely be an occasion for some tears – and how she would lay to rest her guilty secret once and for all!

How lovely Mary looked now, as her soft rosy lips parted with a little smile and her dark eyes sparkled at the thought of dropping the veil of deceit which stood between her and the man she truly esteemed and loved! All of blooming nature around her seemed to be in harmony with her thoughts, the very daffodils in the meadow nodded their heads in approval, the rustling leaves of the trees were like a thousand little pairs of hands clapping in gentle acclamation of her greatness of spirit. She clasped her hands together as the warmth of her feelings animated her heart, and discovered she was still holding on to the little parcel entrusted to her, by Edmund, the present he had chosen for Fanny.

It was to the credit of her willpower, she thought, that she resisted opening the parcel for a full further hour. She untied the ribbons, pulled off the paper, opened a neat little box and pulled out a simple gold necklace, a suitable gift for a young cousin entering upon womanhood. Mary congratulated herself on her future husband's good taste, but Fanny was not to expect such extravagant gifts in the future, not after *she* became mistress at Thornton Lacey.

There was of course a letter with the necklace, in which Edmund told Fanny of his engagement to Mary, expressed again his sorrow that Fanny had never written him, and spoke of his wish that she might return to attend his wedding. He then dilated on the charms and perfections of his bride-to-be, and Mary, enchanted, read that passage again and again, in a perfect warm glow of contentment, before finally turning the page, whereupon she came to a passage which destroyed her good humour as assuredly as a heavy rain shower blotted out the sun:

.... for, Fanny, as I have so frequently confided my misgivings to you in the past, you are entitled to know my thoughts, now that Mary has consented to be my wife. While I now repose every confidence in Mary's essential goodness and benevolence, I confess that her warm and passionate spirits led her to commit a wrongdoing, one which shook me, however briefly, from the conviction I had long held that she is the only

woman in the world whom I could ever think of as a wife. The particulars need not be related, but in short, she was led to dissemble at the request of a friend. The greater fault lies with the friend who asked her to stoop to deceit, for I believe this friend was as deceitful to Mary as she had been to her own family. But, further reflection convinced me, that although Mary was careless as a woman and a friend, she gained nothing personally by this falsehood – her intention was only to oblige.

However, to my knowledge, no lasting harm has arisen, at least none has appeared, so to judge by both Mary's intent and the result, I cannot condemn her. She was only too ready to fall in with the inclination of others, and that is in itself perfectly amiable. If persuadableness and complacency be her only faults, as I am now convinced, how readily she shall be able to correct herself, once removed from the polluting influence of her uncle and her unscrupulous friends. They have been leading her astray for years. Even her prejudice against the clergy may be removed – in time – when I am able to show her, by gentle and patient example, that the life is not a contemptible one.

You can bear me witness, Fanny, that I have never been blinded. How many a time have we talked over her little errors! For I can never be ashamed of my own scruples; and if they are removed, it must be by changes that will only raise her character the more by the recollection of the faults she once had....

Scruples! Talked over her errors! For a time Mary was so angry, at Fanny and at Edmund as well, that she looked wildly about her but observed nothing. Her glance alone should have blasted the spring blossoms from the trees and withered the bluebell on its stalk. To think of Edmund discussing her faults with that milksop of a girl! And many a time! Was Fanny Price, of all people, to be her judge? Was the opinion and estimation of a Fanny Price the means by which her future husband measured the worth of his bride?

Mary gave vent to her spleen by folding the note over again and again and then ripping it into shreds with the strength of outrage. She pictured her own nails tearing into Fanny Price's pale little face, peeling away the false mask of humility and exposing the sly, calculating creature who lived within. She could scarcely keep her seat in her carriage, she knew not how to contain herself, and looking around wildly, even greatly alarmed her lady's maid and Henry's manservant, who were sitting on the platform behind her, until, upon finally perceiving how these two servants were shrinking away from her and endeavouring to avoid falling under her gaze, (for they had borne the brunt of her tempers before) she finally mastered herself enough to sit silently, facing forward, as still as a statue, although her angry passions did not subside for several hours more.

Now she rejected with scorn the idea of asking Edmund or Fanny to forgive her. The two of them had secretly conspired against *her* – speaking of her behind her back! No doubt Fanny, between soft murmurings of assent to whatever Edmund had said, had poured her own brand of poison into his ears, saying whatever she could to destroy Edmund's affection and confidence. Mary's own heart felt like stone within her breast, and it was some time before her feelings towards Edmund softened, and procured him something like a pardon, while the blame all shifted toward Fanny Price and her flattering insinuations.

She thought of the letter she had written to Fanny, thinking her to be in Portsmouth, in which she had made Fanny understand that she, Mary, saw through Fanny's assumed façade of innocence, candour and modesty, and recognized her as being devious and cunning, though all the rest of the world was blind! Although the letter had been written in anger, she meant every word of it, and would retract not a jot – only, it still would not do for Edmund to ever know of it, and she must retrieve it, if it was to be found.

***

As it happened, it was as futile to find a missing letter in the Price household as it was to find a clean dish, or an unwrinkled shirt, or a stocking that didn't need darning. Little Betsey, however, had not forgotten her commission from the beautiful lady, and when the Crawfords called briefly at the household, she brought Miss Crawford the newspaper, pulled out of her own father's hands, and a street ballad about a sensational murder that Susan had purchased, and demanded a shilling for each. Henry, laughing, urged Mary to pay the little hoyden, so Mary handed over two shiny coins, smiled sweetly and murmured, "Remember, it is letters that I need. Keep them for me. I shall come back for them." Betsey, obviously eager to oblige, disappeared and reappeared, downcast, with no letters and Mary felt increasingly certain that she must be safe.

She and her brother declared themselves, as friends of Sir Thomas, to be the well-wishers of William, and proposed to take him away to the Crown Inn to ply him with roast beef and good ale to celebrate his safe return to England. To Mrs. Price, nothing could be more natural than that her eldest son deserved such a distinction, and a cheerful William was soon seated in a private dining room with the Crawfords where they unhurriedly made his acquaintance.

Henry Crawford's encouraging questions, and Mary Crawford's admiring glances, soon had the unsuspecting midshipman relating some of his adventures. Young as he was, William had already seen a great deal. He had been in the Mediterranean; in the West Indies; in the Mediterranean again; had been often taken on shore by the favour of his captain, and in the course of seven years had known every variety of danger which sea and war together could offer. With such means in his power he had a right to be listened to; even Mary found herself liking the unpretending brother of Fanny.

Henry Crawford discovered that this young man actually aroused feelings of jealousy within his breast, – and yet something more, a feeling he was unaccustomed to, which was self-reproach. He longed to have been at sea, and seen and done and suffered as much. His heart was warmed, his fancy fired, and he felt the highest respect for a lad who, before he was twenty, had gone through such bodily hardships and given such proofs of mind. The glory of heroism, of usefulness, of exertion, of endurance, made his own habits of selfish indulgence appear in shameful contrast; and he wished he had been a William Price, distinguishing himself and working his way to fortune and consequence with so much self-respect and happy ardour, instead of what he was!

The wish was rather eager than lasting. He was roused from the reverie of retrospection and regret produced by it, by some inquiry from his sister about the missing Fanny, and he returned his attention to the matter at hand, finding it was pleasant to have the sole command of his own time, and to choose where, when and how he could come and go, for Mary asked William Price if he had visited Fanny, and the young man answered in the negative, explaining that he was waiting to be paid out for some prize monies and needs must remain in Portsmouth to receive his share.

"I dare say that your parents were anxious to know everything *you* know about your sister's whereabouts," Mary speculated thoughtfully.

"Why, no, in fact, ma'am," William looked confused. "My parents – my parents hadn't thought to ask me if Fanny had written to me. They have been that happy to see *me*, begging your pardons, for I have been away from England for so long, and my father was a sea-going man, before he was injured, so....."

"Ah, of course," Mary murmured, noting to herself that to be a daughter in the Price household was obviously to be an afterthought for both mother and father. So Fanny Price was as forgotten at home as she was neglected at Mansfield.

Henry explained that he had promised the Bertrams he would find Fanny and reassure the family at Mansfield Park of her safety; and return her, if possible, to the bosom of her family. "She is in Bristol, or thereabouts, is she not?" Henry asked nonchalantly, refilling William's glass.

"I must beg your pardon sir, but my sister asked me not to disclose her direction to anyone, even though −" he broke off and chewed his lip.

"What is it, Mr. Price?" asked Mary, all concern.

"My sister has not written me this month. I know that letters can miscarry, and in fact, it is a wonder to me how the navy can bring me a letter from my sister, from hand to hand, from boat to packet, from packet to ship, all over the globe, and while sometimes the letter must chase around after me for a while, it does find me in time, and me just a common midshipman, so now that I am on shore, I am sorry I don't find a letter from her waiting for me here at home. She must know I am back in England, and I would sorely like to see her after all these years. But without leave, I cannot go to − to where she is, and so…. I have a letter ready to send to her, but I was hoping every day to see something from her…."

Henry smiled and Mary placed a sympathetic hand lightly on the midshipman's well-muscled forearm.

"We do have some knowledge of the family, and are only asking for your confirmation. Fanny herself told us that she was to meet a wealthy widow − in Oxford, I believe it was, and go from thence to Bristol. Will that satisfy your sense of delicacy, as regards your sister's confidence?"

William's honest face brightened up. "Oh yes. Fan never told me she had confided in you as well. Yes, she wrote me about Mrs. Butters − a very kind lady."

"Well then," continued Henry, "my information is that she is with a family by the name of Simpson, is that so?"

William's brow clouded, "Simpson?"

"Oh, no, no, no, I misspoke. It is *Smallridge*, isn't it?"

"Yes, sir. That's right, sir. Smallridge, at Keynsham Hill, just outside of Bristol. She says she is contented there, sir, otherwise I'd have sent her funds to come home to our mother. And if you was − were − to see my sister, could you ask her, can she come to Portsmouth to visit her family?"

"Have no fear. We will bring her to you, young man. May we convey your letter to your sister?" Mary offered her most charming smile, which was rewarded by an unaffected, open grin from the young midshipman.

Chapter Sixteen

Fanny lay on a wicker chaise under the trees, watching the children play nearby with the nursery maids. She was able to read and talk to them a little, and wanted to do more rather than less, for her conscience smote her that a se'nnight had elapsed since her recovery, yet she was still too weak to take up her duties. But she was still very tired and pale. At least she had summoned the energy to wash herself thoroughly, over Anna's shocked protests, and even wash her hair, so that her natural soft curls now covered her head. Her eyes looked large in her face and her cheekbones were more pronounced than they had been before her sickness. She was in nervous anticipation of the visit from Mr. Gibson – the blanket was drawn up to her chin – and she hoped he wouldn't be too dismayed at her altered appearance.

He arrived, and he *was* alarmed by her thin frame and her pale countenance, but he hid it well, with his usual warm smile, and he sat down, cross-legged, on the grass beside her with no ceremony.

At his request, she gave him a short description of her illness and recovery, and they sat silent again for a while, and a footman brought them lemonade to drink, and a cushion for him to sit on, then he asked – "What is it like, to almost die? Did you see heaven? What were your thoughts?"

"I have thought about that, Mr. Gibson, and I believe that I profited more while caring for Caroline and Edward than when I was ill myself. *Then*, I was rational, and I had time to think about a great many things, such as how childish I have been in the past – I mean, as regards my own little difficulties. Oh, and I thought of you, as well."

"Really?" he sat upright, pleased and attentive.

"You will recall that you asked me if I had read the Old Testament. When I was younger I read the book of Job. And I will acknowledge to you, it appeared unfair and unjust to me at the time that the children of Job should have perished, to test the faith of their father. Why was Job's soul of more consequence than the souls of his children, and his servants? They were spoken of little differently than his camels and all the other animals he lost. He suffered, yes – but did they not suffer *more*, by losing their lives? Both Caroline and Edward could have died, and they have already lost a younger brother – but still, am I to believe the common cant that losing a child is truly a test, sent by God, of the *parents*?"

Mr. Gibson decided to say nothing, partly because he did not wish to attack Miss Price's faith, especially not at such a time, and also because he was a little disappointed to understand, after her having made so promising a beginning, she had not thought on him much at all, except as someone who had posed a question. But he could have said much about how frequently and how earnestly he had been threatened with the terrors of hell for the most minor transgressions when a young child, and as an unlooked-for consequence, he had very early come to doubt the justice of the God of Abraham. The overweening interest which the Almighty Jehovah took in the misdeeds of a small lad who daydreamed in church, the apparent eagerness of the Lord of Hosts to consign Master William Gibson to a lake of fire for all eternity, did not lead the rebellious boy to draw those conclusions which his uncle intended that he should.

"But," Fanny continued thoughtfully, "If we reject the idea of punishment as being sent by God, how gladly we accept the blessings of Providence! You cannot know with what heartfelt joy and gratitude we greeted the recovery of the children, and how thankful we were to Heaven for having spared them! The world on that day seemed a surpassingly beautiful place, and I believe that having their children restored *alive* to them has done more for my employers, than being chastened with the *loss* of them ever could. I do not pretend to understand the ways of Heaven.... " She trailed off, too tired to speak, or at least, too tired to find the words to express her meaning, and lay quietly watching the boughs of the trees gently sway above her, and beyond that, the blue sky studded with clouds.

"Where wast thou *when I laid the foundations of the earth?,"* Mr. Gibson recited softly at her side. *"declare, if thou hast understanding. Who hath laid the measures thereof, if thou knowest? or who hath stretched the line upon it? Whereupon are the foundations thereof fastened? or who laid the corner stone thereof; When the morning stars sang together, and all the sons of God shouted for joy?"*

Fanny turned her head and smiled at him. She waited for him to go on, but he merely smiled back at her. After a moment of comfortable silence, she continued. "However, *I* have learned from the sufferings of others. That is, I have been brought to comprehend that my own solicitude for myself, my own self-pity, was for concerns that were mere trifles, in comparison to the burdens other people must sometimes bear. I have been so..... so all consumed with my own problems, so selfish, silly and.... weak."

"No," he said gently. 'You have been young, that's all. And you are still young. Do not berate yourself for the faults of youth. I am sure that

174

whatever you have done, or didn't do, was nothing to *my* faults, for example. My good uncle brought me up, and paid for me to go to Cambridge, and what did I do? I left school early, and refused to enter the law or the ministry, and brought his grey hair with sorrow down to the grave."

"I'm sorry."

"How kind you are, not to preach to me, but simply to listen! And as for you being weak, nonsense. What strength you must have, Miss Price, to be still alive today, despite the best efforts of the finest physician in the county! You must be stronger than you know, stronger than you ever imagined."

It warmed his heart to see that his encouraging words brought a faint blush to those pale cheeks.

"And I will accuse you of being *un*selfish, Miss Price, extraordinarily unselfish, for after being so very ill yourself, your thoughts are all for the sufferings of others – for these children, for their mother and father."

"Oh! Who would not be moved, who sees a child suffer?"

"Ostrich mothers. Some take human form."

"I beg your pardon, I do not understand you."

"*Gavest* thou *the goodly wings unto the peacocks?,*" Gibson recited slowly, trying to recall the verse, "*or wings and feathers unto the ostrich? Which leaveth her eggs in the earth, and warmeth them in dust, And forgetteth that the foot may crush them, or that the wild beast may break them. She is hardened against her young ones, as though they were not hers: her labour is in vain without fear; Because God hath deprived her of wisdom, neither hath he imparted to her understanding.*"

"*Her labour is in vain without fear,*" Fanny repeated. "A loving mother *must*, alas, endure fear for her children."

"Thus endeth the lesson," Mr. Gibson intoned, and another comfortable silence continued between them for a few minutes, until he resumed, "Miss Price, you were not offended, I hope, by my writing you directly? I like talking with you, my little friend, and I thought we could form our own circulating library, as it were, and share books and discuss them by letter. Or I could write the first part of a story, and you could write the next part and send it back to me, and so on. Would you think it improper?"

"Well... if we entered into a correspondence, would we not lay ourselves open to the suspicion, or expectation...." she coughed, he leaned closer to hear her. "Mr. Gibson, you were candid enough to say that you have resolved against – against entering upon domestic life, because of your commitment to your cause, and I just wanted to explain that I... that I..."

"You love someone," he said, with that same gentle smile. She was surprised, but nodded, feeling a flood of relief upon sharing her secret with someone.

"Mrs. Butters and I, we each thought as much, after hearing you recite Helena's speech so beautifully that evening. We did differ on – well, let's just say that Mrs. Butters owes me a shilling. Does this gentleman know his good fortune?"

"Oh! No, no, that could never be."

"Why?" Mr. Gibson let the question hang in the air.

Fanny furrowed her brow. "Well, he is – I am not..."

"Let me ask you something, Miss Price. I am very curious. Just over a week ago, you almost left this vale of tears behind and went to sit at the Right Hand, perched on a cloud, no doubt, with wings on your back and a harp in your hand." She rolled her eyes at him, knowing that he was teasing her. "Or, we must await further bulletins on the precise conditions of the life hereafter, because, to my intense disappointment, you don't recall seeing heaven or angels or anything but, if I understood you correctly, only the ramparts around Portsmouth, and the sea beyond it, and I refuse to believe that the eternal reward for God's righteous servants is to bob about in the Spithead.

"At any rate, at the time you were so very ill, didn't you regret the fact that the gentleman was in ignorance of your affection for him? Did you regret that your secret would die with you? Because, truthfully, if I loved, and if I thought I might never see the young lady again, whether or not I had any hope whatsoever of a return, I believe I would unburden myself and tell her as much."

"But that is different! You are a man, and women don't...." her voice trailed off.

"Indeed. You wouldn't want to be indecorous. It would be too shocking altogether." He started idly pulling up some nearby wildflowers and stripping the leaves from them absent-mindedly. "Still, I would like to know, what is the worst thing that could happen if you informed the gentleman? You would be exchanging uncertainty for certainty, would you not?"

Fanny closed her eyes.

"Forgive me. I have over-tired you, and asked questions which were none of my business. We scribblers are like that. Beware of making friends with any of our tribe, Miss Price, or you may find yourself inscribed within the pages of some novel whether you will or no. I can control your destiny as a puppet master pulls the strings on his puppets! So, I will take my leave, most reluctantly. But may we correspond?"

"Yes, I would like that very, very much. No-one here seems to care about books. I'd like to discuss them with you."

"Good afternoon, then, Miss Price." He rose, and took her little hand carefully, and placed it gently back on the blanket which covered her. He rode away slowly, with a borrowed pony cart, and thought to himself that Fanny Price must have had a mother who forgot that her children could be crushed underfoot, because someone had evidently crushed Fanny under their foot, to make her think so lowly of herself. He knew not how he had survived a childhood of neglect and severity to be so independent, so confident in himself, so certain of the way he wished to conduct his own life. He had been planted in rocky soil and yet, by his own estimation, he throve, though he was poor and obscure. But Fanny was different – she was a delicate plant, and she had been badly bruised, and a man naturally felt the urge to protect and shelter her, and to see that she came to no harm.

***

"Only three months more, Maria," Julia said consolingly. "It is now April, and surely father will relent by July, if not earlier, and allow Dr. Grant to publish the banns." And then she carelessly added, "any man who *truly* loved would not object to waiting only three months."

A heavy rain having suspended all plans for an outing, the Bertram sisters were passing a dull and seemingly endless afternoon in their bedchamber. Mrs. Norris was muttering over her needlework in the parlour, their brother Edmund was in his father's study, puzzling over some ambitious drawings from Henry Crawford concerning alterations that Mary wanted done at the parsonage at Thornton Lacey, and the servants were keeping themselves well out of sight below stairs. Something of an unhealthy east wind had made both sisters feel dissatisfied and anxious, too restless to choose some useful pursuit but too troubled by a prickly conscience to abandon themselves to doing nothing at all. Julia's pianoforte sat untouched, Maria's embroidery lay in a tangle, and the letters they had promised to their Mansfield friends would go unwritten another day. Maria in particular only wanted to sit at the window and watch and wait; Julia felt morose because she had no one to wait for. And yet, she acknowledged, she no longer envied Maria. What happiness had her sister's passion for Henry Crawford brought her? Maria was impatient and cross, jealous and fearful, when she ought to be radiant, cheerful and glowing. Julia could truly pity her.

"You suppose, because he has seldom called upon us here, that he is growing indifferent to me," Maria rejoined coldly. "You do not know the whole, so do not presume to judge of his affection."

"And you suppose that I would rejoice to see you miserable and thwarted at last, because I once harbored a foolish little liking for him! Believe better of me than that, Maria! If he is to be my brother, I will learn to love him as a brother, but as for — as for thinking of him as I did last autumn, *that* is all over and done with."

"It is not the delay which frightens me, it is the disdain our father now shows him," Maria confessed. "Henry is a proud man — why should he not be proud? Why should he not resent our father's unwillingness to give his blessing?"

"A sensible man would put it down to a father's affection for his daughter. Is any man worth the name to be frightened away by this little difficulty? Why then, you are stauncher than he, for you know that Admiral Crawford despises marriage and will not even attend your wedding, when it takes place. Why should the disapprobation of *his* relations be less of a hindrance than the reluctance of *yours*?"

"Men are more proud, that is all," Maria replied simply. She could not confess the whole — they had quarreled, she had behaved like a common fishwife — or so she supposed, for she numbered no fishwives amongst her acquaintance — she and Henry had parted coldly and in silence, and now he was gone.

At first she had been so angry that she thought of ending the engagement, despite the humiliations attendant on throwing over two fiancés in the space of half of a year! As she would not be the first to yield, so it followed that it was Henry's duty to yield and to ask for her forgiveness.

But a week had passed with no word from Henry, other than through his sister, who wrote that they were off in search of Fanny again — as though Henry cared two figs where Fanny was, or what she did. And now Maria did wish to write to him, desperately, but as usual, she did not know where to send the letter, for the Crawfords had left no directions. Wherever he was, she suspected, there was a lady looking at him with admiration, laughing and smiling at his sallies, and he was being his most charming self.

* * *

Henry Crawford was a little disappointed that he would not, after all, need to knock on the door of every stately home outside of Bristol, in search of Miss Frances Price, the governess. It would have suited his sense of drama, but, thanks to the information from William, he and his sister knew their destination, and with a little trouble – chiefly because he preferred to race along the lanes at top speed in his carriage and often missed the turnings – they found their way to the neighbourhood of Keynsham Hill.

"Have you considered what we will say to Miss Price *when* we find her?" enquired Mary. "Her family in Portsmouth – and Edmund – both expect us to produce her for them. What if she has fallen in love with the master of the house, as governesses often do, we are told, and refuses to leave him?"

"I have been pondering how we may best get her away," Henry replied. "The simplest expedient, of course, would be to tell her that Sir Thomas is dying, and he wishes to see her before he expires. She will leap into the carriage and we can undeceive her at our leisure."

"Lady Bertram's imminent death would serve even better," sighed Mary. "I believe Miss Price is quite fond of that silly woman. But, for my own ends, I would rather see her in Portsmouth, away from Mansfield Park, until after my wedding. A meeting, or even an exchange of letters, between Edmund and his little cousin before the marriage would be exceedingly awkward for me. She will attempt to dissuade him from the match and represent matters in the worst possible light, I know it. Keep her away, keep her silent, for only one month more!"

"Let us offer to convey her to Portsmouth, then, to see her beloved brother. And we shall not mention your upcoming nuptials, so she will have no alarms on the subject."

* * *

Mrs. Smallridge was feeling the weight of an empty afternoon hanging over her. With no particular talents or pursuits to occupy her mind, she was sitting in her best drawing room, the tall windows open to the broad lawn before, her white curtains gently moving in a warm spring breeze, her needlework lying neglected in her lap. The day and the scene were tranquil and beautiful, but she was feeling restless and dissatisfied, a mood that can

179

sometimes befall even those whose lives appear to unite the brightest blessings. Her role as chatelaine of Keynsham Hill sometimes seemed a dreary and empty one, as there was usually no husband or relative to share it with. What did it matter if she arranged the flowers in the vase with a skillful hand, and for whose benefit did she complete her daily *toilette*?

But then something occurred which was to furnish material for her correspondence for some time thereafter. First there was the unexpected sound of a carriage entering the sweep, and after a suspenseful pause, the butler appeared with two cards to announce the arrival of Henry Crawford, Esq. and Miss Mary Crawford. Mrs. Smallridge was surprised and gratified at the appearance of two young people of fashion who united both ease and elegance in their manner. Introductions were made and accepted, early tea was spoken for, and the Crawfords were invited to take a seat.

"Ma'am, please forgive this intrusion on your household," Miss Crawford began, while her brother contented himself with eyeing his handsome hostess with some complacency. He recognized instantly that Mrs. Smallridge was restless, idle and bored, and most probably neglected, and had he but the time at his disposal, he would have set about curing those ills immediately. "My brother and I are lately residents of Mansfield, in Northamptonshire, and we are — we are distantly related to your governess. That is, we believe that you employ a Miss Frances Price in your household?"

"Indeed, Miss Price has been with us since the end of October."

"As we were travelling through to Bristol on private business, we felt it only fitting that we pay Fanny — Miss Price, that is, a brief visit, and we ask for your indulgence."

Mrs. Smallridge was only too happy to oblige her elegant visitors, and after another moment's consideration, invited them to dinner on the morrow, an invitation politely declined at first, but after being urged and urged again, accepted with pleasure.

"I suppose as I should summon Miss Price, and retire so that you may have your reunion." Mrs. Smallridge pondered aloud, for it somehow did not suit her sense of propriety that a governess should have the best room in the house in which to entertain her visitors, but on the other hand, the Crawfords were the most elegant persons Keynsham Hill had ever sheltered. Henry Crawford, sensing her hesitation, and correctly divining its cause, disclaimed any wish to inconvenience his hostess and declared himself perfectly willing to be led to the nursery, or the offices, or wherever they could greet Miss Price without disturbing the household arrangements. The elegance of his language, his graceful air, and the fact that he seemed to admire her exceedingly, combined to make the decision an easy one: she would not hear of asking them to remove to another room, Miss Price would join them and they could all take their tea together. She was happy to do this for Miss Price, who was a veritable treasure.

Mrs. Smallridge withdrew, told a footman to fetch the governess to the best sitting room, then retired to her bedchamber where, to pass the interval, she summoned her lady's maid to re-arrange her hair.

Fanny thought only that her mistress wished to see her, and the unexpected summons was in itself cause for some apprehension. The footman did not inform her that someone else awaited her, for he had assumed that the visitors in the sitting room were the guests of Mrs. Smallridge, and so, when Fanny entered the room and unexpectedly encountered the two persons she could least wish to meet again, she was almost overpowered. She had not the presence of mind to avoid Mary Crawford's outstretched arms as she exclaimed "Dear, dear Miss Price! How *can* this have come to be? Were you abducted? Thank heavens we've found you!"

Led by Miss Crawford to the settee, Fanny at the last moment resisted being pulled down beside her, and instead took a nearby chair. "How – how, how did you find me?"

Fanny could not have asked a question that Henry Crawford was more ready, nay, eager to answer. The entire escapade, the skill and address of the search, with some embellishments and omissions, was soon laid before Fanny, from the following of her trail at Oxford, and his careful reading of her letter, his researches at the coffee shop, and in short, his dogged pursuit of every possibility that could lead to her.

Fanny grew increasingly perplexed but knew not how to pose the question. At last: "But why? Mr. Crawford, why have you been to such pains on my behalf? You must have been travelling these four months!"

Fanny noted a quick glance between brother and sister, and Mr. Crawford's slight, almost imperceptible, smile.

"Our esteem for your family, of course," responded Miss Crawford brightly. "We have grown close…. so very close since I came to live at the Parsonage." She coloured becomingly and looked down at her lap. "Of course your cousins are also very anxious about you. But Mr. Bertram and Mr. Edmund Bertram have responsibilities, for example, supporting your mother and father, which Henry and I do not."

"My uncle! When did he return? Is he well?"

The Crawfords were the last people from her old life that Fanny wished to feel beholden to, not even so far as to be obliged to them for providing information she sorely wished to know. Her reluctance to appear too effusive before them prevented her from asking many little details which she longed to learn, and she had to content herself with such news as occurred to them to give. Still, much had transpired since she left the family – she was relieved to hear that everyone at Mansfield Park was well, happy to learn that her uncle had returned safely from Antigua, that he had taken a house in London for the season, and surprised to find that Maria and Rushworth were *not* going to be married, but no explanation for the breach was offered, apart from a sneering reference to Mr. Rushworth's dullness. The matters which most occupied her, Edmund's ordination and his plans for the future, were not mentioned by Mary and she could not, would not, bring herself to ask, lest her voice betray her, or she hear news about her cousin which she felt unequal to hearing.

"But, my dear Miss Price, look at you! You are wearing your hair *à la Titus!* How daring! And how slender you are! Have you been well?"

"I am well, thank you, Miss Crawford," was all Fanny would allow herself to say, self-consciously touching the short curls at the back of her neck.

"You look like a little waif, a heroine in a play!" Henry laughed, and, filled with high spirits and self-congratulation at the success of his quest, he struck a dramatic pose and declaimed: "'Having fled from her cruel family, brave little Fanny trembled to recall the wicked Sir Thomas – '"

"Oh, pray, no!" Fanny clasped her hands together in dismay. "Did you tell Mrs. Smallridge about Sir Thomas and the Bertrams?"

Mary raised an eyebrow. "We are as anxious to preserve Sir Thomas' good name as you *claim* to be. So Mrs. Smallridge doesn't know whose niece you are? We may add, 'telling falsehoods,' to the list of your offences? But, you will say, 'it was in a good cause, it was for the right reason,' and therefore, excusable, that your employers, who entrusted you with their children, don't know who you really are.'"

Fanny started guiltily, and knew not how to answer the charges against her, until Mary and Henry began laughing together.

"In fact, Miss Price, we introduced ourselves to the – may I say, very charming – Mrs. Smallridge, as your distant relations, so I'd advise you to refer to us in those terms." Henry fell to devising, *extempore*, an imaginary family tree, complete with elopements, missing heirs who had peculiarly-shaped birthmarks, hauntingly beautiful Spanish dancers and wicked stepmothers, and Fanny had to admire the rapidity of his powers of invention and the flow of his wit.

"But, Fanny," admonished Mary Crawford, "you may as well know that your conduct has astonished, and I am sorry to say, raised some resentment against you amongst your cousins. It was my hope that in finding you, we might help to reconcile you with your family.... one day."

Fanny trembled involuntarily and she felt the tears stinging, which she tried to control. "One day? Are they so very angry with me, Miss Crawford?"

Mary looked out the window, as if recalling a painful interview. "*One* in particular, so disapproves of your behaviour, that I would advise you not to attempt to communicate with him at this time." She made a slight gesture to her brother, who swiftly moved away, picked up a newspaper and pretended to be absorbed in it. Lowering her voice, Maria said to Fanny, "You left Edmund – Mr. Edmund Bertram a letter, did you not?"

Fanny nodded dumbly, unable to trust her voice.

"I have never seen him so discomposed as he was then. He has said very little to me on the subject, but I believe he thought your communication to be.... what was the word he used? Ah yes – *presumptuous*. Something about you presuming to give him advice on an important subject. I do not know to what, in particular, he referred. – And of course the entire family unites in thinking you ungrateful and lacking in respect."

Fanny turned her head for a moment, wishing to die on the spot rather than let Miss Crawford witness her humiliation and dismay. With an effort, she blinked away her tears, and moved toward the windows. She caught a glimpse of Miss Crawford's face in the pier glass. Miss Crawford was regarding her curiously, eagerly, anxiously. While her voice proclaimed sympathy and sadness, her countenance told of machination and deceit.

Fanny remained for some moments with her back to Miss Crawford, undecided what to do or say. *She is lying – exaggerating – deceiving me about Edmund. How could she think I would believe Edmund would speak of me so cruelly? What is she about?* At last, Miss Crawford broke the silence.

"My dear Miss Price – Fanny. May I call you Fanny? Edmund Bertram and I are in such sympathy on so many points, we agree together so well, we have become, in short.... such..... *close friends*, that it pains me that we differ on this one subject. I trust that in time I may bring about a reconciliation, but for now, please be guided by me, and do not provoke him."

"It matters not," Fanny heard herself say. "I do not desire to return to Mansfield Park. This is the new life that I've chosen." Had she not turned her back to both of them, she would have perceived the looks of astonishment on the faces of both her auditors, and the glances they quickly exchanged with each other of perplexity and dismay.

Fanny would have said more in her own defense, she could have expressed her belief that she would be reconciled with her family one day, but she shrank from sharing her hopes and fears with two people for whom she felt neither affection or confidence. Let them think of her what they liked. The less they knew of her true sentiments, the less they could impose on her.

The entrance of servants with the tea board put an end to all conversation and Fanny gratefully used the interval of preparing and serving tea to compose herself further. At last, she ventured, "Will you be returning to Northamptonshire or to Norfolk, Mr. Crawford? Or perhaps London?"

"After travelling across the breadth and almost the length of England in search of *you*, Miss Price, some quiet solitude at home is all I could wish for," replied Mr. Crawford with some archness of manner.

"It was indeed very good of you to go to such an effort, sir," cried Fanny, forcing herself to speak calmly, "but I do recall that in my last letter to the family, I explained that I was safe and well and that I would let them know where I was, in due course – I hope your journey was enjoyable for its own sake. Have you been to Bristol before, Miss Crawford?"

"Fanny, you may wish to resort to polite nothings, but believe me, we did not travel this far to debate the merits of Kings Weston versus Blaise Castle. We wish to see you reconciled with your family but we believe, my brother and I, only time – along with, I need hardly add, every show of contrition and remorse on your part – can heal the breach." Mary Crawford hesitated over a plate of small triangles of bread and butter and chose a slice.

Fanny could not help but smile as she thought of what form "forgiveness" would take with her aunt Norris. Perhaps censorious hints of ingratitude, dropped only every half hour, as opposed to every quarter. A breeze, coming through the window near where she sat, ruffled her new curls and tickled her ear. *You are stronger than you know,* the breeze seemed to whisper.

"Thank you. Now that my whereabouts have been discovered, if any members of my family wish to communicate their sentiments to me *directly*, they will do so."

"Is this Fanny Price?" exclaimed Mr. Crawford, laying down his newspaper in astonishment.

"Upon my word, Fanny, you *are* quite an altered creature from the girl we knew in Northamptonshire!" his sister added. "I recall once conversing with your cousins about the revolution in manners produced when a young girl comes out in society, but this – this new indifference, this coldness, is astounding."

Fanny looked at them silently, thinking *'And did you really know me in Northamptonshire? Did anyone know me, save Edmund? Did anyone care enough about me to know me? Did I even know myself?'* But aloud she said only, "I am very obliged to you – I am sorry, exceedingly sorry, for the exertions you have undergone on my behalf, but it was unlooked for by me." She stood, and gave a slight curtsey. "I hope that you are now satisfied that I am well. In my estimation, I have brought no disgrace upon the family by taking on the responsibility of my own maintenance."

"Well, even though you are intent on turning your back on those at Mansfield, what of your family in Portsmouth? Did you know that your brother William is there and anxious to see you?" asked Miss Crawford.

Fanny trembled with surprise. She thought it abominable and condescending for Miss Crawford to speak so freely of her relations, calling her brother 'William,' but the news that her brother, the so long absent and dearly loved brother, was in England again, filled her with joy. Henry made idle note of the fact of how Miss Price's face lit up when her brother was mentioned.

"We stopped in Portsmouth on our way to Bristol. Here, Fanny, is a letter that we are pleased to convey to you from your brother, who also sends his love and his earnest desire that you come to Portsmouth. Your mother is of course *longing* to see you, and worries about you daily." And Miss Crawford handed over the letter, which, the reader will note, was the only letter, of all those which fell into her hands, that she actually conveyed from sender to recipient in the entirety of our story.

Fanny thought Miss Crawford's representations of her mother's feelings were highly doubtful, for as she well knew, her mother was not of a doating disposition, at least not where she was concerned.

"Well, Miss Price, what do you say? Henry and I would be pleased to convey you there…. how long has it been, Fanny, since you have seen your own family? Should you not like to be amongst them again?"

Perplexity and anger now followed pain and humiliation. Why were the Crawfords so intent on meddling in her affairs? Fanny intently longed to go see her brother, but did not wish to put herself in the power of this brother and sister, who, every instinct told her, were not her friends. "I am very much obliged to you, but – I have undertaken to stay with the Smallridges for no less than a year – barely half that time has elapsed – it would not be proper to ask them for leave to go to Portsmouth. Please, please do not trouble yourself further on my account."

With a nod of thanks, and clutching the precious letter, she was about to make the plea of a headache, when Henry Crawford intervened.

"Do not run away, Miss Price, as I perceive you are longing to do. We have not finished our tea, and you should know that the amiable Mrs. Smallridge has invited us for dinner on the morrow – yes, she has, and no doubt you will be at the table also," Henry Crawford extended his cup to Fanny for her to refill. Although he and his sister had decided to refrain from informing Fanny of Edmund's engagement to Mary, he could not forebear, out of mischief, from telling her something of how Maria came to discard Mr. Rushworth. "You have shown very little curiosity about Miss Bertram's ruptured engagement with the estimable Mr. Rushworth," he ventured. "You see, Maria discovered herself to be in love with me – "

Fanny nodded, unsmiling.

"And so, we are to be married – or so I am told!" He laughed, but Fanny received the information with grave silence.

"What? No 'congratulations'? No 'best wishes'?"

"I do sincerely hope…… that my cousin Maria, and you, will both be very happy, sir."

"But you doubt it will be so?" Henry was intrigued. "Or… you doubt we will be happy *together*? Is that what you think?"

Was this jealousy? He asked himself. *My sister believes that Fanny harbours* a tendresse *for her cousin, but – it appears she does not like to think of me being married.*

"Now, don't teaze her, Henry. You know that our Miss Price is too upright to engage in making artful inferences."

But Mr. Crawford decided to try some flattery, to test if Miss Price felt a secret affection for him.

186

"Yes, Maria threw over poor old Rushworth while we were rehearsing *Lovers' Vows*. Poor Rushworth and his two-and-forty speeches! Nobody can ever forget them. Poor fellow. You were Mr. Rushworth's best friend. Your kindness and patience can never be forgotten, your indefatigable patience in trying to make it possible for him to learn his part—in trying to give him a brain which nature had denied—to mix up an understanding for him out of the superfluity of your own."

Fanny coloured, and said nothing, but she did not appear gratified by his praise. The recollection of last October, however, led Henry to exclaim, "It is as a dream, a pleasant dream! I shall always look back on our theatricals with exquisite pleasure. There was such an interest, such an animation, such a spirit diffused. Everybody felt it. We were all alive. I never was happier."

With silent indignation Fanny repeated to herself, *Never happier!—never happier than when doing what you must know was not justifiable!—never happier than when behaving so dishonourably and unfeelingly! Oh! what a corrupted mind!*

Now Fanny's mild blue eyes were fixed steadily on Henry, with no very benignant expression.

"Nothing to say? I think, my dear Fanny, that you *have* been unwell," Miss Crawford interposed. "You must be very tired. Henry, we shall not detain her longer today, nor prevent our hostess from the use of her own drawing room. Fanny, my dear, we shall see you again tomorrow and we hope to find you in better looks." She rose and moved to the door just as Mrs. Smallridge reached it, with her dress and hair newly arranged. Mr. Crawford's smile told her, her efforts had not been in vain.

Fanny curtsied and departed swiftly, under plea of returning to her duties, and after exchanging further civilities with Mrs. Smallridge, the Crawfords then excused themselves, having much they wished to discuss with each other as they continued to Bristol to find a hostelry for the night.

At least Fanny had the consolation, the more than consolation, of a long letter from William to delight herself with. The letter had been begun at sea, and continued in Portsmouth with a description of the family and their doings, and contrary to Miss Crawford's assertion, contained no longing message from a worried mother, who, by William's description, was busily engaged in her usual pursuits of complaining about the servants, coddling Betsey, and lamenting the unmended parlor rug.

The chief of William's letter consisted of telling her all his hopes and fears, plans, and solicitudes respecting that long thought of, dearly earned, and justly valued blessing of promotion. *Everybody gets made but me,*

Fanny, he wrote despairingly. *And this war will end before I am ever more than a worthless midshipman. Our family has no influence at the Admiralty. I hope I am not boastful when I say that I* have *earned a promotion through merit and diligence, and I passed the lieutenant's exam with distinction, but without patronage.... as you know..... I fear I it shall never be.*

Fanny's disposition was such that she could never even think of her aunt Norris in the meagreness and cheerlessness of her own small house, without reproaching herself for some little want of attention to her when they had been last together; much less could her feelings acquit her of having done and said and thought everything by William that was due to him

Gladly did Fanny lay aside her own sorrows and perplexities to think upon William and to wish with all her soul that she could contrive some way to help him. Her own prospects for a happy, successful life were irredeemably blighted but her brother, uniting as he did, intelligence, fortitude, talent and enterprise, deserved every happiness which public fame or private domestic felicity could bestow. If it were possible, through any sacrifice on her part, to obtain a promotion for her brother, she believed she was equal to it. But no amount of earnest contemplation could suggest an answer to the problem.

***

"Now I am at a loss, Henry," exclaimed Mary in vexation as soon as they were alone again. "I had assumed that she would return with us and that I could so work upon her to make her afraid to speak to anyone by the name of Bertram! If we leave her here, she is beyond my control, and Edmund will write to her, perhaps even visit her, before our marriage – I am certain he will."

"You desire that Fanny Price be removed somewhere that will satisfy her cousin Edmund," Henry pondered aloud, "but be so situated that he feels under no account obliged to visit her, or even write her, nor she him."

"While you," smiled Mary, "wish that your marriage to the lovely Maria remain a distant event, but the one reason that you advanced for postponing it – the disappearance of her cousin – has been removed, thanks to your own ingenuity! And did you not observe how discomposed Miss Price became when you spoke of your marriage to Maria?"

"Is it at all possible that she is jealous? Could she be acting a part, hiding some regard for me? How well do you know this girl? I had very little to do with her at Mansfield Park and now I find, to my surprise, that she appears to dislike me. It's neither here nor there of course, but – "

Mary was grateful for an occasion to laugh, given the hardships which enveloped her. "My dear brother, you cannot make a hole in every girl's heart, you must rest content with making the Bertram girls and Margaret Fraser and half a dozen others miserable!"

"Either she is affronted because I did not distinguish her, as I did her cousins," Crawford mused aloud, "or she is prudish and did not admire how adept I was at making love to two Bertram sisters at once."

"The latter, I conjecture."

"If we know her character, we can trim our sails accordingly. I do not despair of persuading her to return to Portsmouth with us – her devotion to her brother is very evident."

"Now that we *have* found her, what shall you tell Maria? Shall I order my dress for your wedding?"

Henry yawned. "Were it not for Boney, I'd be off to go rock-climbing in Switzerland, followed by a leisurely tour of Italy in the winter, perhaps. Ah well, I always wanted to make a walking tour of the Hebrides. I know very well how to place myself beyond the reach of matrimony, but where, where, shall you place Miss Price?"

"The bottom of Bristol harbor does suggest itself," laughed Mary. "No, no, that will not do, even for a jest. However, I am certain she was very ill indeed, and quite recently – her hair all shorn off – and she has lost so much flesh – why are the Fates so capricious?"

"Here is a challenge to confound even our combined talents!"

The pair were indeed silent for some time, and Mary Crawford was feeling very vexed at Fanny Price by the time they returned to their hostelry in Bristol and ate a quiet supper. Henry too, was deep in thought. Mary was about to propose turning in for the night, when Henry clapped his hands and exclaimed, "I have it, Mary. I have a solution that will answer your wishes – and my own."

Chapter Seventeen

Mr. Smallridge escorted Mary Crawford in to dinner, Henry Crawford had the honour of conducting Mrs. Smallridge to her seat, and last of all, Fanny was handed in by Mr. Chatsworth, the local vicar. Mrs. Smallridge was too taken up with entertaining the Crawfords to observe that her governess, the supposed relative of her dinner guests, never looked in their direction or joined in their conversation of her own accord. Fanny could not entirely escape hearing them, of course. Mr. Crawford, with all the skills of address that she herself lacked, was interposing himself in the Smallridge's usual talk about their neighbours and their estate and their dogs, with amusing anecdotes about his own coachman, or the eccentric old dowager who was his nearest neighbour at Everingham, while also asking them questions about their own country – their horses – their pursuits – and his conversation was all that was agreeable and captivating while still being perfectly proper and gentleman-like. He transformed the shopworn topics the Smallridges usually canvassed, that she had been used to think of as tedious, without dominating the table nor showing anything but the most considerate interest in his host and hostess. She could not but allow that the art of being witty, agreeable and charming was, in itself, not to be condemned; it was only when it was placed in the service of corrupt ends that it became an evil. But she had only to recollect his behavior last autumn to her cousins to know to what advantage he had used his charm, and, if his stay under the Smallridge's roof were to last for some weeks, rather than a few hours, she would not have laid a wager that Mrs. Smallridge's heart, or even her virtue, would escape unscathed.

Meanwhile Miss Crawford, in conversing with Mr. Chatsworth, felt again all the superiority of Edmund Bertram's conversation, air and appearance, and again lamented the rash step he had taken in enlisting himself amongst a body of men who were, in her experience, distinguished by their dullness, or their absurd self-importance, or their hypocrisy in preaching Christian forbearance while indulging their own appetites, whims and ill-tempers (and here she was thinking particularly of her brother-in-law). Mr. Chatsworth, labouring mightily to make himself agreeable to both the ladies, did allow, upon a saucy enquiry from Miss Crawford, that an unmarried vicar was a constant temptation to the neighbourhood and he could not be too cautious in his dealings with the fair sex. 'Hadn't a vicar better marry, and set a good example in his parish?' Miss Crawford pursued, and hinted that no doubt more than one young lady in the vicinity would gladly undertake the role.

Fanny, watching as Miss Crawford toyed with the vicar just for the idle amusement of watching him puff up with vanity, began to count the minutes when her "distant relations" would be on their way back to Northamptonshire.

With such condemnatory thoughts as these residing in her breast, she was completely taken aback when, the men rejoining the ladies after dinner, Henry Crawford asked to speak to her privately for a few moments. With a feeling of foreboding, and a resolution to say as little to him as possible, she led him to her own little sitting room-bedchamber adjoining the nursery. Scarcely pausing as they entered the room, Crawford said, "I think that you do not approve of my marrying your cousin Maria, Miss Price."

Fanny only looked her reply.

"*You* have it in your power to prevent it."

Again silence, but now Fanny refused even to look at him.

"If *you* will impersonate the part of my wife, for some definite period of time – it need not be more than a twelvemonth – I can put it about that *you and I* are married. You can come live at Everingham, in every comfort, while I – oh, Miss Price, pray sit down. May I fetch you some brandy? Do you have some salts?"

A few more minutes, indeed, were necessary for Fanny to find her breath and steady her racing heart. The indecorum of the suggestion, the barefaced audacity of it, exceeded even the worst she had supposed of Henry Crawford. She became aware, as one becomes aware of a distant noise and realizes the noise has been continuing for some time, that Mr. Crawford was still speaking, outlining the advantages to her of such an arrangement.

"....your person, of course, would be sacrosanct, I would claim no rights over you. *All* you need do is not contradict the report that we are married. I would settle a handsome allowance on you. As Mrs. Henry Crawford, you could come and go as you please, visit your family, live comfortably at my estate, entertain guests... have you ever been to Norfolk?"

"And what of Maria?" Fanny managed to utter.

"Maria is sure to find a husband within a twelvemonth. She is eager to enter the state, while I, alas...." Crawford spread his hands gracefully.

"Once she is married to some other, and no doubt, much worthier man, we can drop the imposture."

Crawford watched Fanny for some sign that she comprehended the proposal and would not put an immediate negative on it, but she was rendered speechless. "Take your time, Miss Price, consider my offer well. I will return tomorrow morning and I trust you will give me enough of an audience to answer any objections as may occur to you. And remember, the destiny of your cousin Maria is in your hands."

For the better part of a sleepless night, Fanny pondered and occasionally wept over the corruption and impiety of Henry Crawford. At first, her only concern was to find the words to tell him what she thought of the recklessness of his scheme. For herself, for her own reputation, she had no doubt that impersonating a married woman, after running away from home to be a governess, might so confirm her eccentricity in the eyes of the world as to necessitate her removing herself from society altogether.

The more she condemned Mr. Crawford's character, however, as immoral, careless and even vicious, the more justifiable it appeared to her that preventing a union with Maria should be a prime object. Should the marriage be effectually prevented, the sacrifice on Fanny's part, of her own peace of mind and reputation, in exchange for the certain good of preserving Maria – as seemed certain to Fanny – from a lifetime of the bitterest regret, was a reasonable price to pay. Since she, Fanny, would never know earthly happiness, being separated forever from the man she loved, she could at least derive some satisfaction in assisting others. In her humility, she still rated her own claims to worldly happiness so low, and her cousin, being a Bertram, as so high, that once she became convinced the scheme would preserve Maria from a fatal step, she thought that her willingness to undertake this sacrifice for her cousin would be a proof of her gratitude toward the family that even Mrs. Norris, should she ever comprehend the whole, could not gainsay.

But – but – deceit was deceit, and falsehood was falsehood. How a false marriage with the brother might affect her cousin Edmund's courtship of the sister, Fanny could not guess. She felt the Bertrams would be disgusted with Henry Crawford for throwing Maria over after she had spurned Rushworth for him, but if her own innate sense of justice prevented her from holding one responsible for the sins of the other, so too should her family not blame Mary Crawford for the actions of an Henry. In fact, if anything, if Edmund supposed his cousin Fanny to be Henry Crawford's wife, the relationship should draw him ever closer to Miss Crawford.

However, Fanny also reflected with a sigh, as Edmund so disapproved of deceit and prevarication of any kind, so her involvement in such a scheme would damage her, perhaps irreparably, in her beloved cousin's eyes, whatever the imputed cause that impelled her to it.

This was, undoubtedly, the chief argument *against* agreeing to Mr. Crawford's proposal. But there were others – she instinctively shrank from the idea with such true maidenly modesty as made her feel almost ill, and in addition, there was the sorrow of leaving her new friends in Bristol. In all probability she would never see Mr. Gibson again. She was truly fond of Caroline and Edward and flattered herself that her gentle affection helped to shelter them from all that was unpleasant and unhappy in the pronounced lack of harmony between their mother and father, which the advent of Henry Crawford had done nothing to improve.

But, on the other hand, if Fanny were to have the handsome allowance Mr. Crawford promised her, she would have an opportunity to assist her brothers and sisters. She did not doubt that she would see little of her sham husband – his motive in proposing this scheme was to secure his freedom – so he would be in London and Bath and all the fashionable watering places while she, the titular wife, stayed at Everingham in seclusion, away from the wondering eyes of the world.

The clocks were striking two in the morning as she dimly realized she was tempted to accept Henry Crawford's offer – perhaps this is how the gamester feels when he is convinced that he will win back his lost fortune, she surmised. Perhaps everyone who stoops to some wrongdoing thinks they have very good reasons for doing it! She saw herself living in comfort and seclusion, able to save up more monies in a year than she could in a dozen years as a governess. She saw herself attaining some measure of independence, the independence she dreamt of. But then she contemplated herself looking Edmund in the face and telling him that she was Mrs. Crawford, and she was again wide-awake and pacing the floor in her dressing gown.

The sun appeared on the horizon and she thought she had faced the temptation and faced it down, and resigned herself to staying with the Smallridges, with only a tranquil conscience to console her, when another thought occurred to her – if she could, by this sacrifice, benefit Maria Bertram and her family, could she not benefit *another*, infinitely dearer to *her* heart?

Mr. Crawford had supposed that the offer of being mistress of Everingham, even if in name only, was enough inducement for Fanny to quit her post as governess, and so he was quite unable to comprehend that Fanny, for reasons of honour and integrity, could not easily abandon what she had agreed to do. But, as *he* sought to benefit from this arrangement, could *she* not do likewise? Could she not benefit her own brother, William? The household was beginning to stir when Fanny gasped at a *new* thought – could she meet the Crawfords in audacity, as regarded taking care of her own best interests and of those she loved? In a wild flight of bravado, she yielded – she resolved – she told herself, that the prize she would obtain, was worth whatever she might have to pay.

Henry Crawford returned, true to his time, and sought another private conference with Fanny. He noted that although her eyes were a little red, she was pale and composed.

"Well, madam, what have you to say to me this morning?"

"Mr. Crawford, amongst our acquaintance, who would know that we are not really husband and wife?"

"My sister only. You will be introduced to everyone else, my friends and my servants, as Mrs. Crawford, and I need hardly add, treated by me with all the respect due to you."

Now came the time! Fanny steeled herself to look into his eyes, and mildly but firmly recited the short speech she had just been practising before the mirror. "I have a condition, Mr. Crawford. You have met my brother William. You are acquainted with his excellent qualities. He has no interest to help him further his career. Sir Thomas has been very kind to him, but my uncle has no influence at the Admiralty. Please introduce William to your uncle and ask *him* to use his influence to get William made lieutenant. If William sends me a satisfactory account of his meeting with your uncle, I will enter into this false marriage with you for so long as you require."

She shivered, and blushed, then saw with gratification that Crawford was regarding her with surprise and, she thought, a degree of respect. It was as though he was looking at her for the first time.

"I say again, is this Miss Price? By heaven, I think running away from home has done a great deal for you. I agree to your terms. But, as soon as my errand is accomplished, you must be ready to leave Keynsham Hill. I can't have my wife working as a governess. With your permission, my sister and I will take our leave and I will set about immediately to fulfil my part of the bargain. And, my dear Miss Price, please," he added with a faint smile, "consider yourself an engaged woman and do not enter into any other entanglements in my absence. Also, it were best that you continue to communicate nothing to the Bertrams at this time. Rely on me for making the necessary communications."

Fanny nodded her agreement and after taking her hand and examining the delicate little fingers as though to judge the size of wedding ring he must purchase, Crawford bowed and withdrew, leaving Fanny to exult in the hope that, while she was a monstrous sinner for lying to the world, she might be the means of helping a beloved brother to that long deserved, long delayed, promotion.

With the stamina of youth, mixed with the agitation produced by the recent turn of events, Fanny was able to attend to her duties with the children after her sleepless night to a degree that surprised even herself. The possibility that she might soon be leaving Caroline and Edward inclined her heart to them even more tenderly. At last, after the children were put to bed, and despite her lack of sleep, Fanny wrapped herself up in her cloak and paced upon the terrace for an hour. To think of herself as someone who could act, persuade, and command others, was entirely novel and not a little intoxicating. Anna the nursery maid observed her and wondered if the elegant gentleman who had visited her was only, as he claimed, a distant relation. Ah, poor Mr. Gibson! What chance did he have now?

***

William Gibson, for reasons he could not well explain, had decided to attend a public sermon by that well-known nonconformist divine, Dr. Lant Carpenter, concerning Unitarianism, even though his own views as regarding religion had been fixed pretty firmly since his youth. But, since the authorities were opposed to the growth in popularity of Unitarianism and Methodism, he decided he must be in favour of both, and could profit by learning more. He had a long walk home, after dark, to his lodgings, which was not at all unusual for him at any time of the year, and it was no hardship to enjoy the freshness of the night air after a warm day in which the head was assailed by the usual Bristol smells and sounds.

He was deep in thought, wondering if the Unitarians, like the Quakers, were inclined to champion the cause of abolition, when he suddenly found himself accosted by what he assumed to be a gang of footpads – a half-a-dozen big burly men, wearing the sailors' attire of short jackets and wide-legged pants, some of them swinging formidable-looking cudgels with a practised air. He turned to run away, and found himself surrounded on all sides.

"Gentlemen," he greeted them calmly, "to expend your labours on me would be, in the words of the Bard, much ado about nothing. You may have the few coins I possess, and then we both may go in peace, I trust, without any undue exertion on your part or suffering on mine."

"Do we have the honour of addressing Mr. William Gibson, the noted abolitionist?" said one of the thugs, with an exaggerated bow.

"Who enquires?"

"Stay, brothers, let's give him three guesses." The circle of men tightened around him, and he was grabbed and then casually pushed, back and forth across the circle, as in a child's game. It was humiliating but he could neither break free nor regain his balance.

"It's the Hotwells Cotillion Society," cried one. Another shove across the circle.

"It's the League for Teaching Jumped-up Whoresons a Lesson," followed by a shove.

"Still can't guess, Mr. Gibson? It's the North Bristol Press, of course. By special request, sent to apprehend one William Gibson, of no known occupation, and no income, and moreover, of known seditious tendencies, an enemy to our established religion, and a danger to the peace and good order of the City of Bristol, and therefore, the same William Gibson is hereby to be pressed into the service of His Majesty, King George the Third – "

"God bless him!" interjected a confederate of the speaker.

"And send him long to reign over us," added another.

"Because better a lunatic than that fat pig, the Prince," opined a third.

"– as I was saying, to wit, William Gibson is to be pressed into the service of His Majesty's Navy forthwith, as provided by the laws of Great Britain, and the argument of this cudgel –"

A cudgel was expertly smashed into the back of Gibson's right leg, just below his knee, and he fell helplessly to the pavement.

"One moment, good fellows – here is some error! I am not a sailor!" Gibson managed to gasp, before two beefy pairs of hands firmly seized him by both arms and yanked him to his feet again.

"You were sought out particularly, Mr. Gibson, on account of your tender solicitude for our dusky heathen brothers. As you will see."

Though taller than any of his captors, Gibson was fairly pinioned by two and surrounded by the other four and the entire gang was moving with practised efficiency down the street, hauling him along in their midst away from the main thoroughfare and down unlit alleys, elbowing aside the street prostitutes, and stepping on sleeping beggars, but no one they passed raised a cry of protest on his behalf. Escape seemed entirely unlikely. He could shout for help, but who would come to his aid? Sailors and merchants often intervened to help their own friends and free them from the press gang, but the streets seemed peculiarly free of impecunious poets at that hour, nor were they, as a tribe, able to match the press gang in terms of strength.

Gibson could only hope that he could appeal to a magistrate before he was deposited on board one of the Navy's ships and taken out to sea. He looked up at the narrow vault of the night sky through the looming buildings on either side and thought, *I will write about this one day... only a scribbler would think about writing at such a time....*

"Nothing to say, Mr. Gibson? I was told you could talk the legs off a pianoforte. Well, let's have a song then, mates. Mr. Blunt, you'll give us the pitch, please, and the time."

"Come, cheer up, my lads, 'tis to glory we steer," came a strong baritone voice from the darkness, soon joined by the others, as the group arrived at a courtyard unknown to Gibson.

To add something more to this wonderful year;
To honour we call you, as freemen not slaves,
– Gibson's arms were released, and he staggered, trying to regain his balance–
For who are so free as the sons of the waves?
– a mighty kick to his groin sent him flying backward to land on the slimy pavement, followed by laughter as he doubled up in agony. But just as swiftly, a man seized each of his limbs –
Hearts of Oak are our ships,
Jolly Tars are our men –
As his head dangled upside down, and stars danced across his vision, he could just make out a driver pulling up before them with a pony cart, with a large, lidded box placed in the back.
We always are ready:
He was rocked back and forth, to the cadence of –
Steady...... boys...... Steady!......
He was released and flew through the air, to land in the box with a jarring thud, cracking his head against the side.
We'll fight and we'll conquer again and again!
The hinged lids of the box were flipped closed, and he was in utter darkness.

"*Bon voyage*, Mr. Gibson!"

And he knew himself to be headed for the dockyard and a cell called the 'rondy,' or 'rendezvous,' where impressed men were kept under guard until they could be loaded aboard one of His Majesty's ships and taken to sea.

Chapter Eighteen

Fanny had only to wait ten days – the longest ten days of her life – before a letter, postmarked from London, arrived from her brother William, confirming that Mr. Henry Crawford, who must be ranked among the best of mortals, had abstracted him from Portsmouth and sped him to Hill Street, where he had dined several times with the Admiral, and that, in his modest opinion, he had acquitted himself well.

She was so overjoyed and filled with fine naval fervor, that she decided the weather was warm enough for little Edward to take his new toy ship out to the duck pond. As he ran about on the shore, shouting: *Hands make sail! Away aloft and loose the royals and topgallant sails! Layout and loose the flying-jib. Board your fore and main tacks!*, in her own imagination Fanny could hear and see William, resplendent in his lieutenant's uniform and his bicorne hat, issuing the same orders from the quarter deck, and the entire crew leaping to obey him.

A following letter from Crawford himself confirmed that his uncle was much taken with the midshipman and promised to act swiftly on his behalf. Then came the exaction of the promise Fanny had made – Crawford would follow the letter in three days' time, accompanied, for propriety's sake, by a lady's maid, to escort Miss Price to Everingham where she would pretend to be his wife.

Now it was for Fanny to fulfill her part of the bargain. She had fled Mansfield Park in the grey light before dawn, unable to tell anyone of what she felt; now she must look her employer in the face and tell an utter falsehood, and only her devotion to William enabled her to persevere through the guilt of it.

With all the fortitude that she could muster, Fanny unfolded the news of her matrimonial good fortune to her mistress, who, fortunately for Fanny, was of a romantic disposition and attributed Fanny's scarlet cheeks and averted eyes to a different cause than shame. At any rate, there could be no doubt that any governess, even one so fortunately situated as Fanny, would resign her post immediately upon being solicited to become Mrs. Henry Crawford, so Mrs. Smallridge could not bring herself to feel resentment on that score.

Fanny's gentle demeanour had recommended her to all the servants of the Smallridge household, and though they were sorry to part with her, she was regarded by the housemaids as the heroine of a fairy tale and they helped her pack her portmanteau with much giggling and some sly comments. She bestowed what little she had to give away – a spare petticoat and some collars – to Anna the nursery maid.

Fanny's greatest regret would be in leaving little Caroline and Edward. Far from selfishly hoping that they would not love their next governess as much as herself, she hoped that whomever took her place would be as tenderly inclined toward her charges as she was. Fanny wept, indeed, during her final farewell to the children, who, when learning that she was leaving, clung to her legs and begged her not to go, but when told she was to be married, immediately clamored to be sent a piece of the wedding cake.

She was sorry, and not a little surprised, that she received no letter from her new correspondent Mr. Gibson, in the two weeks since his visit. She had expected him to be more prompt in beginning their correspondence, but did not feel herself equal to writing the first note to him instead. She did, with some trepidation, write to Mrs. Butters, to announce the change in her circumstances. She hardly knew what to say in reference to her new husband, as she could not bring herself to write that she was the happiest woman in the world, or to enumerate his good qualities, but on the other hand, if she were only to state his income and possessions, she would undoubtedly be set down as a mercenary bride. She could only give her new address in Norfolk and express the humble hope that both she and Mr. Gibson might be so kind as to write her there in future. Mrs. Butters' lively imagination, assisted perhaps by Madame Orly, could fill in the rest as they wished.

A beaming Crawford arrived as promised, in excellent spirits, as befitted a happy bridegroom. His good humour arose not only from the capital joke he was about to play on Maria and all his acquaintance but he had, quite accidentally, discovered that it was a pleasant thing to help his fellow creatures, to recognize and reward energy, activity and merit, and to change the destiny of a deserving young person, and all it had cost him was several swift trips across the country and several dinners at his uncle's well-kept table, all activities he thoroughly enjoyed for their own sakes. He was therefore in a full glow of self-congratulation when he saluted Fanny with the news: "He is made."

She took the letters as he gave them. The first was from the Admiral to inform his nephew, in a few words, of his having succeeded in the object he had undertaken, the promotion of young Price, and enclosing two more, one from the Secretary of the First Lord to a friend, whom the Admiral had set to work in the business, the other from that friend to himself, by which it appeared that his lordship had the very great happiness of attending to the recommendation of Sir Charles; that Sir Charles was much delighted in having such an opportunity of proving his regard for Admiral Crawford, and that the circumstance of Mr. William Price's commission as Second Lieutenant of *H.M.S. Solebay* being made out was spreading general joy through a wide circle of great people.

Henry Crawford was well aware that Miss Price was always on her guard when in his presence, but when she read the letters, her habitual reserve fell away and he beheld a vivacious, happy, laughing girl. She never looked prettier than she did at that moment and she even thanked him, profusely, for what he had done. Such a girl, lively, intelligent, with colour rising to her delicate complexion, might be plausibly presented as the wife of Henry Crawford, whereas the drab, disapproving governess would certainly perplex all his acquaintance. His own vanity required that Fanny Price be kept content, if she were to be introduced to any of his friends in future.

Fanny's raptures also helped her through the farce that was to follow – indeed, if it were not for her pleasure and pride over William's promotion, it is doubtful whether she could have sustained the deception long enough to bid farewell to the Smallridges and walk from the front hall to a post chaise, where the coachman, two postillions, a manservant and a blonde, buxom lady's maid, awaited.

Mr. Crawford charmingly apologized to the Smallridges for depriving them of their governess, and he had so ingratiated himself with the mistress of the house, that Mrs. Smallridge was impulsively moved to propose that the wedding be held there, in Keynsham Hill, with a special license. Fanny had time for only one thrill of horror, before Mr. Crawford gracefully declined the offer, explaining that his relatives were anxious to witness the sacred ceremony in their dear old village church, of which he spoke so tenderly and with such veneration that Fanny could hardly contain her indignation.

Fanny's little portmanteau was placed in the carriage, and Mr. Crawford kissed Mrs. Smallridge's hand, and fixed her with a look she would long remember, particularly when alone in her bath, then shook hands with Mr. Smallridge, and escorted Fanny to the carriage, placing his bride-to-be inside as carefully as though she were made of cut glass. Fanny's eyes were indeed streaming when she left.

(This was the first, but not the last occasion, when the Smallridges had difficulties retaining a governess. Something remarkably similar would happen again in five years' time, and their friends remarked that if a poor girl sought a rich husband, she need only engage herself to the Smallridges!)

"Well, it's too bad, Honoria, you must look for another governess," Mr. Smallridge consoled his wife as the carriage pulled away. "But Miss Price forgot to ask for her half year's wages, so you are ten pounds to the good."

No sooner had the carriage cleared the sweep, than Henry Crawford sat back and laughed uproariously until tears came to his eyes. Fanny wondered if she would have to remind him that no-one was to suspect they were not an engaged couple, when he finally collected himself, still chuckling, and wiping his eyes, exclaimed softly, "That was capital! Capital! You played your part very well, Fanny —" then seeing her stiffen at being so addressed, added "oh very well, Miss Price. Now, let us calculate the days — how long would it take to travel from here to Gretna Green, and back again, at my usual rate of speed? How long before you will permit me to address you as 'Mrs. Crawford?' We shall spend the intervening days in Portsmouth and London, actually. I thought you might like to visit your family, and see William before he ships out." And he fell to laughing anew as his bride's countenance changed from frost back to sunshine, as she expressed her raptures at the prospect of seeing her beloved William, her parents and her younger brothers and sisters.

But even the best news in the world could not sustain Fanny's spirits forever, even the prospect of seeing William in his lieutenant's uniform, and knowing that it was her own doing, was still not enough to prevent her from worrying about the rash step she had taken and whether she had one one-hundredth part of Mr. Crawford's audacity sufficient to pull off the imposture.

Fanny's eyes brimmed over again, as she thought about deceiving her own father and mother, although she tried to weep silently. Her eyelashes were still wet when she composed herself to sleep, and as the late afternoon sun filtered in through the coach window, Henry Crawford found himself speculatively evaluating her -- as any young man in the full prime and vigor of life will adjudge the worthiness of any female old or young enough to come within his observation, in terms of being a possible bedmate.

She was, in point of figure and height, not to be compared to the Bertram girls, who possessed the type of beauty that he favoured. They were full-figured and fair, and either one could be an artist's model for a statue of Britannia. Miss Price was slender and delicate, and somewhat less than the middle height. Her short hair, curling about her forehead, was brown – simply brown, not chestnut or light brown shot through with golden strands, and he could barely recollect the colour of her eyes, now closed, but thought they must be blue. But as she lay sleeping, her head thrown back against the seat, he could acknowledge that, taking her all in all, she could be considered pretty enough. The nicely arched little eyebrows for example, and the neatly formed head with its close-set ears, the delicate lines of her jaw, the long, vulnerable fair neck presented toward him, some might think pleasant to nibble upon, her small but high bosom, her slender waist.... perhaps if the two of them spent any time together at Everingham, he would amuse himself by making her overcome her dislike of him. It might be entertaining to draw her on, to be the first man to kiss those soft pink lips, to slide his hand up under her skirt, to watch her eyes open wide with surprise and perhaps a little fear, but, soon yielding to his skillful caresses, the very reserved little Miss Price would receive her first lessons in the arts of love.

Ah, well. He shifted in his seat and thought about cricket. More than likely, Fanny Price would behave like a heroine in a three volume novel – she would reject him with horror, call on Heaven to protect her, and then faint dead away at his feet – that last part, he had always thought a peculiarly ineffectual strategy for heroines hoping to escape ravishment.

And, in fact, the buxom actress whom he had hired to impersonate a lady's maid – who was sharing his bedchamber in the various inns they stopped at on their journey -- was more suited to his tastes.

***

On the day after leaving the Smallridges, Henry Crawford and Fanny were in the environs of Portsmouth while there was yet daylight for Fanny to look around her, and wonder at the new buildings. They passed the drawbridge, and entered the town; and the light was only beginning to fail as, guided by Mr. Crawford's recollection of his previous visit, they rattled into a narrow street, leading from the High Street, and drew up before the door of the small house now inhabited by Fanny's family.

Another moment and Fanny was in the narrow entrance-passage of the house, and in her mother's arms, who met her there with looks of true kindness, and there were her two sisters: Susan, who had been barely five years old when Fanny had gone away, and little Betsey.

They were then taken into a parlour, so small that Fanny's first conviction was of its being only a passage-room to something better, and she stood for a moment expecting to be invited on; but when she saw there was no other door, and that there were signs of habitation before her, she called back her thoughts, reproved herself, and grieved lest they should have been suspected.

Fanny then performed the office, which she had been dreading, of introducing Mr. Crawford to her parents, as her husband! The first exclamation of surprise was not over before Mr. Crawford smoothly took the conversation into his own hands, and Fanny found that she need not do more than sit and watch, as at a play, while Mr. Crawford described their first acquaintance at Mansfield Park, his growing admiration for Miss Price, his anguish at her disappearance, his search for her through the length and breadth of England, his joy at finding her and his impetuous proposal that they be married in Gretna Green. He was also prepared to speak, eloquently and at length, about the charms and virtues of his new bride, but he was, as always, sensitive to the minutest shades on the faces of his audience, and he discovered that when he came to speak of Fanny's perfections, he pretty soon lost their attention entirely. He moved ahead to the bland announcement of his yearly income and the extent of his estate at Everingham, to which they attended with incredulity and pleasure, and which rendered the concluding part of his speech -- his plea for forgiveness for marrying Fanny without reference to them, and his request for their blessing on the union -- a mere formality, as he well knew it would be.

His narrative had forestalled most of their questions, and the Prices had only to express their approval: "By g-d, you've knocked us on our beam ends, Mr. Crawford, and no mistake! Fan, if your husband has half the gilt he's told you he's got – you've done very well for yourself!" Mr. Price pounded his daughter on the back approvingly, she began coughing, and the subject of her husband's wealth, as fascinating as it was to the Prices, was soon dropped completely by the entrance of William, complete in his lieutenant's uniform, with the happiest smile over his face, who walked up directly to Fanny, who, rising from her seat, looked at him for a moment in speechless admiration, and then threw her arms round his neck to sob out her various emotions of pain and pleasure.

Here was her triumph indeed, though her brother would not, could not, know the secret pain it had cost her. Now it was William who took the centre stage in the family – all conversation now moved to his commission, his prospects, and when he might ship out – William explained over the growing din, as three younger Price brothers ran downstairs to admire him, he was soon to sail in the *Agincourt,* and he knew not where or when he would join the *Solebay,* but perhaps at Sierra Leone, and suddenly Fanny's marriage to Mr. Crawford was no longer the main wonder of the evening. Mr. Crawford, not deficient in his knowledge of the Navy, thanks to his uncle the Admiral, joined in, and all Fanny had to do was sit and listen and long for some tea! She smiled inwardly to recall her anxieties on the subject of her first parental interview, mixed with some mortification at seeing herself so quickly overlooked and forgotten after a ten years' absence.

Finally, Susan and a servant appeared with everything necessary for the meal; Susan looking, as she put the kettle on the fire and glanced at her sister, as if divided between the agreeable triumph of showing her activity and usefulness, and the dread of being thought to demean herself by such an office. "She had been into the kitchen," she said, "to help make the toast, and spread the bread and butter, or she did not know when they should have got tea, and she was sure her sister and her new brother must want something after their journey."

Fanny was very thankful, and Susan immediately set about making it, as if pleased to have the employment all to herself; and with only a little unnecessary bustle, and some few injudicious attempts at keeping her brothers in better order than she could, acquitted herself very well. Susan had an open, sensible countenance; she was like William, and Fanny hoped to find her like him in disposition and goodwill towards herself.

It was not to be wondered that the bridegroom -- and not the bride -- was the more honoured guest during Fanny's brief reunion with her family; as it was Mr. Crawford who had put William in the way of obtaining his promotion. He was the first to be served tea by Mrs. Price, the first to be toasted with madeira by Mr. Price, and while Fanny's brothers did suffer her to kiss them, they all lined up eagerly to shake Mr. Crawford's hand when the new-married couple excused themselves for the evening. Her father's final benediction on the match was to make a coarse remark to her new bridegroom and to slap him heartily on the back as they left.

When bidding Mr. Crawford 'good night' at the Crown, Fanny thanked him heartily for his great kindness in bringing her to Portsmouth, and he, once again, enjoyed the sensation of being a fine fellow who had actually done some good for his fellow creatures, so that despite the vulgarity and disorder of the Price household, he retired to his separate chamber feeling well-disposed toward mankind in general and even all persons named Price.

And when he grappled with his buxom actress, for the first of several lively encounters that night, in various postures, he reflected that his wedding night exceeded his most sanguine expectations and his only regret was that he could not tell all his acquaintance about it – at least not for the present.

The next day was the Sabbath, and Henry had already resigned himself to staying in Portsmouth another day, as Fanny made her reluctance to travel clear; it was no great hardship, as he had a number of naval acquaintance in Portsmouth and was happy to call on them while his new bride spent the day visiting with her family.

Mrs. Price took her weekly walk on the ramparts every fine Sunday throughout the year, always going directly after morning service and staying till dinner-time. It was her public place: there she met her acquaintance, heard a little news, talked over the badness of the Portsmouth servants, and wound up her spirits for the six days ensuing. Fanny attended chapel with her family, and afterwards walked with them as she had not done for almost ten years. Before she'd been sent away to Mansfield, she had been the little shepardess to her younger brothers and sisters, but she was sorry to discover that, of the children still at home, only Susan retained any faint memory of her.

William was free to walk with them for an hour, and Fanny gloried in being once more on the ramparts with her brother. He pointed out the ugly hulk that was the *Agincourt*, anchored far out in the harbour, but since it was not the *Solebay*, Fanny could not be interested in taking a boat to go and tour it, nor did William think it was appropriate for his sister, who appeared too delicate for the rough-and-tumble atmosphere on the ship. As they parted, and over his protests, Fanny gave him all of her paltry savings, knowing that he would need ready monies more than she, for he would have to pay for his share of the officer's mess, and while Fanny was inexpressibly sorry to part with William, she preferred to make her *adieux* in the open air, in the haunts of their childhood, than back in the crowded, noisy, squalor and disorder of their Portsmouth home.

William hurried back to the 'rondy,' to escort a batch of new recruits to the launch that would carry them to the *Agincourt*. A detachment of marines with baleful expressions and glittering bayonets prodded the victims of the press gangs out of a dismal holding cell to the docks, and they were rowed out through the harbor, past graceful frigates and plump merchant ships to the great, black, hulking shape of the *Agincourt*, already surrounded by small boats bearing sailors' wives, and those who claimed to be sailors' wives. The boats bearing these dainty damsels competed with merchants steering bumboats piled high with all sorts of merchandise and gimcracks, who likewise intended to separate the sailors from their earnings. The rowers on the launch shoved their way through the throng and accompanied by enthusiastic swearing and prodding, everyone was sent climbing up a rope net to the gun deck.

Price idly took stock of the impressed men, and noticed one slender young man with glasses who was taller by a head than everyone else. *No tattoos, no tar-blackened hands*, he thought to himself. *He doesn't walk like a seaman, nor dress as one.*

William Gibson barely had time to look around him before he and his fellow pressed men were forced to climb a series of ladders down to the orlop deck – a gloomy, airless hole in the bowels of the ship. As the last of them clambered down – including two little boys who had run away from home and volunteered to be cabin boys and who were now trying not to weep for fright – an iron grating was dropped over the hatch.

The ceiling was so low that Gibson could not even stand up. He tried to find an unoccupied spot to sit down in the dark, and to avoid calling attention to himself, surrounded as he was by men who appeared to be mostly experienced sea-faring types of one sort of another. By sitting back and listening, he hoped to learn as much as he could about his strange new world, but he soon found himself intervening when some of the men, to pass the time, were amusing themselves by telling the two little cabin boys about what awaited them.

"Here are two new powder-monkeys for the gunners' crews, mates. I remember when that 18 pounder exploded in the *Bulldog*. The gun crew disappeared, we found little pieces of them blowed t'other side of the gundecks, we did."

"There was my old mate, Sam Polly. He was no taller than the two of you youngsters, and he said the cannonballs would go over' im, but lor' if one didn't take his head clean off, right above the ears!'"

"Better a clean death than having both your legs off with grapeshot, I say. Then comes the sawbones to finish the job."

"Here, here, chaps, this is all very interesting," Gibson's calm, pleasant voice rang out in the darkness. "Tell me about it, I am a true landlubber. How long shall we be kept in confinement? I've never been pressed before."

A chorus of groans went up in the darkness. "Oh, spare us. A landsman."

"We'll be put before the ratings committee," a raspy voice issuing from about Gibson's left elbow explained. "You'll give your name —"

"Or some other name —" put in another, which brought some harsh laughter from some of the men.

"—and *you'll* be rated as a landsman, see, and most of us are able seaman. We'll be paid more because we've got tar on our hands, see? Then we will each be assigned somewheres."

"We are not to serve on this ship, then?"

"This is just a transport ship."

"I heard the *Agincourt* is a victualling ship, going to the African coast," another voice chimed in.

"God help us. I'd rather fight the stinking Frenchies than face those mosquitos again."

"Why are they sending us to fight the mosquitoes?," asked a laughing voice. "Not that the bastards don't deserve it."

"Not mosquitoes, you blockhead, it's to stop the slave ships leaving Africa."

"Piss on that. I want my bonus money for fighting Jack Crapaud."

"That's all you know. The Navy is paying a fat bonus for every slave that's rescued, see, and every slave ship that's captured."

"Will they pay my wife a bonus if she comes to rescue me? I do appear to be held against my will."

More bleak laughter.

Through patient enquiry, Gibson learned that some of the men were merchant seaman, newly arrived back in England after months or years at sea, and snatched up for service in His Majesty's Navy, sometimes within sight of their long yearned-for homes. Some were fisherman, some were drunkards, some he would have crossed the street rather than encounter back in Bristol, and all could speak to each other in a language, or using terms and expressions, he could not begin to understand. Finally, he leaned back against a barrel and softly recited to himself:

I would not have a slave to till my ground,
To carry me, to fan me while I sleep,
And tremble when I wake, for all the wealth
That sinews bought and sold have ever earn'd.
No: dear as freedom is,—and in my heart's
Just estimation priz'd above all price,—
I had much rather be myself the slave,

And wear the bonds, than fasten them on him.

We have no Slaves at home—

"Here – you're a gentlemen, aren't you?" asked the raspy voice at his elbow. "You're scot free, my lad. When they start asking you questions, answer them in Latin or Greek like that, see. They'll have to let you go."

"And if they don't?"

"Then, you're off to boil your brains in Africa, my boy. Or the West Indies. Or maybe freezing your arse off near Copenhagen."

The grating was briefly lifted while a keg of water and some ship's biscuit was lowered down, then a cheerful young man, who Gibson recognized as being the young lieutenant on the launch, peered down at them.

"Lads, I don't wonder that you want to kick at your fate," said William cheerfully, looking down at the glowering men packed below. "But consider – you will see the world, and the rate of pay is better than you will get ashore, and the prospect of prize money for all. So if you sign up and volunteer, you will receive the joining bonus."

"Shove your bonus up your arse, my little captain's pet," snarled one of the pressed men under his breath, following up with a vulgar reference about what he could do to the young lieutenant if he could corner him, which caused Mr. Gibson, out of an abundance of caution, to move a little away from the grumbler. But it seemed the young lieutenant was quick-eared.

"You will address me as Mr. Price. And I have served in His Majesty's Navy since my twelfth year and have eluded more nimble fellows than you. I am second lieutenant of His Majesty's frigate *Solebay*, assigned to the West African Squadron, whither perhaps some of you are bound, along with me." The grating slammed down again and Gibson wondered – *Price? Miss Price spoke of a brother in the Navy, but he was a midshipman, as I recall, in Gibraltar*. He closed his eyes and tried to get some rest, but the foul, close air was sorely trying.

***

After dinner, peace and calm descended upon the Price household as all of its male members were abroad, and Fanny sat sewing with her mother and Susan, helping to get William's shirts and linen ready. Although Fanny had not been among her family for ten years, she was not an object of curiosity or solicitude for her mother, a fact that both surprised and grieved her but to which she could do nothing but resign herself. Mrs. Price had no questions for her long-absent daughter even about the doings of her sister Bertram. Only Susan showed some curiosity about life at Mansfield Park, and how Fanny's life there differed from the family she had left behind. She asked Fanny about the kitchens at Mansfield and "were they not prodigious big"? and Fanny could hardly reply, having scarcely ever been in them, and Susan silently wondered how her sister could have attained the age of eighteen without knowing how to make an oyster stew or even boil an egg. She supposed that her sister, though a grown woman, must have to sit and wait helplessly for someone to come along and feed her, a circumstance she could hardly comprehend or respect.

By Susan's questions, however, Fanny understood that Susan saw that much was wrong at home, and wanted to set it right. This accounted for her impatience with her mother, her angry remonstrance of her brothers. That a girl of fourteen, acting only on her own unassisted reason, should err in the method of reform, was not wonderful; and Fanny soon became more disposed to admire the natural light of the mind which could so early distinguish justly, than to censure severely the faults of conduct to which it led. Susan tried to be useful, where *she* could only have gone away and cried.

In the late afternoon, Mr. Crawford came to fetch her and was invited to join the family for tea, and she was grateful for the tranquility and good humour with which he took his seat and waited, without appearing to wait, for tea which in all probability might not come until darkness fell. He made himself very agreeable to the three Price boys as they came rattling in, and even took little Betsey up on his lap to admire her.

As Fanny now sat looking at Betsey, she could not but think particularly of another sister, a very pretty little girl, whom she had left there when she went into Northamptonshire, who had died a few years afterwards. There had been something remarkably amiable about her. While considering her with these ideas, she saw that Betsey was holding out something to catch her eyes, meaning to screen it at the same time from Susan's.

"What have you got there, my love?" said Fanny.

It was a silver knife. Up jumped Susan, claiming it as her own, and trying to get it away; but the child hopped off of Mr. Crawford's lap and ran to her mother's protection, and Susan could only reproach, which she did very warmly, and evidently hoping to interest Fanny on her side. "It was very hard that she was not to have her own knife; it was her own knife; little sister Mary had left it to her upon her deathbed, and she ought to have had it to keep herself long ago. But mama kept it from her, and was always letting

Betsey get hold of it; and the end of it would be that Betsey would spoil it, and get it for her own, though mama had promised her that Betsey should not have it in her own hands."

Fanny was quite shocked. Every feeling of duty, honour, and tenderness was wounded by her sister's speech and her mother's reply.

"Now, Susan," cried Mrs. Price, in a complaining voice, "now, how can you be so cross? You are always quarrelling about that knife. I wish you would not be so quarrelsome. Poor little Betsey; how cross Susan is to you! But you should not have taken it out, my dear, when I sent you to the drawer. You know I told you not to touch it, because Susan is so cross about it. I must hide it another time, Betsey. Poor Mary little thought it would be such a bone of contention when she gave it me to keep, only two hours before she died. Poor little soul!"

Fanny watched in surprise as Henry Crawford immediately reached into his pocket, extracted his watch and fob, and removed from its chain, a very elegant little mother-of-pearl knife which he promptly and with ceremony, presented to Betsey, who snatched at it with cries of joy. Susan, now confirmed in the undisputed ownership of Mary's knife, thanked him warmly, and Fanny envied the decisiveness of a character which so quickly saw a solution to the dilemma and acted upon it.

Acknowledging her smile of thanks, Crawford reflected to himself that there were some young ladies in the world who were pleased by other things than idle flattery.

On the following day, the Crawfords, man and wife, called one last time at the Price's door, but only to bid them *adieu*. Susan and Betsey and Mr. and Mrs. Price lined up outside the front door to watch as the hero of the hour, Mr. Crawford, assisted Fanny in to the carriage and tucked a travelling robe carefully around her. At the last moment, Mrs. Price held up her hand, signaling them to wait, ran inside, and a few moments passed before she returned with a little package. "William left this for me to give to you, Fanny, and he should have been very put out if I had forgotten!" Fanny opened the package and found a little amber cross that William had bought for her while in Sicily, and Fanny looked at it affectionately, then looked up at Mr. Crawford, who silently mouthed the words "one… two…three…." and she knew he was counting off the time before her tears would start to flow, so she smiled, and checked herself.

No sooner had the carriage pulled out of sight when Mrs. Price exclaimed, "Bless me, I forgot to give Fanny those letters for her! I found them and put them away most carefully in my wardrobe so no-one could lose them again. I don't suppose it signifies any more. She's no longer our Fanny, but Mrs. Crawford now."

Shilling! Betsey exclaimed to herself.

***

"Now, Mrs. Crawford, what do you think? We will stop off in London and get your wedding clothes made up and your portrait taken, shall we? Then heigh ho, for Norfolk and the peace and quiet of the countryside! For you, that is."

Fanny's eyes widened with alarm. "But – London – my cousins – Maria!"

"Never fear, Mrs. Crawford," he said, leaning forward as though to impart a great confidence. "London is a great place, and we need not worry about encountering them."

"Still – are there not mantua-makers and portrait-takers to be found in Norfolk? In fact," she added, thinking she could appeal to frugality if nothing else, "isn't everything twice as dear in London?"

"By heaven, that's so," agreed Henry. "But, you see, if it was put about that Mrs. Crawford had *not* had her wedding clothes made in London, then all my acquaintance would wonder what sort of wife I had married. Any woman taking the name of Mrs. Henry Crawford would expect nothing less – and in addition, new livery for the servants and a carriage for herself."

Fanny knew not how to dispute with this line of reasoning, so she fell silent, resolving to let as little money as possible pass through Mr. Crawford's fingers on her account, and trembling at the thought that by some accident, she might spy Edmund or his sisters coming out of a shop. What could she say? How would they look? How could Maria greet *her* as 'Mrs. Crawford'? It was past imagining.

Henry Crawford was in the highest spirits as the carriage sped along, loudly singing,

A North Country maid up to London has strayed
Although with her nature it did – not –agree.
So she wept and she sighed and bitterly she cried,
"Oh, I wish once again in the north I could be."

For the oak and the ash and the bonny ivy tree
They all grow green in the North Country.

"By the bye," he added presently. "Would forty pounds be suitable for you? Could you manage on that sum?"

"To – to pay for the servants, and the victuals in Everingham? And what about candles and, and —"

"No, you little ninny. For your pin money. Your new bonnets and your gaming stakes and your trinkets."

"Oh! More than amply, I'm sure. I don't spend twenty pounds in a year, so I wouldn't know how to spend forty."

"A year!" More roars of laughter. "You will have forty pounds every quarter, my frugal little bride. Be as miserly as you like with it, but don't expect any more than forty."

Fanny was stupefied at the thought of commanding such sums. She knew that Christopher Jackson was paid thirty pounds a year by Sir Thomas, and according to Aunt Norris, was very generously paid indeed. And she would have more than five times that amount to spend on bonnets and trinkets? She sat quietly, looking out the window, thinking of her family and the poor and needy of Mr. Crawford's estate, and how materially she would be able to help them, and thus fortified, was able to travel to London as the acknowledged wife of Mr. Henry Crawford without resorting to much use of her handkerchief.

Chapter Nineteen

Mary Crawford had pressed for an early marriage, arguing that her fortune made caution and delay unnecessary. Living as she had been, as a guest of her friends and her sister, she had saved the greater part of her yearly income, and she proposed to use those funds to pay for some alterations, which Henry called 'absolutely essential,' to be done at Thornton Lacey. The farmyard was to be cleared away and re-located, and trees planted to shield the house from the blacksmith's shop; the principal rooms would all be altered to face the east, a new portico would be built on the east side, and finally a new garden would be planted behind the house. Edmund Bertram had left London, at Mary's bidding, to go to Thornton Lacey to direct the commencement of the work, and knowing that she had a horror of living amongst half-finished alterations, mud and disorder, he was happy to acquiesce.

Thus confident that the two cousins would not meet before she was Edmund's wife, Mary Crawford called on Fanny at her hotel.

"Fanny, Henry tells me you refused him when he wanted to give you a gift of some jewelry," she began. "And I'm sure your disinterestedness does you great credit, but how shall you wear your brother's amber cross without a chain?" And as she spoke she was undoing a small parcel, which Fanny had observed in her hand when they met. Fanny acknowledged she had no means of wearing the cross, except for a simple ribbon, and she was answered by having a small trinket-box placed before her, and being requested to choose from among several gold chains and necklaces. [I]n the kindest manner Mary now urged Fanny's taking one for the cross and to keep for her sake, saying everything she could think of to obviate the scruples which were making Fanny start back at first with a look of horror at the proposal.

"You see what a collection I have," said she; "more by half than I ever use or think of. I do not offer them as new. I offer nothing but an old necklace. You must forgive the liberty, and oblige me."

Fanny found herself obliged to yield, that she might not be accused of pride or indifference, or some other littleness; and having with modest reluctance given her consent, proceeded to make the selection. She looked and looked, longing to know which might be least valuable, until Miss Crawford felt she could wrap her hands around Fanny's little neck and shake her head until it wobbled off. She exclaimed with some irritation, "For the love of heaven, Fanny Price, will you force me to attend on you all morning while you make a parade of your humility? Why must your modesty take such a tiresome form and be such an imposition on others?"

Blushing with shame, Fanny quickly chose a necklace more frequently placed before her eyes by Miss Crawford than the rest. It was of gold, prettily worked; and though Fanny would have preferred a longer and plainer chain also laid before her, she hoped, in fixing on this, to be choosing what Miss Crawford least wished to keep. Miss Crawford smiled her perfect approbation; and hastened to complete the gift by putting the necklace round her, and making her see how well it looked. Fanny had not a word to say against its becomingness. She would rather, perhaps, have been obliged to some other person.

Mary was preparing to depart when she suddenly recollected another matter: "Oh, Fanny! I was coming out of a shop on Jermyn Street and there, on the pavement, was none other than the Baron von Wildenhaim himself – Mr. Yates, that is. He has heard the news of your marriage and asked me, rather impertinently I thought, when you and Henry might receive him at Everingham?"

"Oh Miss Crawford, must I entertain guests at Everingham?" cried Fanny anxiously.

Mary shrugged. "Depend on it, my dear, you will receive many enquiries of this sort. I have heard it said of Mr. Yates, particularly, that once he has arrived at your home, he will ignore all your hints that it is time for him to depart."

Fanny began to pace up and down, wringing her hands. "Miss Crawford, I do not think I can do this. I cannot impose this lie on the entire world. I had thought I would be left alone at Everingham."

"There, there," Mary soothed her. "They are unlikely to travel all the way to the wilds of Norfolk without your invitation. Do you have some writing paper? Allow me to dictate a letter to you. With some slight variations, you can send this reply to all enquiries."

Fanny sat down at the desk and wrote as Mary dictated:

Dear Sir:

Many thanks for your kind remembrances of the pleasant times we spent together at Mansfield Park.

It would be my pleasure to welcome old friends to Everingham, but, as my husband will be called away on business shortly after my arrival there, and my new obligations and duties will necessarily occupy my time, I must regretfully await a future day when he and I, together, can welcome guests to our home.

I am, obliged, etc.

F. Crawford

"There. No one will fail to understand your sentiments and yet it is polite enough, I think, for the likes of Mr. Yates. I will give this to him for you – we meet tomorrow afternoon at Lady Delingpole's reception. Do not make yourself uneasy any more, Fanny. As you see, I will do everything in my power to assist you."

Fanny entreated, and Henry Crawford assented, that their sojourn in London be as quiet as possible – that she not be introduced to any of his acquaintance, nor go to any public places. Thus, although this was her first visit to the great city, Fanny denied herself the pleasures of the theatre, or parks or even the bookstores. In the evening she rested in the room Crawford had engaged for her, and the five days they spent there were largely taken up with the business of ordering new clothes, shoes, headdresses and bonnets and having her portrait taken, all of which was tiring enough.

The mantua-makers of the great London warehouses were not kind in their appraisal of Mrs. Henry Crawford, and did not scruple to express their surprise that Mr. Crawford, well-known about the town, should have settled on such a demure little bride. If Mr. Crawford and his bride had made a love match, how to interpret the smiles, the glances between Mr. Crawford and his wife's lady's maid? And the seamstresses were *not* called upon to disguise a growing thickness at the waist, as sometimes did occur in their profession, so *that* could not explain this strange marriage.

Mrs. Crawford was at best, only tolerable-looking, with only youth and gentleness of manner to recommend her. If she was of noble birth, why did she speak of visiting a younger brother who toiled as a clerk in Wapping, and if she was an heiress, why was she not dressed as one?

Still, the groom was undeniably a charming gentleman, and one with a good eye for lace and muslin and silk. His daring taste was wasted on Mrs. Crawford, however, who blushed as red as a beet root at some of the sheer night gowns he laughingly held up for her approval.

The mantua-makers did conclude that pink was her best colour, she looked dreadful in mustard – although it was the fashionable colour that year – and she was in fact correct that simplicity and modesty suited her best. She had little in the way of *embonpoint* to show off, but her *décolletage* could be cut to emphasize her delicate collarbones, and her neck and arms were not contemptible. The high-waisted gowns of the day were made for slender frames, such as hers, but she lacked the height, the assurance, the carriage, that would mark her out as a leader of fashion.

***

Lady Bertram was reclining in her usual place when Sir Thomas entered with a letter and a small parcel in his hand. "This has just arrived, my dear, from Mr. Crawford in London. He may have some intelligence of our little Fanny."

Lady Bertram sat up and pushed her sleeping pug to one end of the sofa with an alacrity which startled Sir Thomas no less than the animal, and invited her husband to sit down. They read the following:

My dear sir, the letter began,

I trust that this letter finds you and all your family well. I know that you, and especially Lady Bertram, have been very solicitous on our account, so may I assure you that my sister and I are both well, and that we were fortunate, for the most part, in the weather and the roads during our travels in search of your niece. But I will sport with your patience no longer – I take the greatest satisfaction in informing you that she has been located and she is well.

We discovered your niece toiling as a governess for a respectable family near Bristol. I should assure you that she had not revealed herself to be the niece of Sir Thomas Bertram. My sister and I likewise, wishing to spare you and your Lady any indignity, did not mention the name of 'Bertram' to her employers.

Upon our private representations to Miss Price of the distress of your family since her departure from your midst, she agreed to quit her post. Her employers were saddened to part with her, but as she had, one month previously, devotedly nursed their two little children through a grave episode of illness, she had thereby secured their affection and gratitude to the highest degree. They kindly consented for her to depart without the customary notice given in these circumstances.

To continue, I naturally had occasion to hold many conferences with your niece, first at the home of her erstwhile employers and later as we retraced our path to Northamptonshire. I was well aware of your niece's maidenly modesty and gentleness when I first made her acquaintance, but I

217

*soon became sensible as never before of her sweetness of temper –
qualities which any man of sense desires to have in a wife. Impelled by the
strongest feelings of love and respect, I declared myself to her and am
humbled to relate that Miss Price consented to make me the happiest of
men. We therefore diverted my carriage north to Gretna Green, and were
there confirmed as husband and wife.*

*Mrs. Crawford sends you her love and begs you to accept this small
watercolour portrait to in token of her affection and gratitude. The full-size
version will hang over the fireplace in the main sitting room at Everingham.*

*So, having located your niece, as I pledged to do, may I reiterate it was
an honour to render this service to your family, whose warm friendship I will
forever hold in the highest esteem. If I may ever be of assistance again, I
am, of course,*

Your humble servant, Henry Crawford

(When Henry had composed this letter, his sister had exclaimed, "*Must
you take your little fling at Maria, Henry! Is it not enough to throw her
over! I fear that none of the Bertrams will ever speak with me again!*")

Before Sir Thomas could send someone to gently break the news to her,
poor Maria, sitting down to breakfast, had the misfortune of seeing a small
notice which Henry had caused to be placed in the papers on his last day in
London: *Lately, Mr. Henry Crawford, Esq., of Everingham, Norfolk, to Miss
Price, niece to Sir Thomas Bertram, Bart., of Mansfield Park,
Northamptonshire.*

Her eyes swam with tears, her heart threatened to burst out of her
chest, she felt she was choking to death, but, she did not doubt the truth of
what she read. Only Henry himself would have published such a notice – it
must be so.

***

William Price attempted in vain to assemble his features into what he
supposed was the appropriate and serious mien for a lieutenant. He
couldn't not entirely keep a smile from his lips as he showed himself in the
dockyard for the first time in his new uniform, nor could he forebear
contemplating the appearance he would make at the Assembly dance later
that week. He thought as well of Lucy Gregory and her sisters, who had
snubbed him at the last Assembly, when he was still a midshipman.
Fortunately, implacable resentment formed no part of his character,
especially not when Lucy Gregory had grown up into such a fine pretty

young lady, with such jolly dimples and blonde curls, and he was picturing himself whirling her about in a country dance, when suddenly he heard his name being called by the *Agincourt's* purser. He fairly flew, weaving his way around barrels and bales being loaded and unloaded, and under ropes pulled by straining men, but resisted the urge to leap over coiled rolls of rope as being incompatible with his new dignity as a lieutenant, and finally finding Captain Henderson speaking to his first lieutenant, waited respectfully for the Captain's eyes to fall on him. The pair were discussing something with great animation, and William could make out the words "new orders" and "west coast," but he kept a respectful distance, until, the Captain finally noticing him, he was summoned to step forward.

"Mr. Price, I am leaving Lieutenant Bayly here in charge. You shall accompany me to the Admiralty on behalf of your captain."

"Yes, sir."

London! William exclaimed to himself. *The Admiralty!* When he had been in London with Mr. Crawford, he had been driven past the Admiralty, Mr. Crawford had pointed it out to him – now he was to step inside, perhaps actually set eyes upon the First Lord…. And then… possibly he would be permitted to visit his younger brother John, or perhaps Fanny was still in the city. Given leave to go home and prepare for the journey, his thoughts alternated between pride and dismay, picturing himself calling on Wimpole Street in his uniform, and wondering if his mother had washed and mended his linen.

His announcement threw the household into more than usual heights of alarm and disorder, and Susan was urged to find dear William's shirt and mend it, and perhaps it could be washed and then dried before the fire, and his mother thought that her sister Bertram had mentioned exactly where her family were staying in London in her last letter, at which Betsey looked conscious and turned and ran upstairs, and William followed her, to find her hiding inside a small packing box in the attic which she had fitted up with an old blanket, a dish, a cup, half of the household's teaspoons and, unaccountably, old newspapers, handbills and – what were these? Letters?

He reached out for them, and narrowly avoided Betsey's teeth clamping down on his hand.

"Shan't!" She exclaimed. "The beautiful lady is going to give me a shilling for them!"

"Betsey," he said. "Give me those letters, there's a good girl."

"Shan't!"

"Will you give me one letter for this big shiny penny?"

Since Betsey didn't know the value of coins, only that they were coins, she happily assented, and handed him a letter from the top of the pile, which proved to be Lady Bertram's. In his haste to prepare for his trip to London, William didn't stay to examine the others, but went back downstairs to help Susan find the scissors.

"Mother, I know why we can't find any paper to use in the necessary – Betsey has it all in the attic," he reported, as he and Susan turned the workbasket upside down and pawed through its contents. Another thought struck him; "By the by, do the Bertrams know about Fan's marriage?"

"Why, not from me, I'm sure. I've had no time to write a letter this week, but I should think it's for Fanny herself to tell them."

"Susan, you have my leave to go over the railing, as Fan did," laughed Mr. Price, "so long as you come home with a rich husband like your sister. By g-d, William, my boy, we'll see if you are as skillful at catching prizes as your sister, hey?"

Susan muttered under her breath that she would love nothing so much as to run away from home, rich husband or no.

***

For four full days, Maria had refused to leave her room, and could barely be persuaded to take anything more than a little tea and some brandy. She wailed aloud if anyone attempted solace in any form, or tried to persuade her to return, with all her sorrows, to Mansfield. She refused to speak to anyone, nor even allow her maid to open the curtains. Finally, on the fourth day, her father arrived in London, sent for by Julia, for Mrs. Norris would not acknowledge that anyone but she had the ability, or even the right, to console poor Maria. For the first time that Maria could remember, her father enfolded her in his arms, and she burst out weeping anew.

Edmund had been alerted to the surprising news of his cousin Fanny's marriage by his brother Tom, who rode over to Thornton Lacey where Edmund had been living in a house torn apart with alterations. The brothers then travelled swiftly to London, Tom to Wimpole Street, and Edmund to visit his fiancée, wondering what she could tell him of her brother's sudden preference for Fanny over Maria.

"As you can imagine, Mary, I am of two minds about this news. Fanny surprised us all when she left to be a governess – this is equally perplexing," he exclaimed to Mary after the first raptures of their reunion had passed and they were able to contemplate some other creatures than themselves.

Mary raised an eyebrow at the perceived slight to her brother. "What girl of Fanny's low rank would not accept such a proposal, and become mistress of Everingham? It is a tremendous match for her."

"When we were all together at Mansfield last autumn, I saw no indication that she bore him any affection, or even esteem. Perhaps you observed something, with your quickness, that I did not. And if there is a young lady in this nation who would decline to form an alliance for mercenary reasons, I would say that young lady is Fanny Price. Still, he did that for her brother, which I should suppose would have been almost sufficient recommendation to her, had there been no other."

"In other words, you think that he is to be obliged to her, for *her* stooping to marry *him*?" Mary knew she ought to have quietly assented to all, but she could not restrain herself. "You must excuse a fond sister, but I should think most people would view matters quite differently — they would wonder why a man of his sense, temper, manners, and fortune, would marry a portionless girl with neither great beauty nor accomplishments to recommend her."

Edmund smiled down at her. "I congratulate him on his choice. While I am heartily sorry for Maria, the fact that your brother married without regard to rank or fortune speaks as eloquently of Fanny's virtues as it does his discernment of them. And my dear, as I have been fortunate enough to win your affections, I know how perverse the ways of the heart can be."

"Yes," Mary nodded. "For example, you know how I dreaded the day you would take orders, and now that it is done, I can only admire how very handsome you look, all dressed in black!"

"Playfully said, and you illustrate my theorem that, in marriage, the tempers had better be unlike: I mean unlike in the flow of the spirits, in the manners, in the inclination for much or little company, in the propensity to talk or to be silent, to be grave or to be gay. Some opposition here is, I am thoroughly convinced, friendly to matrimonial happiness."

"Fanny will be the anchor line to Henry's hot air balloon, I have no doubt!" Mary sounded not entirely convinced by this line of reasoning.

"Well, I hope with all my heart they shall be very happy — but I confess, speaking as a man who has loved only *one* woman, and *will* love no other, I wonder how it came to be that your brother transferred his affections so rapidly. And knowing of Fanny's delicacy as to conduct, how could my cousin have been comfortable accepting the addresses of a man who was in honour bound to my sister? Maria is in a very bad way, by the bye."

"Oh, dear. Poor Maria." Mary paused here, for though she had joined her brother in laughing over Maria's downfall, and scorning her for her jealousy, her flights of temper, and her imprudence in allowing Henry to make so free with her before marriage, she saw by the grave features of her beloved that he saw nothing to amuse, and much to lament, in Maria's humiliation. She ventured a new approach.

"Edmund, you will recall Maria threw over poor Mr. *Rushworth* without any ceremony. I believe you did not condemn *her* at that time, but rather, thought it was all for the best."

Edward nodded. "But, my Mary, this is a privilege reserved to womankind, and not to a man of honour. The understanding between Henry and my sister was of some months' duration."

"Or so we believed, we who approved of the match. But – *were* they engaged? Didn't your own father withhold his consent?"

Edmund took her hand, in acknowledgement of the point. How could this beautiful creature be so bewitching, so feminine in all her ways, and be withal so clear-sighted, so intelligent, so discerning, so unsentimental and practical when confronted with difficulties? There was simply not another such a woman upon the earth – and he had won her.

Mary intertwined her slender fingers with his broad, strong ones, and stood very still, looking up at him, willing him to kiss her again and change the subject from his cousin Fanny. But his mind still ran upon his cousin.

"My love, did Fanny like the necklace I got for her? Did she have some message for me?"

Mary's face fell. "Oh, my dear, I am so sorry to tell you this. From the time that we first found her in Keynsham Hill she evinced the most complete coldness toward your family. I spoke to her of your affection, how the entire family regretted her absence and wished her to return with us. I recall how shocked we were at her reply, 'I do not desire to return to Mansfield Park. This is the new life that I've chosen.' And, when I placed your necklace before her, she would not take it."

Edmund's countenance bore testimony to his sorrow, surprise and disappointment. "Ah. Well, you may keep the necklace for yourself, my dear. And did she leave me no note, no message?"

With every show of reluctance, and a little sigh, Mary handed him the note intended for Mr. Yates, whom, in fact, she had not seen on Jermyn Street, or anywhere else. She watched his face eagerly as he read it, hoping to see such resentment as would lead to a final breach between the two. Instead, he appeared perplexed and saddened. He read it carefully, then slowly folded it up and put it in his breast pocket.

"There is a double breach between our families now, and who knows what evils it will produce! Your brother will not attend our wedding, nor will Maria, and, it seems, his new wife wishes to turn her back on *all* of us! I hope that you can help me to plead my case with Fanny. I am at a loss."

"Perhaps you should forebear for a time, dear Edmund. And, of course, when the time is right, I will do everything I can to restore the good understanding you once had with your little cousin."

She watched him as he paced up and down, deep in thought. Then: "No – this is madness. I know Fanny too well – it is inconceivable that she should be so estranged from me. Where is she? I must speak to her today."

"No, that is not possible, I'm afraid. They are on their way to Everingham now."

***

Henry Crawford had been alternately amused and perplexed by Fanny Price, as though he had suddenly been handed an exotic jungle animal, or a wailing infant, that he knew not how to care for, and the challenge of keeping the creature fed and happy; of learning, by trial and error, what it liked and disliked, what frightened and what pleased it, sufficed to entertain him for a time, but the novelty of travelling, day after day, with a girl who was so easily disconcerted, yet so stubborn on the smallest points, who preferred to read books rather than converse with him, a girl entirely indifferent to fashionable dresses, or jewelry, or his routine gallantries, had long since worn away, and he was counting the hours when he could resume his accustomed habits.

She was, for example, gravely perusing some grim-looking pamphlets while they were baiting the horses at Cambridge, so he entertained himself by flirting with the serving-girl, a bonny redheaded charmer.

For her part, Fanny tried to ignore her companion, but she could not help glancing up now and again, wondering what a real bride would say to her groom if he conducted himself before her in public in such a fashion. Here was again a want of delicacy and regard for others which had formerly so struck and disgusted her. Here was again a something of the same Mr. Crawford whom she had so reprobated before. How evidently was there a gross want of feeling and humanity where his own pleasure was concerned; and alas! how always known –

223

"By heaven, Mrs. Crawford," Henry broke upon her thoughts. "You were worried that you would not be able to act your part, but I assure you, you give a perfect impression of a married woman! No one, seeing you, could doubt your complete indifference towards me. I believe you have not addressed three words to me this entire morning! What ghastly thing are you reading?"

"It is some abolitionist literature given to me in Bristol. It is most affecting, but more than that, I think it is well-argued, from a theological and moral point of view, that we English must lead all the other nations in exterminating the trade in human beings."

"Sugar plantations in Antigua being excepted?"

She looked up at him calmly. "I do now comprehend, Mr. Crawford, that much of that ease and comfort which surrounded me in Mansfield Park, is owing to the sugar trade. I have not seen my uncle since I was sixteen years of age, but when I meet with him again, I will endeavour to better inform myself as to his sentiments on the matter. In my youth, he was an advocate for what was moral, and upright and just – his sense of honour is so strict, that I cannot reconcile in my mind how he could countenance this." And she held up a printed engraving of captured Africans packed tightly into a ship for the Atlantic crossing.

Crawford slouched back in his seat, with his hands behind his head and replied with a tolerant smile, "This slavery debate has gone on in the public sphere for some time, so I can put some thoughts to you for your consideration, Mrs. Crawford. First, you have been in correspondence with your dear brother William for many years now, haven't you? He has sung to you the praises of the Navy, hasn't he? Has he *never* happened to mention to you, Mrs. Crawford, that our own sailors, our own Englishmen, are sometimes tied to the grates, then flogged with a cat o' nine tails, until the blood streams down their backs, and so are our soldiers in the army, and if a primitive heathen is too good to be flogged, the same as an honest Englishman, why the world is topsy-turvy, I would say."

"As you like, Mr. Crawford, but the slave is taken by force away from his home – "

"Nor has your brother ever once mentioned press gangs to you? You grew up in Portsmouth, did you not? Surely you know about the press gangs?"

"Why, y-yes," Fanny admitted, hesitantly. "Although we always supposed that the gangs were rounding up sailors who had deserted their posts, or who were not doing themselves any good on shore, being drunkards, and who were the better for being on ship and under discipline – " here she paused, unhappily, thinking of her own father.

"And, have you never heard of the miserable, brutish life of our own coal miners? Have you never seen the little children who earn their living by crawling down our chimneys and brushing out the soot? Is there not enough suffering here in our 'precious stone set in the silver sea' for you to bestow your benevolent concern upon, without troubling yourself over beings half a world away?"

Fanny shook her head, "Which would *you* rather be, Mr. Crawford? A tin miner in Cornwall or a slave cutting down sugar cane?"

Crawford laughed, and tipped his hat to her. "I would rather be who I am – but look out the window, Mrs. Crawford, if you please. There you will see, walking along the road, a family of farm labourers, dressed in rags, miserably drenched from the rain, with no home, nor steady employment. Observe how they run up to the passing carriages, and hold out their hands, begging for some coins. On the other hand, the slaves on your uncle's plantation are fed and clothed from birth until death, even after they are unfit for heavy work by reason of injury or old age. They are not used for one season and cast aside like the free-born men of England."

"Life is unjust, indeed, Mr. Crawford, and it is our duty to relieve the suffering of the poor and to teach them how they may improve their own condition. But by your arguments, have you sought to excuse one injustice with illustrations of other cruel situations? Shall we despair of remedying *any* evils, because we cannot remedy *all* of them? These abolitionists have chosen this cause, and renounced eating the products of slavery, to help eradicate – "

"Oh, L-rd bless us no, no, no – no wife of mine is going to become an anti-Saccharite!" Crawford laughed. "My dear Mrs. Crawford, the first thing I plan to do when we arrive at Everingham is to instruct my cook to stuff you full of good things, like puddings, and cakes and trifles and syllabubs, in the hopes of getting some flesh on you, for er…. for the sake of your health, so please don't tell me you will refuse to eat sugar!"

"My resolution is weak, Mr. Crawford, I own, nor would I want to be a hypocrite and pretend, as I said, that the home comforts we enjoyed at Mansfield Park were not as a result of sugar. I simply wish to study and understand this question better."

"Pray consider this, Mrs. Crawford," Henry leaned forward and took her hand. "If your uncle, in a fit of benevolence, were to release all of his slaves, what do you suppose would be the result? In all likelihood, none of them would know how to take care of themselves, and would be reduced to worser straits than they were on your uncle's plantation. The more brutish among them would threaten the lives of the Englishmen and women, and yes, even the children. Our own peoples would be overthrown and massacred, as happened to the Frenchmen in Saint Domingue. It is easy to say, 'free the slaves' but responsible men must consider the consequences."

Fanny nodded, not intending to agree but simply to show that she was attending to what he had to say, and acknowledged it was a difficult question, and privately wished that her friend William Gibson was there, so that she could simply sit quietly and say nothing, and listen to a debate betwixt them.

"And one other thing," her companion added, as he settled comfortably back in his seat. "Who d'you suppose provides those slaves in the first place. Their own rulers, back in Africa. They round up their own people – or whoever is in a different tribe from their own tribe – and sell them off for trinkets. I dare say they are better off under English management than under their own kings. And of course," he added complacently, composing himself for a nap. "The Negroes are brought to a knowledge of our Christian religion – they are brought out of the darkness of their heathen ways." He yawned.

Fanny smiled politely, and resumed reading her pamphlets. The thought occurred to her that a few months ago, she would have maintained her silence because she felt too abashed to interpose her own judgment against anyone else's. Now, she kept her peace only because she felt that it was futile to debate the issue with Mr. Crawford; had she felt inclined to want to try to change his views, or at least oppose them, she might have said more. The ability to hold one's peace was no bad thing, and Fanny rejoiced to feel that she had grown in confidence in the past half-year.

***

My dearest Fanny,

For dear you will always be to me, although we are, unaccountably to my mind, estranged. Fanny, I miss you more than I can express.

We have been friends for ten years now, by my count, since that day I found you weeping on the staircase, for homesickness and love of your brother William. Little did I expect that in befriending my little cousin, that I would be doing such good for myself, for as you grew, you became my most loyal friend and confidante. How often have we sat over the same books together, or admired the same stars in the night sky! Can you have forgotten, cousin, what simple pleasures we enjoyed together as we grew up? Is it nothing to you now? I know your tender heart too well – you have not forgotten me, and although some misunderstanding or resentment has arisen between us, I swear before Heaven that I have the warmest affection for you, my little cousin, and would consciously do nothing to cause you pain. Please, break this cold silence and speak to me!

I have also to express to you my best wishes on your wedding to Mr. Crawford. May he always cherish you as he ought, may he always listen to your counsel and become the man he could become, with Fanny by his side to guide and support him! May he always understand that he is the most fortunate of men in having Fanny for his wife!

As a married woman now yourself, you perhaps have reflected that as we all have our own faults, we ought to choose our partners in consideration of which faults we can tolerate and which faults we cannot. It seems that I can tolerate those little faults which I still see in Mary because I love her – I must love her, she is the only woman I could love. She has a tendency to speak lightly of serious matters, but of her essential kindness and sympathy, I have no doubt – as you yourself can attest, for she travelled across the country to find you! How happy you must have been to see your good friend! I wish that I could have witnessed that reunion!

Now, when I consider my many, many shortcomings – notice I do not nominate my own faults as 'faults,' but shortcomings – my shortcomings, as I said, which Mary must tolerate in me! I do not know how to flatter or court her, I am not ambitious, nor witty, nor lively, and can only sit and admire her as she brings grace, joy, and life to everything she touches. My father, in particular, delights in his new daughter-in-law. In one week – but one week more – I will escort my new bride to Thornton Lacey, there to begin our lives together as man and wife. You know how I barely allowed myself a hope of making her my own. I cannot find words sufficient to express my felicity.

Only one thing would complete my happiness – to repair my friendship with you, Fanny. Pray, let me know how you are. I think of you daily. With love, I am always,

Your,

Cousin Edmund

"Edmund, I am sending a parcel to Fanny – the last of her *trousseau* which has now been finished. I can send your letter with it."

227

"Thank you, my dear."

***

Tom Bertram still harbored the guilty secret of Crawford's seduction of Maria on the night of the dress rehearsal of *Lovers' Vows*. He hoped that Julia had remained discreet, and that Maria could escape from the debacle with some credit. The uproar, at least, helped him to know his own mind better — he dreaded the day when he must assume headship of the Bertram family, and be responsible for the happiness and prosperity of all its members, the honour of its daughters, the credit of its sons. Although he tried to reason himself into acceptance of his responsibilities as the first born, in truth, he wanted no part of such burdens.

Tom arrived at Wimpole Street to a house in virtual mourning. The Bertram girls, so lately the ornaments of London society, were now 'at home' to no-one. There was no question in Mrs. Norris' mind as who was to be charged as the daemon of the piece — it was Fanny, Fanny Price, who had somehow tricked Maria's intended husband into marriage. This idea she seized on with tenacity, while admittedly at a loss to understand how it could have come about, for Fanny was no rival for the beautiful Maria.

"It is astonishing, aunt," cried Tom. "Crawford has taken her for her hand alone — not a word about wanting any monies settled on her. When he might have had Maria and ten thousand pounds."

"Well then," his aunt retorted, "she must have more of her mother in her than we knew, more imprudence and less self-command, for how else could she have beguiled Mr. Crawford?"

Tom thought firstly, that if his aunt truly cared for Maria and her sufferings, she would refrain from canvassing the subject, again and again, before her niece, and secondly, exercise his imagination though he might, he could no more picture Fanny as a seductress than he could picture his own mother riding to hounds. With a hurried glance at Maria, who sat huddled in a shawl in a corner of the sofa, apparently insensible to all that was being said on the subject, he awkwardly added, "At least, my father is now relieved of her support, which must have been a prodigious sum, considering how often you lamented the cost she represented to our household."

His aunt looked at him sharply, but he only looked back at her with the blandest of expressions on his face.

"Beware yourself, Tom! You cannot be too guarded with these types of designing females, as handsome and as eligible as you are. Our dear Maria has such a strict sense of propriety, so much of that true delicacy which one seldom meets with nowadays – but how readily a young man can be brought to forget himself when a young lady behaves in a shameless fashion!" She fetched breath and continued, "Depend upon it, Tom, Fanny Price will rue the day she ever aspired to become Mrs. Henry Crawford, for people are never respected when they step out of their proper sphere. The nonsense and folly of people's stepping out of their rank and trying to appear above themselves – how ridiculous she will be, and how the servants at Everingham will laugh at her behind her back, when she tries to make herself its mistress!"

***

"What shall you do we arrive in Everingham, Mr. Crawford? That is, will you return to London?"

"Indeed I shall, Mrs. Crawford. You will not have heard of the Four-in-Hand club, but I have had the honour to be proposed for membership. They meet during these spring months, twice a month, and we ride with our teams in procession."

"Ah, it is a society for gentlemen who enjoy driving coaches, I apprehend."

"Yes. We even have our own clothing," Henry laughed self-consciously. "Something similar to the coachmen who drive the mail."

"Should I need to communicate with you, shall I write to your hotel?"

"You may," he said carelessly, "but I shall be everywhere, you know."

Fanny surmised they must be approaching Everingham, when Mr. Crawford suddenly called the coach driver to stop. Fanny waited quietly for an explanation, as she knew him well enough by now to understand he loved to cloak his doings with mystery and drama. She had not long to wait. He pulled from his pocket a little box, lined with velvet, containing a simple but pretty gold ring, small enough to fit the third finger of her left hand.

"We will be in Everingham in about half an hour," he explained quietly. "All the servants will be lined up along the sweep to meet you. I forgot about *this*, and thought I had better give it to you now, to give you time to recover from weeping before we arrived. And here – I ordered you two dozen extra handkerchiefs. You see, I have thought of every detail."

Fanny was deeply abashed, but his mockery, though almost affectionate, was not enough to stop her from crying, just a little, at the shame of wearing what should only be worn by those who have taken the most solemn oaths before their Creator. The ring burned her finger like fire.

Chapter Twenty

Henry Crawford stayed barely a week, only long enough to see Fanny settled in her new home, to assure himself that she was able to carry off the imposture, and long enough to see the response from Sir Thomas, to the news of the supposed marriage.

Dear Mrs. Crawford:

I thought it not inappropriate, on the occasion of your marriage, to convey to you my sentiments. It is the usual custom, I believe, to proffer "best wishes" to a bride. However, I think it is my duty to mark my opinion of your conduct. I am in no small doubt as to how you shall receive this letter as you have recently shown, by every means possible, that you disdain the deference that youth and inexperience owes to wisdom and authority. You have disappointed every expectation I had formed, and proved yourself of a character the very reverse of what I had supposed.

Firstly – and if the fact had not been confirmed by Miss Crawford herself I could scarcely credit it – you assumed the role of a governess in a household near Bristol. That a niece of Sir Thomas Bertram, raised under his roof, would stoop to this expedient, and would flee from home, from family, from safety, honour, comfort and ease, to repay our generosity with resentment and scorn, is past all my powers to comprehend.

Secondly – you have flouted the laws of England respecting the marriage of underage persons, and entered into the state of matrimony, with a man who was in honour pledged to my daughter Maria. Time alone will reveal who will be the greater sufferer as a result of this rash action – the daughter who lost Mr. Crawford as a husband or the niece who gained him as one.

You do not owe me the duty of a child. But, Fanny, if your heart can acquit you of ingratitude on this occasion, then your heart must not be as tender as I once supposed.

While my judgment in this matter has been severe, depend upon it, I remain your well-wisher and friend. May you never know the pain of being so grievously disappointed by those to whom you are bound by the tenderest ties of affection.

Your sorrowful uncle, Thomas Bertram

Fanny had been making some progress in training herself not to cry every time her feelings were wounded, but a letter such as this from her uncle, a man whom she had always feared and respected, caused her to retire to her bedchamber to weep until slumber brought her some relief. It appeared that Miss Crawford had told her nothing less than the truth – she was rejected by her family – she was cast out of Mansfield Park – she was nothing to them now!

Henry Crawford, partially out of resentment at being thus insulted by Sir Thomas, and partially out of actual pity and good feeling for Fanny, instructed the steward that any letters from her Bertram cousins be kept away from Mrs. Crawford and locked up in his study until his return, so that he could peruse them first.

The following morning, he told Fanny he was off again, adding that the lady's maid would accompany him, as she had decided she did not wish to live in so remote a place as Everingham. Fanny did not regret this in the least as the maid was a singularly clumsy and vulgar woman, and in answer to Fanny's enquiry about engaging a new lady's maid, Mr. Crawford had carelessly told her she was the entire mistress of the place and could hire and dismiss as many servants as she wished!

During their brief stay together in Everingham, he had been as good as his word in every respect – he treated her with the liberality and good-breeding of a gentleman, she retired to her own bedchamber at night unmolested, he made no overtures or insinuations, he left her with generous funds and, as though she were truly his wife, instructed the steward, housekeeper and butler to obey her every command. The fact was that Everingham sorely needed a mistress, as was apparent to Fanny from her first night, when she could not help comparing the quiet and smooth order of Mansfield Park with the bustle and confusion of Everingham, and the ensuing days did nothing to win her approbation.

She noted the cobwebs that festooned the chandeliers, she saw the unpolished furniture, the sooty fireplaces, she lightly partook of the greasy meals laid before her, but, unaccustomed to command, and moreover, intimidated by the housekeeper, who clearly resented her presence, Fanny kept to her room in those first days and ate her fatty pork and syllabubs in solitude, sighing for some plain biscuits and cheese and apples. She was exhausted by her recent illness, the abrupt change in her fortunes and her rapid travels, and she trembled at the rashness of the step she had taken. At least her bedchamber was comfortable and, after several nights' good sleep, she resolved within herself to think only of the benefit to her brother

William, and the ancillary good she might do to her family and the tenants of Everingham, instead of tormenting herself over having succumbed to perpetrating a falsehood. But no matter how she tried to put such pictures out of her mind, she was tortured with anxiety over what would Edmund's reaction be to the news of her marriage. He would undoubtedly be surprised and curious, but would he be censorious like his father? But greetings from Edmund, alas, never came, and Fanny was too timid to write without having first received a letter from him. She interpreted his continued silence to mean that he disapproved, probably for Maria's sake.

Fanny attempted to recover her health by walking alone in the beautiful parks and gardens of the estate, which were reasonably maintained, and she admired, despite herself, Mr. Crawford's taste in designing them. She wondered that a man of such intelligence, talent and ability should be so abandoned in character. She felt very alone at Everingham, if being surrounded by three dozen curious, gossiping servants can be called being alone.

After nearly a fortnight spent in this manner, the mild weather and the peace and solitude restored something of Fanny's health and spirits. She had not been called upon, as she had feared, to entertain neighbours, as the estate was truly secluded, with few in the surrounding villages claiming the rank of gentleman.

With some temerity, she decided to occupy her time by trying to learn if she, at not quite nineteen, could manage a country home. Her talents of observation served her well, as did her memories of the smooth, orderly harmony of Mansfield Park. Fanny thought too lowly of herself to resent any lack of attention and deference on the part of the servants, but she did disapprove of idleness and waste, as she regarded it as a species of theft, and so gradually and then more pointedly, she began to question the housekeeper, visit the offices, inspect the stores, ask for inventories of the plate, linen and etc. She observed many shoddy practices in her new home, and many wasteful doings to be investigated and corrected, and sometimes laughed aloud to think that what she had observed of her Aunt Norris, over the years, would aid her more effectually than any example set by her Aunt Bertram, who seldom troubled herself over any part of the management of Mansfield Park.

Her memory being excellent and her manner gentle, she soon learned the names of everyone who attended her, their duties and their histories, which endeared to her many, if not all, of her servitors. Those amongst her servants who would rather serve in a well-run house rejoiced at the advent of a mistress, and those who preferred to skulk in corners and cadge what they could, showed their resentment more pointedly. It was these last that she daringly thought she might dismiss when their year of service was up.

She learned from the steward, Mr. Maddison, who was all smiles and complaisance, about the neediest of Mr. Crawford's tenants, and directed that those in want of food and fuel be supplied from Everingham. She also finally steeled herself to appear in public, making her first appearance on Sunday morning at the village church. The townspeople marveled that for the first time in twelve years, a Crawford was in attendance in the family pew, and Fanny was, as she feared she would be, of more interest to the congregation than the sermon!

Then came some news which drew all of Fanny's solicitude back to her friends in Bristol and London — Mrs. Butters wrote with the shocking intelligence from her Bristol correspondents that William Gibson had been press-ganged. At first, his friends did not know what had befallen him — he had failed to return to his lodgings one evening, and almost a fortnight elapsed before the news escaped from an unfriendly quarter, that he had been seized by the press. His friends had applied to the local magistrates in great indignation — Mr. Thompson, in fact, was nearly arrested after brandishing his walking stick and bellowing imprecations at the authorities — and they had spoken to everyone they knew in any way related to the Navy, but he was not to be recovered. He was no longer being held in Bristol and no-one knew, or would reveal, where he had been dispatched. He could be on his way to the Caribbean for an absence of five years or more, or he could be held in some other port, awaiting assignment to one ship or another.

Fanny was disconsolate to think of Mr. Gibson, with all his accomplishments, being snatched off the streets and forced to become a common seaman, though she naturally regarded the Navy more benignly than did the Bristol abolitionists. She wrote an anxious letter to her brother, giving a description of Mr. Gibson and asking him to be on the lookout for her friend.

***

Blinking in the harsh sunlight after so many days held below decks, William Gibson was lined up with the other pressed men on deck, to be interviewed by a serious young lieutenant with what he supposed were midshipmen or clerks on either side of him. He listened as the men ahead of him were interviewed, until his turn came.

"Name?"

"William Frederick Gibson."

"Age?"

"Twenty-six."

"Place of birth?"

"Cambridgeshire."

"Occupation?"

"Writer."

"A writer? A writer of what?"

"Anti-slavery tracts, mostly. And poetry."

"Religion?"

Gibson was tempted to say 'none', just to see the expression on the lieutenant's face, but having watched the previous pressed men being interviewed, he knew there was only one acceptable answer, one which he refused to give. He prevaricated.

"My uncle, who raised me, was a clergyman."

"Begging your pardon, Mr. Bayly," said a voice behind Gibson. "But this man is a gentleman. He's no sailor."

"Silence! No-one is to speak unless spoken to."

Bayly scrutinized Gibson, who was wearing the same clothes he had been wearing more than a fortnight ago when he was seized off the streets in Bristol. Well, few gentlemen could look like gentlemen after such an ordeal.

"Are you, sir, a gentleman?"

Gibson had struggled for several days, locked in the hold with his conscience. The fact that he could put on a show of outrage, speak of having attended Cambridge, declare himself to be a gentleman in education, birth, breeding, everything but substance, and escape the fate of his fellow captives, struck him as a trial or a temptation comparable to that faced by St. Anthony. *He* might walk away; *they* could not. Neither could the Africans he had pledged his life to fight for.

"Well?" demanded Lieutenant Bayly. "Do you contend that you were impressed illegally?"

"*Civis romanus sum*, sir. But I contend that the fact of *my* being impressed, is not more unjust than the impressment of any of my fellows here." There! It was said, and he wanted to feel glorious and noble for having stood by his principles, but he felt tired, grubby, hungry, thirsty, and possibly foolish to the point of insanity.

A long cool stare from Bayly. Then -

"Any previous seagoing experience?"

"None."

"Will you volunteer?"

"No. No, thank you."

"Landsman Gibson, you are assigned to the West Africa Squadron. Many vacancies have arisen there. Dismissed."

Gibson turned around, expecting to see awe and respect in the eyes of the other pressed men, but most were watching him with looks of disgust or perplexity.

"What's that? He didn't try to get off — Now we've got to look after this lubber — touched in the head — you take care of him, I won't take him in my mess."

Gibson was unceremoniously shoved aside. His eyes were finally adjusting to the sunshine, but he saw to his dismay he was being taken below-decks again. He looked around for the friendly young Lieutenant Price, but he was nowhere to be found.

***

Sir Thomas was visiting his bankers, Mrs. Norris was gone to pay her morning visits, and Julia elected to stay home with Maria, who was feeling unwell. However, Maria made it clear that she desired nothing more than to be left alone, and Julia was descending the stairs to the parlour, hesitating between practicing on the piano, or writing a letter to her mother, when there came a knock at the front door, and, out of curiosity, she answered the summons herself.

She beheld a tall, broad-shouldered, suntanned young naval lieutenant, with a cheerful and open countenance, whom she had never seen before, yet there was something about him which was oddly familiar to her. She was taken aback, but also could not help returning the artless smile he bestowed upon her. It would be fair to say that each of the young people surveyed each other, and each was not displeased by what they saw.

"I beg your pardon, Miss — do I have the honour of addressing one of my Bertram cousins?" ventured William Price (for of course it was he).

"Oh! You are Cousin William! I mean — Mr. Price," Julia exclaimed, then reddened. "Do — please — " the lieutenant was ushered in with no further ceremony and shown to the parlour. She was briefly alarmed that she had perhaps greeted her cousin with more warmth than was proper, considering the vast gulf between the Bertrams and the Prices, but William Price was so unselfconscious in his manner, so free from either cringing

236

servility or assumed *hauteur*, that she soon was chatting with him without reserve.

Captain Henderson had kindly left him at Wimpole Street and his carriage would return in twenty minutes' time. The visitor declined all offers of tea, and there was but time to tell how Mr. Crawford's uncle had obtained his long-desired promotion, for which Julia congratulated him heartily, not even blanching at the mention of the name "Crawford," and she listened with great attention, though not much comprehension, to his animated description of the fifth-rate frigate *HMS Solebay*, the number of her guns, her dimensions, her history, the many ships she had captured in her past and his great fortune in being assigned to her, though she had been re-fitted and commissioned at least four times, to be sure, and probably would scarcely hold together when encountering a gale. Julia exclaimed against the possibility, which led to young Price's modest acknowledgment that he had lived through several hurricanes and a shipwreck, to say nothing of several engagements with the French, and at her invitation he was expanding on his adventures, when too soon, alas, the young people heard the sound of the hackney coach come to collect the young lieutenant and return him to his duty.

Julia then happily recalled that Fanny used to share some parts of William's letters with the family [William blushed to recollect how warmly he used to abuse Aunt Norris, and trusted that his sister had been discreet in which portions she read], and she surprised herself with the impulsive suggestion that he ought to correspond with his uncle, Sir Thomas, who, she was sure, would be pleased to hear from his nephew. William pronounced it a capital idea, as his uncle had in fact been his first benefactor, even before Henry Crawford. He promised to write regularly, and dared to hope that his uncle might have time to write him a line in reply, as letters were very precious things to sailors far from home, and with a final warm smile and a bow, he left his fair cousin.

Julia skipped upstairs, feeling more light-hearted than she had in weeks. Whether or not she ever saw that pleasant William Price again, the fact that he gave her heart a little flutter was proof that she was in a fair way of recovering from having it broke by Henry Crawford. She went into the bedchamber she shared with her sister and found Maria being sick into the washbasin.

"Whatever is the matter, Maria?"

Maria looked at her with despairing eyes. "Nothing. Some bad mussels, I think. I'm going to lie down now."

***

Dear Fanny, I am forwarding a letter from Mr. Gibson for your perusal, as I'm sure you would like to read of his adventures first-hand — Yours affectionately, H. Butters.

Apr 15 —

My dear Mrs. Butters,

Madam,

I am writing to you from the deck of the victualling ship, Agincourt, *currently at harbour in Portsmouth. Would you please inform our mutual friend, Miss Price, that I have now seen the ramparts of Portsmouth and the sea beyond and can confirm that it in no way resembles Heaven, at least not to my eyes. She will understand.*

The mystery of my impressment has now been unfolded to me — some of our merchant friends in Bristol, seeking revenge over the loss of their profitable trade in human souls across the Atlantic, and the corresponding end of their trade in trinkets and cloth to the corrupt African chiefs in exchange for the unhappy victims, paid a bribe for me to be abstracted from the streets.

However, Fate may have hoisted my persecutors on their own petard. They arranged for me to be swiftly transported to Portsmouth, evidently to thwart any efforts by my friends to effect my release, but in so doing, they put me in the way of being selected for the West Africa Squadron. Think of it — the merchants of Bristol have paid to send another man to help put an end to the diabolical slave traffic. Therefore, please inform our Bristol colleagues that I am growing daily more resigned to this unexpected adventure. For, imagine if you will, Ma'am, the account I could write for the public, once I have witnessed the reality of the slave trade in person! I feel, in all modesty, I could be of signal aid to our cause. Further, I shall be paid wages while I collect material for a book, and a man must live upon something, as I can attest, having attempted to live upon nothing for several years now.

I am no sailor, but I am trading on what little I have learned over the years just by breathing the sea air of Bristol and hearing the talk of nautical folk.

I know that you will keep me in your thoughts and I will write to you as events permit. And now for my most urgent request — may I beg you to send me, as swiftly as possible, a quantity of Jesuit bark? The more experienced sailors have impressed upon me the hazards of the miasmatic air of the

238

African coast, and the high probability that I may contract fever. That, and protecting my one pair of spectacles from being broken, are my chief concerns. A ream of paper or some notebooks would also be a godsend.

Thank you for your kind solicitude and also please tender my regrets to Miss Price, as we had planned to establish our own little circulating library, and exchange our thoughts by correspondence, which is now, alas, impossible unless the bluestocking females of the Ghana tribe write three-volume novels on coconut fronds. [Here, Mr. Gibson had written several lines but had crossed them out completely so they were impossible to read.]

your devoted servant, Wm. Gibson.

ps –. Apr 17 – This letter is being conveyed to London by my new friend, second lieutenant William Price. And to answer your next question – yes, he is. He is her brother. And he is a fine fellow, not yet one-and-twenty, cheerful, encouraging, and he has been extremely helpful to me and has prevented me from making many 'lubberly' errors which would have earned me the derision of my shipmates. He has informed me that his sister has recently married. Will you please tender her my congratulations on having exchanged uncertainty for certainty. And don't forget that you owe me a shilling. Wm. G.

***

Apr 21, at sea

Dear Fanny,

I trust this letter finds you happy and in the best of health, and Mr. Crawford likewise. I am still on the Agincourt *as I write this – I am sharing a wardroom with Lt. Bayly but expect to join my own ship within the month. We are sailing south at last to meet up with the* Solebay – *my ship – (with what pleasure can I write – "my ship!") – along with the sloop* Derwent, – *those two ships together comprise the entire mighty West African Squadron!*

The West African Squadron is charged with patrolling the coast, principally from Cape Verde to Benguela – I know my dear sister will consult an atlas – and stopping any English or French ships carrying enslaved Africans. We can't stop ships under other flags, you see, because our English laws don't apply, but we can stop English ships and the Frenchies as well because we are at war with them. This is why, do you know, that so many traders are using American ships now-a-days!

You can imagine my surprise when your letter informed me that we had a common acquaintance on board ship here. To think, you were in

Portsmouth and never knew that your friend Mr. Gibson was also there! He has been pressed into service – in fact, Lt. Bayly told me all about this curious fellow he had assigned to the Solebay, *before I ever knew he was your friend! He – Mr. Gibson that is – says you are a very thoughtful person, and said much in your praise. He's a splendid chap, good-natured and curious about everything but I have been at some pains to teach him that he mustn't talk or ask questions when he's on duty. The other able-bodies were hostile to him at first, but he has won them over – as he is so friendly and obliging and does not hold himself out as better than the others – he will write a letter home for any sailor who only knows how to mark his 'x' and, what do you think? He has offered to give me private lessons in Latin for free, or rather,* gratis. *I dined at the Captain's table for the first time last week, and rather wanted to crawl away and hide, as half the time the other officers were speaking to each other in Latin tags, and then the chaplain would turn to me and say, "Ain't that so, Price?" so I rather think he was trying to score a point off me. Gibson says he can teach me so I can* quid nunc *and* quid pro *with the best of them soon....*

We should make the Isle of Gorée (no, I never heard of it before, either!) by the middle of May, if all goes well...

Fanny had decided against engaging a lady's maid because she had come to regard the sanctuary of her bedchamber as a place where she could drop the mask of being the chatelaine of Everingham and become just Fanny Price again. It was there that she retreated to read what little private correspondence she did receive – from her brother or Mrs. Butters, for, though she daily hoped for a letter from Edmund, none arrived.

She was therefore alone in her room when she opened a note from Henry Crawford which brought the news of the union of Edmund and Mary. *While I was not myself at the ceremony, I can answer your undoubted anxiety that on that most essential point – the radiance of the bride. The bride herself assures me, she was a vision of modesty and beauty, all in white with a veil to match. The happy couple are now residing in Thornton Lacey....*

Fanny had again that strange floating sensation she had experienced the morning she quit Mansfield Park – she could see herself, as though from a great distance, standing in her bedroom by the window, holding the letter, looking out across the fields. She thought to herself she might faint, and when she didn't, she thought, *I am glad I never told him.*

Chapter Twenty-One

The day that Edmund Bertram took Mary Crawford to wife was the happiest of his life. Mary had declared she cared not a fig for a fashionable wedding at Hanover Square, as it would be injurious to the feelings of poor Maria and further, neither her brother nor the Admiral would attend; she was, against all expectations, a country bride in Mansfield with her sister, Mrs. Grant, as her only attendant. Nor did she condition for a bridal trip to Brighton or the Lake District; her new husband handed her into their smart new gig, a gift from Sir Thomas and his lady, to travel the short distance from Mansfield Park to take up their new lives in Thornton Lacey.

That night, Mary Bertram, as she was now, attired in a sheer night dress, her dark hair unpinned and flowing around her shoulders, lay in bed in their small bedchamber, awaiting her husband. She was nervous – and perhaps that was all to the good. Although her brother's coarse jests had angered her, the truth was that she must not betray any knowledge of what was to come.

Her new husband slipped into the room, and smiled at her as though he beheld an angel in his bed, and started to extinguish the candles, though he left a few burning which spread small soft pools of light, enough for her to admire him through half-lowered eyes. She saw that his hand was trembling slightly as he lifted the covers to slide in beside her.

"Mary," he said softly. "Let me hold you, my dear."

She moved into his arms and rested her head upon his chest. She wondered if she could unbutton his night shirt and stroke his bare skin, but decided to wait. *Ah, he was so handsome, so well-made. no! wait…. wait…. wait …lie still…*

He put his hand under her chin and tipped up her face to receive his gentle kiss. She kept her eyes lowered.

"Look at me," he whispered.

She looked up at him and saw the love shining in his eyes, a love without guile, a soul without secrets. *Oh Edmund. You lovely, lovely man.*

His breathing thickened as he brushed her hair back and pulled her closer for a more insistent, longer kiss. She melted against his body. Then he slowly untied the ribbon at the top of her gown. His slow, deliberate, gentle movements drove her wild with anticipation; she quivered with hunger for him.

"You're trembling! Don't be afraid, my love," he murmured in her ear. "I will be very careful and slow."

Ah, she thought she would go mad.

***

At Edmund's request, their families stayed away from his first sermon, but the pews were full of the curious, of course. Those of the congregants who preferred their clergymen to be tall, dark-haired, handsome and possessed of a pleasing, resonant voice, found nothing to complain of in the Reverend Bertram. His wife won general approbation for her pretty looks and her ready smiles.

"I am conscious of being far better reconciled to a country residence than I had ever expected to be," Mary wrote to her brother shortly after her wedding. *"I can even suppose it pleasant to spend half the year in the country, under certain circumstances, very pleasant. An elegant, moderate-sized house in the centre of family connexions; continual engagements among them; commanding the first society in the neighbourhood; looked up to, perhaps, as leading it even more than those of larger fortune, and turning from the cheerful round of such amusements to nothing worse than a tête-a-tête with the person one feels most agreeable in the world. There is nothing frightful in such a picture, is there?*

Alas, while it was no small source of gratification to know herself to be the first lady of refinement and gentility in her neighbourhood, Mary Bertram soon discovered that she had no acquaintance in Thornton Lacey whose society was not a punishment of some form or another. While most of the residents of the village kept a respectful distance from the vicar's wife, there were some prosperous farmers and a few merchants who fancied themselves not so far removed from the Bertrams in point of birth, manners or wealth, to make them at all reticent about paying a morning call on the bride, or extending invitations to their homes for tea or dinner, the prospect of which filled Mary with dismay.

The alterations to the parsonage afforded Mary with an excuse for refusing most of the unwanted solicitations – until she could return hospitality in kind, she was resolute in declining it, but many a farmer's muddy boots disgraced her parlour floor and many a gossiping housewife had to be endured nonetheless. She philosophized that such minor irritations were to be preferred to the *ennui* of having only the servants for company, and hoped that the end of the Season in London might bring more eligible families within visiting distance to their part of the country.

She attempted to content herself with the novelty of managing her own household, overseeing the alterations to the house and the yard, and spending whatever time with her husband that he could spare from his duties. Together, they become acquainted with their parish through walks and horseback rides, until they could count every cottage and name every family that dwelt therein.

Mary's chief source of happiness derived from the knowledge that her husband adored her, was proud of her, and delighted in her company. To commence married life in the country in the springtime, was surely a recipe for contentment.

***

Although she was unable to make anyone her true confidante, Fanny nonetheless yearned for a companion, and she formed the wish of inviting her sister Susan to come and stay with her. The letter was dispatched – the offer joyfully accepted – monies were provided – and Fanny's father himself, finding it no hardship to leave his fireside when his married daughter was paying the fare, brought Susan to Everingham within three weeks of Mr. Crawford's quitting it. Her father stayed long enough to admire the home, sample its wine cellar, observe that the servants were all a pack of idle, shiftless thieves, and then returned to the familiar haunts of Portsmouth, there to boast of his well-married daughter.

The arrival of Susan, with her energetic disposition, gave Fanny many funds of gratification. She could think of someone other than herself, by seeing to Susan's comfort and enjoyment. At first it was enough to watch as Susan reveled in the beauty, the air, the light and freedom of the country in the springtime, and to laugh as her sister ate her fill of whatever the cook put in front of them (and it was no surprise that she rated the cook much higher than did Fanny.)

Fanny soon realized, to her surprise, that Susan looked up to her, and wanted to acquire her elder sister's quiet ladylike manner, and no tutor could be kinder and more patient than Fanny in smoothing away Susan's little rusticities while teaching, chiefly by illustration, the arts of courtesy and feminine deportment. Nor could any young girl fail to be delighted by being provided for with a new wardrobe, shoes and bonnets. Fanny of course derived far greater pleasure in giving these things to Susan than she had felt when Mr. Crawford purchased her wedding clothes.

Susan was amused and delighted with Fanny's short hair, and offered to trim it herself, as she had, for several years, served as the family barber for

243

her younger brothers. She then resolved to cut her own hair off likewise, releasing the soft curls which both sisters were favoured with. "You said you don't want a lady's maid, so you have no-one to dress your hair at any rate," Susan reasoned. "You can keep it cropped, as we shall always wear our bonnets in church and in company, and you can wear your married lady's caps while at home." Fanny had grown accustomed to her shorn hair style and even suspected that it flattered her.

Because Susan's eyes were upon her, Fanny was forced to exert herself. Susan was direct, impatient and curious – when Fanny lamented the over-rich fare and wished she could have something simpler, her sister asked her, *then why don't you say so*? Susan forced Fanny to confront her own foolish timidity and her fear of giving offense to anyone, even her own servants.

Fanny was candid enough to acknowledge that her younger sister had qualities that she lacked – among them a good head for figures – and together they began to establish, in fits and starts, a new regime at Everingham. It was a joint project they undertook, at first out of motives of imposing better order and thrift, then out of increasing sensations of pride and accomplishment. They pored over the account books for the estate, marveling at how much in the way of butter and eggs, wine and meat, candles and fuel had been consumed while the master was not in residence. It was Susan who discovered that many of the servants were relations of the steward, Mr. Maddison – in fact, most of the servitors at Everingham were supplied from the ranks of his nieces and nephews and cousins, and many of them, in the frequent absence of Mr. Crawford, were obliged to work for the steward in *his* residence, although of course their wages were paid by Everingham. Then came the day when one upper housemaid guilelessly revealed to Susan that she had to turn over a portion of her wage to Mr. Maddison to thank him for having found her employment!

Fanny resolved to speak seriously to Mr. Crawford, when she next saw him, about some needed reforms that she believed should only be undertaken by him, but in the meantime, she and Susan took the greatest pleasure in observing the gradual amendment in the manners and activity of the servants, the improvement in the comforts of their home and the small economies made on behalf of their absent host.

Susan attributed Fanny's occasional fits of mental abstraction to the continued absence of her husband Mr. Crawford, and kindly refrained from mentioning him, as Fanny appeared to derive no comfort from the subject.

***

May, Isle of Gorée....

To Sir Thomas Bertram,

Dear Sir,

I trust this letter finds you and all of your family well. My sister Fanny often wrote to me of her anxieties for your health, during that period of time when you were resident in Antigua. I myself served briefly in the West Indies, and now that I and my fellow shipmates are arrived at the African coast, I fully apprehend her concerns about the insalubrious climate, and the enervating heat of the Tropicks, which has a most enervating effect upon the crew. May your nephew prove to have as strong a constitution as his uncle, and return to England the better and wiser for this experience and may the words of Horace, Caelum non animum mutant qui trans mare currunt, *not apply to him!*

I am finally aboard my ship, the HMS Solebay, *and very content to be under so good a commander as Captain Columbine. He is a man of science as well as a mariner, being a hydrographer who surveyed the island of Trinidad. We are currently anchored at the Isle of Gorée, undergoing some repairs to the ship, as best as can be contrived so far from home. We are then to proceed to Sierra Leone, where Captain Columbine will assume the office of governor there.*

Our officers dined with the commander of the British garrison here, and he informed us that the French have an outpost nearby in the Gambia River from whence they send privateers to harass our shipping....

..... to close with my most sincere thanks, sir, for everything you have done for me, my sister Fanny and my family. Will you please give my respects to Lady Bertram and the Misses Bertram. I hope to have the honour, sir, of calling upon you and your family upon my return to England.

Your nephew and devoted servant,

Lt. William Price

"Pretty good, Price," said William Gibson. "You have used 'enervating' twice, but taken as a whole, a fine letter."

The two Williams were enjoying a rare moment of peace, sheltering from the sun under a small tarpaulin, in a little corner of the deck which was designated the schoolroom aboard the *HMS Solebay*. Their table was an empty crate and their seats were cut down barrels, and the schoolroom walls consisted of wire cages stuffed with chickens destined for the officer's table. Their rustling and clucking provided a running commentary on the efforts of Lt. Price. He didn't complain about the distraction because after all, he would have the last word – or rather, the last bite.

"Here is another one for you, Price: *causa latet, vis est notissima* – 'the cause is hidden, but the result is well known'. You are learning Latin, you told me, to converse with your brother officers, but perhaps there is another reason – perhaps, you wish to impress a certain uncle, who is father to a certain young lady....."

William Price grinned. "It's like that fellow you told me about – that fellow who wrote *War in Disguise*. He saw that people can have more than one motive for doing a thing."

"Mr. Stephen. Yes. Clever fox – he saw that Parliament could not be persuaded to outlaw the trade in slaves for moral reasons. So, he made the French slave trade a *casus belli*, if you will –

"A *casus bell-eye*?"

"Look it up in your grammar, Mr. Price. First, Parliament made it illegal for we English to have anything to do with the French slave trade – to hurt Napoleon. From there, the Abolitionists in Parliament were able to outlaw the English trade as well. Why does Parliament vote the funds for the West African Squadron to patrol the coastline here, when you might suppose that no ships could be spared from the war with the French? Perhaps the actions of His Britannic Majesty's government are entirely benevolent. Or perhaps, there is this advantage to be gained by driving the French and their slave ships from the coast of Africa. England's navy will control this entire coastline, which means that our ships will have a monopoly on palm oil and ground nuts and other trade items which are becoming more valuable."

"Such as ivory," added William Price. "And perhaps even some of their curious manufactures. I have a small statue I bought in Gibraltar off of a chap who had rounded the Horn, I must show it to you."

"I should be more grateful if you had anything at all to read, lieutenant. Anything besides your Latin grammar and the *Young Midshipman's Instructor*, that is."

"Sorry, Gibson. I have owned some books coming and going, but the only thing I keep with me is my sister's letters. As a matter of fact, I have the letter she wrote which describes her first meeting with you in Bristol."

"Oh, indeed?"

***

The calendar proclaimed that summer reigned, but the London skies were overcast and gloomy. Sir Thomas had returned to his study on Wimpole Street, and was reviewing the terms of his sale of the majority of his Antigua properties, when a timid rap at the door was followed by the entrance of his daughter Maria, whose countenance caused him to set down his papers and focus his attention on her with the alarm of a truly fond and affectionate parent. She had not been in good looks or temper since that day when she read of Crawford's marriage to Fanny; but he had hoped to see, by this time, some improvement in her health and spirits.

"Father….." Maria began, with a voice and manner so truly agitated, so expressive of despair, that Sir Thomas could not keep his seat, and came forward to take her hand, press it affectionately, and offer her a chair. These small tokens of kindness undid her completely, and she began to weep. To his amazement, she sank to the floor at his feet, crying, "Forgive me! Oh father, do not abandon me now!"

Sir Thomas could not bring himself to utter the awful presentiment that occurred to his mind. It was too terrible a thing to pronounce, and he shrank from asking, in the forlorn hope that it was some other distress which thus brought his daughter, penitent, to her knees before him.

"Maria, what is it? What is the matter?" Was all he could bring himself to say. But his hopes, and very nearly his reason itself, were to be shattered, as his daughter, unable to look at him, uttered through her sobs…

"Oh, father! Oh, father! I am carrying Henry Crawford's child!"

A long silence followed as Sir Thomas struggled to regain his composure. A black tide of misery swept over father and daughter alike, she struggling with shame and fear, he with anger and sorrow. If Sir Thomas had been applied to the day before and asked, what was to be done if a daughter of good family had sacrificed her virtue, he would have answered unhesitatingly that death was to be preferred to a dishonour so complete, comprehending as it did the reputation of the family, the happiness of its members, the respectability of all of its daughters, and the defiance of a morality whose strictures he had endeavoured to live by and imbibe in his children.

But as Maria had not spontaneously expired under the disgrace of her condition, as she lived, and would live, and so in time, might bring forth a living child, Sir Thomas's thoughts rapidly turned to where he might send her to reside until she was safely delivered, and to consider where she might live hereafter.

"Maria, I trust you understand that it is impossible for you to ever live under the same roof with your sister again," he began, and Maria nodded, remaining where she was, eyes downcast, at his feet. "We will spare no exertion and there will be no loss of time in making those arrangements which are necessary. You will be provided with a secluded but comfortable lodging in some neighbourhood where the name of 'Bertram' is unknown. You could represent yourself as being the wife of a ship's officer – should you be forced to converse with anyone, which, under any circumstances, I advise strongly against. But the servants I shall engage for you will be so informed. Heaven help you to uphold this necessary deception! You will be provided with sufficient funds, of course, as would be consistent with your pretended station in life. But...."

Maria shuddered, and waited, head bowed, for the lacerating tongue of her father to outline, in his formal and measured way, why she was a disgrace to the name of Bertram, how he wished she had never been born, and how she was never to address him as 'father' again, when an unusual sound caught her ear. She looked up and beheld to her astonishment that her father was weeping! He gathered her up in his arms and said, "You asked me to consent to your marriage to Mr. Crawford, more than once you beseeched me – I refused, repeatedly. Had I acquiesced, you would now be honourably married, albeit to a man I must forever regard with detestation. I knew he was an unprincipled cad – but never did I suspect the depths of his depravity! Your happiness and credit were my only consideration, my Maria!"

Father and daughter wept together, then, after looking in the hallway to see that no servants were about, Sir Thomas led Maria back to her bedchamber, where with his own hands he helped her to pack her travelling trunks.

To completely conceal the truth of what was happening would most likely be impossible. The servants who had waited on Maria these past few months might be in the secret of it, perhaps Julia also. But everything that speed and discretion could do, would be done. He and Maria left London together, by post, and he arrived at Mansfield Park eight days later, alone. The story was given out that she was staying with friends at the seaside to recover her health and spirits after the failure of her second engagement within the span of six months. The necessity for dissimulation to his household, to friends and neighbours, to his own wife and his own family, sickened Sir Thomas until he wondered whether his constitution could withstand the shock and horror of it.

248

Tom Bertram was dispatched to bring Julia home, as Sir Thomas was disposed to gather what remained of his family around him. It was a more sober and generous Julia who returned home after her season in London. Henry Crawford had wounded her, but she had pride and spirit enough to recover, and though the experience was dearly bought, she felt the wiser for it. She came away with vows of eternal friendship and promises of faithful correspondence from some of the other young ladies she'd met during the Season. Home now wore a more attractive aspect; her mother greeted her with something approaching animation and pleasure, and Julia was ready, after the late hours and bustle of London, for country air, horse-riding, and long walks.

In the ensuing days, the household servants understood it was best to avoid Sir Thomas, to exit through one door if he entered at another, to keep their eyes to the floor if passing him in the hallway, and to move about their tasks in utter silence. Some suspected the reason for his severity – and some remembered the housemaid, Sarah, who had been dismissed from service and publicly disgraced by this same Sir Thomas a few months before. Did the master of the house ever spare a thought for her?

Sir Thomas reflected that Maria had kept her dread secret to herself, until *after* the wedding of Edmund and Mary, so as not to alloy the happiness of that occasion. Sir Thomas' anger at Henry Crawford in no way comprehended his new daughter-in-law Mary. She was sweet, virtuous, and loving and not to be compared with Crawford, who no doubt was making his niece Fanny's life miserable. Crawford of course, was not to be found – he was thought to be at Brighton, then at the races at Newmarket. Accusation or reparation was futile now that he was a married man and public disgrace would only fall upon Maria should her secret become known.

Sir Thomas' implacable anger, without that immediate object before him, was diffused and general; it comprehended Henry Crawford, Maria, himself – for his failings as a father – and, after a few days of consideration, Mrs. Norris as well. She had been supposed to be Maria's particular chaperone when in London – how imperfectly had she discharged her duties! Yet he could not relieve his feelings by questioning her minutely about Maria's comings and goings, nor by condemning her to her face, for he wished to keep Maria's disgrace a secret even from Mrs. Norris, if not particularly from Mrs. Norris, for the woman could not guard her tongue at any time.

Sir Thomas had a sudden inspiration; to offer, in such terms as left his sister-in-law without the power of refusal, to send her for that long-desired visit to see her 'dear sister Price' in Portsmouth. An industrious, managing woman such as herself might be a positive benefit to the Prices, but even if it were not so, even if she proved to be as great a plague to the Prices as she had been to the Bertrams, he cared not. He heartily wished her gone, and so she was gone, very soon after he had formed the idea, sent by post chaise to take up her abode with her sister and family. He ensured that her stay would be a long one by informing her that, to his very great regret, he must begin charging rent for the White house, but should she find a respectable tenant, she could keep half the proceeds for so long as she lived elsewhere! The speed and alacrity with which Mrs. Norris found and installed her tenant and packed her trunks for Portsmouth proved an object lesson in how swiftly persons will act, when a way to appeal to their self-interest may be found.

Sir Thomas thereby obtained a not inconsiderable benefit to himself and his household, and if he had known of the degree of rejoicing in the servants' hall when the news reached their ears, he would have been enlightened as to how cordially the woman had been detested by his faithful servitors. Christopher Jackson laughed and offered to build a bonfire in the lower meadow, and the housekeeper looked the other way when a ration of wine was poured out for both the upper and lower tables and "May God keep Mrs. Norris" was proposed, and no-one needed to add the old tag, "far away from us," for everyone understood.

Thus this blackest of all black clouds proved to have a silver lining.

***

William Gibson dropped a heavy armful of wet branches and roots, wrestled from the mangrove swamps, into the cutter and straightened his aching back, while sucking in a lungful of the muggy, heavy air. Rivers of sweat streamed into his eyes. Shore duty was one of the few manual tasks he could perform without getting tangled up in ropes, or striking his head on a low beam, in other words, without dangerously injuring himself or others. He had not shown himself unwilling to work, but the combination of his height, poor eyesight, and inability to adapt to the heat had held him back from acquiring the requisite skills of an able seaman. Nevertheless, his fellow sailors had grown fond of him, working together to protect him from the worst errors, and laughing at him for the rest. He gave himself no airs, he asked for no special treatment.

Captain Columbine swiftly sized up the earnest young scribbler and appointed him as the ship's schoolmaster, in charge of teaching geometry and geography to the young midshipman and cabin boys, for the previous schoolmaster had been a worthless drunk who had died of putrid fever. Captain Columbine also called on Gibson's talents as a clerk, and soon Gibson had enough honest work wielding a pen or drumming the rudiments of antipodal points into young minds to excuse him from most other duties.

No-one escaped shore party duty, however, and as Gibson and his mess mates rowed back to the *Solebay* with fuel and full water barrels, he tried to take what pleasure he could in the blueness of the sky and the green glimmer of the waves. They were leaving behind the sandy beaches that were so white they hurt his eyes, and the innumerable hordes of tiny biting insects which descended in a cloud on the mariners as they collected fresh water at the riverbank. Away from the shore, one could almost persuade oneself that the sea breezes brought some infinitesimal relief from the smothering heat. Gibson's habit was to think back to his days as a young child, in his old bedroom at his uncle's rectory on a January morning, performing his ablutions with ice water, his feet and hands numb, his teeth chattering aloud– and he would gladly have exchanged places with himself, if only for a few moments.

The *Solebay* was still anchored at the Isle of Gorée whilst Captain Columbine was in conference with Major Maxwell, commander of the British garrison. The topic of the meeting was the cause of much muttered speculation amongst the crew. The sailors who were already on board the *Solebay* before Lieutenant Price and William Gibson had joined them were bitter in the failure of the expedition to find any slave ships to intercept in the vast expanse they patrolled, for only by doing so would they win prize money. Gibson was disappointed as well, for without seeing a slave ship with his own eyes, the narrative of his life as a sailor would be to very little purpose for the abolitionist cause.

Regaining the ship, he joined some of the men bathing in the sea, protected from drowning by a large net draped over the sides. The plunge into the ocean brought a few moment's relief from the heat, that is, until he exerted himself to climb back aboard ship again. There he spotted Second Lieutenant Price looking excited, obviously the recipient of important news, and had to remind himself to say nothing until spoken to, until he and Price were off duty.

251

Gibson could not imagine what could transpire out of the ordinary for the *Solebay* and her crew, but he was not to be in suspense for long; he was summoned to Captain Columbine's cabin to write out orders for the rest of the naval ships anchored at the garrison: The fleet was to join forces with the garrison soldiers, travel up the Gambia River and attack and wipe out the French settlement of St. Louis, one hundred miles upstream.

Soon, the ship's cannons would be fired in earnest, and they would be fired upon, in their turn.

That night, Gibson wrote: *every schoolboy of my acquaintance, not excluding myself, thrilled to tales of battles, of heroism and glory. As the good doctor himself said, 'Every man thinks meanly of himself for not having been a soldier, or not having been at sea.' But faced with the reality, would I rather think meanly of myself, or instead, face cannon, grapeshot, bayonets and cutlasses, before this week is out? Do my fellow ship mates feel the alarms, the regrets, the anxieties that I cannot reason myself out of? They, poor souls, are an exceedingly superstitious tribe, seeing omens in the clouds, or if a bird lights on the rigging, or even if someone absent-mindedly whistles while on board. They attribute their misfortunes, after the fact, to the indubitable sign that appeared prior to the catastrophe. While in my mechanical universe, it is largely a matter of chance whether or not I am mowed down by grapeshot or stop a musket ball or a bayonet blade. How fortunate for me that I have no choice in the matter, so I will never know what I might do to escape this trial!*

I am also paying the penalty for the independence of my habits, and my neglect and indifference of family ties, for I find myself wondering – if I do fall, who would be there to mourn for and remember me? Oh indeed, I can count many people as friends and comrades, but solicitude for myself compels me to ask, is there anyone on this vast sphere for whom my death would occasion more than passing regret?

***

June 25, 1809
To Lady Bertram:
Dear Maria:
One day I may find it in myself to forgive Sir Thomas for sending our Sister to live amongst us, but that day is still a distant one! She is being her intolerable Self, that I remember from our Girlhood days. It tries my Nerves to the greatest degree that Elizabeth will always remark unkindly upon the most trifling matters, and must have Everything done to her satisfaction!

Rebekah has given her Notice rather than bear with it and will leave us at Michaelmas – I was planning to Dismiss her myself at any rate, but it is still most Provoking to find oneself no longer Mistress of one's own Household! ! My Husband goes abroad even more than usual, to seek some respite from her carping Tongue.

She has not offered us so much as a farthing toward the cost of her Bread and Board, by the way, but nonetheless finds fault with every meal laid before her. I told her plainly that if she wants better Beef and more Sugar, she must reach into her own Purse to procure it.

As disordered and harassed as I am, I must take some Pains to relate a most extraordinary Incident which occurred yesterday. Sir Thomas will, no doubt, read of it in the News Papers, and will be anxious on our behalf, so I assure you that we are all Alive and Well – that is, we still have our heads and limbs attached to our bodies, which is more than –

– but I am getting ahead of my Tale. Your Sister and I, and my Boys, were walking along the foreshore on Point Beach yesterday morning, for she wished to go to the Post Office – but we first turned down to the beach because Tom and Charles clamoured to see the 8th Regiment, who were embarking for the Isle of Jersey.

The soldiers and their followers were all camped along the shore, in the greatest Disarray and Confusion. We were in the midst of this Throng, and I was determining that we had best come away, owing to the disreputable appearance of many of the Wives, Laundresses and what-have-yous following the Regiment, when our Sister spied a young Woman, great with child, with an older infant hanging in a sling on her back and leading yet two more young children with both hands (such a picture as I myself presented in the early days of my Marriage, alas! I feel immensely weary just recalling it!)

"What, Sarah! What brings you here!" Our Sister accosted her.

And the saucy wench answered her most Disrespectfully, saying that she herself, our Sister, was the Reason she found herself there. It appears that through some Indiscretion she had lost her Position with you and Sir Thomas, and she subsequently had fled to her Brother, a Corporal in the 8th, having No-where else to go, and through his Good Offices she had recently been taken under the Protection of one of his comrades, a newly-widowed Sergeant with three young Children.

Our Sister fell to haranguing the girl and abusing her for the practise of smoking Tobacco – for she had a clay Pipe clenched in her teeth – until I grew weary of listening and interposed:

"Pray, Sister, do not trouble yourself about the ways of Soldiers' wives. Tobacco has many medicinal qualities and it will carry away hunger when there is no meal to be had. This young person is off your hands – are we, your own Family, not enough for you to scold, without tormenting those who have Nothing to do with you?"

At which, this Sarah laughed and said that interfering in other people's business was all that Mrs. Norris ever had done and that she, our Sister, was a crotchety old b—tch (and some other terms too vulgar to relate). And with that she sauntered away, still Laughing. This Impertinence disconcerted our Sister not a little, especially as my own boys were also laughing heartily, and I could not find it in my Heart to rebuke them.

We repaired to the Post Office, where our Sister mailed a letter to you, I believe – no doubt full of remarks about my management of my own household – and we were just regaining the sidewalk when a tremendous noise, followed by a great blast of Wind, nearly deafened us and knocked us off our feet. The Windows of every building in the street were Shattered – fortunately our hats and capes sheltered us from any Injury from the falling glass – but then the most frightful, unlooked-for thing occurred – a human Leg, a severed Leg, fell from the sky and dropped on the pavement right in front of our Sister, splattering her with Gore!

Her Constitution is such that she did not faint – and neither did I – but she was robbed of the power of speech and movement for some time. We led her Home and she has been a-bed ever since, and I have urged her to Remain there, as you may well suppose, and would gladly bribe an Apothecary to advise her not to stir for a Fortnight, had I the means to do so.

To return to the Incident, we at first feared an Invasion by the French, as you may imagine, and were in the greatest Perturbation for some time, but my husband, seeking out his informants in the Dockyard, returned with the Intelligence that the infernal noise was caused by the accidental alighting of a vast quantity of Gunpowder amongst the stores of the 8th Regiment. It is said that the spark came from a pipe of one of the soldiers' wives, who knocked her pipe out against the stones on the shale because it would not draw. Some of the lit tobacco fell out and chanced to ignite some loose cartridges, which exploded and in turn ignited a quantity of barrelsful of Powder, with the deadly result – more than a Score of persons killed, and Scores more injured!

I do not know of the Fate of your former Servant as I am too much occupied with care and concern for my own household to seek further particulars about her. Had we not come away when we had, we might well have been blown to Oblivion, and as heartily as I thank Providence for our Preservation, my nerves are too disordered for me to dress and attend Divine Services this morning. Thank Heavens I left my little Betsey at home yesterday to watch our Servants and she was spared the ghastly sight! Whenever I close my eyes I can see that severed limb on the pavements in front of me, and I pray the Shocking spectacle will cause no lasting damage to the Constitutions of my poor darling boys. They are running up and down the Stairs as I speak, causing me to have a most frightful Headache, and in consequence, I shall conclude and sign myself,

Your Martyred Sister,

Frances Price

***

As the summer advanced, so Edmund Bertram advanced in confidence in his new role as clergyman. He had feared that he was too young to give advice to the aged, too sedate to captivate his youngest parishioners, and too diffident to command attention from the pews, but as the weeks went by he began to wear his new responsibilities naturally and lightly. His wife, alas, with her rapidity of understanding and impatience of boredom, began to feel, and to show, that she was already growing tired of the confines of the parish and the unvarying routine of country life. She felt, too, with some resentment, that every eye in the village was upon her, and making note if she arose late, or did nothing all day but read novels and play the harp.

Owing to the alterations to the landscape and the principal rooms as proposed by her brother, there was, as yet, no garden for her to enjoy — she was surrounded by an acre of mud and disorder without, and sawdust and noise and loose planks within. Unexpected expenses arose as well, for the removal of the farm-yard necessitated the digging of a new well, and the projected costs for the improvements proved to be easily twice what Henry had calculated.

Mary's temper suffered as a result, and she was not infrequently disposed to quarrel over trifles. Edmund winced when he heard her scolding the servants and arguing with the tradesmen over their bills. Nor was he spared the sharp edge of her tongue. Sadly, she and her husband had very different modes of disputation — she could speak cuttingly one moment, in a brief flight of anger, then, having relieved her feelings, resume her wonted cheerfulness, as though nothing had occurred. But

Edmund was of a different stamp – he was his father's son – he loathed quarrelling, and would leave a room rather than betray any loss of composure, and after the storm clouds had passed, he felt no small difficulty in laying aside the remembrance of his wife's unkind language. He reflected, with some regret, that their dispositions were very different in this respect, and here were two temperaments that, although opposed, were not always conjoined in mutual sympathy.

Barely six weeks after entering into Thornton Lacey, Mary proposed that she pay a trip to London to choose wallpapers and draperies for their home, and because the lease on the house on Wimpole Street had not yet expired, Sir Thomas was happy to indulge his new daughter-in-law by placing it at her disposal.

***

Mansfield Park, July 29

My dear sister Norris,

Do not be alarmed at the receipt of this letter, even though it is not a fortnight since I last wrote you. But I have some news to impart, which I make no doubt, will surprise you. Edmund has informed us that Mary has extended the lease on the townhouse in Wimpole Street, and intends to live in the city, at least until the alterations are finished at Thornton Lacey. Mary has assured me their home is quite intolerable because of the alterations now in hand, so I will defer my visit to Edmund's new parish until all of that is done with.

Edmund has given his consent for Mary to do as she wishes, and he will divide his time between city and country, travelling up to London at least twice a month. I am not a little astonished at this – what think you, Sister? I own that I cannot help reflecting, I would never have thought to go abroad without Sir Thomas by my side.

It is almost a full three months since you have been living in Portsmouth with our sister Price and her family. I am sure you are very often thought of here at Mansfield – yesterday I overheard Baddeley remark to one of our footman, who had chanced to drop a plate, that he was sure you heard the sound of the plate shattering on the floor, all the way in Portsmouth! Although your hearing is remarkably acute, especially for your age, I fancy he was speaking in jest.

In the absence of yourself, Fanny, and my oldest daughter, I remain quite desolate for want of company. Dear Mrs. Grant from the Parsonage is a frequent visitor. Speaking of hardships, I trust that you are completely recovered from the dreadful calamity that befell you last month, which I shudder to recall.

The weather continues remarkably fine, and Pug and I have sat outdoors more than once this month to enjoy it, when it is not too hot. However, I greatly fear that you cannot say the same, living as you are close by the docks with all of their dreadful odours. I remember how I used to dread the heat of the summer months in Huntingdon! Heat disagrees with me terribly.

Please give my love to my sister Price and her family. How many of them are still at home?

Yours affectionately,

M. Bertram

Mrs. Norris had not allowed the ill-temper of her sister Price to dissuade her from directing and managing the children and servants of the Price household – mere peevishness from her hostess would not prevent that worthy lady from carrying out what was most evidently any Christian woman's duty – but after three months amongst them, Mrs. Norris felt that she had done all that one woman could do. To the unfeigned relief of the Prices, Mrs. Norris took the unprecedented step of travelling from Portsmouth to London at her own expense, in anticipation of returning to Northamptonshire in her nephew's carriage – after a pleasant sojourn with Mary Bertram in London. The new bride could undoubtedly benefit from the advice of an older and wiser head. She arrived at Wimpole Street in early August with all her luggage, in good time to dress and then join her nephew and his wife for dinner.

Very pleased at being back in the fashionable world, Mrs. Norris was merrier than usual over her wine, and spoke confidingly to Mary, as though the two of them shared a private joke.

"Mary, I believe it is only a year ago last month that you and your brother first came to Mansfield Park, is it not? And how long was it after that, when Edmund made you a proposal?"

"I asked Mary to become my wife only last March, Aunt Norris," replied her nephew. "Mary and I are not advocates of long engagements!"

"But you two had an understanding *long before that*, did you not?" And she nodded meaningfully at Mary. "Last autumn?"

"I am fortunate that not everyone has your penetration, ma'am," exclaimed Mary with a smile. "I had thought, last autumn, that the depth of my regard for your nephew was known only to myself."

"And I ardently wished for Mary to be my wife from that time," added Edmund, "but had not the courage to declare myself."

"Oh, no need to be so coy," said Mrs. Norris. "Many persons form an understanding upon a few weeks' acquaintance. It was not, of course, the case with Mr. Norris and myself. I had known him for many years before determining upon marriage with him. But, truly, I have a romantic nature at heart, and so, when I discovered your letter to Fanny – "

"My letter, ma'am?" asked Mary, her smiles vanishing.

"Yes, your letter which I found in that den of disorder which my poor sister Price calls her home. Before I left, you may be sure that I saw everything scrubbed and scoured and set to rights, from cellar to garret. I found some letters in the attic, including some letters to Fanny, one from my sister Bertram, and one from you, Mary," she nodded to Mary.

"Ah, I think I recall the letter you speak of. We thought Fanny had decamped to Portsmouth but she had in fact, deceived everyone on that point. I had written a few lines to her at Portsmouth. What became of that letter, ma'am?" asked Mary, in indifferent tones.

"Why, as the seal was broken, I read it myself and I must congratulate you, Mary, on your perception. You saw through Fanny's machinations, as no-one else has."

"Oh, please say nothing of it, ma'am. Will you have some more *ragout*?"

"No, there is no need to be modest, my dear Mary. I *will* speak of it." It was clear that their guest had been eager to unfold this topic, and had only waited until they were all seated at dinner to bring it forward. Turning to Edmund, Mrs. Norris added eagerly, "Fanny had written you a letter upon quitting the house, had she not? A very sly, insinuating letter, I gather, isn't that so?" Before Edmund could reply in the negative, Mrs. Norris went on. "Well, your future wife understood that this so-called farewell letter was actually an invitation to an assignation in disguise. Fanny wanted you to chase after her, to find her, because she had the presumption to aspire to be – your wife! Moreover, Mary quite rightly shamed Fanny for her lack of gratitude to your father and us all. It is all there in Mary's letter. Here," and to Mary's horror, she pulled a much-crumpled note out of her pocket and handed it to Edmund, who took it gravely.

"This is my wife's private correspondence with my cousin?"

"Oh, that doesn't signify – I was reading it quite unawares, I do assure you, before I saw who it was from. But do read it, and congratulate yourself that your future wife warned Fanny off in no uncertain terms. Didn't I always say that Fanny was always trying to put herself forward? To form such a design on you, Edmund, is the height of mercenary ambition, and only someone as presumptuous as Fanny could have thought herself capable of succeeding in it. And of course," Mrs. Norris nodded at Mary, "you preserved Edmund from her designs but then your own brother was not proof against her ambitious schemes. I believe that she would marry any man of means who would have her, you know."

Increasingly perplexed, Edmund was preparing to hand the letter, unread, to his wife, when he beheld her expression. He paused, and gently asked, "Is there any reason, my dear, why you would wish me not to read this letter?"

Mary coloured, "I believe, Edmund, that you and I, for some time, have not shared quite the same opinion about Fanny, so my letter may cause you some pain. On that account, I ask you to return it to me, as many events have occurred since then, and none of us are the persons that we were last autumn, when that little note was written. I can barely recall what it said, at any rate." Edmund held it out to her, feeling it only right, and Mary, with every show of casual indifference, was about to take it, when Mrs. Norris, leaning forward, snatched it back.

"Then allow me to read it to you now, Mary! You were so correct in what you said!"

"Pray don't trouble yourself, ma'am. Please, allow me to help you to some roast vegetables."

"Hmmm….. hmmmm. Here: '*Edmund has shown me the letter you left for him upon your departure from Mansfield Park, Fanny, and as a friend, I must caution you that although you may think that your wishes and your designs are too subtle to be detected, both Edmund and I see through your feeble plotting. Therefore, you will* not *see Edmund follow you to Portsmouth, and you will not enjoy any private* tête-à-tête *with him, for he is astonished at your presumption in supposing that he would ever think of you in any other light than as a member of an inferior branch of the family.*' Oh, well said, Mary!"

"A letter from Fanny to me – that I showed to you, Mary?" said Edmund slowly and quietly.

Mrs. Norris ignored the interruption, exulting that Fanny's character was exposed at last: "Let's see…. ah, yes: '*I write to you candidly as a friend and, soon to be a relation of yours, for Edmund has chosen me as his future partner, in despite of your efforts to blacken my character to him, as your letter so clearly evidences. Your arrogance in presuming to give advice to Edmund on the question of whom he ought to marry is of a piece with your mistaken notions of your place in the family.'* Too true, Mary, didn't I always say so, she was forever imagining that she was the same as dear Maria or dear Julia. Well. I wish she *had* received your letter, Mary, and profited by it."

And so on and on spoke Mrs. Norris, who did not perceive, by Edmund's grave silence and Mary's lowered eyes, that a dangerous and silent conversation was unravelling between her host and hostess.

"This would be a letter which Fanny left for me in…. the East Room, where you, Mary, were so good as to go in search of her, after we had first discovered her to be missing?" Edmund could not resist asking, as he endeavoured to keep his voice as level as possible.

Mary looked back at him defiantly. "If there is any point of confusion about those events which occurred so many months ago, I can assure you that whatever I did, was done for the best. Now, I pray, both of you will excuse me. I find I have a violent headache."

Mary did not ordinarily flee the field of battle, but she wanted to speak to Edmund privately, without having to contradict herself in front of Mrs. Norris. *You knew this must come to light sooner or later,* she reminded herself, *and, you are now married. There is nothing he can do.*

Edmund remained at the table, unmoving, and still able to respond, occasionally, to his aunt, as she exulted in the fact that in Mary, she had found another person who saw through Fanny Price's machinations. When she finally rose from the table, he asked her if she could entertain herself for the rest of the evening, as he wished to go for a long walk. "And I find that I must return to Thornton Lacey early in the morning, Aunt Norris. I should be very much obliged if you could remain here, and keep Mary company for so long as she stays in London? I should dislike to leave her with no companion." Mrs. Norris had never been backward about proposing herself as a guest in the homes of others, and she in fact had had it at her tongue's end to suggest the same; she happily assented, and settled herself down in the parlour with her needlework. She heard Edmund slowly walk down the front steps, and she congratulated herself on being back in the bosom of her family, and being as useful and necessary to them all as she had always been.

It was unseasonably cold, and raining steadily the following morning when Edmund left Wimpole Street soon after the dawn, and before anyone else in the household had stirred. Edmund was grateful for the rain and the solitude of his own little carriage. He needed time to be alone with his thoughts, on this, the greyest morning of his life. He was most grievously convinced that he had never understood his wife before, and that, as far as related to mind, it had been a creature of his own imagination, not a real woman, with whom he had fallen in love and married. He had often praised the sweetness of her disposition and the openness of her temper. These, along with the superior endowments of her mind, were what had beguiled him into loving her. Now he discovered that rather than possessing those advantages, he would be obliged to put up with exactly the reverse for the rest of his life. He had already discovered her to be short-tempered and artful; but worse, she was deceitful.

There could be no mitigation, no palliation to explain the letter which last night, he had examined with his own eyes, again and again. His wife's handwriting, speaking of a letter from Fanny to him – a letter that she claimed *he* had shown to *her*, a letter they had discussed together – how often had he lamented to her, how often had he spoken of his regret that Fanny had left him no note! How often had she comforted and distracted him! How often had he consoled himself that, whatever else, in Mary he had a loving and sympathetic companion. It was all falsehood, all lies.

And then, unbidden, he began to think of everything that could be said to extenuate, to excuse, to explain, his wife's conduct. Jealousy, it appeared, had impelled her to the course she took. Her apparent love for him, her choice of him as her husband, she who had been sought by so many, and further, the more than unfortunate childhood she had endured, the polluting influence of her friends – did not all of this urge him to seek a reconciliation? To understand and to forgive?

But, her carelessness for the safety of Maria this past spring, her indifference when Maria was abandoned by her brother, her willingness to say anything false about his cousin Fanny, the ease with which she lied to him to secure her own ends, all of this spoke to severe faults of principle, of blunted delicacy and a corrupted, vitiated mind.

He began to catalogue all the ways that the Crawfords, between them, had deceived and hurt his family. The list of their crimes grew and multiplied in his mind – the destruction of Maria, the injury to Julia, the calumnies directed toward Fanny.

And after thoroughly canvassing the character of his wife and her brother, he began to examine himself and he could nearly despair. He castigated himself for his own folly, and as he revolved the events of the last half-year, he reviled his own blindness and complacency in believing everything Mary had told him about Fanny's coldness toward him. He wished to write to Fanny, but even more ardently, wished to see her in person.

Then, with growing self-condemnation, he asked himself if he had been as blind as regards *Fanny* as he had been towards *Mary*, assuming Fanny's complaisance and agreement with him on all points, including his regard for Mary Crawford. What silent wounds had he inflicted on Fanny, when praising Mary Crawford to her face? Supposing that she indeed held him in tender esteem, as Mary evidently believed, how painful must it have been when he, without her leave, forced her to be his confidante as he discussed his growing love for Mary, along with his doubts as to her character, and thus forced her to witness as his attraction to Mary triumphed over his scruples?

He recalled their final private conversation when he had in fact *compelled* her to agree with him in his decision to take the part of Anhalt, to spare Mary from the indelicacy of playing love scenes with a stranger in *Lovers' Vows*! Perhaps Fanny knew, but could not suggest to him, that Mary was far from fastidious as to points of delicacy and modesty. Perhaps her sudden departure –

He could only hope that this suggestion, that Fanny loved him as more than a cousin, was an invention of Mary's jealous mind. His love for Fanny had always been as a devoted brother, for they were, so far as he was concerned, as close as brother and sister, though merely cousins. Now, he could never atone for the pain he had unconsciously caused her, nor, as a married man, ever return that devotion which might have been his for the asking. They were both married to others now – out of delicacy, he could not pursue the supposition.

Chapter Twenty-Two

Fanny was learning that the objects of our benevolence do not always conform to our conception of them. She had supposed that she and Susan would spend hours studying books together, as she and Edmund had done, but discovered that Susan was no reader, and preferred to learn by watching and doing, and her younger sister declared that she did not aspire to be a fine "useless" lady, but preferred to learn how to manage a household. She petitioned to be allowed to follow the housekeeper, and help in the kitchen, and learn how to cook, instead of being cooped up in the library poring over *The Theory of Moral Sentiments*. The cook and kitchen maids at first regarded her as a spy and a sneak, and indeed, as she had grown up in her mother's house, Susan had no other conception of servants but as persons to be watched and reported on, but when the servants saw that she truly wished to understand the doings of a great house, they were happy to relieve themselves of the tedious chores, such as beating egg whites, in favour of the eager apprentice.

Fanny then engaged a music master to teach them both the pianoforte, and she and Susan practised companionably together for a time, until Susan grew weary of the monotony of playing scales, and gave up the enterprise. Nor was Susan of a contemplative character; although she loved the freedom of the outdoors, she would rather run through the shrubbery, than walk sedately while exchanging quotations from favourite poets in praise of the sublimity of Nature.

Susan earnestly desired to learn horse-riding, but Fanny had qualms — she feared the horses in Mr. Crawford's stables were too high-spirited. The coachmen and stable-grooms undertook to let the ladies take turns on the oldest and most docile mare on the estate whilst they escorted them about in the paddocks. Fanny would not permit anything more daring, out of her sense of responsibility for Mr. Crawford's possessions, as well as her anxious fears for her sister.

To have someone to talk to, to sit down to meals with, and to have by her side when she ventured about the neighbourhood, was inestimably precious to Fanny. She was forced to exert herself daily for Susan's sake and not brood over the news of her cousin's marriage. In fact, Fanny had never been in such good health, or looks, as in that summer in Norfolk. She was, for the first time in her life, in command of her own time, mistress of her own affairs and household, and these new freedoms and responsibilities engrossed her entirely.

Fanny and Susan were at breakfast one morning in late August when they opened a letter from Mrs. Butters with no sensation other than happiness and curiosity, but how swiftly did an ordinary day, with its little projects, plans and pleasures, turn into a day whose terrors and fears they would long recall. Mrs. Butters had sent a note reading:

Alarming news, my dear Mrs. Crawford. My home is open to you if you wish to travel hither. We await further bulletins. She had copied out a small notice from the *Times* of London of 23rd August:

Yesterday *Captain Columbine arrived at the Admiralty with dispatches announcing the surrender of Senegal to his Majesty's arms. Captain Columbine commanded the* Solebay *frigate, which, we regret to state, has been lost on the coast of Africa, but in what way we do not know.*

Fanny endeavoured to keep her composure for the sake of her younger sister, but her anxiety was severe, and with one accord, they both left the table to walk in the garden and exclaim over the letter, trying, if it were possible, by reading it again and again, to find some detail which would allay their anxiety. "We see that Captain Columbine is alive – why should not our own dear William have survived likewise?" asked Fanny, her voice trembling.

"This report is two days old – by now, more will be known," offered Susan. "Fanny, could we not go to London, and then to Portsmouth? Oh, I want to be home if something has happened!"

"But how shall we travel to London?" asked Fanny, forgetting that as a married woman she could travel without a chaperone, indeed, she could be a chaperone for Susan. Susan's perplexed look reminded her that she had the independence, the servants, and the means to travel anywhere in Great Britain.

"Yes, of course – we will hire a post chaise! Let us be off immediately! Change into your travelling clothes, Susan, and send for the servants to pack our trunks. I will inform the housekeeper."

The agitated pair were at the front door with their luggage not long after the coachman drove round. Mr. Maddison, with feelings known only to himself, handed them in, whilst assuring Fanny that the affairs of Everingham would be managed scrupulously in her absence. She had hardly time or sense to make an intelligible reply – Fanny and Susan left Everingham behind, determined to reach Mrs. Butters' home in Stoke Newington as soon as possible. In Thetford they bid farewell to the old coachman and, attended by one manservant, engaged a post chaise, whose postilions obligingly hurried the horses along as swiftly as Fanny's nerves could bear.

Fanny had her younger sister's spirits to support – but oh! Susan could not know of the remorse that tore at Fanny's heart, which she dare not share with a living soul. For she felt that she, Fanny Price, had been the one who placed her brother on the deck of the ageing frigate; it was done by her agency, her intervention – had she not challenged Henry Crawford to help her brother, he might still be alive and well, a midshipman in Gibraltar rather than, as her fears betokened, lost beneath the deep, his last thoughts, as the waves closed over his head for the final time, of home and the ones who loved him so dearly! She felt dreadful anxiety for William Gibson, and sorrow for the prospect of his loss, but it was the thought that by *creating* Lieutenant William Price she had also *destroyed* him, which brought tears to her eyes, despite her best endeavours at self-control. She had yielded to the temptation of trying to extract a benefit out of deceit and prevarication – what if she had, in fact, brought about her own brother's death? Could the judgments of Heaven be so swift, so cruel? Was her brother to be punished for her

***

Edmund Bertram warily climbed the stairs to the townhouse on Wimpole Street. Some other men might have brought flowers or even jewels to a reunion with an unhappy wife, but Edmund Bertram could never be brought to regard women as a species of irrational creatures whose affections could be bought with trinkets. He had thought his own wife in particular was above the petty female vices of jealousy and vanity and, while possessed of acute sensibilities, was also a creature of reason. He had written to her from Thornton Lacey, announcing his return to London after preaching his usual Sunday sermon, and expressed the hope that they might reconcile. The butler welcomed him gravely; his Aunt Norris, still tenaciously in residence, ordered tea for him, but no wife appeared, and upon his enquiry, he learned that Mary was visiting her friend Lady Stornoway in Richmond. He was embarrassed to be exposed in this fashion – he said, clumsily, "Ah yes, she had written to me of the invitation but I must have misremembered the date."

"As you men so often do," returned his aunt, "I made it a rule with my late husband to inform him of everything *at least* three times, so I could be certain he would recall it."

"A wise precaution, aunt, and no doubt he was grateful for it."

"Your brother Tom is in town, I believe," his aunt replied, unperturbed, as she retook her seat and resumed her sewing. "I wonder he does not stay here with us, we have bedchambers enough and I have seen that everything has been scrubbed and aired out and put in order. Your wife has engaged this house until the New Year, I suppose you know – and I do not wonder at it, for we are so well situated! The offices are too small, and the bedchambers are oppressively warm in the evening, but taken all in all, we are fortunate to have this for our family home in London."

Edmund was going to raise his eyebrow at his aunt's use of "we" and "our," but, as he had invited her to stay, he had only himself to blame.

***

July 29, at sea

Dear Fanny,

I hope this letter finds you and Mr. Crawford well. Even though in all likelihood I will hand this letter to you in person, as we may reach England before the next packet, I can relieve my feelings by noting down some lines about the adventures we have undergone. The first ship to which I was assigned as a lieutenant has gone to a watery grave, and although the poor old Solebay *was a rotten old tub, unfit to cross a duck pond, let alone go to sea, I shall always feel a sentimental tenderness toward her and lament that my career on her was so short. I was not aboard her at the time, nor were any of the officers, for I was placed in command of a launch, carrying a detachment of soldiers to attack the French outpost of Barbague – I doubt you will find that in the atlas – and the ship was left in charge of the Master.*

We left her anchored in the Gambia River, close enough to bring her guns to bear upon the Frenchies, but overnight, she shifted in her berth and went aground. These African rivers are treacherous, barely navigable but, we had to risk encroaching as far as possible upstream if we were to bring Maxwell's troops to attack the settlement, and on the bright side of the matter, we took the Frenchies by surprise when we showed up at their doorstep with a frigate and a sloop, and commenced firing on them, so that they took tail and ran, and none of our men injured, though a few sadly were drowned. So that is one nest of slave traders cleared out, and Senegal is now a British colony!

So now we are bobbing about in the ocean, two ships' crews crammed aboard the one, the Derwent. Therefore, we must land frequently for more water and firewood, which, unfortunately, exposes us to the unhealthy air of the coast. Many of the men have fallen, including, I am sorry to tell you, our mutual friend, Mr. Gibson. I searched his possessions to find his supply of Jesuit bark, only to discover that he had given almost all of it away, when our cabin boys, his students, fell ill last month. So typical of his generous nature! He has contracted a severe case of putrid fever, and is in the ship's infirmary with many others. I pray that he will hang on until we reach Portsmouth, and more can be done for him there, I trust.

But may I tell you of a signal service he performed for us just before he fell ill, one which will give every man on board some prize money – we have captured a slaver! The lookout spotted a brig last week, we gave chase and the ship heaved to, flying the Portuguese flag. Captain Columbine chose Gibson and me to go with the first lieutenant as part of the boarding party. I speak a few words of Portuguese that I picked up in Gibraltar, and we get aboard and meet with the captain, who is as friendly as you like, and says, to us, why yes, they are transporting Africans to the Indies but, as the vessel is neither English nor French, there is nothing that the British Navy can say about it.

While the officers were talking and me attempting to translate, Gibson was looking around him at some of the sailors, and observing their tattoos, and he sees one or two that were tattooed with English words, such as 'Roast Beef & Liberty' or 'Heart of Oak' and suchlike. So, he whispers to me, "say something provoking to them in Portuguese, Mr. Price," which I did – I shan't repeat what I said – they all just looked away and refused to answer me, and I thought, the Portuguese sailors I met in Gibraltar would have had their knives at my neck for such a remark and no error. So I said it again, with illustrative gestures, and one of the cabin boys swore a stream of oaths at us – in perfect English, or at least perfect English of that particular sort – and, the game was up!

It was an English ship, the Clementine, from the Bristol dockyards, but flying under a false flag, and the so-called captain was the only Portuguese on board! We turned up her real captain and her papers, all English, and below decks, we discovered – well, Fanny, I cannot find words to express it and, I hate to think of my sister even knowing of these things, as I know your gentle heart would break over it. I will leave it for Gibson, for he says *he will write a book about it when we return. But our crew, who are hardened sailors, were weeping for pity and anger when the poor shackled wretches, men, women and children, were brought up on deck, naked, covered in their own filth and vomit, and just as frightened of us as they were of their captors, as they knew not what was going to happen to them. The place of their confinement was something horrible, and the stench and the close air was enough to make a man faint. There were over five hundred of them, and some of them already dying or dead, but still shackled to the living.*

We arrested the brig's crew, and Captain Columbine assigned Lieutenant Tetley and a prize crew to sail the brig back to Sierra Leone where the Africans will be set free. (Although what they will do after being abducted from their homes and then cast ashore with nothing even on their backs, is beyond my knowledge.) The owners of the brig will be fined and the ship confiscated – that will send a message, won't it?

I would it had been me, of course, in charge of the prize crew and commanding that beautiful new brig, instead of Tetley, but we will all be in Portsmouth by the middle of August, perhaps before you even see this letter, so I do rely upon meeting with all my family again and I hope that you and Mr. Crawford can visit from Norfolk. Perhaps we could meet together in Northamptonshire? I should like to pay my respects to Sir Thomas and all of his family, if I can get leave.

I look in frequently upon our friend Mr. Gibson and I trust that we can bring him safely home to England. I own that I am in some anxiety about him.

Until we meet again, I am,
Your loving brother, William

***

Fanny and Susan, thankfully, were not long left in ignorance and suspense concerning the fate of the 'two Williams,' as on the late afternoon of the first day, stopping to change their horses in Newmarket, they happened to meet in the inn-yard, a traveler lately from London, and Susan, spying a newspaper under his arm, eagerly questioned him. He was able to inform them that the *Solebay* had run aground during an action against the French colony of Senegal, but that the crew had survived the engagement and had landed in Portsmouth, aboard the *Derwent*, five days previously.

With many fervent ejaculations of thanks to Providence, the sisters allowed themselves to rest at the Inn for the night, confident that surely their brother and his friend numbered among the sailors safely returned to England.

"There will be a court-martial, you know, Fanny – there always is when a captain loses a ship. All of the officers will be questioned. I fancy that our brother must remain in Portsmouth until then," Susan explained, and Fanny promised to take Susan home to support their brother, although they had no doubt between them that far from being in any way culpable in the loss of the *Solebay*, the court-martial testimony would reveal that Second Lieutenant Price's skill, devotion to duty and exemplary courage had forestalled some greater disaster.

"Will we see dear Mr. Crawford in London?" Susan next enquired, and received, to her astonishment, another perplexed look from her sister, who, to all appearances, needed a moment to recollect the name of her husband! Fanny looked doubtful, she was not sure, but at Susan's prodding, undertook to write Mr. Crawford at his usual hotel.

The following day brought them to the airy, pleasant country neighbourhood of Stoke Newington, and the handsome home of Mrs. Butters, whom Fanny was extremely pleased to see after so many months. Fanny delighted in the warm and charitable welcome she received from her friend, and mutual reassurances and congratulations were exchanged on the good news respecting the crew of the *Solebay*.

Fanny was proud to see how well Susan bore her introduction to Mrs. Butters. Susan was wearing one of the new dresses Fanny had provided for her, and her entry into Mrs. Butters' parlour, her curtsey and her polite replies to her hostess shewed that Fanny's gentle tutelage had not been in vain. Susan acquitted herself well, even when introduced to another guest of Mrs. Butter's – her neighbour, Mr. James Stephen, an older gentleman with an intelligent and penetrating gaze. When the girls came to understand that he was a lawyer, and a Member of Parliament, and had, moreover, been the author of the celebrated Act that banned all Englishmen from trading in slaves, they were both pretty well awed into silence.

Mr. Stephen and Mrs. Butters were not indisposed to carry the conversation while the young people listened respectfully; naturally, the adventures of Lieutenant Price and Mr. Gibson were touched upon, but as Mr. Stephen had spent part of his early life in St. Kitts, he tended to view travel and its attendant hardships as salutary for male character, and he declared he would not be who he was today if he had not seen, with his own eyes, scenes of suffering and injustice meted out to the black slaves which, in consideration of the young ladies at table, he would not dwell upon.

After dinner and tea, Susan was discovered to be nodding off in her chair, and she was kindly led upstairs by the maid for a long rest, while Fanny, still delighted to be amongst such interesting conversationalists, felt she could listen all night. But now that Susan was gone, Mrs. Butters, with an emphatic look, demanded of Fanny that she tell everything relative to her recent marriage. She knew something of Henry Crawford by reputation, and could not imagine that he and Fanny were in any way suited to be husband and wife, although she acknowledged that Fanny had never looked so well and she must, therefore, be well content.

Fanny's all-too-evident discomfort upon being applied to in this manner was of course immediately noted by both her auditors; even taking into account Fanny's gentle and reserved manner, she did not appear to be a newly-married woman in love, and Mrs. Butters was by no means inclined to leave off pursuing the matter, especially since she had determined (it must be no secret to the reader) that Fanny was to have married William Gibson, and she was therefore a little disappointed in Fanny, and began to suppose that Fanny had made a loveless, mercenary match. She even hinted as much.

"Now, my dear hostess, don't condemn the girl if she's married for money," Mr. Stephen put in bluntly. "We all must have something to live on, and Mrs. Crawford may be in the way of becoming a patron to Mr. Gibson, if she will not have the pleasure of starving with him in a garret. And by 'patron,' I do assure you I mean the word literally, Mrs. Crawford, and nothing that would redound to your discredit."

To have her private affairs canvassed so openly by the two older people, especially after weeks of solitude in Everingham, was such an unexpected turn of events for Fanny, and took her so aback, that she did not even blush or stammer, but found herself confessing that one of her motives in "becoming Mrs. Crawford," as she put it, was to help her brother's career. And having said that much, recklessly added that Henry Crawford was a man of good understanding, education, wit, imagination, and address, but......

"But?" prompted Mrs. Butters, truly interested.

Fanny confessed that his fault was a liking to make girls a little in love with him. What a relief it was to her, to say aloud even a small part of the truth! But she could find no words to explain why she did not know where her husband was – for she lacked the guile to dissemble on this point – though only four months' married.

Mrs. Butters had heard enough, and started to condemn him as a rake and a libertine, when restrained by Mr. Stephen. "He may yet turn out well, my dear Mrs. Butters, if Mrs. Crawford will be as patient and show as much forbearance and forgiveness as my own poor first wife. Mrs. Crawford may yet make something of her husband. The most abandoned rake may reform his ways, although in my case, to be honest, I think it is the operation of time, and the consequent extinguishment of the passions of youth – not repentance or reflection – that has changed me from an ardent young man to a philosophic old one."

The flickering firelight, casting its shadow on the wall, the deepening shades of night without, the silence of the household, all lent themselves to a confessional mood, and Fanny found herself listening with amazement and horror to his story:

"Many years ago, I was secretly engaged, to a lovely girl. Her parents objected to me – as well they should have! She was the sister of my dearest friend, Tom, then away in the Navy. Tom was pledged to marry a beautiful girl, Maria. While I was formally engaged to Nancy, while the sweet trusting girl waited for the day I would take her as my wife, I was so powerfully attracted to Maria's charms that I began secretly courting her as well. I overcame Maria's virtue and got her with child."

Fanny gasped and clasped a hand to her mouth.

"I was then courting two women, and promising to marry *both* of them. My friend returned to England and learned that I, his good friend, had destroyed all his hopes in this world. He left for a distant post. I never saw him again. Nancy, meanwhile, was driven to despair, almost to suicide.

"I determined to escape to the Caribbean, and as I could marry only one of the two women I loved, I vowed to marry whichever of them could not find herself another husband. But, in the meantime, I fell in love, briefly and violently, with a Scottish girl."

Fanny's eyes rolled in her head but she stayed silent.

"As that affair came to a close, the lovely Maria was courted by another man and taken as his wife. Nancy was great-hearted enough to forgive me and adopt Maria's baby as our first child.

"There, Mrs. Crawford. Would you say that my character was the same, or worse, than your husband's? And yet, I have lived to make myself useful to my fellow creatures – " here, Mrs. Butters nodded her head vigorously, –

271

"without, indeed, overcoming many, or any of my faults. My temper is bad, my language often vile, and I was more apt to be ashamed of my lack of classical education, than to remedy that lack through constant study. Still, I am proud to be the ally of Mr. Wilberforce, and Mr. Clarkson, and to be one of those who will accomplish the mighty work, please God, in our lifetimes, of making the thought of slavery so detestable to civilized men that we will see it eradicated from the globe.

"So, don't despair of your own husband, Mrs. Crawford, with the talents you say he possesses, he may yet redeem himself."

***

The next morning, Mrs. Butters and her guests prepared for their day's diversions. Madame Orly insisted on helping Fanny with her toilette: "We are in London now, Madame Crawford, we must look creditable!"

Mrs. Butters kindly offered to take Susan to see the Tower of London and then to Wapping New Stairs to look in on their brother John, who was a junior clerk at the Marine Police office. Fanny requested to be let off at Wimpole Street to call on her cousins, with a promise to meet her brother another day.

With trembling and apprehension did Fanny descend from the carriage. She did not know which members of the Bertram family, if any, she would find there. She was most afraid of meeting Maria, and in fact would not have been surprised if Maria had slammed the door in her face!

"Pardon me, are any of the family within?" she enquired of the butler who opened the door.

"May I take your card in, madam?"

"Oh – I have no card, but could you please inform them – that Fanny is here. I mean, Miss Price. I mean, Mrs. Henry Crawford."

The butler startled slightly, then nodded his head, and bowed her in to a small but elegantly appointed entry hall. "Please wait here, madam, if you please."

Fanny stood in terrific suspense, not knowing who, if anyone, would appear and acknowledge her as a relative. She heard some low murmured voices, and then she thought she heard a commotion, as though a chair had been scraped back suddenly – even knocked aside – she heard a firm rapid footstep, a man's voice saying, "No, I shall greet her myself," a door opened and there appeared –

"Cousin!" she exclaimed.

Edmund approached rapidly, looking at her carefully. He saw an elegantly dressed little woman, looking up at him with joy on her face. It was his own Fanny whom he had last seen the previous October but oh, how the intervening months had changed them both!

"My Fanny!" He watched her countenance carefully for some signs of the disdain which his wife had assured him Fanny felt for him and all the Bertrams. She stepped up lightly to meet him, and to his infinite relief, she embraced him and laid her head on his chest.

"Thank goodness! Fanny, there is so much to explain, so much I need to apologize for – "

She stepped back, startled. "Apologize? You, cousin? I rather think I need to apologize to you!"

"No, never, Fanny, for you could never do anything harmful to anyone. Please, please, come in and sit down. You cannot know how comforting, how wonderful it is to see you again. Please come and talk with me."

He led her gently to the sitting room, closed the door behind them and led her to a chair, all the while looking over her carefully and with the warmest affection on his countenance.

"Fanny, I need not ask you if you have been well, you look very well indeed."

They had not met for three-quarters of a year, and Fanny had altered from a girl to a fashionable young woman in that space of time. Her hair curled charmingly under her stylish little bonnet, coral earrings dangled from her neat little ears and the high collar of her burgundy jacket set off her pale, slender neck. But was she still his friend, still his greatest confidante in this world? With an eagerness which bespoke the warmth of his affection, he begged her to tell him all of her story, from the day of her early morning departure from Mansfield Park.

"Fanny, you need not tell me anything you might find disagreeable to relate, but please, I must know one thing – did you leave a letter for me when you left the house?"

Startled, Fanny replied, "Yes, *of course* I did, cousin!" and to her astonishment Edmund sat back abruptly, then leaned forward and buried his head in his hands. "Fanny – Fanny, I never received that letter."

Fanny sat in stunned silence for a moment. Then ventured – "why then, you must have believed that I disappeared without a word of explanation to you and the family, and the first news you had of me was my letter from Bristol? How sorry I am! You must have wondered and worried – But stay – no, cousin – Miss Crawford – that is, as she was then, when she found me in Bristol, she told me that you *had* read my letter and you were very angry with me....." she trailed off in perplexity and embarrassment.

Edmund sighed. "I cannot explain.... wait...... no, Fanny – with you I can have no reserve, particularly if these horrible misunderstandings and blunders are to be set aright, I must explain, I must tell you the truth. Believe me, only my desire to do right by you compels me to cast aside all reserve, all decorum, and all the discretion which I ordinarily uphold as every person's duty toward those whom they are bound to honour. You will understand my reticence, and all of the motives which *would* enjoin me to silence. I am not proud of confessing what you will soon perceive – how matters stand with me and mine! At least I will obtain some comfort, some happiness, by confiding in you. How I have missed you! And so I will be direct, and trust upon your generosity and candour.

"We did have your letter to my *father*, on the morning you left. But, Fanny," he added, speaking with obvious reluctance, "only recently did I learn of the existence of your letter to me, and that it was kept from me by..... by she who is now my wife."

A long silence ensued. Edmund sat gravely, looking down at his hands, and Fanny studied him carefully, while her feelings of tenderness and compassion for him threatened to overpower her. He looked older, somehow a little harder, and there were lines about his mouth and on his brow which had not been there before. She now saw the sorrow and disillusionment which had placed those lines there. She was not surprised, and certainly not triumphant, in knowing that she had been correct as to the hidden venality of Mary Crawford's character, while Edmund, once deceived, was now......

Tears arose to her eyes. Though she remained perfectly silent and still, he nevertheless felt the full force of her sympathy, though he could barely endure to glance at her during the next part of his confession.

After a time, Edmund sighed and continued. "Fanny, I want so much to hear your voice again, but allow me to explain a little of what happened. When we discovered that you were not – not among us, my wife – then Miss Crawford – went to the East Room, in search of you. It cannot be denied that *she* found your letter to me and removed it; she gave me only the letter for my father. I believed that you had left without leaving a word for me, she allowed me to continue in that error. And worse – but no, pray continue, let us retrace our steps, both of us, since that day. What a relief it will be to talk with you, whatever the outcome of this conversation!"

And so, in halting fashion, step by step, Fanny unfolded her story, and Edmund his, and as well, he recounted the progress and destruction of Maria's engagement to Henry Crawford.

Edmund's courtship of Mary Crawford in London, their quarrel and reconciliation, and the final abandonment of his scruples in the face of his strong attachment, were but briefly touched upon. He wished not to cause *Fanny* any pain; she wished likewise to spare him the agony of describing a union which began with every expectation of felicity and which now, even if she had only his altered features as her authority, was clearly a cause of disillusionment and regret.

Fanny described her winter and spring with the Smallridges, the kindness she had received from Mrs. Butters, her serious illness and recovery, but when, in her recitation, she came to the time when the Crawfords surprised her by appearing at Keynsham Hill, she paused in embarrassment. She felt that, even under these circumstances, she could not betray Henry Crawford's confidence and the agreement she had made with him. But Edmund took up the narrative and did not ask her about her supposed trip to Gretna Green.

"Once again, Fanny, I must ask – when Mary and her brother departed to seek you out, I gave Mary a letter to give to you. And I gave her a present for you, a gold chain. Did you receive them?"

Fanny shook her head in the negative. Then, recollecting, added, "Wait, cousin, she did bring to me a parcel containing some half-a-dozen gold chains, which she said all belonged to her. She said she wished to make a gift of one to me, and asked me to make a selection of one of them, but she made no mention of a gift from *you*. I am wearing the chain she gave me," and she held it out for Edmund's inspection.

He looked at it briefly, smiled sadly, and said, "that is a necklace I have seen around her neck before. It is not the chain I bought for you. She told me that you had refused to accept my gift."

"I? No, cousin, never."

"But wait, Fanny, you *did* write me a short note from London in response to mine – it was in your hand, and it said, "Dear Sir... Many thanks for your kind remembrances...." – and Edmund began to recite from memory the brief letter that Mary had dictated.

Fanny's face was suffused with blushes. Her lips started to form the words, 'Mary."

Edmund looked, nodded, then stood up and began to pace around the room. "Pray continue."

275

In a soft but steady voice, Fanny explained that she had supposed she was writing to Mr. Yates.

"What happened next?" asked Edmund.

"Well – Mr. Crawford and I, that is – Mr. Crawford and I went on to Everingham." Edmund turned and looked at her enquiringly. Now, surely was the time for Fanny to unfold her reasons for entering into matrimony with a man she had hitherto disliked, and for him to extend his best wishes in response. But she remained silent. At last, Edmund ventured, "And you have lived with him there since that time?"

"*I* have lived there, but I have seen very little of Mr. Crawford since – he did write to inform me of your marriage." Fanny looked down. She knew that she should, in her turn, be wishing Edmund great joy in his marriage. But they both knew the words would be worse than hollow, they would be actually cruel. A sudden inspiration allowed her to change the subject. "Edmund, I am so happy and proud that you are now ordained! I have wanted so much to hear a little news about you – I have thought of you very often, you may be sure. I was assured that you were very angry with me, which I sometimes doubted, but I had some hope of receiving a line from you, and did not."

"I did write to you Fanny – I wrote you, at Everingham, several times, including this past month."

"You did? You did?" Fanny also stood and clasped her hand to her mouth. "Oh, Edmund, we have been completely imposed upon! Those letters never reached me!"

Another round of questions and wonderings. The agitated pair stood, sat, paced, held hands, embraced, exclaimed, then paced the room again, questioning, wondering, and in Fanny's case, shedding a few tears of relief mixed with remorse for all the lost times when she might have had Edmund's counsel and had denied it to herself, believing the entire family was estranged from her. Edmund was thunderstruck at the confirmation of deceit and machinations more complete, more thorough, than even his darkest suspicions. As a clergyman, it was his calling to encourage and guide the families in his parish, to warn them from the paths of sin and danger. Now he felt as helpless as a babe in the woods, wholly unaware of where duplicity resided, unable to conceive that such malevolence could occur outside of a gothic novel, and incapable of recognizing the evils that had been brooding by his own fireside.

There followed reassurances of their mutual good feeling, and exclamations over the revival of that sorely missed, that best comfort, which if known, might have been claimed at any time this past half year. Edmund wondered to himself if Fanny could possibly have loved Henry Crawford when she entered into marriage with him – she appeared to be learning here, for the first time, of his cruelty in intercepting her letters. And had she any inkling of the worst of her husband's conduct?

Finally, Fanny also thought of her cousins and asked about Maria. Edmund's countenance fell again and out of an overflow of grief, he murmured, without any preamble, "Maria is lost to us, Fanny. She is ruined."

Fanny looked searchingly into his eyes. He could not tell her, in so many words, that the man who seduced Maria was the man whose name she now bore, but she knew Edmund too well – she saw it written plainly on his countenance.

"Mr. Crawford," she whispered, and turned ashen white. Edmund stepped forward to catch her as she began to faint away. He gently led her back to the sofa. He knew she felt tender solicitude for her cousin Maria, but he could damn himself for being the one who revealed the truth to Crawford's wife. Concealment was impossible, but how he despised himself for being the one to destroy Fanny's peace of mind forever.

"Is it so?" asked Fanny in a faltering voice, sick with horror, "my cousin? Where is she?"

"Truly, Fanny, I think only my brother Tom and my father know where she resides, but I believe it must be north of London. They both visit her on their way between London and Northamptonshire. There is a conspiracy within the family to shield my mother from all knowledge and, so far as possible, to spare each other the grief of canvassing this matter. I believe she will have her child in October."

Fanny closed her eyes and thought, *Maria, I only meant to help. I only meant to protect you. What have I done?* And she burst into tears. She had succumbed to the temptation of telling a falsehood – and not only had it nearly brought the death of her brother, she had brought disaster upon Maria. How bitterly did she regret acting in concert with the likes of Henry Crawford! She recalled Julia's contemptuous words from last winter – *'Have you never succumbed and done what you knew to be wrong? No? I tell you why. It is not because you are more virtuous than the rest of us – though I know you think you are. It is because nothing tempts you.'*

She had denied it at the time, but she *had* thought herself better than the others, until tempted to do something she knew was wrong, to help her brother. Never, never, could she think herself more virtuous again!

277

It was some moments before she was coherent and rational again. She raised a tear-streaked face to Edmund and said, "There is only one thing to be done. Henry Crawford must marry her. Don't you agree? He *must* marry Maria so that the child may have a name."

"But Fanny," Edmund gently took her hand. "How can this be? It cannot be done expeditiously, and you would destroy your own reputation to save hers. Crawford must accuse you of adultery and then obtain an Act of Parliament before he can marry again – "

Fanny shook her head desperately. "It was all false. All falsehoods!"

Now it was Edmund's turn to grow pale. "What do you mean, Fanny? In the name of heaven, what are you saying?"

Fanny could not hold back her tears, her face a picture of contrition. "Oh, cousin, how can I bear to tell you? I am *not* married to Henry Crawford. We were *never* married. It was a deception. He – he told me..." She could not speak more, she was overcome with sobs of remorse and she buried her face in her hands. *With what arrogance did I propose to arrange the destinies of others!* She thought to herself. *I allowed myself to believe Mr. Crawford when he said that Maria would forget him and marry another. I have destroyed Maria's life – she has been in agonies these – how many months? Thinking me married to the man she loved, while she carried his child! I am abominable!*

She remained for a moment, almost insensible, when the sound of a door being slammed shut, caught her attention. She stood up and ran to the window and beheld Edmund running down the front steps while putting on his jacket and jamming his hat upon his head. And he was gone, pacing briskly down the street.

Fanny stood at the window, unable to move. She knew not how much time elapsed until the door creaked and a gentle cough caused her to turn around. The butler, not meeting her eyes, said apologetically, "Is there anything I can do for you, Madam?"

"Where has Mr. Bertram gone?"

"He enquired for the whereabouts of Mr. Crawford, Madam. That is all I know." Fanny resumed looking out the window.

Another gentle cough.

"Pardon, how may I assist you, Madam?"

"Is Mr. Bertram here? Tom Bertram? I believe something terrible is about to happen."

"He is at his private club, I believe, madam. We can send the footman with a message."

"Please, please ask Mr. Bertram to come immediately!"

Chapter Twenty Three

In only a few minutes' brisk walking, Edmund reached Cavendish Square, where a row of a dozen brilliantly decorated open carriages, all painted yellow, and each harnessed to a handsome team of four horses, were lined up in the street. The pavement was crowded with admirers, with more watching from the windows of the houses overlooking the Square – some spectators were there to admire the teams and the equipage, and others to admire the young men preparing to drive them, and still others to admire the fashionable society beauties in attendance, for this was a special meeting of the Four in Hand Club, preparing to set out for their procession to Salt Hill, twenty-four miles away. Edmund quickly scanned the young drivers, lounging, laughing and chatting with each other and with the throngs of spectators. He soon spotted the man he was searching for. Henry Crawford was at his gayest, standing proudly next to his barouche, while the groomsmen held the reins of a splendid team of four matched bays. The horses and the equipage were the best that money could buy, and Crawford himself was proudly sporting the blue and yellow striped waistcoat that only members of Mr. Buxton's driving club were permitted to wear.

"When will you start for Salt Hill, Mr. Crawford?" one of the young ladies asked coquettishly. "It will be frightful if we must be the last in the procession."

"As the newest member, my dear Miss Campbell, I shall take my place at the rear, or wherever Mr. Buxton is pleased to place me, but, depend upon it, whether we are first or last, all eyes will be upon you." Crawford replied cheerfully, then broke off when he saw Edmund Bertram's approaching form and more than that, the expression on his brother-in-law's countenance.

"Crawford, I must speak with you privately, sir, on an urgent matter."

With feelings most unwilling, Crawford led Edmund through the crowd and found a secluded spot in the park, under some plane trees.

"Crawford!" Edmund spat out in contempt as soon as they were out of hearing of the others. "Crawford, I call you out to defend your infamous conduct."

An observer might have thought Henry Crawford turned a little pale, but his bearing remained as graceful as ever, his voice languid and unperturbed.

"Sir? Do I understand you correctly, are you issuing me a challenge?"

"For your destruction of my sister Maria – and my cousin Fanny – "

Crawford's eyebrow shot up. "Fanny?"

"Did you not enter into a sham marriage with her?"

"Yes, but depend upon it, I only requested her services for a short period of time -- "

With a cry, Edmund launched himself on Crawford and would have borne him to the ground had not Crawford's friends, watching the pair with interest, intervened. Edmund struggled to regain his composure, then, through clenched teeth, said only, "My brother Tom will be my second. Do not fail to meet me tomorrow morning." He left the Square and regained the street, to commence walking, he knew not where.

Crawford brushed himself off and attempted to make light of the matter, but Charles Buxton, the president of the Four in Hand Club, hastening into the park in response to the commotion, would not be satisfied without some explanation. Understanding that the challenge concerned the honour of a young lady – nay, two young ladies, for the affair proved to be twice as scandalous as the first report – Buxton exclaimed, "and some of my friends did warn me about you, Crawford! I will appoint one of our members as your second, to whom you will confide every detail of the events leading up to Mr. Bertram's challenge, and by every means in your power, you will seek an honourable resolution without resorting to the folly of settling your dispute with a duel. In the meantime, you will not accompany us today, nor ever will, until this matter is satisfactorily resolved. This is a club for gentlemen, Crawford, and I will not have us become notorious for being rakehells and seducers."

"Sir, I understand you perfectly...." Crawford began, but Buxton brushed him off contemptuously and stalked away.

The humiliation of having to leave Cavendish Square with all eyes upon him enraged Henry Crawford, and it was some time before he could command himself to explain and attempt to defend his conduct to Mr. Stanhope, whom Mr. Buxton had appointed as his second. He soon discovered that what he had regarded as a light-hearted escapade – pretending to be married to thwart the designs of a young lady who had herself broken through her prior engagement – was viewed more seriously by Mr. Stanhope. Stanhope saw an offer of marriage to Miss Bertram, along with a handsome settlement on Miss Price for the injury to her reputation, as the only solution likely to satisfy the Bertrams.

In vain had been the precepts of his religion, as taught by his late mother, in awakening Henry Crawford's conscience. In vain were the pleadings of his sister, in vain were Maria's tears and Fanny's frowns; none of these had availed to awaken Henry Crawford to a sense of his duty to his fellow creatures. But now, faced with the loss of his blue-and-yellow waistcoat, threatened with being an outcast from the exclusive society of gentlemen four-in-hand drivers, he agreed to everything.

"You had better see a solicitor, Crawford, and draw up the marriage articles and make some provision for Miss Price. I will meet with the Bertrams," Mr. Stanhope offered, in a tone that brooked no opposition.

But, by the time that worthy man learned where the Bertrams resided and called at Wimpole Street, neither Mr. Edmund Bertram nor Mr. Bertram were declared to be at home by the butler, and he came away only with a note, fixing the meeting at dawn on the following day, at the West Meadow on Hampstead Heath.

***

Tom Bertram had responded to Fanny's note by hastening to Wimpole Street, about the time that Mrs. Butters returned to pick her up. After a brief but anxious conference, he saw Fanny packed safely back to Stoke Newington – she had to be almost lifted up into the carriage, so oppressed was she with grief and horror – with a promise to send word the next day. Dusk was falling when Edmund returned and Tom persuaded him to leave home and have supper with him at his private gentleman's club near St. James's Square.

Tom had bespoken a private dining room and to Edmund's surprise, four of Tom's particular friends – Anderson, Yates, Sneyd and Hedgerow, were all in attendance. "As it happens, Edmund, I *was* hosting a special supper tonight, and I think you will soon perceive why you were not one of the guests. But, events have necessitated a slight change in the evening's entertainment."

"We *were* to have been playing cards," put in Mr. Yates, evidently disappointed.

Tom, as usual, was a gracious host, spirited and witty, and Edmund would have enjoyed himself thoroughly had he not been completely consumed with pictures of facing down Henry Crawford on the morrow and watching the bastard fall backwards, with a crimson stain spreading over his shirt, and his eyes staring sightlessly at the dawn sky. Tom's friend Charles Anderson sent a servant to retrieve his prized dueling pistols, and they were passed around and admired by the men.

The clock struck nine, the ninth bottle of claret was opened, when Edmund stood and made to excuse himself, pleading the need to get a few hours' sleep before the contest in the morning.

Instantly Tom's countenance changed from mirth to the utmost gravity. "No, Edmund, you are not going anywhere." Suddenly, four pairs of hands seized Edmund's arms and he found himself firmly pinioned between his brother's friends who had leaped from their lounging postures with an alacrity that took him completely by surprise.

Edmund struggled, but in vain.

"Dear fellow, you are at risk of tearing my lace. Pray relax and submit." said Mr. Sneyd.

"My faith, Tom, if you'd told me that your brother was such a well-built fellow, we'd have more volunteers for this pleasant duty," jested Hedgerow.

Tom laughed. "Pay them no mind, Edmund."

"Yes, your virtue is safe with us," added Mr. Yates.

"I have asked my friends to ensure that you are kept away from the dueling grounds. They will stay with you tonight. You will be released tomorrow morning.

"What does this mean, Tom?" Edmund gasped, although he had already formed a good idea. "What are you about?"

"Simply this, Edmund. I will fight the duel with Crawford on the morrow. Do not think I am doing you a favour. I am performing this one office of an elder brother, and you will soon agree it is a paltry enough service when you understand that in exchange, should I survive of course, I will abandon my life here in England. I will not marry, and I will have no heir. You, Edward, are the heir presumptive. Stay away from duels, and after I die, you will become Sir Edmund Bertram one day – if not you, then your son. I will depart for Virginia with my stable of stud horses and begin my life anew, free from the responsibilities, the expectations and, I need hardly add, the continual cloud of our father's disappointment in me that has hung over my head ever since I can remember."

"Instead of being covered in shame, you will be covering mares in Virginia?" laughed Sneyd.

"I believe only his horses will," Hedgerow answered, with a friendly jab of the elbow.

Edmund stopped straining against his captors for a moment, hoping that Tom's friends would relax their hold, then he tried suddenly to break away. Instantly the hands tightened on him, and he was dragged without ceremony to a parlor chair, and his arms and legs were bound to it.

"I haven't had this much fun since Lord Ravenshaw's masked ball," laughed Yates.

"Tom," begged Edmund. "Consider what you are about. *I* challenged Crawford, not you."

"I have considered it, dear brother, and you cannot deny that, firstly, I am a much better shot than you are. Secondly, had I listened to your warning about that damned *Lovers' Vows*, none of us would be where we are tonight. It brought Crawford and Maria into a dangerous intimacy. Without the play, Crawford would not have had so fair an opportunity to insinuate himself into Maria's − good graces, and life would not have imitated art. Because I was ashamed, I never informed you of what happened on the night of that final dress rehearsal. Instead, I allowed Crawford to pretend he was going to marry our sister."

"I too, watched complacently as Crawford flirted with *both* of our sisters," responded Edmund in anguish. "But Fanny! Who could have imagined that he was so base as to promise her marriage, and through some ruse − doubtless with a confederate posing as a clergyman − deceive her into surrendering herself to him, thinking herself his legal wife! There are not words strong enough to express my horror and detestation of the man. My blood is at the boil, Tom, I must meet him and hold him to account!"

"Ah…. pray do not distress yourself on Fanny's account, she will be none the worse for her adventures and from what I have seen, she is decidedly improved."

"How dare you speak so callously!" And Edmund began to struggle again.

"No, no, there has been a misunderstanding. There was no sham wedding ceremony. Listen to me. She agreed to *pretend* to be Crawford's wife, for completely selfless motives, and he − and I have this from Fanny − never touched her, nor made any attempt upon her person. I think we can trust our cousin's word on this point. *His* motive, as you may surmise, was to avoid matrimony with our sister."

"This becomes more and more interesting," exclaimed Sneyd.

"What motive would induce Fanny to deceive the world with a sham marriage?"

"I'm sure she would have explained it all to you had you not rushed out of the room to challenge Crawford to a duel."

Edmund listened, transfixed – and so did his captors, for all hope of keeping their domestic affairs from the world was now at an end – as his brother explained how Fanny hoped to protect Maria from a man who was unworthy of her and, at the same time, help her brother. "I believe that the second motive was paramount. She was willing to make any sacrifice to help her brother get his promotion, and having obtained, so unexpectedly, the means to do it, she acted. I always said she would be able to *act*, if she tried, if you'll recall."

"You speak very lightly of – of such a tissue of deceits and falsehoods."

"Well, condemn her if you must, judge her if you will, but I am rather more astonished at her temerity. Little Fanny, cold-bloodedly extorting a promise from an infamous rake, to help her brother! Who would have thought she had the *sang-froid* for such an enterprise!"

Edmund groaned aloud. "So Crawford is innocent of harming our cousin in – in the fashion that I had supposed. That was, indeed, why I sought him out so impetuously. But, now that we know the whole story, he still stands condemned for seducing and abandoning our sister, and pretending to be married to avoid doing his duty by her. Maria's life is ruined. But it was my blunder, my error, which led to the challenge being laid. Surely it is my responsibility to carry it out."

"Don't suppose that *I* have any objection to putting a bullet in Crawford's chest on behalf of my poor deceived sister – or even for Fanny's sake – but I wanted you to understand that Fanny's virtue is intact, if not, as *you* reckon these things, her honour and reputation."

Edmund shook his head. "If I have been too quick to judge others, brother, my own affairs have brought, and will bring, for the rest of my life, a lesson in humility. I believe I was too apt to look upon the foibles of others, too apt to condemn, but now, with the examples of my own errors and blindness before me, I must be more compassionate of my fellow creatures."

"With the exception of this Crawford fellow, of course," put in Anderson. "There is a limit, after all."

"Come to remark on it," Tom interposed, "The bare fact that I am *not* in such a passion as Edmund over this whole business, provides another reason why it is I and not he, who should meet Crawford. Mine is the cooler head. Edmund is so determined to punish Crawford he has forgotten that, if he kills him, he is killing his own brother. I believe his marriage has already been a source of some disappointment – what will it be if his *wife* regards her *husband* as the murderer of her *brother*?"

Edmund's head snapped up, astonished. He had indeed forgotten, in the intensity of his fury against Crawford, that he was bound to him by marriage. "Tom, if you finish what I began, how could I ever repay you? How to surrender this duty to you, how can I watch you put your own life in peril, to spare me from the consequences of my own folly?"

"Please view the matter as I do – I will take on the responsibility of protecting the honour of the Bertram family for this one contest. I may fall, and if I fall, I will atone for much. If I live, watch to see how completely and utterly I relinquish those duties and expectations which are the lot of the first-born son. One hazard in exchange for the life I want to live. I'll wager everything on those odds, gratefully."

Edmund, who lately had only been able to view life as a series of duties, was dumbfounded at the apparent insouciance with which his brother was able to walk away from title, estate, and family. Finally, he croaked, "But you are a Bertram. Can you truly ever forget it?"

Tom smiled, "And, if I never mentioned it, I'm proud to be your brother, Edmund Bertram. Let us not pretend that our dear father doesn't regard you as the steadier character – and who, in all candour, could disagree with him? But I do not harbour any resentment against you on that account. I wonder if he will be proud of me for this night's work – what a novel sensation that would be!

"You cannot know for how long I have struggled with this dilemma. It is not merely that I have the greatest antipathy for the responsibilities and restrictions attendant on becoming Sir Thomas Bertram, the baronet. There is more. I think, Edmund, I *think* you know that I am a confirmed bachelor. Our father will never cease urging me to enter into matrimony, and the thought of deceiving some poor innocent girl, tricking her into marriage, for her to spend the rest of her days feeling unloved and disillusioned, sickens me. You know I have always been interested in horses – "

"—and the handsome young fellas who ride 'em – " put in Hedgerow.

"Shush, Hedgerow. As I was saying, the plain truth is that horse bloodlines interest me more than perpetuating the Bertram bloodline. So, from tomorrow, it's up to you, brother."

"Hear, hear! Up to you, Edmund," from his friends.

"But to leave your family, Tom, to leave us all and go to Virginia. We may well never see you again."

"So please don't be hurt when I say I can barely wait to be off. My horses are stabled near the Liverpool dockyards and as soon as I've taken my shot at Crawford, I will bolt across country for my new life. A life where I can breathe free air and follow my own pursuits."

"And," added Yates helpfully, "in Virginia those pursuits are not capital crimes, as they are here in England. Only one to ten years' imprisonment!"

Edmund blushed at this open reference to Tom's propensities, which he had suspected since their school days. "Tom, I trust you know that your family loves you."

"Of course they do. I'm a lovable chap. Who wouldn't love me? If anyone had cause to hate me, however, it would be you. That reminds me, I owe you another apology, for all the debt I ran into a few years ago, so that father had to give your living to Dr. Grant. That was unspeakably selfish of me. At the time, I was unhappy and confused, and tried to lose myself in drink and at the gaming tables. I promise you, our father will never have to pay my debts again at your expense. He has generously given me, the prodigal son, the funds to start my horse-breeding venture, and what remains of the family fortunes will henceforward be in your hands, Edmund. You may keep the fatted calf, with my compliments – don't worry that I'll come back to claim it."

Edmund yielded, and added, sadly, "Then, friends, please untie my right arm so that I may drink a toast to my brother."

His wish was obeyed, the port was poured and the two brothers toasted each other.

"God bless you and keep you, Tom."

"The same to you, Edmund. I wish you a long and happy life, with many little Bertrams clustering about your knees, and a never-ending procession of disgruntled tenants and dissatisfied servants to bother yourself with. You cannot know how I feel tonight, having finally shucked this unwanted weight off my shoulders."

"I will pray for you, brother."

"Oh, of course you will, dear Edmund. I will let you know if anything transpires as a result."

And he was gone, with Anderson as his second. Edmund heard the clatter of hooves in the courtyard, then silence.

"What shall we do, chaps? Cards?" asked Yates.

Sneyd, eyeing Edmund's countenance said, "No, that won't do. Let us just keep vigil, and watch and wait for news of our dear friend Tom."

"Gentlemen," answered Edmund, "Do not think I would imagine that *you* feel less than *I* do on this occasion, should you choose to relieve the suspense of this night with a game of cards. Please, do as you wish. It occurs to me that it might not be appropriate for a clergyman to spend the night bound to a chair in a private gentlemen's club, but something tells me I may rely on your discretion, as you may rely on my sympathy and friendship."

"Thank you, Mr. Bertram," said Yates, refilling Edmund's glass.

***

The candles burning in the windows at Mrs. Butters house in Stoke Newington testified to the fact that someone in the household was awake and keeping vigil. Fanny was in an agony of soul as she had never before experienced. Her failure to explain herself to Edmund, the immediate cause of the duel, haunted her grievously. She imagined only one returning alive – then condemned herself for wishing it were Henry Crawford that lay dead, rather than Edmund; then she imagined Edmund dead at Crawford's hand, she imagined them *both* mortally wounded, and she powerless to do or say anything. She hoped that Tom had found Edmund in time, she prayed that cooler heads could prevail at the last moment and return them both home unscathed, for only then could she attempt to set right the wrongs she had done against Maria and persuade Crawford that the path of honour and duty would ultimately be the path to peace, tranquility and happiness. Fervently she prayed, silently she wept, ardently she hoped, aware of Mrs. Butters' sympathizing presence but too overwrought and too ashamed to seek comfort from any earthly counsellor.

The first glimmers of dawn appeared in the east; she imagined the combatants meeting – oh, if she only knew where! – she imagined Edmund removing his jacket to reveal a silk shirt underneath, nodding at his opponent, trying not to shiver in the cold; she saw the smile play across Henry Crawford's face, jesting and laughing to the end, the two of them pacing out their steps, then turning and – she covered her face with her hands and trembled with horror. Her heart pounded furiously, she sometimes had to jump up from her knees and pace back and forth on the hearthrug, she massaged her own temples, she wrung her hands, then glanced at the window again. It was lighter! It was surely dawn now! Undoubtedly, the contest was about to commence and a few more moments would decide it all! But how long, alas, how long before someone could bring word to her?

"I say, it's beautiful here, isn't it, Anderson?" asked Tom Bertram, surveying the open glade of the West Meadow through the rising mists of early dawn and taking a deep breath of the fragrant woodland air.

"Certainly. Makes you glad to be alive, doesn't it?"

Both men laughed aloud. "Gad, I will miss you so much, my particular friend – with your particular sense of humour," said Tom, embracing his friend one last time.

They stood silent for a few moments, listening to the birds awaken and call to each other in the trees, as they had ever done and would ever do, whether Tom Bertram would be alive to hear them the following morning or not.

"D'you think he will send his second ahead of him, to offer to make amends?" Anderson asked.

Tom wrapped his cloak more firmly around him. The cold morning air bit into him and he was chagrined to discover he was shivering. "He is a proud fellow, Anderson. And further, we can't take him at his word, even if he were to swear to marry my sister. He may need a pistol in his back to get him into the church. In fact, like me, he may prefer to take his chances in a duel, rather than submit to a life he doesn't want."

"Still – healthy, wealthy, and married to your beautiful sister – I do not think that Henry Crawford would be an object of pity."

"Nor am I, yet –"Tom broke off, laughing. "You might be surprised to know, how much solicitude I am feeling for myself, just at this moment!"

Another long silence. Then Tom sighed. "As a rational man, I know myself to be very fortunate. The world we live in can essentially be divided into two classes, those who do not empty their own chamber pots and those who do."

"And, I suppose, those who empty the chamber pots of others."

"Three classes, then. And I, Anderson, I have been to Antigua. I have seen the slaves who toil so that I may enjoy comfort and ease. Dante missed out on one level of hell in his damned book – there is a place called a sugaring-down shack, where the cane liquor is boiled down – this is in tropical heat, mind. The cane is fed into mills and the slaves toil there for twelve hours a day – the overseer and his whip keep them at their posts, but sometimes they are so exhausted that they fall into the vats or are crushed in the rollers that extract the liquor of the cane. So many die, in the shacks and in the fields, that even though every white man there, who is so inclined, takes his pleasure upon any slave woman he fancies, there are not enough babies born on the island to maintain the slave population.

"I have seen this, and more, and now, when I contemplate the manner in which I threw away the sums earned by such toil and misery – with gaming and drinking and idle spending – I suddenly find the question of whether there is an eternal judgment, to be more than an academic one."

There seemed to be nothing more to be said, so the two friends stood companionably, watching through the openings in the trees which encircled the glade where they stood, for some sign of an approaching carriage.

"What shall you do if he does not meet you, Tom?" Charles Anderson began to wonder, then squinted into the pale light of dawn…. "stay, is that his yellow barouche?"

It was indeed Henry Crawford, who, having spent the night with some good friends and, affecting nonchalance about the coming meeting with the Bertrams, had elected to delay his departure until the last moment. He fully expected that Mr. Stanhope would speak for him and make a contest unnecessary, and that the marriage articles and promissory note to Miss Price he carried in his waistcoat pocket would convince the Bertrams that he was at last in earnest. But, having left himself very little time to reach Hampstead Heath, and suddenly fearing that his late arrival at the dueling-grounds might be attributed to cowardice, he pushed his horses to greater efforts. The fresh, invigorating night breeze, the empty roads, and his conflicting thoughts all led to a kind of elated frenzy, and he unrestrainedly pushed his team to their uttermost limits, as though signifying to himself *'this is my last moment of freedom before I must put on the yoke.'*

He could barely perceive the two small figures in the distance, who he supposed to be Tom and Edmund Bertram, waiting for him in the meadow. He had expected to see his second, Mr. Stanhope, arrived ahead of him, presenting the offer of marriage on his behalf. But, come to think on it, he would be pleased to dispense with tradition and speak for himself. He had always held that no man was his equal in turning an indifferent acquaintance into a friend, or in disarming an enemy with his ability to charm and persuade. The forthcoming interview would be the crowning glory of his career – Edmund Bertram, who sought to murder him, would become his loving brother – he and Maria, and Edmund and Mary, would spend Christmas and Easter together, now at Mansfield Park, now at Everingham, now in London, and this morning on the heath would become a fond memory to be talked over and laughed about, and as for Tom – well, he had never been sure about Tom, but they at least could always talk about horses. Laughing out loud, and in final show of careless bravado, he urged his own team to greater efforts even as the narrow rutted road curved and rose into the meeting-grounds.

His rapid approach amused, then alarmed, both Tom and Mr. Anderson.

"By g-d! He is laying on the whip – that must be Crawford. He's the wildest driver in England, I vow."

"He is driving like a man possessed – watch him, look how he is taking the corner – "

Both men watched, transfixed, as Henry Crawford left the narrow road to travel directly to them over the uneven ground. They saw the barouche tip dangerously to one side and almost overturn, then recover its balance. Alas, a moment later, when he was almost upon them, they watched in horror as the barouche flew into the air – undoubtedly one of the wheels had come into contact with a stump or a boulder – he landed on one wheel, overturned and, still pulled by the panicked team, was dragged across the meadow to the other side of the clearing where all came to a halt in a tangled mass of horses, reins, mangled carriage, broken axle, and, somewhere in that carnage, a man.

Chapter Twenty-Four

Mrs. Butters finally persuaded Fanny to take some tea – any kind of nourishment was impossible. She waited, miserably, as the parlour clock chimed the hours. Oh, would that it were Edmund who rode up to the door, healthy and well. Or Tom, with a hopeful message. And what if the combatants escaped with their lives but then were arrested for dueling?

She heard the sound of horse's hoofs, but at an unhurried pace which proclaimed the advent of another day for traders and travelers, all going about their business in calm indifference. She heard window shutters opening, and street vendors crying and all the sounds of a world awakening to another ordinary day. But no matter the outcome, the world would never be the same again for her.

Six o'clock came! Seven! Eight! There was no possibility of rest. The morning arrived, without pause of misery. She passed only from feelings of sickness to shudderings of horror; and from hot fits of fever to cold. Although straining to listen with every nerve of her body, she was barely aware when Susan was escorted out, to pass the day with the wife and children of their neighbour, Mr. Stephen. With every moment that crawled by, Fanny felt her spirits sinking. Surely this silence meant that Edmund was dying or dead, with Tom attending him, too distracted to send a message to her. If Henry Crawford was triumphant, supposing he had even made note of where she was to be reached, he might have decided to leave her in cruel suspense. Her suppositions and speculations grew ever darker. It seemed only too probable that she would never see Edmund again – what other explanation could there be for this long delay?

At nine, when her poor suffering frame could endure no more, and she was resting on her bed, there came at last a knock at the door. Fanny sprang up, flew down the stairs and ran into the waiting arms of a weary Edmund Bertram. He held her tightly, without saying a word, for a long moment. Fanny stifled her questions and stood quietly in his embrace, laying her head upon his heart, instantly changing from being the one who sorely needed comfort and relief, to being the one who gave it. Whatever had transpired or was to come, he was drawing strength from her.

***

Henry Crawford was lying in agony at The Spaniards Pub, close by the Heath, whose proprietors were accustomed to receiving injured parties from duels. A surgeon was swiftly summoned and pronounced what no-one needed a surgeon to perceive – although the injuries to Mr. Crawford's head looked alarming and bloody, they were inconsequential as compared to the injuries to his legs, which were mangled and crushed beyond repair. He would require amputation, which he refused. "That's right, the young gentlemens always refuses – at first. And when they changes their minds, it's often too late," said the surgeon philosophically, packing up his bloody tools into his satchel.

Upon hearing the grim news from Edmund, Mrs. Butters swiftly offered her own home to receive Mr. Crawford, who she still supposed to be Fanny's husband. "What agonies the young man will be in!" exclaimed the kindly widow. "Oh dear, and his horses – I expect they were all put down, poor things."

A few hours later the injured man arrived at their door, laid upon a blanket which had been ingeniously suspended by four corners in the back of a hay wagon to protect him, to some extent, from the bumping and jostling of a hazardous trip over country roads. The full extent of his injuries were not apparent until he was brought inside and laid upon a mattress placed on Mrs. Butter's dining table. His pain was severe; he had been well plied with brandy, to little avail. Both Mrs. Butters and her housekeeper received their unexpected guest with composure, having had experience in years past with the injuries suffered by shipwrights on the Bristol docks; the sight did not overpower them, but even Fanny, to Edmund's surprise, placed herself at Crawford's side and took his hand, offering him calm reassurance. He was half-delirious, and more concerned about the fate of his team of horses than himself.

Others crowded into the room – Edmund, Mr. Anderson, and Mr. Stanhope, who had followed Henry Crawford to the dueling grounds to act as his second, but who had fallen behind when Crawford unaccountably whipped his horses into a frenzy.

"Fanny – waste – waste – waste! " Henry gasped out through his pain. Fanny moved closer to listen.

Mrs. Butters supposed that Crawford, facing his own extinction, was lamenting his misspent life, and was about to exhort him to think on eternity, but Fanny said, "No, ma'am, I believe he is saying 'waistcoat.' Something about a waistcoat.' An answering squeeze to her hand confirmed that she was correct.

"Do you want your club waistcoat, Crawford?" asked Mr. Stanhope. "Your blue-and-yellow? It is not here, but I can have it brought to you," he promised, though thinking within himself it was a trivial request from a trivial man facing his final judgement. Crawford shook his head and moaned. Fanny placed her head closer to his mouth, he whispered something, and she reported, "He says, look in the pocket of his waistcoat."

Crawford's bloody waistcoat had been cut from his body at The Spaniard Pub, and was located with some difficulty, half-hidden under the blood-spattered hay in the wagon. Inside were found his settlements, sworn before a lawyer, on Miss Maria Bertram, to be his wife, and on Miss Fanny Price, in reparation for the injury done to her reputation. Fanny was to have three thousand pounds.

With a great effort Crawford exclaimed, "Where is Maria? I may die under the surgeon – need to take my vows first. For God's sake, bring her swiftly."

Mr. Stanhope volunteered to use his influence to obtain a special license as quickly as possible. Edmund offered to fetch the Admiral or Mary to the bedside but Crawford refused vehemently –"You don't want the Admiral at a wedding, and I don't want Mary to see – " before fainting away.

Mrs. Butters was dumbfounded to learn that Fanny was not Henry Crawford's wife, but to Fanny's relief, she did not condemn her for telling falsehoods. Mrs. Butters had her own reasons for being pleased that Fanny was a free woman and although she was no poet, she could hardly wait to find a quiet moment to put pen to paper and inform some of her correspondents that Mrs. Crawford was in fact still Miss Price, and would be three thousand pounds richer into the bargain.

In the almost twenty-four hours of agonizing waiting that followed, Fanny tried her best to comfort and support Henry through his ordeal, as Edmund hastened to fetch his sister from the secluded village where she lived, whose location he had learnt from Tom just prior to his brother's hasty departure for Liverpool.

The entire household watched anxiously for Edmund's carriage, which finally arrived in the late morning the day after Mr. Crawford's accident. It rattled swiftly up the street, a heavily veiled lady climbed down awkwardly and was carefully escorted inside. Fanny had hardly left Henry Crawford's side through his ordeal, but shrank away when she saw her cousin Maria arrive. She did not see the lovers reunited, did not see Henry Crawford take Maria's hand and kiss it, did not see the tears falling on her cheeks, as she guided his hand to her belly so he could feel his child kicking under her heart.

"Ah, Maria, he has good strong legs," Henry jested weakly.

It had taken a substantial fee to obtain a special license that waived the reading of the banns, and moved the ceremony from the church. Edmund anxiously watched the clock on the mantelpiece, as the hands crept toward noon, for weddings had to be solemnized before that time. The minister was found and hurried to his place, Henry waved away the proffered brandy and laudanum, so that he might clearly speak his vows, which he did, through a haze of excruciating pain, and after being pronounced man and wife, he could even make a jest about disappointing his bride on his wedding day. The bride was led back to the carriage to rest at Wimpole Street, so that she should not hear what was to follow, as the surgeon stepped forward to tighten his tourniquets and sever both of the bridegroom's legs above the knee.

Now the house rang with the screams of the injured man! Fanny wept and buried her head under her pillow until sudden silence fell upon the household.

***

William Gibson held his hand and forearm up before his eyes and thought, impartially, that he wouldn't have recognized the limb for his own, it was so browned from the tropical sun, and so thin and wiry – just bone and gristle. He lay back, closed his eyes and thought of the delicious food available to him in Portsmouth, if he could only leave his hammock and obtain it – fresh bread and butter, fried eggs and ham, roast chicken, frothy ale, perhaps some oysters, or an apple tart.

And that was supposing that he had the ready funds to buy something in Portsmouth, and the clothes to be seen in amongst decent folk. The Navy was fairly nonchalant in the matter of what and when he would be paid. More precious than the pay, though, was the fact that Captain Columbine had procured his discharge from the Navy. "You are no sailor, and never will be, Gibson," he'd said with a smile. "You can do more good for the cause of abolition if you stay ashore. I'll write you from Sierra Leone after I've assumed the governorship and let you know how matters prosper there."

Gibson remembered little of the last two weeks, after succumbing to the fever and dysentery that swept through the crowded sloop. He thought he could remember the nightmares more vividly than the waking;

nightmares of struggling in a dark cave through green water, chest deep, sweating and panting in the stinking heat, as he frantically pushed barrels and bales through a hole smashed in the side of – the side of what? He blinked, confused. It had been no cave. It had been no nightmare. There had been an exhausting and totally futile hour of working the pumps in the bowels of the ship to try and keep the hold from flooding. He could feel the *Solebay* slowly listing beneath his feet, could hear the planks crack and separate and the warm water rush in. The pumps were abandoned and he and his mates turned to trying to save the stores of food and rum and ammunition. At last, as the waters surged around his waist, he climbed out of the hold and struck out for the shore, limp as a rag and gasping for breath.

Other fragments of the expedition against the French came back to him; the pathetic little boats attempting to ferry the soldiers and sailors across the sand bar at the mouth of the river, fighting the river currents as they plowed into the ocean tides, watching one of the boats flip and seeing seven men from the *Derwent* tossed out, clawing at the waves and swept under to rise no more; the misery of the soldiers, who were, of course, compelled to wear the same wool jackets and rigid stocks around their neck that they would have worn on a cool morning back in Merrie Old England, except now they were in the middle of a steaming jungle where no-one in his right senses would wear more than a loin cloth if he had any choice in the matter; the poor old sergeant, overcome by the heat, falling face down, never to rise again, the cabin boys, round-eyed and silent, poised by their gun crews, ready to run on command to fetch more gunpowder, the deafening sound of that first salvo sent across the river to smash into the French defenses, the general joy when it was realized that the French had abandoned their posts and withdrawn into the jungle, and the smile on Captain Columbine's tired, sweat-streaked face when he returned with the articles of surrender from the French encampment, and the answering cheers of the crew.

Gibson hoped that his illness had not wiped out other details, for he needed to recall everything for his book. Did he remember correctly, or was it some feverish fantasy, that the surrendering French were allowed to keep their own slaves, because they were, after all, the *property* of the French?

Gibson had spent the last part of the voyage home to England crammed into a stinking infirmary with other stricken sailors, some of whom had been carried out wrapped in a shroud. Now safely anchored in the

Spithead, Gibson was still lying on board the *Derwent*, gently bobbing in English waters, for lack of anywhere else to go. His friend Lieutenant Price had been granted shore leave to arrange lodging with his family, but he could not flatter himself that the Price family would want to take in an invalid stranger, as the ever-sanguine William Price assured him they would. Should that fail, he would write to his old friend Mrs. Butters for the name of some friend of the abolitionist cause in Portsmouth – a friendly and compassionate Quaker, perhaps – for he doubted he could survive the journey to London or Bristol, as he couldn't even crawl to the head and back without fainting.

He allowed himself to briefly feel some pity on his own behalf; he had no anxious family waiting for him on the pier upon his return – no parents, no cousins, no relations who were obliged to take him in while he recovered his strength – and certainly no one with soft blue eyes who looked up at him with admiration for everything he said. He managed a smile, and admitted to himself that in certain circumstances it might be very useful, even pleasant, to have such a thing as a family one day.

There *were* women within hailing distance, surrounding the sloop, bobbing in the harbour on little boats, a small army of gap toothed, grimy, blousy and vulgar dolly mops who would instantly claim to be his wife, should he wish. Fortunately, he was too tired to consider coming to grips with any of them.

He was asleep again when Lieutenant Price returned, waving the discharge papers which would permit him to remove William Gibson from onboard ship. His mother had been unenthused, but was unable to refuse her beloved son's request – "And just when we were returning to our ordinary ways, after having your aunt Norris amongst us. I've had enough of company for three lifetimes, may I tell you. And I have enough to do, without nursing an invalid on top of the bargain!"

William promised he would help take care of his friend, if only a corner could be found for him upstairs, and finally his mother sighed, "all right, you may place him on a pallet in the attic. But he's your responsibility, mind," as though her son was asking to bring home a guinea pig, or a puppy.

"And," added his mother, "he'll pay for his lodging, and his food, or he'll be back on the street right sharply, I can promise you that."

Lieutenant Price represented his mother as being of course in every way delighted to welcome her son's good friend into her home, so Gibson thankfully bid farewell to the *Derwent,* and with the help of some friendly

Marines he was carried to a bosun's chair and lowered away to a launch. The sun was bright but the breeze was deliciously cool, wonderfully English and, by Heaven – whether or not you believed there was such a place, of course – it was good to be alive.

***

The funeral for the late Henry Crawford was held at St. James, Piccadilly, with Admiral Crawford serving as chief mourner. Edmund Bertram slipped quietly into the rear pews, wanting to pay his respects, feeling it proper, but unsure of how he would be received. His brother Tom's friend, Charles Anderson, was the only sympathetic face he saw in the church – the other men, all friends of the Admiral or of the dead man, upon seeing him, nudged each other with their elbows, whispered in each other's ears, and gave him icy stares of contempt.

After Crawford survived the amputation – he had thankfully fainted dead away during the operation – Edmund had informed the Admiral, over Crawford's objections – and the Admiral, over the objections of everyone, insisted on transporting his nephew from Stoke Newington to Hill Street. Once there, no one by the name of Bertram, not even Mary, was admitted to see the patient. A week later, came the word that the wounds had turned putrid and Henry Crawford was dead after a week of intense suffering.

The service concluded, Edmund and Anderson waited respectfully for the others to leave before they departed.

"A chilly reception, bigad, Bertram," whispered Mr. Anderson after they shook the vicar's hand and turned to walk down the stone steps. "I am accustomed to my relatives watching me in church as though they expect me to burst into flames, but you, sir, this must be a novel experience for you."

"A great many people loved Henry Crawford," Edmund reflected.

"Yes, and for every man here there must be at least two or three young ladies at home, weeping their eyes out."

They were but a few steps from the church when a shrill and angry voice assailed them. They turned to see the Admiral bearing down on them, with half-a-dozen or more angry supporters behind him.

"Hey! Ahoy! You blackguard Bertram! I ought to beat your brains out here in the street!" The Admiral waved his walking stick emphatically.

"Sir," Edmund bowed. "Pray allow me to convey my most sincere condolences and sympathies, on behalf of myself and all – "

"Be silent, you quivering poltroon." The old man fixed Edmund with a venomous stare, his cane clutched at the ready in his fist, the veins in his neck throbbing. "You Bertrams are bent on the utter destruction of my family! You challenged my nephew to a duel with the false and scurrilous lie that he deflowered some little whey-faced cousin of yours. When in fact, he never laid a finger on the little b—tch, and she was living in luxury at his expense, calling herself "Mrs. Crawford," ordering his servants about and helping herself to everything that wasn't nailed down – along with a parcel of her poxy Portsmouth relations! Then, when my nephew was lying in his death agonies, your lying whore of a sister showed up and claimed that the bastard in her belly was his child, so she could inherit Everingham away from Mary, the rightful heir. You wouldn't allow the surgeon near him, nor let him have any brandy or laudanum, until he was forced into marriage with the slut!"

By now a small crowd had gathered, and were listening intently. The Admiral took a deep breath, fumbled with his false teeth, and resumed: "As for Mary, she told me she believed you actually loved her – more fool she – and that you cared nothing for her fortune, when in fact, before the ink was dry on your marriage license, you began draining her pockets to turn your wretched country hovel into a palace, while at the same time installing your thieving aunt in Mary's house in London, living at *her* expense. She told me you abandoned her last month, over some trumped-up quarrel you invented and you've left her to die of a broken heart. My family, sir, has reason to curse the day we ever heard the name 'Bertram.'"

There were some disapproving murmurs in the crowd and angry looks directed toward Edmund and his companion. He removed his hat and bowed again, deeply.

"Sir, I very much regret the circumstances of the accident which claimed your nephew's life. As to the rest, sir, time and Providence must be my judge."

"Don't 'Providence,' me, you black-robed jackal! My niece, married to a clergyman! G-d help us all! By g-d, if I had you on one of my ships, I would lash you to the gratings and flog you to the bone! I'd flog you, just as your father, the honourable Sir Thomas, flogs his slaves, you sanctimonious prating hypocrite!" The Admiral's voice raised to a crescendo, the false teeth nearly slipped out and were retrieved, and the crowd now completely surrounded the old Admiral and the object of his hatred.

"Sir," Edmund finally ventured, "We all regret the mischance that befell your nephew, but it is not in my power to –."

"Mischance! You pharisaical whoreson! Give me my nephew back! And you may go to the devil, with all of your tribe of vultures!" The Admiral raised his cane, but just as Edmund lifted his arm to ward off the blow, the angry old man spun around abruptly and scuttled away as quickly as he had come, leaving the murmuring crowd to discuss whether the impudent bastard ought to be hung from a lamppost or merely pelted with the dung from the streets.

Mr. Anderson seized his arm and hurried him away before the crowd could decide on the correct course of action. "By my faith," Anderson panted, "I thought the apoplectic old fellow would drop right there on the pavement and you'd have the death of another Crawford on your conscience! What a final oration, though, begad! Not since Antony has a man stirred up a crowd like that, eh?"

"There is enough truth in what he said to discompose me and enough clever falsehoods to illustrate the malignity of the mind that invented this version of events. And yet, is it invention, or do the Crawfords regard this as a true history? How wonderful are the workings of the human mind when the desire arises to justify oneself to others!"

"A little less philosophy and a little more velocity would be to the purpose, Bertram," cautioned Anderson, looking over his shoulder. "We haven't shaken the last of the Admiral's claque yet." And a clump of horse dung caught Edmund squarely between the shoulder blades. Still, he refused to run.

***

Several evenings of quiet retirement at Mrs. Butter's fireside, and several days devoted to long walks in the park, were needed to tranquilize Fanny after the events of the past fortnight. She had elected to remain in the peace of Stoke Newington, now that the alarms over her brother and Mr. Gibson were got over; they were known to be safely in Portsmouth, and she felt she could know neither good spirits nor good health in her parents' house, nor in the Crown Inn, for any tolerable length of time. Mrs. Butters had promised to escort her and Susan to Portsmouth in plenty of time for the court martial, and after that ordeal was over, she knew not where she would reside – and yet, that question, which ought to have occupied her the most, concerned her the least.

She was still very much inclined to blame herself, not the principals themselves, or the vagaries of chance, for the sufferings of Maria and the tragedy of Henry Crawford's death. She prayed for him earnestly, believing

300

that his courage and steadfastness in doing right by Maria, undertaken at a time of such physical suffering as made her weep to recall, was eloquent testimony that he intended to be a better man. Had he lived, she firmly believed, he would have become a better – if not perfect – husband and father, a good landlord and master. The admiral had snatched his broken body away, but he could not hang on to his soul – he was lost to his family, to his uncle, before his death – he had awakened, he was beginning to turn his back on all that was reprehensible in his past. That was why the old admiral was so vicious, so unreasoning in his anger.

Fanny wrote long penitential letters to William, Sir Thomas, and Maria, explaining how it had come about that she had pretended to be married to Henry Crawford, and the considerations that had impelled her to do it. She shrank from the task – she would far rather that someone, anyone, speak on her behalf, but Mrs. Butters firmly urged her to be her own advocate.

Her cousin Edmund was gone, escorting his sister Maria to Everingham. The family's old nursery maid, Hannah, was with them as well, to give Maria the comfort of a familiar, loving face in her new home. Fanny was grateful that she was not to be of the party, for she admittedly had not the courage for the ordeal of explaining to the vicar, or to Mr. Maddison and the rest of the servants, why *one* Mrs. Crawford went up to London in August and a *different* Mrs. Crawford, now a widow, came back in September.

It was impossible to keep any part of the affair from the newspapers, a prospect that filled her with shame, most particularly for Sir Thomas and Lady Bertram, and yet, the provision of a home for Maria and a name for her child was a happy resolution unlooked-for by the family only a week ago. Maria herself, Fanny had been assured, had courage and spirit enough to assume her new role as mistress of Everingham, and sufficient tender feelings subsisting for her late husband to raise his child so as to honour the memory of the father.

Everingham was uncongenial to Fanny, but Thornton Lacey was forbidden to her. Although she and Edmund had re-established the most perfect sympathy, friendship and understanding betwixt them, although she had had the joy of being with him, talking with him, and just listening to him during several evenings at Mrs. Butters' table, she knew that she would never be welcomed across the threshold of the parsonage by its mistress. She would like nothing better than to hear Edmund preach a sermon, and he promised that it should be so, on some future occasion, but it was impossible to foretell when favourable circumstances might arise. Fanny sighed at the necessity of the separation, but was resigned to it.

As for returning to live in Mansfield Park, she disliked the idea, as being a falling back, a withdrawal from the world, and a return to too many things she had fled. She and Sir Thomas had yet to meet, and she must await his invitation and his forgiveness, should he be inclined to extend it, before she could enter his halls again as a visitor. She looked to time, and Sir Thomas's sense of justice, for forgiveness and reconciliation.

The bequest from Henry Crawford might be enough, with careful management, for her to live modestly, in independence and obscurity, a prospect as beguiling to her as a palace would have been to many another. But in the vague scenes of the future that her fancy painted, there was always another one living with her; sometimes it was Susan, sometimes William, perhaps even Miss Lee, retired from her labours, some congenial person with whom to talk and walk. For the present, Mrs. Butters did not speak of Fanny ever leaving her side, and Fanny was grateful to remain with the kind old widow.

***

Mary Bertram, clad in the deepest mourning, lay prostrate on the sofa, her lovely eyes red-rimmed. The old Admiral, whom she had always detested, had proven to be her staunchest ally in the catastrophe, and to her surprise she found herself inviting him for tea a few days after the funeral so that she could once again review the disastrous events of the past year. She could not think of enough bad things to say about her husband's family. Who would have thought that the meek little Fanny Price could have authored such devastation? She must have brazenly lied to Edmund about being deceived and seduced by Henry, and her brother was dead in consequence.

Even as Mary spurned Edmund and refused to answer his messages, he was all she could think about, and she realized that she longed to feel his arms around her again. She couldn't bear the company of her old friends, such as Mrs. Fraser. The Earl of Elsham had sent flowers and his card; she was at home to nobody. Yet, she hated being alone. She wanted desperately to feel as secure and loved as she had when she was first married. "Tell me again of my husband, uncle. What did he say to you after the funeral?"

"Very little to the purpose, child, he bowed and stammered and said he was sorry. The pious fraud. I gave him a piece of my mind, you may be sure!"

"Thank you, uncle. When I think of how that wretched Miss Price connived against us – my brother in his death agonies, our family estates stolen away from us!"

"Mr. Stanhope said that Miss Price would not leave your brother's side while he lay there."

"Yes, so as to keep him prisoner until he could be forced into marriage with Maria!"

"Aye, and the grieving widow has already hastened to Norfolk to seize control of Everingham."

"And what of Edmund's father or his brother Tom – did they dare to show their faces at my brother's funeral?"

"Sir Thomas, I believe, is hiding away in his estate. As for his elder brother, that reminds me, I've significant news for you. This morning I had it on good authority, –

"– by 'good authority' I know you mean that woman who lives with you, yes?"

"Sneer if you will, but Sophia is very reliable. I have never known her to be in error in her information. The older Bertram son, the one *they* call 'Tom,' but whom *I* will call a – [and here the Admiral used a series of colourful naval epithets that made Mary wince] – fled to Liverpool on the morning of the duel."

Mary frowned. "The duel wasn't actually fought, was it? Why would Mr. Bertram need to evade the law?"

"Ah, he's not fleeing from the law. He's fleeing from his life, don't you know. He has set sail for America where he plans to breed horses. But he'll breed nothing himself – if what Sophie hears of him is true, he will make no heir, so your husband will be the heir presumptive. Or, if you have a son, Mary, he will be a baronet one day. That ought to please you. What a revenge that will be for losing Everingham! Please promise me you'll cuckold him."

Mary sat bolt upright, alarm in her eyes.

"Uncle, what *did* you say to Edmund after the funeral? Tell me everything."

303

Chapter Twenty-Five

"We have a proposal for you, Fanny," said Mrs. Butters in her direct way, one morning at breakfast. She had yet to explain who 'we' were, but Fanny knew the rest would follow shortly. She and Susan exchanged glances – and Susan took the precaution of selecting another muffin and buttering it well, in preparation for whatever news befell them.

"My relations – not the high and mighty Smallridges – I mean the Blodgetts – those folk who sell fabrics and lace in Bristol – you have been to their draper's shop with me, haven't you, Fanny?"

"Yes, ma'am. You and I and Madame Orly, last winter."

Mrs. Butters leaned forward confidingly.

"They have plans, Fanny. Plans to expand their trade to London."

"I see."

"Not yet, you don't. I have yet to explain. We shall also be opening a dress-maker's shop before the next Season commences, and engaging the most skilled mantua-makers. Our scheme, as well, is to provide honourable employment for girls in reduced circumstances."

Susan's eyes grew wide in horror, wondering if she were a girl in reduced circumstances, and if Mrs. Butters meant to tie her to a stool and have her stitch away from sunrise until midnight as so many seamstresses did. As though anticipating her, Mrs. Butters added, "My relations, the Blodgetts, will offer the prevailing wage, comfortable working conditions, adequate light and air, and healthy meals, in exchange for diligent labour and exemplary skills. They are partnering with Mr. Wilberforce's Society for Bettering the Conditions and Increasing the Comforts of the Poor, to create a workplace founded upon humane conditions."

"This all sounds most commendable, ma'am, and there are many young persons who – "

"These young persons will require persons not quite as young to supervise and train them, and I had proposed your name, Fanny..."

"Oh! Mrs. Butters! You must excuse me, I could not undertake such a responsibility," Fanny responded, almost automatically.

A piercing look from Mrs. Butters.

"Do you mean to say, you do not care to accept this offer of employment, or you feel yourself unequal to it?"

"Well, I.... I.... "

"Do not decide now. Consider it. I was under the impression that you would like something to do with yourself every day, now that you are neither a governess nor pretending to be married. And I *have* told my relations that you are somewhat frail, and could not be expected to work the long hours customary in the trade, but nevertheless your talents could be put to good use."

"Thank you, ma'am, I am most obliged to you for your thoughtfulness. I would like to learn more of your scheme – I suspect that you, in your benevolence, were actually the one who proposed the entire idea."

***

Edmund's wife was waiting for him at Thornton Lacey when he returned from Everingham, as the cheerful housemaid informed him at the door – "So good to see the mistress again sir, I'm sure you were missing her, you were that quiet when she was away." She was not in the parlour, which was still in a half-finished state, so he climbed the crooked staircase to their bedchamber and wondered, would she be penitent? accusing? conciliatory? And he found her sitting on their bed, looking more beautiful than he had ever remembered, clad only in a flowing silk brocade wrap with her hair unbound. She waited for him to close the door behind him, then commenced eagerly, in her low, soft voice:

"Edmund, you remember when I said that selfishness must always be forgiven, because there is no hope of a cure. I could not bear to share your love with anyone, not even your foolish little cousin. That is why I tried to keep you apart. It was just a trifling jealous game on my part, with no harm done to anyone."

Edmund watched her, fascinated, waiting to see what she would say next. "Even though my brother is dead because of you and your family, I cannot bring myself to leave you. I need you still. Please tell me that you still need me. I am your wife. Why will you forgive your brother Tom for being what *he* is, but you shrink away from me?"

"Mary, this estrangement is dreadful to my feelings, and contrary to everything we looked and hoped for in the marriage state," Edmund began, suddenly feeling like a pompous fool, "but the most important bond between a husband and wife is mutual confidence, sympathy and trust. We took a sacred vow before God to be loyal to one another. What can this mean, but to be truthful, to have no secrets worth the name, no reservations, no holding back. A wife who will lie to her husband, repeatedly, about one particular, may well lie to her husband about many other things – or so he will come to fear. Doubt and reservation will inevitably chase away – "

Mary sprang from her seat, her countenance changing from supplication to disdain, with a rapidity that startled Edmund. "A pretty good lecture, upon my word. Was it part of your last sermon? At this rate you will soon reform everybody at Mansfield and Thornton Lacey; and no doubt you will rise from your present obscurity to become a celebrated preacher in some great society of Methodists. Tell me, Edmund, if you cannot trust *me*, why do you trust Fanny? *She* deceived everyone, did she not, by pretending to marry my brother? She lied to you, to Sir Thomas, to your sister, to the world. Have you forgiven *her*? Do you respect and trust *her*? There is no question, is there? *She* may do as she pleases, so long as she fawns on you like a lapdog. She feeds your vanity and you will not hold her to account."

Edmund did not need to be reminded that his wife was one who, in flights of passion, made remarks which she was likely to regret when her temper cooled. He abhorred this type of temperament, even as he acknowledged her skill in inflicting deeper wounds in every sentence. And at the same time he was engaged in these unhappy thoughts, he was also aware of her slender white neck, her bare shoulders, her firm high breasts, heaving with anger, thinly clad by the sheer silk robe, and how he could, with one swift caress, send that robe shimmering to the floor.

He turned away, determined not to dispute with her when she had lost her composure so utterly, and to seek the solitude of his study downstairs. Again, like quicksilver, his wife changed from resentment to contrition -- so quickly, that he had to doubt the sincerity of any of her feelings – did she love him? Could she love?

"Please, Edmund." She stood, beautiful and beguiling, and gracefully untied his cravat. She had started to tug at his sleeves, to remove his jacket, and he grabbed one of her arms to stop her. At his touch, she submitted and looked up at him pleadingly.

"Mary, Mary, how can we make things as they were before? What is to be done?"

She tried a saucy, playful smile, "I promise, I will be a good wife to you here at Thornton Lacey, you will see! You will have no cause for regret!"

"Oh, would to God we had never met!" The bitter cry burst forth from Edmund. In answer, Mary's eyes rolled back in her head, and she started to swoon away so that he had to catch her to prevent her from falling, senseless, to the ground. He stood irresolute for a moment, looking down at the lovely form lying helplessly in his arms, then her eyes fluttered, and she looked up at him through her long lashes. "If you must turn me away, Edmund," she murmured, "please, be my husband again just for one night." She reached into his shirt to stroke his chest. His knees trembled violently, he almost stumbled; he carried her to their bed and very soon thereafter he made the surprising discovery that, while anger at a wife may cool the heart, it can still heat the blood.

***

Mrs. Butters' carriage, with Fanny and Susan, rolled into Portsmouth in the early days of September, a few days before the court martial, for a happy reunion with friends and relations. William Gibson was retrieved from the Price's attic, where little Betsey had been his principal nurse. She had brought him food and hot water, and, to ensure that she would return three times a day, he told her little stories about a family of monkeys who lived in a cocoa-nut tree.

Mrs. Butters installed him in more comfortable and restful lodgings in the Crown Inn and aggressively nursed and fed him.

William and Fanny had much to relate to each other, and genuine sorrow to share over the death of Henry Crawford. She knew that her brother would not hold her blameable for his misadventures, if they could be so-called, aboard the *Solebay*, and he was thunderstruck at the thought that his upright sister had loved him well enough to stoop to such an expedient to win his preferment.

William Gibson, informed by Mrs. Butters, jested that he had been press ganged into the navy and Miss Price had been press ganged into marriage, and they both were released at about the same time.

Mr. Price was temporarily outraged upon learning that his daughter Fanny had *not* been married – he assumed the worst and threatened to 'give her the rope's end as long as he could stand over her.' In fact, it was not until the he repaired to the Crown Inn and enquired of the landlord, to be assured Mr. and Mrs. Crawford had indeed taken separate rooms when visiting there last spring, that he allowed himself to believe his daughter.

Even though matters were cleared up, Fanny spent very little time with her parents; she usually left their roof as soon as breakfast was over and spent the day with Mrs. Butters, shopping for gifts for her family, and books and sweetmeats to send to her former pupils Caroline and Edward, or walking and talking on the ramparts with William, and hearing, once again, all the details of the trip down the African coast, the attack on the

French at St. Louis, the loss of the *Solebay* and the capture of the slave ship.

"Once the authorities uncover the identity of the owners of that ship, they will pay a fine of one hundred pounds for every African that was on board," William explained to her one morning when they were escorting Mr. Gibson for a brief walk in the sunshine, "and the *Clementine* will be forfeit, and she was a beauty."

They came to a comfortable bench, and Fanny suddenly realized that, by prearrangement between her two companions, her brother was going to leave her there for a *tête à tête* with Mr. Gibson. William Price strolled on, alone, hearing the faint laughter of Fanny and his friend carried on the sea breeze and feeling well pleased with himself.

William Gibson questioned Fanny, in that mild, yet direct way that she fondly recalled from their previous conversations, about her sham marriage to the late Henry Crawford. Fanny blushed and demurred, "You warned me, Mr. Gibson, that you might drop me into a three-volume novel, but I had no fears of this so long as the life I led was unexceptional – but now – please promise me that you are not inspired to weave a story about my cousins and Mr. Crawford and me! The papers have been full of the scandal of the late Mr. C_____ and his erstwhile bride, Miss P_____, to my everlasting chagrin."

"You ask a great deal, Miss Price, given that I have the advantage of being acquainted with one of the principals. I had even thought, when the news of your marriage first reached me, that it was *I* who had brought it about – that you had taken up my advice to confess your love to the object of your devotion. I had supposed that, thanks to my timely counsel, you were embarked on a lifetime of the greatest felicity with the man of your choice."

Fanny shook her head and replied with a calmness that surprised herself, "*That* gentleman – he – it will never be, it *can* never be, and I have come some way in schooling myself to feel nothing more than the warmest regard for him."

"If your affections were less tenacious than they are, they would not be worth the winning," Gibson observed quietly, and Fanny could only look away from him and blink back the tears that rose to her eyes. After a pause, he enquired, "Your brother tells me that you and he and your sister Susan are all invited to Northamptonshire, where you grew up."

"Yes – my uncle has written me, most kindly, and so has my aunt. How wonderful it will be to see Mansfield again! Even though, I suppose, it will never be the same, for better or for worse. My cousin Maria is in Norfolk, and my cousin Tom is on his way to America – my aunt Bertram must have been very lonely these past months."

"Mansfield Park is a place of some grandeur, I collect?"

"Yes – and I know what you are thinking. You know the source of a goodly portion of my uncle's wealth, and you cannot think as well of Mansfield Park and my uncle as I could wish."

"My thoughts are even more radical than you could suppose. I want to one day live in an England where a man who grows rich off the toil and agony of slaves is held in greater contempt by society than... let's say.... a young woman who stoops to folly and is gotten with child before her marriage. Imagine that! You may feel required to condemn your cousin and defend your uncle, along with the rest of the world. But, I understand that your uncle was until recently very severe, very severe indeed, upon *you* – and I cannot excuse him for that, considering what he himself is guilty of."

"Oh, you must have heard something from William about it all. Thank you for being my champion, but I only want to be reconciled to my aunt and uncle, and trust I shall be."

"Very well. I shall *say* no more about it to you, in deference to your feelings. If I have learned anything in the past few months, it is that family ties are not to be despised. Your brother's friendship was a great blessing to me, by the bye, and I think I even owe my life to him for his attentions to me when I was struck down by fever."

"Oh dear! William told me he feared that you would expire in the little attic at my father's house, with only Betsey to care for you!"

"Betsey was an excellent nurse and companion, Miss Price. I recognize a fellow scribbler in her. She has a capital imagination and a taste for the Gothic. She entertained me with stories about a horrible apparition that haunted your father's household, a creature that was banished shortly before my arrival, who gave your family no rest by day or by night. She had the eyes and claws of a cat, and she was called the 'An'norris' – "

Fanny began laughing so heartily that tears sprang to her eyes, and Mr. Gibson paused, gratified but perplexed, doubting whether the flow of his wit, alone, could account for his fair companion's mirth.

***

Edmund often had the sensation of being a spectator at a play, but the play was in fact his own life. The Act I curtain arose on a happy married couple at their little breakfast table. His wife Mary ably directed the servants; they were happy to learn from her the little ways of arranging a home and setting out a meal as would distinguish their household in elegance and refinement from all their neighbours; they were pleased to think of themselves as serving the master and mistress that set the mode for the parish and who would one day be a baronet and his lady! The husband read his paper and answered his wife's thoughtful questions about the news of the day and of the parish, she enquired after his comfort and asked, what could she do to help her husband serve his parishioners today? Was there a family stricken with illness? Whom could she visit to bring succour?

In Act II, after breakfast, husband and wife went about their daily duties; he to his study to write and prepare for Sunday, or else he visited his parishioners; she turned to her many tasks as mistress of the parsonage, in which her performance was beyond reproach, or if there was a reproach to be made, it was that she was too extravagant as regards ordering improvements for her husband's comfort – now that the alterations were nearly finished for the front of the house, she set about re-doing the offices, to make them modern, larger and better equipped.

On these fine September days, she would urge her husband to go riding with her; and, when he could not think of an excuse to refuse, he would yield, for she had no-one else to ride with, and they would set out together while she exclaimed on the beauty and freshness of the countryside. In the evening, after tea, she sometimes played the harp for him, which softened his heart toward her as nothing else could, recalling as it did those days, twelve months ago, when he had fallen in love with her.

Act III saw the happy couple alone together, retiring for the night, and as the lights were extinguished, the minister's wife became an altogether different woman, a woman who had acquired, somehow, skills and knowledge which kept Edmund in thrall to her, and the final curtain often found him, the sole observer of the play, staring into the darkness, while his wife slept sweetly beside him, clinging to his arm.

His was a special kind of torment. He could not persuade himself that all was well between them, nor could he maintain a coldness and reserve towards one whom he had vowed to love and to cherish, who was such an excellent helpmeet by day and such a temptress by night, but his esteem for her was severely shaken. Further, he *did* feel, and perhaps would always feel, guilt over his hasty challenge of her brother Henry and the string of blunders that led to his death.

As one who preached the gospel, he knew that he was to ask for and practise forgiveness, but he also felt his wife should atone to Fanny, and he dreaded a resumption of those reproaches and recriminations that had revealed his wife's malignant view of the events of the past few months. He did not raise the subject, excusing himself on the grounds that he and his wife were still wearing mourning ribbons for her brother, and tender subjects should be set aside for a time.

The worst of all was, he could confide his regrets to no other person.

He was a clergyman; and even if divorce had been within his reach, as far as the law went, he would not resort to it. It was a trial on him, a very severe trial of his principles, and one which, as much as possible, for her sake and his, he would not expose to the world. It was as a hair shirt for him to wear – *the world* would congratulate the fortunate man married to the beautiful, intelligent, witty heiress; *he* would know the corruption, the venality and the falsehood beneath the seductive surface. As a vicar he might find himself counseling some or other of his parishioners, urging him to be reconciled with his wife, pointing to the scriptural authorities and the will of Providence on the matter, only *he* would know of the bitter irony, the inner torment as he struggled to practise what he, perforce, must preach!

***

As expected, the court martial was a mere formality, as the Admiralty did not wish to advertise the fact that the crew of the *Solebay* – two hundred and fifty souls – had been sent on their mission in an old, unseaworthy frigate that tore apart like a rotten burlap sack when she was grounded on a Senegal sandbar. No-one was to blame for her loss, least of all the gallant captain and the crew, and William was granted four weeks' leave.

Fanny then took an affectionate farewell of Mrs. Butters and William Gibson, with a promise to him to renew their long-delayed scheme of a book discussion club by correspondence. Mrs. Butters and Mr. Gibson left for Bristol, while Fanny, William and Susan embarked in high spirits for the trip to Northamptonshire.

Fanny then learned another lesson – we are apt to be unreasonably disconcerted when discovering that those we left behind have carried on with their own pleasures and pursuits, and have made their own alterations and improvements in our absence, rather than being, as she had imagined, frozen in amber, and not altering in the least. Mrs. Grant had planted a small rose garden at the Parsonage, Fanny's favourite old oak had been struck by lightning, and Sir Thomas had, at his son Tom's repeated urging, installed a new billiard table. Fanny had fully expected to take her place in the little room in the attic, and found to her gratification that her luggage was delivered instead to Maria's former bedchamber. As disconcerting as these changes were, Fanny had no quarrel with the greatest alteration of all – Mrs. Norris was still determinedly staying on in the London townhome.

Other aspects of life at the park were just as she remembered them; Lady Bertram still reclined in the same spot, and so did Pug; Baddeley and all the servants she knew and remembered, including Christopher Jackson, were all pursuing their usual tasks even though Mrs. Norris was not on hand to superintend and direct them.

Lady Bertram was excessively pleased to see Fanny again after so many months, and, as she had barely comprehended all of the disappointments and unexpected reversals relative to her children, Fanny and the Crawfords, Fanny found that her Ladyship had few enquiries to make, and only frequently exclaimed upon her pleasure that dear Fanny was home, with 'now I shall be comfortable.'

Of the younger Bertrams, only Julia was still at home to welcome their Price cousins. The cordiality with which Julia greeted her cousin Fanny surprised and gratified her.

"Fanny, whatever the world may suspect or say of your false marriage," Julia confided in her as soon as they were alone, "I shall always defend you. I know that you acted for the best, when you tried to prevent Maria's marriage to Mr. Crawford. Based upon what you knew *then* – what you knew of him *then*, you were quite justified in believing that she ought not to marry him – you knew that he had made love to both of us, and – it is not your fault, for as upright as you are, you could never have suspected that both Maria and I were so weak as to...." she trailed off, seeing Fanny's surprised and horrified stare.

"No, no, Fanny, I am not – I am still – I did not lie with him. But I will confess that I allowed him, privately, to take many liberties with me. I am so ashamed to recollect it now!" Julia crossed her arms protectively across her bosom, as though she could *now*, by doing what she ought to have done *then*, erase the memories which shamed her. "How easily he tempted me into hearing words I ought not to have listened to, and receiving attentions I should have repulsed! How readily I agreed! It was only a matter of time before he would have succeeded with me. But when I understood that he was pursuing Maria in the same way – I finally saw him for what he was.

"It hurts me to confess all this to you Fanny, but I want to tell you – I know that your intentions were for the best. I know you wanted to protect Maria. It was very great-hearted of you, especially as, I own, we were not always as kind and sisterly to you as we ought to have been……" This and similar conversations served to bring the two cousins into the most complete confidence and sympathy, and Fanny also told Julia of her belief that Henry Crawford, had he lived, would have reformed himself.

Most precious of all to Fanny's feelings were the quiet moments she spent walking and talking with Sir Thomas in the shrubbery, in the warm autumn afternoons; she, apologizing for having interfered in his daughter's private affairs, and he, acknowledging her good intentions toward Maria, and absolving her of any guilt or blame as regards the outcome.

He assured her as well that Maria bore her no ill will, for Maria was candid enough to acknowledge that it was her own actions, her folly in meeting with Henry Crawford in secret, that had led to her crisis.

"And, Fanny, I cannot but acknowledge, painful though it may be, that perhaps *none* of these untoward events would have occurred if I had not absented myself in Antigua during such an interesting time in my daughters' lives – the time when they were of an age to fancy themselves in love and to think of marriage. Even upon my return, I was too taken up with business to give domestic matters all the attention they deserved. But worse than that, I fear," he added, taking her hand, "were the errors in my system of upbringing of all of you." She protested, but he explained, "Maria, Julia, all of you, repressed your spirits in my presence so as to make your real dispositions unknown to me, and while my daughters were overindulged and excessively praised by your aunt, I know that you, my child, never knew ought of kindness or indulgence from her, nor, to my regret, from me."

"Nevertheless, sir, I always knew you to be a man of good principles, of character, and honour, and it was always my desire to please you and learn from you."

Sir Thomas also shared with her his misgivings about the slave trade, his regret that the family fortunes were bound up in it, and his desire to escape its coils. "My new partners and I have gone into a new venture – the importation of palm oil from Africa, which as you may know, is used for making soap and candles. They expect our investment will yield handsome returns within a twelvemonth and then, I propose to sell the remainder of my Antigua holdings and have done with it."

In this fashion, on really becoming acquainted with each other, the mutual attachment of uncle and niece became very strong.

Together the four young people — Fanny, Julia, William and Susan — made the empty halls of Mansfield Park ring with laughter once again. The weather was fine enough for picnics and riding, and croquet on the lawn, and the evening brought them together for music with Julia at the piano and William's fine tenor voice accompanying hers. Even Fanny was prevailed upon to perform some of the simple pieces she had learned, to much praise and encouragement.

One sunny morning in late October, as the family sat at breakfast, Susan proposed that the young people go for a long walk along the hedgerows and gather rosehips for tea.

"I don't care for rosehip tea," observed Lady Bertram, shaking her head and making a little grimace. "It is very disagreeable."

"As you like, ma'am, but if you have no objection, we shall go gather some for ourselves," Julia returned. Upon William's professing himself to be an enthusiast for rosehip tea, it was decided.

Fanny kindly volunteered to remain behind to attend on Lady Bertram. "You will find it more pleasant than gathering roses in the heat of the summer," she smiled, privately remembering a miserable afternoon last year with Aunt Norris.

"Oh, but only a ninny would pick flowers in the heat of the day!" declared Susan with a laugh. "Everyone knows that the best time to cut flowers is early in the morning." Fanny nodded and said nothing, but thought — the younger sister could speak for herself in a way that the older sister would not have dreamt of. How helpless and overwhelmed had she been last year when faced with the demands of her aunt! How silly, how trifling, these disputes seemed to her now, how easily swept aside by a character possessed of firmness and resolution.

The young people, armed with scissors and baskets, having departed, Sir Thomas sat with the ladies, and placidly read his book, until a special dispatch arrived for him, whereupon he excused himself and retired to his study, and the family did not see him again until they all sat down to dinner. Fanny was acutely aware that something grave had occurred, but it seemed only she shared a consciousness of feeling with her uncle — William and Julia being too engrossed in each other's company, laughing and comparing the scratches on their hands from their encounters with the wild rose bushes, Susan was too young, and Lady Bertram too indolent, to be aware that the head of the household was more silent and thoughtful than usual. Fanny boldly followed him into his study at the conclusion of the meal and asked him, "Sir, is there anything the matter? Will you be needing Edmund? Shall I send William for him?"

"In good time," was all Sir Thomas would say at first, and Fanny saw that he was deep in thought. In a moment he roused himself, smiled weakly and said, "It is of no use, I perceive, to attempt to evade you, but the intelligence I have received is not easily comprehended in one afternoon. The full consequences are yet unknown. Fanny, I have learned that the Vice-Admiralty Court in Sierra Leone has found that the brig *Clementine* was unlawfully engaged in the slave trade, contrary to the new Act, and its owners will suffer the confiscation of the ship, in addition to heavy fines."

"Oh, yes, sir, that is the brig which William captured, from on board the *Derwent*."

"Yes, that much was not unknown to me. And until today, my only reflection upon the matter, was that those persons who had sent a new brig to convey more slaves to the Indies, uninsurable because engaged in unlawful trade, were all of them reckless fools, whose greed and cupidity overcame their prudence. But today I discover... " He paused, rose and strolled to look out the window.

"Sir?"

"Today I discover that *I* am one of those reckless fools. I am a silent partner in the enterprise which, unbeknownst to me, acquired this new ship, and was heavily indebted for its purchase price, and sent it to acquire its illegal cargo – instead of palm oil, as I had been led to believe – in anticipation of handsome profits. My partners did not inform me of this stratagem. I shall be liable to pay the debts of the partnership as well as the Crown penalties. At this juncture, I cannot say with exactitude what portion will fall to my share, but the debt will be prodigious, far exceeding my investments."

"But sir! If you knew not of this venture, how could you be held responsible?"

"There is justice, Fanny, and there is the law, which are sometimes two different things. What once was legal, is now illegal; and we are all bound by the laws of Parliament. The law will deal harshly with me now. As for what we may consider to be *just* and *fair*, I cannot deny that I once believed that an African brought to the West Indies exchanged a life of barbarity, of lawless warfare and subjugation, for one of order and security

– yet, now I must acknowledge that no one, not even a savage, will voluntarily assume the shackles of slavery, no matter what I or anyone say in its favour, and a practise once accepted as necessary, as expedient, and which moreover, formed the basis of the prosperity of many households including our own, is swiftly becoming detestable in the eyes of all Englishmen. However much I may wish to shield my family and my dependents here at Mansfield Park, a new epoch is dawning for us."

Fanny felt for him most acutely. She silently resolved that she would take the position offered by Mrs. Butters, so that he had one less dependent relation to be responsible for, in the face of the financial crisis that now threatened to overwhelm them.

Chapter Twenty-Six

A full year of our story has passed since those events transpired, which commenced it – a year since Fanny Price had fled from the Bertram's roof, a year since Maria ended her loveless engagement to Mr. Rushworth, and a year since the fortunes of the Bertrams became inextricably intertwined with those of the Crawfords.

After the tragedies and disappointments of the past twelve months, and most particularly the latest calamity, Sir Thomas determined upon giving up Mansfield Park. The mansion had been built in his father's time, when the income from the sugar plantations appeared to offer a never-ending source of wealth; it was intended to be the seat of the Bertrams for many generations to follow, and so to abandon the dwelling was to abandon the assumptions, the expectations and the hopes that had animated his every waking hour.

His heir Tom, Sir Thomas was now fully persuaded, would never take his place as the head of a household. Likewise, while Maria had, by the most unlikely of circumstances, attained to some degree of respectability, she would never be the mistress of Sotherton, never be within a carriage ride of her parents' home. Nor, to his regret, did he find himself welcome at Thornton Lacey. Miss Crawford had been all affection and complaisance before her marriage, and Sir Thomas had congratulated himself on the acquisition of such a lovely daughter; but now, Edmund's wife never invited them to visit, and declined all invitations to Mansfield Park, even to visit with Fanny and Julia. Sir Thomas supposed that the death of her brother was the cause of the estrangement, and being helpless to provide redress, accepted the breach with resignation.

The prospect of growing old while living in the great mansion alone, in severely reduced circumstances, surrounded by memories and empty rooms, pitied by the more kind-hearted of his neighbours and mocked by the rest, made an utter removal appear as the least of several evils. Life has he knew it would never return again, both in consequence of the advent of the Crawfords and because of the change of sentiment overtaking the nation in regards to slavery and those who profited from it. What would have been unthinkable only a year before was now almost to be preferred.

Always preferring the countryside to the city, Sir Thomas now sought even greater seclusion from the world. Therefore, at Maria's urgent invitation, Sir Thomas and Lady Bertram prepared to take up residence with her in Norfolk.

Sir Thomas took this step in consultation with his son Edmund, who approved of the measure, as the cost to maintain Mansfield Park, without the additional income from the Antigua plantations, often exceeded the income from the rents attached to it.

Once resolved, Sir Thomas did not hesitate; he promised Maria that he would celebrate Christmas with her at Everingham, and he was as good as his word. Christopher Jackson was put in charge of boarding up the windows, Fanny superintended the packing and removal of the books, plate and paintings, the faithful Baddeley and the old coachman Wilcox received pensions, while a handful of groundskeepers and servants remained to maintain the gardens and safeguard the property.

Edmund, the heir presumptive of what little remained, agreed to assist the steward until a new tenant could be found. He did not foresee a future day when a Sir Edmund might take occupation of Mansfield Park once again. As he explained to his wife, not without some trepidation, "I cannot promise you that we will return to Mansfield Park one day because I cannot promise anything which must be so completely beyond my power to command." As matters stood, he added, he intended to live and die as a clergyman, making Thornton Lacey his home, and upon Dr. Grant's retirement, he would prefer to appoint another clergyman rather than move to the Mansfield Parsonage within sight of his boyhood home. She was greatly discomposed by the news, he saw, but she said only, "I see," before withdrawing to their bedchamber.

***

One sunny afternoon shortly thereafter, Fanny was alone in the East Room, filling a small trunk with her own belongings, those she had left behind a year ago – her beloved books, and her writing desk. Some of her supernumerary sewing chests and netting-boxes would go to her sisters, but she was happy to claim these remembrances from her cousins, reminding her of all that was bitter and sweet of the past.

There came a soft knock at the door, and she turned to behold Edmund.

"What? Still no fire in the hearth, Fanny?" he began cheerfully enough, but soon, the consciousness of what had transpired a year ago in that room, served to silence them both for a time. Here was the table on which Fanny had left her farewell letters, to be intercepted by his now-wife, here were the chairs in which he, and Mary, and Fanny sat, reading through *Lovers' Vows* together, here they had stood while he compelled her to agree with him that he ought to take the part of Anhalt in the play – here, in this room, had young Fanny worked and read, and grown and dreamed, and what, exactly, she had dreamed and wished for, could not be enquired after by him, nor be confessed by her, but it seemed to her that the truth hung in the silence between them. At last, with a shake of his head, and a slight laugh, he gestured toward the windowsill and asked, "did you not wonder what became of your geraniums? I took them to the head gardener, and he assured me that geraniums are a remarkably tenacious plant, and can be revived almost from the dead. I think you will find them in the greenhouse."

"Thank you, cousin," Fanny replied as she resumed wiping a dust cloth over her volume of Lord Macartney's Journal from China, before placing it in her trunk.

"Are you not feeling a little melancholy, Fanny?"

"Oh yes, but it is to be expected – how could we feel otherwise? Your mother is being remarkably stoic about everything. Susan is with her now, they are sorting through all her old letters." She straightened up from the trunk, pushed some curls back from her forehead, and paused to look out window. "I fancy this is what I shall miss the most about this room – this view of the park – but I shall always be able to remember how it looks on an autumn day like this, with the sun illuminating the golden leaves on the trees like stained glass – and so long as I have my memories, nothing else matters. But you, cousin, what must you be feeling?"

"I feel a great many things – to relate them all might tire even your patience, but there is one thing in particular – I will stay overnight here and have supper with you all – my father wants to discuss some of the details of the estate with me – but first, Fanny, I want to speak with you alone – I want to apologize to you Fanny, for my blindness –"

"Oh! Cousin! No, you need not, indeed you must not –"

"No, let me say this much, let me overrule you this one last time, and I will have done. I was too much in the habit of taking you for granted, for assuming that you would agree with me in every thing. I flattered myself that our thoughts, our sentiments, our tastes and our principles accorded so well that we would never differ on any point. And, it fed my vanity to suppose that I had indeed played some part in shaping your tastes and convictions. So, when we did differ – as we did on the question of whether I should join the play-acting – I would not do you the justice of even *permitting* you to disagree with me.

"How often did I silently berate others in my family for treating you as a doll, as an automaton, without due respect for your independence and dignity! Yet, after we were separated, I examined my own conduct and discovered that I was no better – very little better, at any rate! I was blind to my arrogance.

"I do not say that, had I behaved differently, had I listened to you, instead of compelling you to agree with me, events would have transpired differently. I do not place that great of a burden upon your shoulders. The choices that I made were mine, and mine alone.

"I will not ask your forgiveness, for I know you would give it to me instantly. But will you do this for me," he added, taking her hand. "Will you always be my friend, Fanny? Will you promise me that we will never allow time, or distance, or mischance, to make us forget all that we are to one another?"

"Never, never!" Was all Fanny could trust herself to say.

"And, also, Fanny, would you leave your labours here long enough to come for a walk with me in the shrubbery? It is very fine outside, and it may be our last opportunity to walk those familiar paths together and talk about books and poetry as we used to do."

"I shall just collect my shawl and bonnet from my room," Fanny said, starting for the door, when Edmund smiled.

"No, Fanny, I sent a servant to fetch them for you before I came here to find you. I assumed you would fall in with my wishes – as you *nearly* always do."

***

Edmund returned home from his overnight visit with his parents in tolerably placid spirits. He led his horse to the new stables behind his house, and saw to his surprise that the new gig was gone, along with the little mare. Returning to the house, he gazed in stupefaction at his entry hall, bereft of furniture. He pushed past his housekeeper to the parlor, and found it likewise empty – the paintings on the wall, the draperies in the window, the new furniture – all gone.

"Her uncle, the Admiral, came with men from the city," the bewildered housekeeper explained. "For, she said, she knew she could not get the hire of enough horses and carts here in the country. She took everything, sir – the furniture, her clothes, her harp – everything."

Edmund walked slowly upstairs to his empty bedchamber, to examine his own feelings. He felt sorrow and some guilt for having so thoroughly disappointed his wife's hopes in marriage, but since his *own* hopes for domestic felicity had dwindled to ashes, he could and did acknowledge to himself, that he felt as a captive feels once released from prison.

***

Lady Bertram astonished all who knew her, or knew of her, by her fortitude in quitting Mansfield Park and travelling to such an alien place as Norfolk. The great inducement to leave was the prospect, very pleasing to her Ladyship, of having a grandchild to love. And as is so often the case, the grandchild was doted on more unreservedly than the actual child. The infant son of Maria Crawford, born not long after her parents had joined her in Everingham, brought a second spring of felicity to Sir Thomas and his lady, who both thought him the cleverest, handsomest baby in England.

As for Maria, she had once sought marriage as a means of escaping her parents, most particularly, her father. But upon finding herself on the brink of motherhood, alone without a husband or loved one to share her joys and burdens, she underwent no small revolution in character. Although her temper was still sometimes ungoverned, she learned to appreciate and truly love her father's solid worth, to bear with her mother more patiently, and to devote herself to her duties as mistress of Everingham.

Sir Thomas took up the judicious management of Everingham and its estates with a competence and disinterest that swiftly won him the esteem of his neighbours and the gratitude of the tenants. He had heard enough hints from Fanny to be wary of the steward, Mr. Maddison, and indeed, Mr. Maddison was gone within a twelvemonth and the affairs of Everingham prospered as never before.

As for Mrs. Norris, she experienced the indignity of being unceremoniously turned out upon the London streets by Mrs. Edmund Bertram, when that lady arrived from Thornton Lacey. Mrs. Norris was the last of the family to be undeceived as to Mary's true character, and alas, was much humiliated. She fully expected to accompany her sister and brother-in-law to Everingham, and was further mortified when Maria wrote to her to discourage her removal from Northamptonshire. Maria had discovered that life *without* her overbearing and overpartial aunt was far more congenial than life *with* her, and so wrote that 'she knew her own dear Aunt Norris would be much more content to remain in Mansfield village,' where she was such a valued and important neighbour. The hint was too broad to ignore, the slight too great to forgive. Mrs. Norris' curiosity and anxiety over who would be the future occupant of Mansfield Park was in itself almost enough of an inducement for her to remain where she was. She re-installed herself at the White house, to await future events and to act as the custodian of all the memories of the past.

Susan had passed several months as the guest of Lady Bertram; but she rejected an invitation to continue in the unpaid service of her Ladyship – being useful and wanted, assuredly, but only for fetching and carrying, and ministering to her aunt's trifling solicitudes, tasks which could not satisfy Susan's active nature or her restless mind, and she wondered at the docility of any girl, not excepting her sister Fanny, who could have endured it.

Susan's half-year's absence from Portsmouth – and the contrasting misery of having Mrs. Norris with them during the interval – led her mother to finally comprehend how much Susan had contributed to the comfort of them all when at home, and how little thanks she had received in recompense. Susan therefore was welcomed back most affectionately, and enjoyed a greater measure of respect and consequence than she had before. She became the acknowledged manageress of the house and it was remarkable how, even with the same limited means, the family lived in far greater comfort and had better food to eat. It was no longer considered an insurmountable task to wash the windows inside and out with vinegar and water and paper, and the front steps were scrubbed daily. Even her father acquiesced in taking his evening pipe outside when the weather was clement, and her brothers had the dining room table – cleaned thoroughly every day – for their school work. Sir Thomas sent a good carpet from Mansfield to grace the Price's parlour, and the old carpet was cut up and made up into portmanteaus, which Susan used when she visited her sister and Mrs. Butters.

The Bertrams heard infrequently from their brother Tom in Virginia, but when he did send them a line, it was to assure them that his affairs prospered in the fresh air and soil of the New World. He professed himself to be content, and he was never heard to regret his decision to leave his old life in England.

Dr. Grant and his wife continued in the parsonage in Mansfield. Edmund Bertram did not shun their company, nor they his; rather, he visited and dined with them frequently and discussed parish business with Dr. Grant, and occasionally Mrs. Grant would tell him, *sotto voce*, that 'Mary was thought to be staying with Lord and Lady Delingpole at their country estate in Wales' or 'Mary had returned to London but had given up the Wimpole Street house.'

Edmund Bertram devoted himself to his parish and his duties, and found therein some measure of peace. With the death of his brother-in-law and

322

the departure of his wife, he found himself liable for the cost of the extensive alterations which they had thrust upon him, and which would have plunged him into debt for years. He sold his hunters to meet the debt and his father paid off the balance, because, unlike many men of pedigree, they regarded any debt, even a debt to a tradesman, as something to be honoured. Edmund did not resent the fact that the home served as a kind of memorial to the genius and taste of Henry Crawford, a man of many faults but also of many talents, whom he did not cease to regret, or to remember.

As for Julia, she did not wish to live in Norfolk, nor did her father desire that she should live with Maria. He settled an allowance on Julia, and entrusted Edmund with her supervision. Julia divided her time between acting as a hostess for her brother at Thornton Lacey and accepting invitations to visit the homes of the friends she made during her season in London. And while some assumed that Mrs. Norris would also take up residence with her nephew, sadly, a lack of bedrooms – for, Edmund informed her, he must always keep a spare room for a friend – prevented him from offering her permanent shelter under his roof.

Although Julia Bertram of Thornton Lacey might not make as brilliant a match as Miss Julia of Mansfield Park, and although the previous year had been an unhappy one for her, she had gained juster notions about the sort of man who was best calculated to make her happy, and such a man would be as different from Henry Crawford as could be imagined. An open temper, a quiet dedication to duty, a warm and sympathetic heart, were all she prized now and held out as her secret ideal. Out from the shadow of her older sister, who had always been considered her superior in beauty and accomplishment, Julia gave every promise of growing up to be an affectionate and thoughtful woman. Her temper was naturally the easiest of the two; her feelings, though quick, were more controllable, and education had not given her so very hurtful a degree of self-consequence. Her cheerful companionship supported Edmund's spirits, and at her artless suggestion, he began a correspondence with his cousin Lieutenant Price, which led to a deep and sincere friendship between the two young men.

Lieutenant William Price continued his service under Captain Columbine aboard the frigate *Crocodile*, which returned to the African coast, to the great anxiety of his family and friends, who regarded his being stationed in a climate so deleterious to the European constitution as more likely to be fatal than direct warfare against the French, an apprehension that was well founded, as the rate of death amongst the sailors of the anti-slavery squadron was by far the highest in the fleet. Nevertheless, the ever-sanguine William saw in such a situation only the increased chances for promotion, and in rescuing Africans from the toils of the slavers, an activity he relished for its own sake, he anticipated the acquisition of handsome bounties.

William's participation in apprehending the *Clementine* did him no disservice in the eyes of his uncle or his family, who all understood that he was doing his duty, and it provided a reassurance to Fanny that even the best-intentioned actions can have unexpected consequences, and that fear of the worst ought not to deter us from prudently acting for the best.

After the breakup of the establishment at Mansfield Park, Fanny was invited to reside with Mrs. Butters in Stoke Newington. Mrs. Butters was very careful of Fanny's health, and would not permit her to over tax herself. Fanny spent her mornings in helping to establish a sort of academy for young seamstresses, choosing her fellow instructresses, interviewing the many applicants, and educating herself in every detail of the dressmakers' trade. The work stimulated her, and she took a kindly interest in the welfare of the young girls who relied on their skill with a needle to keep themselves and their families from penury. Fanny came to love Mrs. Butters almost as a mother, and Mrs. Butters was likewise very attached to Fanny, and was happy to provide her with a home until the circumstances arose in which Fanny could enter a home of her own.

Although Fanny was reconciled with Maria and Julia and wished them well, her heart, her inclinations, her warmth and interest were more for her own brothers and sisters. Children of the same family, the same blood, with the same first associations and habits, have some means of enjoyment in their power, which no subsequent connexions can supply; and it must be by a long and unnatural estrangement, if such precious remains of the earliest attachments are ever entirely outlived. Although William would always remain her favourite, she established correspondence with her brothers John and Richard, and as with Susan, was amazed to learn how the more fearless disposition and happier nerves of the younger Prices aided them as made their own way in the world. John worked as a junior clerk in the rough-and-tumble world of the police who patrolled the London docks. Though only seventeen, there was not much of human frailty he had not witnessed at first hand. Richard, at sixteen, had been at sea for four years, and was shouldering the responsibilities of a man while still a youth. Fanny gave all of her heart and pride to her brothers and sisters, acknowledging

324

the advantages of early hardship and discipline, and the consciousness of being born to struggle and endure.

William Gibson was some months recovering his health and strength from the effects of the malarial fever contracted from the pestilential shores of Africa. He used his time as an invalid to arrange his notes and write his account of the brief but eventful last voyage of the *Solebay*, and the capture of the slave ship *Clementine*, as the guest of Mr. and Mrs. Smallridge, who offered him a small cottage on their property. After so many months sharing the cramped quarters on board ship, the absolute solitude and peace of the countryside revived his spirits and his enthusiasm for the great struggle for the eradication of slavery which still lay ahead.

Whatever the expectations of her friend Mrs. Butters, Fanny, while harbouring feelings of the greatest respect and regard for Mr. Gibson, did not believe that *he* was ready to enter upon married life, nor, in truth, was she. A few more years were wanting to replace her girlish timidity with the quiet self-confidence of an intelligent, well-judging woman, and to replace her habitual self-doubt with the conviction that she was worthy of attaching a man of serious merit, principles and character. Furthermore, she believed that he to whom she gave her hand, deserved to have her entire heart as well. She hoped that time and fortitude would do away with any tendency on her part to regard Edmund as more than a beloved cousin. While her girlish love for Edmund was by no means blameable, she was teaching herself to regard it as merely the natural consequence of having no other objects to love, other than he who had been her only childhood friend. She had been too apt, to the detriment of them both, to serve as the mirror for his opinions and beliefs, and by pursuing the new career offered to her by Mrs. Butters, she hoped to gain a greater knowledge of her own true self, before submerging that self in marriage. However, it remains to be seen what the determined Mrs. Butters will be able to bring about, in the fullness of time.

The following year, Mr. Gibson, as all the world knows, became a literary lion with the publication of his book describing his adventures in fighting the slave trade. Subsequently he became a celebrated author of novels, which were unlike anything else offered to the public, for they described life in a fantastic future, where the monotonous but necessary chores needed to support civilized life were all performed by steam-powered machines, and thereby, slavery was no more!

This story, as it closes, will not pretend to foretell so far into the distant future but will offer a few glimpses of the immediate years ahead:

325

Julia Bertram, fond of activity, and missing the gardens of Mansfield Park, carried on with the plans for Thornton Lacey as delineated by Henry Crawford, and superintended the establishment of a small garden on the south-eastern slope beside the parsonage, a project which occupied several years, and which brought her great satisfaction.

When her son was three years old, Maria Crawford took a house in London, where her beauty and wealth brought her many admirers, and it was generally believed that a second, and more successful, marriage would be her eventual reward for atoning for the one great error of her youth. Of her own free will, she brought little Henry to meet his great-uncle, the Admiral, who was charmed into acknowledging the dark-haired, clever, lively boy as a Crawford.

As for Edmund's estranged wife, she was often to be seen at Bath or at Brighton, a member of the Prince of Wales' set, in the company of her good friend the Earl of Elsham. Her beauty and wit ensured that she was a favourite, and although she kept her fortune, as Edmund refused to make a claim on it, she also retained all her bitter regrets.

Of all of the principals in this story, the one most often to contemplate 'what if,' was Edmund Bertram, whose most important decision – his choice of a wife – turned out to have such unhappy consequences. He blessed the suffering that made him more compassionate of others, the adage about the mote and the beam was always on his lips, but he could not help asking himself of an evening, while looking into the fire, what would have happened if that contrary wind across the Atlantic had not prevented his father's ship from arriving home in time to stop the rehearsals of *Lovers' Vows*, or how might events have unfolded differently if Fanny had not left home, early that October morning?

For my part, I like Mansfield Park *best. I recognize that its heroine is a little prig and its hero a pompous ass, but I do not care; it is wise, witty and tender, a masterpiece of ironical humour and subtle observation.*

-- Somerset Maugham

Foreword or Afterword

I usually just skim the forewords, don't you? Or read the first few paragraphs, then skip on ahead to chapter one, feeling a bit lazy or guilty. To spare you, gentle reader, from the faintest whisper of self-reproach, I leave it to your inclination. Please feel free to read this before, after, or even not at all.

I've been a Jane Austen devotee ever since my mother introduced *Pride & Prejudice* to me, and on one memorable Christmas gave me a complete Penguin set of her books. Over the years, I have read and re-read Austen's six novels, sometimes to find consolation in a distressed hour, but mostly because she only left us six novels, plus two fragments and her juvenilia, before her untimely death.

For years, I thought about writing an ending to one of Austen's two unfinished novels, – this was years before the internet, when Austen fan fiction really exploded. Then I discovered that it was *Mansfield Park* I returned to, and re-read and thought about the most. But why, considering that – in common with Jane Austen's mother, I find Fanny Price an "insipid" heroine?

Fanny Price, as anyone familiar with Jane Austen and her works knows, is the least popular of all the Austen heroines. Largely because of Fanny, "*Mansfield Park* is the least favourite novel of the six," acknowledges Lorraine Clark, Associate Professor of English at Trent University in Ontario[1] "And yet the pleasures of *Mansfield Park* get deeper, and deeper and deeper on re-reading…. There's a quiet, contemplative, meditative pleasure."

I'll return to Fanny in a minute. She will wait right there on the bench for us, deeply anxious and unhappy, no doubt, but uncomplaining.

Dr. Mary Breen, University College Cork, says "many critics believe [*Mansfield Park* is] the first great English novel…." and I believe this is not just because of Austen's brilliant and subtle handling of the interactions of

---

[1] https://www.youtube.com/watch?v=gONy6lORsQk

the characters through their dialogue, but because Austen is writing in a more somber and assured voice. There are a few passages in which I think I glimpse the emergence of new and even more powerful descriptive abilities, such as the following, when Austen describes the heroine sitting in the tiny, grimy parlour of her parents' home in Portsmouth:

> [Fanny] was deep in other musing. The remembrance of her first evening in that room, of her father and his newspaper, came across her. No candle was now wanted. The sun was yet an hour and half above the horizon. She felt that she had, indeed, been three months there; and the sun's rays falling strongly into the parlour, instead of cheering, made her still more melancholy, for sunshine appeared to her a totally different thing in a town and in the country. Here, its power was only a glare: a stifling, sickly glare, serving but to bring forward stains and dirt that might otherwise have slept. There was neither health nor gaiety in sunshine in a town. She sat in a blaze of oppressive heat, in a cloud of moving dust, and her eyes could only wander from the walls, marked by her father's head, to the table cut and notched by her brothers, where stood the tea-board never thoroughly cleaned, the cups and saucers wiped in streaks, the milk a mixture of motes floating in thin blue, and the bread and butter growing every minute more greasy than even [the servant] Rebecca's hands had first produced it.

In contrast to the "light, and bright, and sparkling" *Pride and Prejudice*, *Mansfield Park* is more serious and more reflective. Author Robert Rodi makes the point that in other Jane Austen novels, the villains and cads are not punished – they get off scot-free. Lucy Steele becomes the wealthy Mrs. Robert Ferrars, the seducer Wickham is paid off, and Mrs. Elton, General Tilney and William Elliott go about their merry ways. In Mansfield Park, Austen created a charming brother and sister team who hover on the brink of redemption, then destroy their own chances, while the sister who falls from grace and becomes an adultress must live out the rest of her life in seclusion. This is closer to the formula for tragedy, rather than comedy, and certainly Mansfield Park has more of a dark, moralizing strain in it, thanks to those indefatigable moralizers, Fanny Price and Edmund Bertram.

Yet, the novel is also filled with irresistible comic touches. The opening might seem staid, an exposition of the marriages made by three sisters, whom we don't yet know and therefore can't care much about, but the opening paragraph ends with this bit of quiet hilarity:

> Lady Bertram, who was a woman of very tranquil feelings, and a temper remarkably easy and indolent, would have contented herself with merely giving up her sister [for having made an imprudent marriage], and thinking no more of the matter; but Mrs. Norris had a spirit of activity, which could not be satisfied till she had written a long and angry letter to [this third sister], to point out the folly of her conduct, and threaten her with all its possible ill consequences. Mrs. Price, in her turn, was injured and angry; and an answer, which comprehended each sister in its bitterness, and bestowed such very disrespectful reflections on the pride of Sir Thomas as Mrs. Norris could not possibly keep to herself, put an end to all intercourse between them for a considerable period.

Or here is Lady Bertram, who can always be relied upon to say something, all unawares, that punctures the delusions and hypocrisy of her older sister. Mrs. Norris is describing her nieces Maria and Julia as being perfect little angels, from whom Fanny will benefit just by being around:

> "That is exactly what I think," cried Mrs. Norris, "and what I was saying to my husband this morning. It will be an education for the child, said I, only being with her cousins; if Miss Lee taught her nothing, she would learn to be good and clever from [Maria and Julia]."
> "I hope she will not tease my poor pug," said Lady Bertram; "I have but just got Julia to leave it alone."

Or picture Lady Bertram and Mrs. Norris gossiping about the wife of the new parson; Lady Bertram wonders that such a plain woman has made such a good marriage, and Mrs. Norris thinks she's an imprudent housekeeper. "These opinions had been hardly canvassed a year before another event arose of such importance in the family, as might fairly claim some place in the thoughts and conversation of the ladies."

It's a leisurely book. For example, Austen uses over 2,300 words – almost the length of a short story – to discuss how Fanny will *not* go to live with Mrs. Norris in the White house after her husband dies. Or 14 paragraphs are devoted to an entertaining conversation about young ladies who change personalities when they "come out" in society, but it's just a conversation, it's not a plot point. However, in these passages, which are chiefly dialogue, Austen establishes characters and their relationships to one another. In the first passage I mentioned, we get our first sample of Edmund Bertram's dry wit, and we learn that while he is intelligent, good-natured and kind, he sometimes wears rose-colored glasses. We also become better acquainted with the selfish hypocrisy of Mrs. Norris and the complacency of her sister. In the second passage, Edmund is the plain-spoken third wheel in a witty exchange between Mary Crawford and his older brother Tom Bertram. This conversation helps us to appreciate the contrast between the brothers. We see Tom's charm and superficiality versus Edmund's quiet maturity.

Let me go on record as saying that I like Edmund Bertram. He can be a prig, but he does have a nice quiet wit, and he is presented as the only one of the four Bertram siblings who is not totally selfish and self-absorbed. The exigencies of the plot require that he be blind to Henry Crawford's seduction of his sisters, to Fanny's love for him, and to Mary's true character, so this puts him in the awkward position of being a bit of a dolt, really, but if we can forgive Emma Woodhouse for her blindness, we should be able to forgive Edmund Bertram.

Referring to *Mansfield Park* in a letter to her sister Cassandra, Jane Austen wrote, "Now I will try to write of something else;—it shall be a complete change of subject—Ordination." We should bear in mind that Edmund's choice to become a clergyman is a central conflict in the plot, and he deserves our sympathy for the sacrifice he must make to become a clergyman – he will lose the woman he loves. He does not give free rein to his emotions – he is like buttoned-down Elinor Dashwood in that respect, but he has feelings, nonetheless. Mary Crawford is discerning enough to recognize him as good husband material.

One barrier that prevents some modern readers from appreciating *Mansfield Park* is that the manners of today are very different from those in Austen's time, so the things that Fanny and Edmund object to as being bad-mannered make them seem prudish and priggish. They criticize Mary Crawford for making a light, passing, disrespectful reference to her uncle in company. Fanny is "quite astonished." Who would be shocked today by a young person making disparaging remarks about their elders? Possibly where I now live and work, mainland China, where Confucian mores still prevail to a great degree, but not in the Western world!

In another episode, the young people are on a pleasure excursion to Sotherton, the stately home of Maria Bertram's fiancé. Julia, the younger Bertram daughter, winds up lagging behind the other young people and she's stuck with Mrs. Rushworth, (the fiancé's mother) as her walking companion. Austen scolds her for chafing at this.

> The remaining three, Mrs. Rushworth, Mrs. Norris, and Julia, were still far behind; for Julia... was obliged to keep by the side of Mrs. Rushworth, and restrain her impatient feet to that lady's slow pace, while her aunt, having fallen in with the housekeeper, who was come out to feed the pheasants, was lingering behind in gossip with her. Poor Julia, the only one out of the nine not tolerably satisfied with their lot, was now in a state of complete penance..... The politeness which she had been brought up to practise as a duty made it impossible for her to escape; while the want of that higher species of self-command, that just consideration of others, that knowledge of her own heart, that principle of right, which had not formed any essential part of her education, made her miserable under it.

Wouldn't most young people today just walk away and join the other young people without a backward glance, regardless of the fact that Mrs. Rushworth is their hostess and she's just fed them a nice meal and taken them on a tour of the house?

It would still be shocking today for a newlywed bride to run away with her lover, but it would not ordinarily result in her exile from society and her own family for the rest of her life, as is Maria's fate in *Mansfield Park*.

By modern standards, virtually nothing Mary Crawford says is objectionable – whether she is making a joke about sodomy in the Royal Navy, insulting the clergy, or complaining about her uncle or Dr. Grant, her brother-in-law. One exception which may be more disturbing *today* than when Mansfield Park was first published, is that Mary jokes about being suspected of trying to murder Tom Bertram, so that Edmund can become the heir: "Fanny, Fanny, I see you smile and look cunning, but, upon my honour, I never bribed a physician in my life." To joke about this to Fanny, to imply that Fanny would laugh along with her, while Tom is struggling for his life! And to do this in a letter which, after all, Fanny could show to anybody. The passage effectually illustrates Mary Crawford's moral blindness, her artificiality and the hollowness of her professed friendship for Fanny, whom she doesn't begin to understand. "[A] mind led astray and bewildered, and without any suspicion of being so; darkened, yet fancying itself light."

Regardless, many readers of Mansfield Park prefer the lively, witty Mary Crawford to the more stolid, timid, humourless Fanny. Some Mansfield Park fan fiction has been written in which the Crawfords are redeemed and take their supposedly rightful place at centre stage as the hero and heroine. In my variation, I have "amped up" their sociopathic qualities to make it clear that they are dangerous people who don't care what havoc they create in other people's lives.

The central example of how modern manners and morals have changed since 1809, is the private theatricals which the young people stage at Mansfield Park, a key part of the plot. Many readers can't understand, as Lionel Trilling put it, "why it is so very wrong for young people in a dull country house to put on a play." In my variation, I have explained more about the play, *Lovers' Vows*, and have included some of the actual dialogue,[2] which should help the reader understand why Sir Thomas, the absent father of the house, would have objected to it. In addition, modern readers might miss how cleverly Austen chose this play and cast the characters in her novel in the various parts. The dullard Mr. Rushworth plays a Don Juan type, while Mansfield Park's real Don Juan, Henry Crawford, is busy seducing his fiancée. Edmund is cast as an earnest young clergyman who shaped and formed the mind of his protégée, Amelia, who falls in love with him, just as, in real life, he guided Fanny's tastes and she secretly loves him. Finally, Maria plays a fallen woman, and becomes one herself when she runs away with Henry Crawford.

***

While some of the morals and manners of the Regency era were stricter than ours, there are other aspects of their life which we find incongruous and unjust – slavery for one! Here Sir Thomas scolds his oldest son for

---

[2] While reading the actual play, *Lovers' Vows*, I made the discovery (for me, anyway) that Mrs. Norris is actually paraphrasing the entry line of the character of Cottager's Wife when she scolds Fanny for refusing to take the part. "What a piece of work here is about nothing!"

going heavily into debt, which obliges him to give a "living" – that is, the income attached to the local parsonage – to someone else, instead of holding it for his second son:

> You have robbed Edmund for ten, twenty, thirty years, perhaps for life, of more than half the income which ought to be his. It may hereafter be in my power, or in yours (I hope it will), to procure him better preferment; but it must not be forgotten that no benefit of that sort would have been beyond his natural claims on us, and that nothing can, in fact, be an equivalent for the certain advantage which he is now obliged to forego through the urgency of your debts.

If one brother drank and gambled away half of another brother's "income for life," wouldn't this create a serious breach in most modern families? We never hear Edmund or anyone else drop a word on the subject.

Internal evidence in the novel suggests that the chief events of *Mansfield Park* take place in 1808, the year after the British Parliament outlawed the slave trade (that is, transporting and selling slaves, not slavery itself). Here is the reference to it in *Mansfield Park*:

> "Did not you hear me ask [Sir Thomas] about the slave-trade last night?" [Fanny asks Edmund].
> "I did—and was in hopes the question would be followed up by others. It would have pleased your uncle to be inquired of farther."

Austen does not reveal what the question was, or how Sir Thomas answered. It's frequently remarked of Jane Austen that she ignored dramatic real-life events such as the Napoleonic Wars, in favour of domestic affairs. This was obviously her conscious choice, so I think it's faintly ridiculous that the merest passing reference to slavery in *Mansfield Park* has led some Austen critics to claim that the book is an anti-slavery tract. I agree with the suggestion that Sir Thomas Bertram's extended absence in Antigua is simply a plot device to get him out of the way, not a means of introducing the topic of chattel slavery into the book. Because of Napoleon, Europe was closed off to English people at that time, so there were comparatively few distant places to which Austen could dispatch Sir

Thomas, to enable her to advance her storyline of the Maria, Rushworth and Henry Crawford triangle.

However, the fact of Sir Thomas and his plantations means that modern readers of the *Mansfield Park* must inevitably grapple with this issue.

Some modern readers may find it impossible *not* to dwell upon the fact that slavery supports the elegant, civilized lifestyle of the family. The critical appreciation of many of our great works of art has been challenged by changing sensibilities about racial stereotypes, cultural appropriation, and sexism. *The Merchant of Venice* has for its comic villain a grasping Jew who gets his comeuppance. *Turandot*, the Chinese princess of Puccini's opera, has three court officials named Ping, Pang and Pong. Even my beloved Astaire and Rogers movies show Fred Astaire behaving in a fashion which would get him arrested for stalking today. If we're going to continue to enjoy these great masterpieces, we have to calmly and rationally understand the times and mores in which they were created. To do otherwise is to deprive yourself of the enjoyment of our cultural heritage, and to subject everyone around you to the irritation of listening to your virtue-signalling. *(Oh, you're against slavery, are you? How courageous of you to speak up.)*

Because of the difficulty of dealing with the slavery issue, because of the grim reality underlying the world of *Mansfield Park*, I frankly wanted to avert my eyes from it; but the more I researched the period in which the main action of the novel is set, the more fascinated I became with the true story of the campaign to abolish the slave trade.

So the abolitionist movement does play a part in *A Contrary Wind*, with consequences for many of the characters, including some new characters I've invented (Mrs. Butters, her lady's maid, and Mr. Thompson) and some real historical people who make an appearance in this variation (Hannah More and James Stephen).

I have also included, unapologetically, some of the real arguments made by people who defended the slave trade at the time. And because I prefer to think well of Sir Thomas, I gave him a troubled conscience. The 1999 movie which portrayed Sir Thomas as a brutal slave owner skews the novel completely out of shape.

Now, finally, to the central problem with *Mansfield Park*: the heroine, Fanny Price. Why is Fanny Price so unlikeable, that in modern film and television adaptations of the book, Austen's timid, long-suffering Fanny Price is excised completely and replaced by a feisty, spunky, rebellious Fanny Price v. 2.0?

Tony Tanner pointed out that the things that irritate us about Fanny Price – her physical frailty, her passivity, her humility, her tendency to cry at the drop of a hat – are presented in the book as virtues. Here are some descriptions of her from some literary critics: "She is never, ever, wrong," (Tony Tanner) she is a "monster of complacency and pride.... morally detestable," (Kingsley Amis), "a dreary, debilitated, priggish, goody-goody," (W.G. Harding), "fiction holds no heroine more repulsive in her cast-iron self-righteousness," (Reginald Ferrar). Author Robert Rodi points out that Fanny "evades possibility, declines to decide, makes no move, lifts no finger to alter her destiny in any way, good or bad; takes no risk, assumes no responsibility, [and] rebuffs all affection." Pretty harsh words about an 18-year-old girl! And I'll pile on by agreeing with Rodi that she is helpless to help herself, whether she has been forgotten and left to sit on a bench, or is waiting for someone to bring her a cup of tea. Her only power is the power of refusal – significantly, refusing to accept Henry Crawford's marriage proposal, despite the enormous pressures brought to bear on her.

Austen devotes much of *Mansfield Park* to describing the inner life, emotions and thoughts of Fanny Price – sometimes even moment to moment, as for example here:

> Dr. Grant was in the vestibule, and as they stopt to speak to him she found, from Edmund's manner, that he did mean to go with her. He too was taking leave. She could not but be thankful. In the moment of parting, Edmund was invited by Dr. Grant to eat his mutton with him the next day; and Fanny had barely time for an unpleasant feeling on the occasion, when Mrs. Grant, with sudden recollection, turned to her and asked for the pleasure of her company too. This was so new an attention, so perfectly new a circumstance in the events of Fanny's life, that she was all surprise and embarrassment; and while stammering out her great obligation, and her "but she did not suppose it would be in her power," was looking at Edmund for his opinion and help.

In less than a minute, Fanny goes from a thrill of pleasure that Edmund is not staying at the Parsonage with Mary Crawford, and will actually be walking home at her side, then, she feels rejected and left out because

Edmund is invited to dinner right in front of her (she feels alarmed and jealous as well because it means he'll be spending an evening in Mary Crawford's company,) but when, a second later, the invitation *is* extended to her, she is so overcome and nervous that she plunges into her most unbecoming trait – everyone must stand around and wait while Fanny Price wallows in humility. The momentous question: "Should Fanny eat dinner with the neighbours?" is finally referred to Sir Thomas and Lady Bertram to decide on her behalf.

Alas, when Fanny Price *does* actually speak, as opposed to stammering, I don't like her any better. Her soliloquies in praise of nature sound faintly ridiculous and pompous to me, [*The evergreen! How beautiful, how welcome, how wonderful the evergreen!*].

I can only view her with sympathy by considering that she grew up in a very isolated setting and doesn't understand how to make ordinary small talk. Who else, when asked, "You have been here a month, I think?" would answer,

"No, not quite a month. It is only four weeks tomorrow since I left Mansfield."

"You are a most accurate and honest reckoner," (responds Henry Crawford.) "I should call that a month."

"I did not arrive here till Tuesday evening."

And what lover would persist in the face of this, if this is a foretaste of the domestic conversation he'll be enduring for the rest of his life?

Podcaster Maggie (of the Jane Austen fandom podcast "First Impressions") who has boldly declared *Mansfield Park* "the best novel ever published," points out that Fanny Price clearly suffers from social anxiety disorder, a common and surely a forgivable problem.

Although I don't loathe Fanny Price as many others do, my beef with her as a heroine is that she is never tempted to do other than what she does.[3] A person who is never tempted to drink is not more virtuous than the alcoholic who must resist the urge to drink. A person who is never tempted to gluttony is not more virtuous than the plump person at the buffet table. Fanny has no *inner* struggle to overcome. She must withstand the *outside*

---

[3] There is a suggestion that in time, she might relent and marry Henry Crawford, but I for one, feel Crawford was kidding himself; he was in love, briefly, with the idea of being in love, and Fanny is right – they are too dissimilar to ever work as a couple. One can't imagine the high-spirited Henry Crawford being happy with Fanny.

pressures upon her, especially the pressure to marry Henry Crawford, to stay true to her own beliefs.

And so, in re-reading *Mansfield Park* over the years, I have been tempted to "tweak" Fanny just a bit. This book came about because I was unexpectedly and suddenly inspired by two particular passages; one, when Henry Crawford wishes that "a steady contrary wind" across the Atlantic had prevented Sir Thomas Bertram from returning home so that the young people could have continued staging *Lovers' Vows*, and secondly, a truly shocking moment when Aunt Norris ("one of the most plausibly odious characters in fiction," Tony Tanner calls her) insults Fanny Price in front of everyone: "I shall think her a very obstinate, ungrateful, girl..... considering who and what she is."

I asked myself, what if Fanny broke away from the truly – to use the modern phrase – dysfunctional situation she's living in? What if Aunt Norris's remark was the straw that broke the camel's back? And what if Sir Thomas *had* been held back by a contrary wind? And finally, what if Fanny was tempted, truly tempted, to do something that was against her strict moral code? What would tempt her? How would the story have unfolded differently?

In *A Contrary Wind*, I started out with making those three variations, placed the characters in motion, and let their actions and interactions play out.

Acknowledgements and References

I wish to thank Jane Austen!

A big thank you to my son Joseph Manning for acting as my copy editor. To switch back to 18th century mode for a moment - his keen eye and his helpful interjections, uniting as they did intelligence, sympathy and wit, rendered an otherwise tedious task more than supportable even though my toleration for lengthy sentences and plentiful commas somewhat exceeds his.

Thanks also to my sister Cara Elrod for reading an early draft and providing helpful comments on the plot and characters.

The following books were very helpful to my research of the period:

Jack Tar: Life in Nelson's Navy by Roy & Lesley Adkins, 2009

Eavesdropping on Jane Austen's England: How our ancestors lived two centuries ago, Roy & Lesley Adkins, 2014.

His Majesty's Ship, by Alaric Bond, 2013

Royal Navy versus the Slave Traders: Enforcing Abolition at Sea, 1808 – 1898, by Bernard Edwards, 2007

Bury the Chains: Prophets and Rebels in the Fight to Free an Empire's Slaves, by Adam Hochschild, 2006

Young Edward's shouted commands to his little toy ship are lifted directly from: *A Middy of the Slave Squadron*, (1910) by Harry Collingwood.

I'm indebted to John Mullan, author of *What Matters in Jane Austen: Twenty Crucial Puzzles Solved*, for daring to ask the question, "Can we think that Colonel Brandon, Mr. Knightley or Captain Wentworth are indeed virgins before their marriage?" That question would also apply to Edmund Bertram; prig though he is, he's only human.

Robert Rodi's *Bitch in a Bonnet: Reclaiming Jane Austen From the Stiffs, the Snobs, the Simps and the Saps* inspired me to add the sub-plot of Sarah, the "idle and dissatisfied" underservant.

The famous abolitionist William Wilberforce does not appear in this novel but he moves behind the scenes. He was also a social reformer, and he and his associates, known as the "Clapham Sect," were devotedly religious and can be seen as the precursors of the Victorian age, an age that was much more concerned with good and evil, public morality, and the reform of public manners, than the Regency Age. The debates and movements that this small group of people set into motion are one of history's hinges or great turning points, and so they have elbowed their way into this story.

Mr. Thomas Clarkson's memoir appeared in 1809, in time for another of my new characters, William Gibson, to read aloud from it at Mrs. Butter's dinner party. The slave "Mary" that the three abolitionists discuss in Bristol is inspired by the story of a slave named Mary Prince, whose autobiography was published in 1831. The abolitionist James Stephen really had two fiancées in his youth, as recounted to Fanny and Mrs. Butters.

St. James Palace really did burn in January 1809 and there was a major explosion in Portsmouth on June 24th, 1809, which happened as described in Mrs. Price's letter.

The poem William Gibson recites to himself while in the hold of the *Agincourt* is from *The Task*, by William Cowper.

The HMS *Solebay* and the HMS *Derwent* were real ships, and were led by the real Captain Edward Columbine against the French colony in Senegal. The brief *Times* newspaper article that Mrs. Butters sent to Fanny is the actual newspaper article with the first news of the loss of the *Solebay*. But the real-life *Derwent* did *not* capture a slave ship during this, the first tour of duty for the African Squadron. In subsequent years, ships of the West African Squadron did apprehend dozens of ships, despite a cripplingly high mortality rate for the sailors serving in the West Africa Squadron owing to malaria and typhoid.

Did you spot all the cameo appearances of characters from other Jane Austen novels? The Smallridges, Sucklings and Bragges are mentioned in *Emma*. The Smallridges were to have been Jane Fairfax's employers until her engagement to Frank Churchill was revealed. William Elliot, the cad who meets Fanny in Oxford, is from *Persuasion*, and Miss Lee's lost love is none other than Mr. Bennet from *Pride and Prejudice*.

The image on the front cover is a detail of a portrait of Madame Fouller, Comtesse de Relingue painted in 1810 by Louis-Léopold Boilly.

A final word: In this version, I've tried to create a Fanny Price who learns and grows and makes mistakes and becomes (I hope) a little more sympathetic. Whether she can become a mature, passionate woman is another question. Who *should* Fanny marry? Also: Did Sarah, the Bertram's former servant, survive the explosion in Portsmouth? Does William Price stand a chance of winning Julia Bertram's hand? Is there any way to repair Edmund's marriage with Mary or is he destined to get together with Fanny? I invite comments from the readers of this book as to what they think should happen next, and will take those comments into consideration for a sequel. Just visit my website (www.lonamanning.ca) or my Contrary Wind Facebook page and drop me a line.

Lona Manning
Zibo City, Shandong Province, China

44012917R00208

Made in the USA
Middletown, DE
26 May 2017